The Adventures of Elizabeth Stanton
Series

Volume 8 The Emperor and Empress

Vic Broquard

Published by:
Broquard eBooks
http://Broquard-eBooks.com
author@Broquard-eBooks.com
103 Timberlane
East Peoria, IL 61611

Artwork by Crooked Willow Studios

For Morgan and L. Ron Hubbard

Table of Contents

Chapter 1 In the Beginning

The date: March 1, 686. The place: Hodenhagen, Annelise. How do I know? My baby body was born today. My head hurts, my face feels squashed, and for a time, I felt frozen, but now I am nursing, wondering about my new name and identity. She is calling me Maren Elizabet Ryker. Of course, I want to be called Bethany or at least Elizabeth so I can shorten it to Bethany. I love that name and have been called Bethany, one way or another, for several lifetimes now.

My name is-was Elizabeth Stanton, originally anyway, my dearest friends still call me Bethany. When that body died, my next lifetime I was called Bethany Madelyn Adid, until I married and became the wife of Jes Amir, who was the Great Messiah. I was then known as Bethany Madelyn Amir and also, I discovered much later, I was called the Blessed Holy Mother. Next, I had a male body known as Ket Bethany. Last lifetime that is until a few months ago, I was known as Elizabeth Ann Rose Weston. Just how I am going to get Maren Elizabet into Bethany I have not yet worked out.

You see, I, like you, am a being — an immortal spirit. I've lived in many bodies and will have as many more as I desire, assuming the world, Tarra, our playground, is not destroyed. It began many years ago; I was part of a group of like-minded people, the druwids. In my group, I was revered as the Wid Bethany — the title that I took nearly nine hundred years ago now as I sit here and look back upon my past. I am Truth and Knowledge. Yes, you may call me a witch, a demon or a heretic, but, in doing so, you mark yourself as just another Blind One. I chose this road — this path I follow — knowingly and willingly. I do it for all mankind, even you.

I've taken this new baby body way down here in the southern potato shaped continent, which, in my last lifetime, we had discovered during our voyage of exploration, in order to become an Empress. Why? So that I can somehow influence the Emperor to not begin another massive war and thus bring about the destruction of the Santi del Dio, the Knights of God. We Santi are trying to maintain peace and tranquility throughout our world called Tarra, so that Jes Amir, the Guardian of the Anuir, can continue to work his miracles, the complete freeing of all we spiritual beings. Yes, the abilities we have potentially available are enormous, I've seen some in action already.

Unless I can do something about it, the global wars will begin around the turn of the century, 700. Thus, I have taken on this unusual assignment in hopes of somehow preventing or minimizing this future war.

However, I am not alone this time. A dear friend of mine has come down here before me and is now my sister, two years older than I am. She is

1

now known as Mia Kallisto and she is pledged to help me out as needed. I will shortly be in dire need of her assistance.

I've learned that the potato continent, as we call it, is called Xanthos by the people who live down here on this southern continent. It is roughly divided into thirds. Where I now live is in the eastern third in a country called Annelise. The middle third is called Vladimir. The western third is Demokritos. Two nearly impassable mountain ranges separate these three countries.

Mia Kallisto and I are the two youngest daughters of King Soren and Queen Lene Ryker, the rulers of Annelise. Our parent's twins are four years old, Cecille and Erik. We all live in the Royal Palace in Hodenhagen, near the center of the country. For reasons I don't yet know, dad's sister Hedda and her husband Gustav live here in the palace, along with their child, Poul, who is two. I do know that Aunt Hedda is very pregnant and is expecting within a few months as well. It seems that I will have many playmates, once this tiny body grows up a bit.

Back home — strange thinking of where I used to live last lifetime as home instead of where I now am — the head of the Santi del Dio is Linda and Chaucer d'Grange. Both have become very free spiritual beings, compliments of the Guardian of the Anuir, who figured that we would need some powerful help in keeping Tarra calm and tranquil so he could continue to free other beings. Linda, Chaucer, and I are very adept with telepathy. Additionally, last lifetime, I taught Linda how to perform the trauma therapy that my mother, Jenna Rose, taught me. Using this method, all harmful effects of the trauma can be completely wiped out, erased, so to speak. Just now, I really could use a short therapy session, if only to get rid of these uncomfortable pains and sensations I have from the birth process.

Linda here. I know that your body just was born. How are you doing? Need a bit of therapy?

Yes! I'm so glad you contacted me. My head hurts and my face feels squashed. Can you help me get rid of the effects of this birth, please?

I figured you would need a bit of therapy. I ran a session for Kallisto after her new body was born. Now I want you to go to the beginning of the recent birth. I told her I was there. *Okay. Now go through it and tell me what is happening.* I did. After several passes through it, I was giggling — well my new tiny body was anyway. My face felt just fine, and my head pressures were gone.

Thanks, Linda. I'll let you know what's going on down here, once I figure it all out. Bye. My tiny body fell asleep and all was well with the world.

The next day, it was day, I could see daylight anyway, I was starving, but mom didn't feed me. I began to wonder why.

I heard dad's voice, very sympathetically say, "Lene, are you really sure that you want to do this to our dear daughter? Once you do it, it cannot be undone. Think of how awful her life will be."

Mom replied, "Soren, we've been going over this for a year now. We both know the prophesy. The Emperor will be coming here to Hodenhagen, looking for just such a Ryker. You and I both know that there is no woman like he's looking for anywhere in our country, let alone here at the palace. Besides, think of what will result from this? We are doing this for the betterment of all our people, our subjects who depend upon us to keep them safe. Now, let's get going. They say the sooner it's done, the easier it will be on her."

I felt arms lifting me up, and I expected that breakfast was on its way. No, I was laid on a cold table with strange people looking down at me. A rag came over my face, I smelled something awful, and my body went unconscious. What were they doing to me? I backed out of the body and looked around. In horror and disgust, I watched them removing my arms!

They had cut around my tiny arms and cut them out of their sockets. My red blood was oozing all over the table. Good god! What have I gotten myself into this time! I had just spent a half lifetime without my arms last life. The mantis creature had eaten them. Now I was having them removed when I was only a day old!

In a flash, I realized that I should have known that this would be happening to me! The prophesy had said that this new Emperor would be looking for a woman of the Old Way, an armless woman. Damn. I wonder if Linda or Kallisto knew this before I agreed to go on this mission and take this body? Maybe that was why Kallisto came down here to be with me. She knew what I was getting myself into this time! I valued her friendship even more now.

Now they were bandaging my body up nicely. I watched as they carefully bathed me clean and wrapped me in warm blankets. Mom then carried me back to my cradle. I stayed out of the blackish drug mass around the body's head for as long as I could. Finally, the body woke up starving. While mom began to nurse it, I ended up smack in that black trauma mass of the surgery. Yes, there was intense pain buried underneath the drugged anesthesia. I felt awful. I lost track of time.

Linda here. Are you receiving me, Bethany? I heard my dear friend speaking in my mind somehow. I muttered something, but I didn't know what I said. *I want you to go to the beginning of the surgery. Okay. Now let's go through that trauma, tell me what is happening as you go along.* Linda was running a therapy session on me! I followed her commands and began to go through that operation, second by second. Each time that I re-experienced the operation, more details emerged. Finally, the black drug veil lifted, and I could re-experience the physical pain that the body had actually experienced. With each additional pass through the trauma, the pain lessened, and finally, the pain and unconsciousness all vanished. I felt alive and cheerful once more. She ended the therapy session.

Thank you! God, I've an armless body again! Did you know that this was going to happen to me?

We weren't entirely sure that it really would. The prophesy led us to suspect it might. Kallisto also though it might happen, so she really wanted to be there for you. Now I'm certain that you'll not have any problems connecting with that Emperor fellow. As I understand it, you have the only armless body in Annelise. At least, we don't have to create special ways and means to have him find you or to choose you over some other woman. Again, all of us thank you tremendously for what you are doing for us and for what you are going to have to endure along the way. Thank you, dearest Bethany. I see they are coming to feed you again. We'll chat more later on.

I watched as mom began nursing me again. I saw Mia Kallisto sitting on the floor watching us. *Hi, Kallisto. Thanks for being here with me. Looks like you will be taking care of me again. Thank you so much! Linda has run out the trauma of the operation already. I feel fine.*

She sent, *I had hoped I was misinterpreting the prophesy, but I wanted to be here with you if this did happen. I promise you, Bethany, I will be here to help you with all your needs. Together, we will succeed. We just have to succeed!*

A small girl's voice said, "Mommy, can I see her? Let me see how she looks. Yew, she really doesn't have any arms!"

"I know, dear Cecille, when she grows up, she will become the Empress of our countries. She will be uniting Annelise and Demokritos and will be a very powerful woman," mom explained.

"Yes, but she won't be able to actually *do* anything. She's going to be completely helpless. What good is being an Empress if you can't *do* anything?" Cecille walked away to go play with her brother, Erik.

I relaxed and allowed the little body to grow up. One interesting side note, the wounds on my shoulders were completely healed in two weeks, shocking everyone, who expected that should take at least six weeks. Therapy sessions work wonders, but my body couldn't yet speak, and I probably wouldn't have told them if I could have spoken.

Later that summer, my Aunt Hedda had twins, Hans and Lise. Was Kallisto ever surprised to find that her dear husband of last lifetime had come to join her here and was now being called Hans! I had no doubt that when their bodies grew up, those two would marry again.

Nothing much happened until I had my fifth birthday party. Cecille stated flatly, "Mom, I am *not* going to feed Maren her cake! Don't you dare try to make me either!"

"I'll do it," Mia Kallisto said, "I've been feeding her every day anyway. I don't mind it at all, mom."

"Well, I'm also not going to open her presents for her either," Cecille declared. "The birthday person is supposed to open their *own* presents. It's not my fault she hasn't got any arms."

"Maren Elizabet," mom completely ignored Cecille, "today you are five years old. Now it is time that we dress you properly. Plus, it is time that we begin your education. Actually, all you children pay attention. Your father and I have hired a tutor to teach you all about everything. From now on, part of each day you will be studying together with Aunt Hedda's children as well."

"Oh mom, you are kidding right?" Cecille whined, unwilling to lose so much of her playtime to studies.

Mom ignored her again. "Maren, since you are going to become the Empress, it is now time that we begin your body training. As Empress, you must uphold all the sacred, honorable, time-proven traditions that we Annelise hold in the highest regard. One of the most important of these is to always dress your finest, to look absolutely perfect at all times."

"We do have one slight problem with this though, your age. You see, Maren, normally we wait until the child is at least twelve years old before we begin body training in earnest. However, if we did that, you would not have enough time to body train and adapt before the Emperor comes for you. Hence, we are going to start in now, on your fifth birthday; and so that the rest of you are not left out, we will also dress you up as well, though your serious body training will wait until you reach twelve years, as is our custom. I know that this will not be totally enjoyable, especially for you, Maren, but always remember, you must look absolutely perfect when the Emperor comes."

"What does this mean, mommy?" I asked, although I already had a very good idea what she meant.

"As the Queen of all Annelise, I'm expected to have the smallest waistline of any woman in our country. As Empress, Maren, you will be expected to do likewise, to uphold our long, proud traditions. Starting today, we will bind your waist with a tight corset, just like mommy wears. See, you will be just like a grownup. Not even Cecille will be allowed to wear one, not until she is twelve. This is a very, very special honor for you, Maren, very special. From now, you girls will also wear on our traditional hoop dresses. You must look totally presentable and at your best at all times, from now on. Yes, Cecille, you will get these fancy and very expensive dresses like your youngest sister."

"Normally, we women wear these thick but high heeled boots, see like mine," she moved one foot out from under her wide hoop skirt so that we could see it. I thought that it was probably at least five inches tall, but the heel was thick, providing some support. "However, since these heels take a good deal of adjustment, learning how to walk in them, we will be starting Maren off in them as well. Only, Maren, I have a very special, very expensive pair of boots for you. These come all the way from Velona, Sea Princes, and way up north. As your feet grow, I will have larger ones for you." She unwrapped the box, and there were the boots that Alexa had made so popular in Velona, her fashion craze. These heels had a tiny metal spike and were even taller than mom's!

"Now the rest of you girls will have to wait until you are twelve for heel training. These are just too expensive for us to buy for all of you — not when you will be growing like weeds and need larger sizes so often. You will just have to be content with your usual flats a few more years. Don't worry, Cecille, you will soon be twelve, just three more years is all. Then, I will get you a beautiful pair as well."

Cecille turned up her nose. However, I saw that she was secretly very relieved that she did not have to wear these heels! Also, she was very happy to have the whole corset training stalled for at least three more years. She loved to run and play, and wearing these tightfitting, monstrous hoops would make that more difficult for her.

"But mom," Mia Kallisto protested, "Maren is going to have an awfully hard time with everything if she has to wear the corset, big dress, and these high heels. She is only five years old mom. She won't be able to do anything." Kallisto was trying to come to my rescue. From the look on mom's face, I could tell her protest was in vain.

"Dear Mia, Maren has got to have a very tiny waist when she is fourteen and the Emperor arrives. She has to be very adept at wearing these heels and our formal dresses when she meets him. Think how awful it will be for her if she is still learning when he comes! She will be so utterly embarrassed! No, we are all thinking ahead nine years. I want my daughter to be just perfect, just absolutely perfect, when the Emperor comes from Demokritos. Surely, you want her that way too, don't you, Mia?"

My sister looked at me and declared, "You don't want to be stumbling and falling down around the Emperor, Maren. I promise you that I will always be around to help you get by and learn."

"Now that's the spirit, Mia, very good indeed," mom praised her. "Cecille, see your younger sister knows what is best. I expect you to be helping Maren as well, just as I will be there when it is your turn in three years." Cecille turned up her nose, but didn't say anything.

"Now you fellows are not to be left out either. From now on, you, too, must look just like perfect gentlemen. Your father has picked out very nice suits for you to wear. See, we are all going to look our very best from now on, as it should be. Here at the Royal Palace, we must set very good examples for our subjects, who look up to us to do so."

I whined, "Don't I get to control *anything* about the way I look?"

"Well, sure you do honey. You can pick the color of your dresses after this one mommy just bought wears out. I'm afraid the boots only come in basic black, but that goes well with nearly everything, except white, which we seldom wear. What would you like to control about the way you look?"

6

She finally became curious enough about what I really meant to ask.

"Can I let my hair grow as long as it can?" I asked. I have always had a fetish for long hair. If I was going to undergo all this trouble, at least I wanted my hair to be long. Besides, I loved the way that Kallisto had hers last lifetime. She let it grow very long and wore it fluffed out over her shoulders, hiding where her arms would have been. The casual glance would not reveal that she had no arms.

"Well, I don't see why not. If you do not give us trouble with the clothing and training, I will allow you to have your hair anyway you desire, as long as it looks good and is presentable, mind you. No looking like some ruffian."

"Thanks mom." I won a very tiny victory.

Just then, dad came in, his hands loaded with packages. "Sorry I am so late. I've all the suits for the little gentlemen. Happy birthday, Maren." He gave me a kiss, and I told him to have a piece of my cake.

A while later mom took me into her sitting room to dress me formally in my new outfit. First, she put on a pair of nickers. Then came the dreaded corset. "Mom! I can't breathe in this. It's too tight," I exclaimed. She would have none of that, I quickly discovered.

"Yes, you can. See, I'm breathing. Just take small breaths, dear. You'll soon learn to adapt. There, this looks good on you, Maren. A while later, she finally got the dress with the enormous hoop on me. It puffed out as much as I was tall, nearly four feet. I could no longer see where I was about to put my feet. Worse, with my waist so constricted, I couldn't even bend over much to see. Next, she had me sit down, and she took off my normal socks and slid a thin hose that went all the way up my legs, fastening them to the bottom of the corset. At last, she slid the boots onto my feet, testing where my toes were located. She seemed pleased with that and then laced them up tightly.

"There, now, Maren, you look absolutely gorgeous, stunning, and perfect. Stand up and have a look in the mirror. Only be very careful while walking, until you get used to these boots. They are a bit higher than even mine are, so that makes you even more special than mommy! There, see how you look?"

I looked at my reflection; I did look las if I were a miniature doll, all dressed up for a fancy ball. "See, you look just great, my dear Maren. Don't ever let anyone tell you differently. You are the most special young girl in all Annelise! You are going to become the Empress! Now walk on out there and show your father just how beautiful you look. He will be very surprised indeed." I grinned and very carefully began to walk back out to the dining room. From last lifetime, I knew that I had to take very small steps from now on, especially since I couldn't even see my feet or anywhere around where they were at, only about three feet ahead of me.

"Wow, look at my little princess!" dad exclaimed, as I walked very slowly into the room. He already had Erik dressed up in his new fancy suit. Erik now looked like a formal, perfectly dressed miniature man. Erik looked very proud with his new suit and how he looked, very similar to dad. He also had a black stovepipe top hat, as did most of the men.

"Maren, you are just perfectly beautiful, my dear. Come, let daddy give you a big hug for being so brave." He gave me a warm hug, which I really appreciated. Mom had now taken Mia back with her, so I carefully sat back down on my chair, trying hard not to fall over in the process.

Cecille turned up her nose, when she looked at me. She added, "Don't go asking *me* to help you, Maren. You have to learn to *do* things yourself."

"Now Cecille, that's no way to talk to your little sister," dad came to my rescue. "After all, she has no arms and you do. I expect that you will help her with things." Cecille frowned and toyed with her dress, brushing off an imaginary piece of lint.

A little while later, Mia came out, smiling and happy. "Look at my new dress, daddy."

My dress was green, and hers was blue. Both of our dresses were very similar indeed, only the color and waistlines differed. Hers was not constricted as was mine. "Okay, Cecille, your turn," mom called out. She got up with a frown and followed mom.

Dad said, "Mia, you look almost as beautiful as your younger sister. Come here, let daddy give you a big hug too. Doesn't she look like a miniature woman, Maren, just like you? You all look so grown up!" We both smiled.

Dad had my cousin, Poul, formally dressed, and he now looked as well dressed as Erik — the two were comparing outfits. Next dad dressed up Hans. A few minutes later Cecille came out wearing a dress identical to ours, only yellow. She purposely banged into the table and chairs, as if to say wearing this was going to be troublesome, but dad ignored that and gave her a hug as well, mollifying her somewhat. A while after that, my cousin Lise made her appearance, dressed like us, but hers was red.

Uncle Gustav and Aunt Hedda arrived, all smiles. After admiring how we now looked and giving each of us a warm hug, she said, "Maren, in honor of this day, your uncle and I have bought you this present." She unwrapped a box which contained a beautiful necklace, which she put around my neck. It lay on my bare chest just above the top of the dress.

"Oh, I love it! Thank you ever so much!" I exclaimed, and leaned over so she could hug me. I would have hugged her, under normal situations, ah well.

"There now, why don't you children run off and play," mom suggested.

"Now we can *really* play party," Cecille suggested. "We look the part. Come on, let's go." All six of them began running out of the room. Until now, I would have been right behind them, only now I could barely walk!

Thankfully, Mia quickly remembered my predicament and dropped back to my side. She put her arm around my waist to steady me, and we slowly followed the others.

As we walked down the long hall, my heels made the familiar clicking sounds on the stone floor, bringing back memories from my last lifetime. I knew that this was going to alter my playtime tremendously. We seven loved to play tag and hide and seek the most. Cecille loved to play either house or party, but the boys only went along for short times, just enough to get her to play tag or hide and seek. By the time we got to the playroom, already the boys had convinced her to play tag instead.

"You cannot *play* tag anymore, Maren," Cecille stated flatly to me as Mia and I walked up to the others.

I replied rebelliously, "Yes, I can. I want to play tag too!"

She reached out with her arm and touched me, "Tag. You're it!" At once, the game was on, and everyone, except Mia and me, ran off.

I tried to run, but nearly fell down, gasping for breath as well. Mia said, "She might be right, Bethany; you might not be able to play tag anymore."

"Oh, I'll just have to become cleverer than they are. Come on, let's try to get someone." She was right; every time I got close to one of them, they could dash away from me far, far faster than I could go now. After an hour, I managed to trick Poul and touched him with my head. Thankfully, the rules said that you could not re-tag the person who just tagged you. I had some time to move slowly away. Later, I discovered playing hide and seek was also going to be much more difficult, not only because of my slow walking but also the noise that my boot heels made. I was not a happy trooper, especially when it was bedtime and I discovered that I had somehow to sleep in this darn corset!

This is not the way anyone should be treating a five year old girl, especially one without arms. No one would listen to me, however. Dad did give me tons of sympathy. I learned that he had done his best to convince mom not to remove my arms at birth, but had failed. Now he at least hugged me a lot and gave me comfort when I needed it.

The next day we gathered in the study for the first of our lessons. Cecille was particularly upset when she found out that these lessons would take nine years to complete! "Good day, children. My name is Mr. Halvor. I will be your tutor. Your parents want to make sure that you seven are the best, most properly educated young children in Annelise. Today we begin the adventure of learning many new things." Cecille raised her nose up and rolled her eyes, but Mr. Halvor ignored her.

"First, I must compliment all of you on just how very well dressed you are, especially Maren Elizabet." He actually bowed to me. Mr. Halvor is around twenty-five, immaculately dressed, cummerbund around his waist, bow tie, and well brushed hair with a tad too much oil for my taste, but then

I am only five years old now, well this body is. I am having a hard time pretending to be only five years old. I remember everything I've learned now for the last several lifetimes. His moustache is very nicely trimmed; his top hat and gloves are on the table, precisely arranged by him when he arrived. His shoes are smartly polished and I can see my own reflection in them when the sun is just right.

"Today, our first lesson is on our dress. Can anyone tell me why we are all dressed so nicely? Why are all our people throughout the country, from the farmer, to the milkman, to the sailor, to the King and Queen — why are we so smartly dressed?"

"How about you, Erik? You are the oldest, along with Cecille. What answer can you give us?" Mr. Halvor asked politely.

"Well, er, people do need to wear clothes. It can be cold out or we can get dirty or we'd look pretty silly running around naked," Erik fumbled for an answer. Every one of us chuckled at his reply.

Mr. Halvor smiled, "Yes, we would at that, though Erik. When you get older, you might not find women running around naked so distasteful." Now we all laughed. Erik's face reddened slightly; he was nine, but at that age where he disliked all things female.

"Now how would you answer that Cecille?" Mr. Halvor asked.

"Well, mom is always saying that we must always look our very best, to set an example for others," she rattled off just what mom kept saying.

"Yes, yes, that sounds just like Lene. Now why do you suppose that we must always look our very best anyway? Surely, you must find that your fancy dress, Cecille, is not the most comfortable clothes in which to run around and play."

She cringed, "No it certainly isn't. I keep bumping into things. It's awkward."

"Ah, yes, but then how do you suppose it is for little Maren? Perhaps more so, eh?" Her face turned beet red; she'd been discovered. Mr. Halvor paid no attention to her reaction. "You didn't answer my question, Cecille. Why do you suppose that we must always look our very best?" She shrugged her shoulders, giving up.

"Poul, would you like to try to answer that for Cecille?"

"Well, because, ah, because everyone can see everyone else," he attempted to make some sort of sense.

"I believe that you are getting slightly warm there, Poul. Anyone else care to take a stab at the answer?" We were all quiet for a bit.

At last, I thought I might test the waters, since it seemed to be more of a discussion than a lesson. "Self-respect may lie behind our dress," I said. Everyone turned to look at me.

"Very good, Maren. However, I can see that others do not quite understand your answer. Could you explain it a bit more fully?"

"Well, if you dress very well, very perfect, very nicely, you feel better, and you have more respect for your appearance. You are saying I am proud of the way that I look. You feel better about yourself and can then have more confidence to do the things you need to do. If you go around dressed in rags, you are saying I don't give a hoot about how I look and how others may see me. You are showing others that you do not have a high respect, a high regard for yourself, your own person, your own body."

"Precisely correct, Maren," Mr. Halvor complimented me. Cecille stuck her tongue out at me when he wasn't looking.

"Can I ask a question, though?"

"Sure, we are all here to learn. Ask."

"What I don't understand is that the clothes do not seem to match the job that the person is doing. I mean, well take the farmer. He is out there plowing in the field, getting very dirty. Surely, leather work clothes would be far more practical than wearing a finely made business suit. These dresses that we are wearing — they are more like very fancy party dresses or fancy court dresses. Yet we are wearing them as everyday play clothes. It seems out of place to me for me to be wearing this kind of dress for play. I've heard that in other countries, people wear clothing that is more appropriate for the job that they are doing. I saw a farmer's wife out helping with the planting wearing a dress similar to mine. She was having a difficult time of it. It seems so impractical for her to wear this party dress while trying to plant crops. That's what I don't understand." Kallisto and Hans nodded in agreement with me; naturally Kallisto, Hans, and I didn't grasp this detail at all.

"Yes, yes, I would agree with you, wearing a fancy party dress while planting a crop makes the task more difficult. Do you not find wearing your dress and your heels, Maren, makes your playing more difficult?" I nodded. "Just as the butcher wearing a fancy business suit finds it more difficult to do his job as well, having to take extra care not to get them bloody. I dare say that every one of us at some time finds some task of theirs more difficult to achieve in their fine clothing. That is very true. So why is it that we all dress this way, the entire country?" None of us had a clue.

"The answer is that, here in Annelise, we all believe that each and every one of us is fit to be a King or Queen. That is not so in most other countries. Maren, suppose that you saw one man dressed in work clothes whose shirt was covered in blood from where he'd wiped his hands, a second man dressed in a very well-tailored business suit, and a third man in leather work pants and white cotton shirt all covered in dirt. One of these men is the King. Which one would you pick?"

"Oh, that's easy," Cecille interrupted. "I'd pick the business suit!" She felt certain she was correct.

"Maren?"

"Well, it could be anyone of the three, actually. Perhaps the King enjoys butchering his family's meat. Perhaps the King loves to garden, to grow his own vegetables. The man in the business suit could well be just a merchant or a moneychanger. I would need to talk with each man to answer the question who was the King," I replied. Cecille gave me another dirty look.

"Precisely so, Maren. Precisely so. In these other societies, very often the clothes make the man or woman. Women dress up in their fancy dresses only to go to a gala ball or dance. Only at that time do they feel special. Likewise, with the farmer, who on Sunday dresses in his suit and goes to church. Likewise with the butcher who wears his finest suit to the dance with his wife. Only then do they feel really special, like they were a king or queen or even 'somebody of importance.'"

"Once we in Annelise were like that, shortly after our ancestors founded our country. Our first King Ane always dressed for his role as King of Annelise. Then, one day he toured the countryside, visiting with his people. He observed that the farmer thought less of himself than he did of the King. The butcher in his rather cruddy clothing felt much less than a king, that King Ane was much better than he was. King Ane, returning to his palace, noticed that his courtly advisors and nobles, who were finely dressed, thought highly of themselves and looked down on the farmer and the mere butcher."

"Now King Ane was a wise man. He knew that we are all good people, that there was no difference between the butcher, the baker, the farmer, the courtly advisors, and the King himself, save perhaps education and knowledge. King Ane then dressed the butcher up in his own clothes and the courtly advisors mistook him for one of them. He dressed the farmer up in his own clothes and again the courtly advisors mistook him for another distant nobleman. Finally, he dressed the farmer's wife in one of his own wife's fine dresses and brought her to his palace. Again, all thought that she was indeed a noblewoman of some importance."

"Right then, he issued the Royal Decree that still stands today. Everyone shall dress in the finest possible clothing at all times, to present a perfect appearance. Every man and woman shall feel at all times as if they are indeed a king or queen. People protested a bit at first. The usual one was, as Maren pointed out, that the clothing was not practical. To this, King Ane replied, 'Aye, that is certainly true, but do you not feel like a king or queen dressed so finely?' To which they all had to answer honestly that they felt wonderful. Yes, we dress this way to make sure that each of us holds ourselves in the highest self-respect, thinking of ourselves as worthy, fit to be king or queen. Through these many centuries now, it has worked miracles. Our people have a high regard for themselves, and crime is very low indeed in our country. Not so in these other countries."

I added, "That's because the criminal has lost his self-respect and can no longer trust himself."

"Brilliant, Maren, positively brilliant indeed." Again, Cecille gave me the dirtiest look yet.

"Surely there are other ways for a person to think highly of themselves," Mia Kallisto stated. "Such as doing a really top quality job of dressmaking for example, or cooking a really fine, delicious meal for others."

"Yes, that is also very true, Mia. In other countries, that is the route often taken by their people. There is nothing at all wrong with that way. However, here we have found that always wearing the finest clothing more uniformly gets the result, increased self-respect. Further, the increased self-respect also increases the quality of the work or product that the person is making or activity the person is doing. Simply put, our way works better and faster, which is why we do it our way."

"Yes, but why such exaggerated dresses, these huge hoops are so difficult to manage," I asked.

Mr. Halvor replied, "You have a point. You may also ask why you women insist on seeing who can have the tiniest waist. No system is perfect. Long, long ago, women just had to be different from each other. I don't know why you all get so upset when two of you discover that you are wearing identical dresses, but you do, let me assure you of that! You girls will discover this on your own soon enough. These hoop skirts have developed over the centuries, slowly growing larger and larger. Frankly, I don't see how they can get any larger at all, but each year at the music festivals, they continue to grow wider. Women!" he jested; we chuckled.

"I can only speculate on why the small waist lines, Maren. I believe that women are conscious of their figures. No one wants to be obese, and some say that it is not healthy for the body to be very overweight. Perhaps this is one way women have devised to ensure that they do not over eat. This question you might ask your mothers."

"Now because Maren is wearing one, she must eat smaller meals and also eat them more frequently. You are all growing children, rather like a weed. Thus, because of her unique needs, we will always be taking a snack break about now. Is that all right with the rest of you?" We cheered! Indeed, I was already feeling a little weak. I was hungry already, having only eaten a third of what I used to eat for breakfast. This time, Cecille gave me a smile as we headed off to grab a midmorning snack.

Hans, Mia, and I trailed slowly behind the others, who rushed off to the kitchen. Each had an arm around my waist, making sure I was okay. "Do you believe all he was saying about the reasons for these stupid clothes?" I asked them.

Hans joked, "Maybe the real reason is that the tailors and seamstresses of Annelise are the real people in control here, behind the scenes, wealthy beyond belief." We chuckled.

"If a person does look and appear so well dressed, they will probably feel better about themselves. Is that enough to lower crime? I surely doubt it," Mia Kallisto added.

"It may be more of an attempt to disguise one's occupation. You know, now you cannot tell the butcher from the farmer when they are in town just by the clothes they wear. Heck, you cannot tell who anyone is from their clothes down here," Hans added.

"No, except the women — whose skirt is the widest, whose waist is the smallest," Mia put in her protest.

A while later we were back at our lessons. This time we dealt with mathematics. I'm afraid that Mr. Halvor was really challenged with us on this one. Quickly, he found that except for Hans, Mia, and me, the others could barely do the simplest arithmetic, whereas we three challenged his knowledge.

In desperation, he asked, "Okay, you are going to bake a very large custard pie for a party. The pie bowl is a very large one, circular and four feet in diameter; its sides are three inches tall. How much custard will you need to prepare?"

I said, "Well, that's an easy one. The radius is two feet, so 3.1 times 2 times 2 is the area of the pie bowl, which is, 12.4 square feet."

Hans added, "The height is a 1/4 of a foot, we have to keep it in feet. So the volume is 3.1 cubic feet. You are making this one too easy to figure, Mr. Halvor."

Mia completed the answer by saying, "A cubic foot is about seven and a half gallons, so the answer is about 23 gallons of custard; that is an awfully large pie, Mr. Halvor!"

Poor Mr. Halvor, his mouth opened to say something, but only a gurgle came out. He swallowed. "That is correct. My, we have three math wizards here. Oh dear me!" After a few more, he definitely had a serious problem with our group and math.

"Let's change the topic for the rest of this period. Let's turn to geography. Does anyone know the name of our country? Lise?"

"Annelise, Mr. Halvor," she said, very glad to have gotten one correct.

"Very good, Lise. What is the name of our continent?"

"Xanthos," Poul quickly replied, happy finally to have one he could answer as well.

"Excellent, Poul. Now is our world, Tarra, flat or round like a ball?"

"Everyone one can see that it is flat," Cecille hastily spoke up, trying not to be outdone by her cousins.

"No, it's a ball, a sphere, Mr. Halvor," I corrected her before Mia or Hans did. I already had Cecille's disdain. I didn't want those two also to get on Cecille's bad side.

"Hum. We have a conflict here, flat or like a ball. Let's have a vote." Three of us voted that Tarra was a sphere, four voted for it being a flat pancake.

"Ah children, here we have a very important lesson, not whether

Tarra is flat or round, but we have a group disagreement. As you grow up, you will always run into disagreements between people. How you settle the disagreements is very important. Could you settle a disagreement you have with another by fighting them and licking them in a fist fight?"

"Sure, you *boys* do that all the time!" Cecille declared raising her nose in the air, as if this was an awful way to settle a disagreement.

"Yes, Cecille, men often resort to fighting to settle a disagreement. Yet, I want to ask you, does beating someone in a fight actually change their view? Let's look more closely at this. Hans, you say the world is round; Poul, you say it is flat. Suppose that you two have a fistfight, and Poul, you being bigger, stronger, and older, win the fistfight. As you are standing there with your fists raised in victory, have you really changed Hans' mind? Hans, you have just lost the fistfight with Poul. Does that make you change your mind that the world is not round, but flat as Poul says?"

"Of course not," Hans said flatly.

"Precisely, children. Fighting another as a method of settling a dispute or disagreement between two people never settles the disagreement. All you have done is enforced your will over the loser, nothing more. You have not changed their ideas or opinions."

"See guys, even Mr. Halvor thinks you shouldn't be fighting!" Cecille retorted. "Fighting never solves anything."

"Very true, Cecille. So how would you go about changing their opinions, Cecille? How would you settle the dispute here between Hans, who says the world is round, and Poul, who insists it is flat?"

"Everybody knows it is flat!" she stated, but realized at once that this would not do. "We would have to talk about it, talk it over, explain to them, and show them why it is flat. I mean, just look around outside; it is mostly flat, except for the hills and such."

"Discussion, yes, that would be a much better approach to take to settle disputes between people. Now how could you show the flat people that the world is actually round?"

"Oh that's so easy, a child could do it!" I declared, and then realized I was supposed to be a child. The body was only five years old! Oops. Cecille raised her nose at me again.

Ignoring her, I said, "Just go down to the docks and watch a big ocean ship, a caravel, come in. If the world were flat, when you first saw the boat, you would see the whole boat, hull, decks, and masts, all very tiny of course. If the world was a sphere, and the ocean was curved, first you would see the tops of the masts appear. As the ship came closer, you would see the middle of the masts, and then the deck and lastly the hull as it got close. Honestly, Tarra is round, a sphere, just go watch caravels come sailing into the docks or leaving the docks. All you have to do is watch. What I wonder is how one could figure out how big around the sphere is and hence what its diameter would be?"

Mr. Halvor gave me a stare of surprise, and said, "Precisely correct, Maren. The world is a giant sphere. One day soon, we will take a field trip to one of our port cities, and we can then see this for ourselves. Would you like to take a field trip?" Cecille, who was halfway into making a funny face at me, stopped and began cheering along with the rest of us.

"Now who can tell me the names of our six largest port cities?" Here, we three were complete dummies. We had no idea. Cecille happily out did us on local geography. In this, we three paid close attention, because we needed to learn all that we could about our new country.

Later we broke for lunch. I overhead Mr. Halvor chatting to mom and dad about us children. "Honestly, Maren, Mia, and Hans are absolute geniuses in some areas. I cannot teach them anything about math! Really, I cannot! It is truly amazing. Yet in some areas, they are as we would expect. They do not even know the names of our port cities."

"See, I told you that Maren would have what it takes to become the Empress!" mom declared certain that all her predictions were going to come true.

As the days passed into weeks into months, I enjoyed our lessons, even though much I already knew. We were learning what we needed to learn. Soon, we took up learning a foreign language, Demokritos, naturally. Besides, I only had to sit, which was about all that I could easily do. Walking and playing were chores for me to accomplish in the getup I was forced to wear.

Playtime was definitely not my favorite time anymore. Cecille constantly harassed me. "Come, let's all play house. Maren, you can't actually *do* anything, so you can be the doll. Or she would say, here is the new baby. Oh, I'm sorry. Maren cannot *hold* her. Here, let's serve some tea. It's your turn to serve, Maren. Oh dear, you cannot *serve* the tea, now can you?" Cecille constantly made me feel uncomfortable, keenly aware of my circumstances.

A year later, formal dancing lessons began. Here was something I could do, though I had to be extra careful not to overdo it and faint from lack of breath. Then came the music lessons. Cecille again rubbed it in on me, telling me that I couldn't play any of the instruments, but I could sing, and that's what I learned to do, sing songs.

Three years after we started our lessons, things changed somewhat. Cecille was now twelve. True to her word, mom gave Cecille a new outfit, complete with corset and high heels, just like mine.

"Mom! I can't breathe in this! Erik! Hold me, I cannot keep my balance!" Cecille complained, both worried and fearful. She looked at me and suddenly realized what I had been enduring all this time. While I could have sneered back at her discomfort now, I chose instead to take her under my wings, so to speak.

I whispered, "Cecille, take really, really small steps — always. You have to look ahead of where your feet are and anticipate carefully because we cannot see our feet with these hoops. Take very shallow breaths often and don't overdo it or you will faint like I sometimes did."

For the next month, I carefully looked out for her, helping her with what wisdom I had worked out on how to do things in this getup. After that, I found that her attitude towards me changed completely. Now she too began to look out for me; I had gotten a new sister. Well, she always was my sister, just now she was actually being a kind, considerate, and loving sister.

Until now, always Mia had to feed me at the table, brush my hair, and help me go to the bathroom and so on. Now, Cecille, who still didn't want anything to do with helping me go to the bathroom, began to take over the duties of brushing out my hair and fixing my clothes, making me look perfect, as mom always would say. In fact, one could say that after this point in time, Cecille was responsible for my overall appearance, doing her best to make me look as pretty as possible.

Cecille agreed with me. My curly, long black hair was down to nearly my waist. "I like it best when we drape it over your shoulders like this, Maren. You are right; it actually does mostly hide your lack of arms. It is not so noticeable this way. There, you look just great. Let's go get some breakfast." She now chose to keep her arm around my waist to steady both of us as we walked in our heels.

Two years after that, mom dressed up Mia and Lise similar to us. Yes, she made sure that our cousins were as well and properly attired as we were. Now Cecille and I helped these two as they struggled to deal with the constriction and heels.

By the time that I finally turned fourteen and of age, we had adjusted well to our constraints. Yes, mom had continually introduced more as we grew older. Our hoop skirts continued to expand with larger and larger diameters. When each of we girls reached fourteen, our skirts reached their normal daily maximum diameters, some fourteen feet across. Only at the formal music dances would we don hoops that spread out to sixteen feet. With arms, these were barely manageable. For me, it was pure torture.

Chapter 2 A Summary of Learning

By now, you have some idea of the way that education is handled here in Annelise. During our education years, Hans, Mia Kallisto, and I learned much valuable information that we really did need to know. Allow me to summarize the more important details here.

Geographically, Annelise occupies the eastern third of the continent of Xanthos, some thousand miles long and five hundred miles wide, that is north-south. It is shaped like a long finger, pointing eastward. Our country has around seven million people according to the year 700 census. The six major port cities, each with a population well over a hundred thousand are, going clockwise, Ringenstad, Viborg, Bjerg, Grenen, Lenvig, and Barborg. Just a hundred fifty miles further west from Ringenstad is the fortress at Betsford, where the Hagan Mountains reach the sea. Here is where occasionally the horsemen of Vladimir raid our country and where our soldiers are stationed, all five hundred of them.

All of the major five rivers run south to north. Originating in the foothills of Hagan, the Silke river flows down past Luborg, and then on into the sea at Ringenstad. The Salbor comes from the southern ice fields up past Nibrehagen, on to Hiborg, and then to the sea at Viborg. The Rund, our largest river, begins at the ice field, near Fruhagen, flows down to our capital city of Hodenhagen, where it splits into two halves. The main part continues down to the sea at Bjerg, although a hundred miles before that point it splits into two halves, E. Rund and W. Rund. Above Hodenhagen, the eastern fork is called the Lille and it runs eastward for nearly three hundred miles before turning north at Mariba and then on into the sea at Grenen. The Feld River also begins at the ice fields and flows northeast to Genser and on into the sea at Barborg.

Between all of these large cities, the roads are paved cobblestones, making passage smooth and swift. Many wagons and carriages travel these roads daily. The climate along the northern coastal cities is temperate, much like that in Velona, Sea Princes. There is significant snowfall in Hodenhagen, where we live, however. We only have one large city near the permanent ice fields, Fruhagen.

Our means of exchange is called the goud, a coin that comes in three types, but one weight for each, an ounce. The gold goud is the most valuable, next come the silver goud. Twenty silvers make one gold. Then there is the bronze goud, of which twenty make a silver. For larger quantities, gemstones are used.

The seasons are backwards from what we were used to during our lifetimes in the northern hemisphere. Spring comes in September, summer begins in December, fall starts in March, and winter commences in June. It took the three of us a good deal of time to get comfortable with the seasonal dates here in the far south of Tarra.

Every March and September, the Summer Collegium Musicum meets in Hodenhagen, for a huge music festival. The place is packed with visitors, for these are the events of the year. At the dance, we discovered that their music was very slow and stately. After all, I realized, what else could we women possibly manage in these outfits? Even so, after one dance, I was gasping for breath, as were all the women. However, they had fans with which to cool their reddish faces off, I didn't. In these heels, too, it was very difficult to look elegant on the dance floor. However, I observed the local women, who did just fine. Practice I concluded, this would take practice, just like any other skill.

Fortunately, after a set of dances, we all sat down a spell, while they played another set of more formal music. Then, it was back to dancing. They timed everything perfectly, giving us enough time to recover enough to avoid fainting or worse.

The instruments were different sizes of stringed instruments, played by holding the body of the instrument between one's legs and bowing across them with a stick with some kind of hair to make the strings sound. These are called viols. A nasal sounding wind instrument added color, a shawm, and several sizes of drums added the percussion.

During the lengthy intermissions, huge tables of food and drink were available, and we made many new friends during the breaks. Everyone wanted to meet us, the children of the rulers.

Incidentally, Hans and Mia chose to learn how to play two of the viols, she the smaller one, he the larger one.

Their boats were called dahabea, about a quarter of the size of our caravel. They had one main mast far to the aft of center, which sported a lateen sail on a long boom attached high atop the mast. A tiny spinnaker hung off the rear and was used for control. The quarterdeck was more like a half deck and their cargo capacity was a fifth of ours.

On our field trip to Viborg, the largest of the port cities, we saw many ships and their crew. The ship's captain wore a spotless blue linen suit, with a perfectly tailored jacket with two long tails falling behind and over his rear end. He looked as if he were ready to go to a fancy party, not captain a sailing ship. Yet, the crew members were just as nicely dressed. They wore white shirts and white pants, tailored to a perfect fit. A blue sash was tied around their waists. The captain wore a blue top hat, like a cylindrical stovepipe, rising at least a foot above his head and with a small brim. The sailors all wore white berets with a blue ribbon dangling from its top.

Again, we were reminded of their motto: Proper clothing brings proper respect.

Everything about the cities was clean and neat. We saw no litter along the sides of the streets. Further, all of the streets were cobblestoned right up to the edges of the buildings. Each of the buildings was well maintained, often built of stone, actually brown bricks. Near the edge of each city was a brick making factory, which we later toured. We also discovered that instead of burning wood or charcoal as we did up north, they burned a black rock called kool, mined down south near the ice sheets.

What did our palace look like? The palace was actually a collection of many large buildings, stone once more. Along the southern edge neat rows of brown brick cottages lay, the guesthouses. One building housed the Royal Diner, where everyone gathered to eat their meals. Another housed their throne room, from which they ruled. However, the largest building was a combination theater, music, and dance hall, capable of holding several thousand at one time. As usual, the musicians played from a raised balcony.

We lived in the Throne Room House, as it was called. Great double doors opened into the red-carpeted room. Two thrones sat at the far end, where mom and dad sat to hold court. Tables and chairs allowed others to sit and plan. Adjacent to this room was the study where we had our lessons. Behind these rooms lay the panty and kitchen, where we often took our meals. Sometimes, we all ate at the Royal Dining Hall, especially if our parents were hosting visitors. Upstairs was the master bedroom for mom and dad. We children had our own large room with and adjoining playroom. Uncle Gustav and Aunt Hedda stayed in the end bedroom, while their children stayed in the other bedroom close to theirs.

There was no bathroom, only chamber pots. However, the Public Bath House served our other needs; it was the next building beside the Royal Palace. At least once a week, we were allowed to remove our corsets and clothing to bathe. This was the time of the week that I treasured the most, for only then did I have my freedom of movement.

At all other times, I was mostly a prisoner in the palace. All doors had knobs, which I could not open. Always I had to be careful to have someone with me, just in case I found myself alone in a room. Twice, Cecille did just this to me, left me alone in a room with the door shut. I was helpless to get out. I dare not use my special powers here.

As I mentioned before, the entire army of Annelise consisted of five hundred soldiers, who guarded the only overland connection the horsemen of Vladimir had with our country. At Betsford, it was possible to ride a horse along the beach, where the formidable Hagan Mountains finally met the sea. Each man wore ring mail and carried huge halberds, used to stop the charging horsemen. Some would raid every couple of years, so this was not a serious threat.

In each town and city, the City Guards, dressed in their finery, mostly red and black outfits, also carried halberds and maintained law and order. However, crime was nearly non-existent in Annelise, mostly the occasional pickpocket. Dad had twenty of these men to provide security around our palace complex, though they mostly handled saddling the horses for the carriages that we used.

During our education years, Mr. Halvor took us on many field trips. We visited every major town and city I've mentioned. Dad thought it was important for us to become familiar with our whole country. After all, I was soon to become Empress, if mom was to be believed. Erik would one day take dad's place as King. If he could not for some reason, then Poul, my cousin would get the opportunity to become King. This potential eventuality was why my aunt and uncle were living here at the palace with us, just in that unlikely eventuality. We women didn't count, only the male heirs.

What of religion in Annelise? Tacitly, these were Sun God worshipers; however, no one was particularly religious about it. We never went to church. Priests were few and mostly ceremonial in nature, marrying people and conducting funeral services. The people of Annelise were not particularly spiritually inclined. Mostly, the country was run on common platitudes, such as: Being well dressed is next to godliness. Work hard so that you can get even finer clothing for your family. Laziness never pays for your next suit. Save for a rainy day. Platitudes served our people in lieu of religion. Strange.

When I was thirteen, I began to get very curious about just what dad and mom actually did here in Hodenhagen, as King and Queen. What was the political situation? Certainly, Mia and Hans were keenly interested in learning this information. What did mom hope to gain with a union with Demokritos anyway? Why had she gone to all this trouble?

We started by talking over what we now knew about our country. To our way of thinking, everything here revolved around the obtaining of ever-fancier dress clothing. This seemed to be the weenie of the society: the goal and target that seven million people were aspiring to attain. Crime was incredibly low, but so were any concepts of spiritualism. Not even status could be considered a goal of people. Indeed, we chatted with various people while on our field trips. When asked if one day they might like to be the King or Queen of Annelise, their reply was always, not really. They were doing what they enjoyed and were happy doing. Yet, if the country asked them, they would become its leader, primarily because they saw that as a means of obtaining an unlimited clothing allowance!

All this had something to do with the Right of Passing, a celebration that occurred on one's fourteenth birthday. In the case of our brother Erik, the ceremony was indefinitely delayed, because he had agreed to one day take over the throne from dad. At least when he turned fourteen, he was allowed complete freedom to come and go as he pleased. He was now gone a lot of the time. Cecille explained that he was off looking for love, someone to take mom's place on the throne.

Cecille, who was not likely to get the throne, did get her Right of Passing ceremony. The entire extended family gathered for her birthday party. Once we finished eating the cake, dad officiated her Right of Passing ceremony. We children paid very close attention to this event.

"Cecille Ryker has now reached the official Age of Consent. From this time forward, Cecille is to be considered an adult in our society, with full rights and obligations, heretofore deigned by our founder, King Ane. We, her proud parents, now present her with her last outfit from us, the finest that we can find anywhere in Annelise." He whispered, "It's entirely made of silk, dear!" Her eyes nearly popped out, so did ours for that matter. Besides being incredible to the touch, a fourteen-foot hoop dress made entirely of silk cost a fortune, well at least five hundred gold gouds.

He continued, "From now on, as a responsible adult, it will be your responsibility to provide for your own wardrobe. Of course, until you are married, you are welcome to stay here with us. However, as a responsible adult, you will be expected to work around here to help earn your keep and goud. Your mother and I would really appreciate it if you would stay at least two more years to help with Maren, that is, unless you have a boyfriend awaiting you."

She blushed. No, she didn't have a boyfriend yet — several possibilities, but she had not fallen for anyone.

Dad continued. "Now as dictated in the Rights of Passing, have you determined what career you most desire to follow?"

Cecille replied formally, "Yes, I have made my decision. I wish to become one of the finest dressmakers in Hodenhagen!" I could see her reasoning. She'd always been in love with dresses. This way, she could make her own and at last have all that she desired.

"Excellent choice, Cecille! I know that you have made your mother proud with your choice. We both wish you all the success in the world!" Everyone clapped for her; she nodded to us. Me, I stomped on the floor. How else could I acknowledge her goal?

"Do you have someone lined up with which to apprentice?" dad asked.

"Not really. I was hoping you could help me. I want to apprentice to one of the best dressmakers, of course. I figured that I would need a bit of political pull that you have, dad," she wrapped him around her fingers.

He beamed, "Of course, my lovely Cecille. I will speak to Madam Grizwoldt tomorrow." G & H Dress Shop was where all our fabulous dresses were made. This delighted Cecille, who talked about this to the rest of us for an entire week! After she was accepted, she continued to expound on the art of dressmaking to us every evening when she came home. We observed that she was now gone for most of the day, returning each evening. She still brushed out my hair first thing in the mornings though, as well as at night before I went to bed.

When Mia and Poul had their thirteenth birthday, me now being eleven, dad took the time to explain to them and the rest of us about the Right of Passing ceremony. He wanted Mia and Poul to be ready when it was their turn to reach fourteen. We learned then that at this age, a person in Annelise was considered to be an adult. Now they could marry and or start a career, usually by apprenticing for a number of years. At this ceremony, they were to announce to the world what career they most wanted to try. It was the parent's last official responsibility to obtain for their child an apprenticeship in their chosen area, or to assist in providing a home if marriage was imminent.

"What if it doesn't work out for them, dad?" I asked. "Suppose they discover that they do not like that career or are not good enough to do it."

"They are always free to choose another career path. However, the parents are not obligated to continue to support them or even assist them in the change. Although realistically, most parents that I know will still help them. It's just that they are not under any social obligation to do so."

"My dear Maren, you will not have to worry about this, because you will become the Empress and a very pretty one too." He gave me one of his wonderful hugs. He whispered to me, "Don't worry Maren. If this Emperor should not come here, you will always have a place right here in our house. We will never abandon you, my love." I smiled and took some comfort in that he really would support me, if the prophesy turned out to be rubbish.

The next year, when Mia and Poul turned fourteen, we again held the Rights of Passing ceremony for them. Again, mom presented Mia with a beautiful green silken hoop dress, again fourteen feet in diameter, her last official dress from our parents. I was anxiously awaiting that point when Mia would be asked to announce her choice of career. However, Poul was asked first.

"Dad, I want to become a ship captain and sail the seas in a dahabea or even better, get my hands on a caravel from the Sea Princes and really sail the high seas. Do you think this is possible? I fell in love with the ships when Mr. Halvor took us to the port on a field trip." It should not have taken anyone by surprise. He had been making ship models in his room for the last five years. Even I have one of his by my bed, a present on my last birthday.

My uncle replied, "The dahabea, that I can manage, son. I am sure we can arrange an apprenticeship for you. However, I surely don't know how we can ever get our hands on one of those caravels of the Sea Princes."

Mom spoke up, "In a couple of years, when Maren becomes the Empress, we should be able to get one of the Demokritos copies of the Sea Prince caravels. Right Maren?"

"Sure thing, Poul, if I can find any way to get one for us, you can captain it and sail the world. That is a very exciting life, very rewarding too. Only I would definitely advise you to take someone along who is very good with languages. These other countries speak very differently than we do." He thanked me, and fortunately did not ask me how I could know that.

He too received his last very fine suit, also made of silk. A little later once Mia and he had changed, he showed it off to us all. He looked stunning, like a real man.

Now it was Mia's turn. When asked, she replied, "I am going to be Maren's Hand Maiden. I have promised her that I will always be there to look after her needs. When she becomes the Empress, I will go wherever she goes to help her with everything. Is this all right with you? I suppose you can also ask me to do other work around here to help out."

"Oh that is so incredibly wonderful of you, Mia, to so sacrifice your life to help our little Maren!" Mom exclaimed before dad could reply. "We have no right to ask you to do this, but since you wish to, why we will support you all of the way. Maren, isn't this the absolutely greatest news?"

"Yes, mom. It would be just awful to sail off to Demokritos with no one coming with me to help me. I would be so embarrassed to have to ask the Emperor to help me pee." I zinged that one in there, just to remind her what her decision to have my arms removed would be costing me.

As usual, she ignored it, continuing to praise Mia for her selfless act. "From now on, Mia, we will give you a worthy allowance for helping Maren through the day with all her needs. We all know how much you do for her, and we've been extremely grateful for your extreme kindness all these years. Now we shall reward you for helping. Thank you ever so much, Mia." Dad just hugged her and kissed her forehead. "Now new adults go and change. Your aunt and I wish to see how gorgeous you look, Mia, and how handsome you look, Poul."

A little while later, mom exclaimed, "Mia, this will never do at all. My, how you are suddenly filling out!"

"What's the matter mom?" I asked, suddenly rather worried that something was wrong with Mia. I depended on her utterly.

"Oh, it's nothing bad, dear Maren. It's just that her bust is undergoing another one of those growth spurts. Her breasts have grown so much since we measured her for this dress that now it is really too tight on her. Yes, she can wear it, but only for a short while. I will take it to the dressmakers tomorrow and get it enlarged a bit."

I felt relieved that it was nothing more than this. I don't know what I would do without Mia. "Mom, is that why my breast are hurting so? They are growing too?" I asked, with this tight corset thing, I could not tell what was really supposed to happen and what might be indicative of a problem.

Mom examined me and declared, "My, oh my, you are growing up too, Maren. It's nothing to worry about. I should give you a massage tonight; that might help, since you cannot do it for yourself. You are both growing so rapidly into womanhood. However, Mia here is growing altogether way too rapidly, it seems."

Mom had very large breasts. What she said next surprised us both. "I have a very full bosom, mind you. Very large, your father often says." We giggled. "He loves them, but don't mention that to him or you'll embarrass him no end!" We giggled even more.

"You see girls, you are taking after the Thorsten line. Your grandmother, Gudrun, my mother, now she died just before you were born, Mia, she had the most enormous breasts I've ever seen! She always said that the Thorsten line produced women with very big breasts. Lord knows mine are very big. However, hers were twice the size of mine. I kid you not! I remember that she always gave the dressmakers absolute fits when she ordered new dresses. When I was your age and my breasts were developing, I prayed and prayed that mine would not reach the size of hers! I got my wish, you see, these are plenty big enough!" We all laughed. I thought that they certainly were.

Then she scared us both. "Now you take Cecille. Hers are pretty much the usual size, but then she looks an awful lot like her father. So I don't expect she will have a problem with hers. My mother, that's your grandmother Gudrun, she explained to me when I was about your age, she says, 'The Thorsten line always produces women with big breasts. So you, Lene, can expect to have large ones too. However, it seems to skip generations. My mother had much smaller ones than I do but my grandmother had huge ones like I do. So dear Lene, yours will be big, but not as big as mine. Do find a husband who likes large ones.' I remember how we both laughed and laughed. Me, I was very relieved to hear her say that." Mom was really smiling over her memories of grandmother that day.

However, Mia and I both looked like mom! We looked at each other and mom's words echoed in our minds, "skips generations." Mia finally was brave enough to ask mom, "Does that mean mine are not done growing?"

"Oh dears, yours will continue filling out for the next couple of years, sometimes until you reach twenty." Mom saw the looks on our faces and realized what Mia had really meant to ask. "Maybe they will just get large like mine," she tried to console us. "Besides girls, think of how fabulous you will look, what with these tiny waists and large bosoms, why, the men will go crazy over your figures!" Well, that's one way of looking at it, I suppose. We were not encouraged, besides Mia's bust was already approaching the size of mom's!

Every morning after that when we two got up, the first thing we did was compare breast sizes. Yes, we did not luck out. Much later on when we were in our late teens, Mia and I both had melons, monster melons! Mia tried to console me, "At least our daughters will have only big ones." Somehow, neither of us felt cheered up.

"Yes, but pity our granddaughters!" I exclaimed. Slowly, life became even more awkward for me as I grew up. I hoped that this Emperor fellow liked big breasts; if not, he was in for a large surprise, but there was nothing, of course, that I could do about it. Heredity was at work; the Thorsten line had struck again.

When I was thirteen, I decided it was time to really get down to work and figure out this society. What did dad do? What did mom have in mind with this Empress thing? What could she possible desire to have result from this union that she had so carefully planned?

The first was easily answered. He took me to work with him, saying I ought to see just how a country was run. I sat in the back; of course, Mia was with me should I need anything. I could not just get up and leave, since I couldn't open the doors. While we found it interesting at first, it quickly became boring. What did dad do? He settled disputes between towns and cities, and occasionally between a person and a company, and once between two people.

Dad worked on advance plans for the country's infrastructure. Which roads needed maintenance and by when? He held extensive discussions between the mayors of the largest inland cities, working out what new roads ought to be paved. Cobblestone roads took a long time to make and were expensive. The criterion was one hundred thousand people. When a town grew that large, at least one paved road was built connecting it to the existing road system. Two towns were rapidly approaching city status, and dad was working out the optimum routes for the new roads.

Dad also worked out the details for countrywide festivals; the musical conventions took top billing. The Mariner's Guild submitted a proposal to purchase one large caravel from Velona. Such a capital expense had to have the King's agreement. I listened in on these men attempting to sell dad on the idea of spending thirty thousand gold goud on one ship. Our smaller ships cost a mere five thousand. In the end, they agreed to wait two years to see if we could acquire one via the new Empress, me. If not, dad promised to grant his okay at that time.

In short, dad was the strangest King I had yet come across. He was more of a business leader of his community, which was the country. I asked him after one session was done, "Dad, who makes all the new laws here?"

"Oh, golly, I guess that falls on me to do. The city mayors make their laws and then pass them on for me to okay. It doesn't happen very often. Now let me see, when did I make a new law?" I couldn't believe what I was seeing. Dad was thinking hard, trying to recall when he had last made a new law in our country. After a time, he finally said, "Now that you mention it, dear Maren, I don't believe that I have actually made one. I've Okayed six from some cities, but I've not invented a new one myself. I guess there isn't much need for any new legislation around here. Things work very smoothly."

"Interesting. Dad, where do you get your funds? I mean do our citizens pay yearly taxes?"

"Oh yes, yes, each year every person in Annelise donates one silver goud to the royal treasury. I expect to get three hundred fifty thousand gold gouds this year. The majority of that goes to build and maintain the roads and our little army. We have to purchase cobblestones for the roads, pay the workers who do the work, pay our few soldiers, pay for our small staff here, and occasionally we need repairs on the palace buildings. Honestly, dear Maren, I think even one silver is too much to ask of our people. Each year, I cannot seem to find ways to spend it to improve our people's lives. I've got a rather large amount of unused funds saved up for some emergency, for a rainy day, as your mom so often reminds me."

This line of inquiry got us nowhere. Next, we asked mom what her Queenly duties were. "Oh, I must set a fine example for other mothers, raising our family properly and perfectly. I must plan our meals, do the laundry — now that *is* a chore — iron your father's shirts and pants. When he has guests, I play hostess and entertain them, dine with them, that sort of thing. I help other women with problems that may arise. Only last week, the Ladies Auxiliary in Hodenhagen needed my help arranging a large social gathering. They are holding a flower show next week. Would you two like to join me? I'm sure you would have a good time."

We agreed to go, but this was not getting us any closer to the answer. Mom continued ironing away. I decided to take the straightforward approach. "Mom, why do you want me to become this Empress anyway? What possible benefit could you or Annelise get from having me married off to this man from Demokritos anyway?"

She stopped ironing and looked at me. Evidently, she saw me as nearly an adult for the first time. "Dear, that is a rather complex question. However, I can see that if you have thought of this, it is time that I am perfectly candid with you. Come. Let's go make us a cup of tea. You too, Mia." We went down into the kitchen for tea. I believe this mundane action gave her time to collect her thoughts. I had startled her with my direct questions.

A little later, over tea, she replied, "You see, King Ane was Demo's son — our founder came from Demokritos. He brought a copy of the *Prophesies of Demos* with him. That original copy is a very valuable and rare book now, stored in the Hodenhagen library archives. According to the prophesies, our two separate countries shall be joined into one sometime in the very early 700's, that's just a year from now. Annelise is completely content to continue as we have for the last seven hundred years. However, when your father first became King, we had visitors from Demokritos, from the Emperor's court, they were."

"They wanted your father to surrender Annelise over to Demokritos! We'd be just another conquered territory for them. Well, we know the *Prophesies of Demos* as well as they do. Your father told them politely, 'Not at this time.' They said that when the Emperor comes, then we would have no choice but to surrender. Dad still refuses to create an army to fight them. He still says, 'Polite gentlemen do not fight. Fighting solves nothing.' After that threat, I studied the prophesies again and saw that if we provide the Empress, then we will be joining Demokritos as an equal, not as a conquered country."

"I am so hoping that you can go to bat for us. I know that in Demokritos, each citizen is expected to pay the King a gold coin each year — that's twenty times the taxes we have here. I hope that you can get that lowered somewhat. Mostly, I am hoping that you can do two things. One, keep the Emperor from trying to conscript our young men into his growing army of fighters, called Centurions. Two, get them to change their horrible attitudes on clothing themselves. They dress as if they are barbarians. Perhaps, Maren, you will be able to get them to become civilized and wear proper clothing."

"Another thing, Maren, if you can find a way to get us a caravel, that would be nice. As you know, we would greatly like increased imports of silk, such as in your dresses. Around here, we just cannot import enough silk to meet the demand. I guess what I am saying, Maren, do what you can that will help us all here. We do not want to be a conquered country, subject to the whims of some distant Emperor. At least, with you as their Empress, we have someone looking out for us there. That's why I had to do what I did to you, your arms. I hated to do that to you, my precious little Maren, but I had to for the sake of our entire country. I hope that you can forgive me."

"I understand mom. I would have done much the same thing. There is nothing to forgive; you acted in the best interests of seven million, not just one person. I promise you I will do all that I can for us." I attempted to put her at ease. She was near tears with her admission. I knew that seeing me every day only reminded her of what she had done to my baby body the day it was born. She hugged me for a long time after that.

"I didn't realize how horrible this would be for you, how hard and impossible your life would be, Maren. I am so sorry," she finally broke down.

"I know mom. I know. Yet, mom, there are seven million of your subjects out there that are depending upon you and me to make this work out. We have to be strong and firm up our resolve to see this through." She stopped crying and began sniffing.

"Yes, yes, Maren, you are right. This is no time for recriminations. We must be brave and make this work for our people. I slipped there a little. I value you more highly than I value the seven million. I guess that is my motherly instincts at work."

I grinned, "Yes, how about a hug, mom?" She hugged me again.

Hans, Mia, and I went to my bedroom. "Well, now we know," Mia stated. "It's actually rather obvious now that she told us why."

"Everything depends upon just how much actual influence Bethany has over this Emperor fellow," Hans pointed out.

"I know," I replied. "Annelise is such a strange country as countries go. I mean they are contented, non-aggressive, totally hung up on clothing and appearances. Yet, there is no crime and no aggression. There is not even an army and only a paltry taxation system. Any general worth his salt could see that conscripting men from such a country would produce the worst possible soldiers. It's highly likely that they would not even fight if forced to do so. I think that I ought to be able to convince Demokritos people of that. Even if they ask for gold, then that could be acceptable, if we can get something from Demokritos in return."

"You know, I've been thinking," Mia interrupted. "It seems to me that the dress designers and makers hold the real power behind the scenes in this country. Have we ever counted their numbers? I did a rough guess with Cecille's help last night. Here in Hodenhagen, we have two hundred fifty thousand people, roughly. One quarter are in the clothing and related industries. Incredible isn't it. What would happen if the dress designers began introducing some new style of dresses, perhaps without these enormous hoops? Within a few years, the whole society would adopt the new style, if only to be modern and current along with everyone else."

"I'd give anything to get out of wearing this hoop skirt!" I declared.

"So would I," Mia replied. "I suppose the change would have to be a gradual one, not a drastic one. I have an idea. Maren Elizabet, I am going to try an experiment here in Annelise. It will take years to work out, but if it works, these hoops may eventually become a thing of the past."

"Can't you make it go faster, like by tomorrow?" I jested. We three laughed.

In the spring of 699, that is September, Mr. Halvor took us on our last field trip. This time, we were going to visit the cobblestone factory in Genser, about three hundred miles southeast of Hodenhagen on the Feld river. He wanted us to see just how they were made, the process from start to finished stone. It illustrated how many different jobs coordinated to produce a final product.

We always enjoyed these field trips, because we got to travel. By royal coach, it took ten days to get from Hodenhagen to Genser. Always, we got to stay at fine inns, meet other people, and chat with them. I enjoyed this immensely, because for a brief time, I could forget that this body had no arms. Mia would carefully arrange my hair over my shoulders as we sat at our table. This way, when someone would come over to chat, they would not notice their absence. Freer conversations resulted, and I felt like a normal person for this brief time.

We were approaching Genser late in the afternoon. A drizzly rain had developed just after we had lunch in a small town and it had been following us the rest of the way into the city. Just as our coach reached the magnificent stone bridge over the Feld river west of the city, our driver unexpectedly stopped the coach. "Looks like someone has had a breakdown at the bridge," he called down to us.

Dad always sent along two of his guards with us on each field trip;

they shared driver duties. Inside, Hans, Mia, Lise, Mr. Halvor, and me, looked at our other guard, whose name was Frederik. "You five stay put; let us check it out," he said, as he climbed out of the coach, joining the driver. The two began to walk up to the coach, which appeared to be somehow broken down.

Hans and Mr. Halvor tried to peer out of the side windows of our coach to see what was happening. "I see a coach at a weird angle. It's blocking the bridge," Hans told us. "Our guards are approaching its driver."

"What's going on?" Mr. Halvor exclaimed, quite shocked.

"Trouble!" Hans called out. "Several more men have just attacked our two guards, both are on the ground. Four men are coming this way with swords in their hands. I thought that there was no crime in Annelise!"

"Shocking behavior! This is outrageous! I demand to know what is going on. What have you done to our driver?" Mr. Halvor yelled angrily, as the four men wearing masks over their heads came up to the coach doors.

"Get out now!" one man said gruffly, and the men opened both doors. Hans had to help me down, while Mr. Halvor assisted Mia and Lise climb out safely, no easy task in our confining clothing and boots.

As soon as we were all outside, the same gruff voice said, "That's the one. She's got no arms." Mr. Halvor tried to say something, but another man struck him on the back of his head with the hilt of his sword. Mr. Halvor collapsed onto the ground as if someone dropped a sack of potatoes. Hans tried to get between us and the men, but he was not armed, and there were four of them.

"Behind you," I called out to Hans. Too late, one struck him on the back of his head as well. I watched as Hans slumped onto the ground.

"You are making a big mistake. We are the King's children," I tried to intervene.

"We know. We came to dispose of you. We don't want the prophesy to be filled. We don't want our Boy Emperor to find you. Gag her and tie the others up." Before we could do anything, strong hands forced Mia's arms behind her, while one tied a rag over my mouth, silencing me. Lise was then tied up as well as Hans. After we all were gaged, the four men picked us up and carried us toward the coach. I wiggled and struggled to break free, but that was futile on my part. I figured they were kidnaping us, going to put us in their waiting coach.

Wrong. As they got to the bridge, the voice said, "Throw them in. It will look like an accidental drowning." I wiggled even harder but found myself falling. I took as deep a breath as possible, which was not much, considering my waistline. I hoped the others were doing likewise. I heard four splashes, and felt my body sinking rapidly, as the huge dress soaked up water and became a dead weight. I knew that we'd never surface and that I had little air to hold.

I backed up out of the body and above the water. Looking down, I latched onto all four of our sinking bodies and rapidly pulled them up out of the water and over onto the cobblestones, lying them as softly as I could onto the hard ground. The four men had already climbed aboard their coach and were just starting up, heading on into Genser.

I was mad — that is putting it mildly. I forgot everything else and let lose a lightning bolt at the carriage. Wham! The bolt hit and shattered the carriage; the horses bolted in fear and ran on down the road, dragging part of their harness with them. Four men stumbled out of the wreckage of the carriage.

Wham! Another bolt hit one of the men. I had not shot that one! I looked down; there was Mia floating up beside me. Hans was too groggy to be effective. Wham! Wham! Wham! I shot another and Mia, two. All four men went down and did not get up. Mia and I looked down at our bodies. She was tied up, and we were all gagged, but all were alive. Lise looked terrified.

I wiggled my body over to Mia's and she pulled the gag out of my mouth. I then used my teeth to undo her bonds eventually. She then crawled over to Hans and freed him, though he was still unconscious. A minute later, Lise was free as well. "Check on Hans, Mia." I ordered. "Lise, can you help me get up please?"

In our soaking wet monster clothing, we weighed a ton. Poor Lise could not get to her feet! Neither could Mia for that matter, she merely crawled over to Hans and examined his head wound. "It's not serious I don't think," she called out. I felt relieved.

I then lifted my own body up and steadied it until I had my footing. Then, I did the same for Lise and Mia. "How did? I don't? Lightning? What's happening?" poor Lise was petrified and unable to even think a straight thought right now.

"Mia, can you walk?" I asked.

"Maybe."

"Check on Mr. Halvor. See if he is going to survive. Lise and I will attempt to check on our guards. Come on, Lise, see if you can walk over to me, and hold on to me. I know I cannot do this by myself. I need your help." I tried to get Lise to do something, knowing that if she could just start to do something, anything, she would start to pull out of her fright. I watched her struggle to take even one step. "Very small steps, Lise," I coached her. She reached me and had already begun to recover her wits. I dare not move a muscle. I knew that I'd just fall down if I tried to move like this, for I weighted a ton!

At last, I felt her arm sliding around my waist, steading both herself and me. Together, we took very small steps toward our two fallen guards. By the time we reached them, Mia called out, "Mr. Halvor is going to be fine too. Out cold."

"Good. Lise, kneel down and see if they are alive. Check their pulse please." That was easy, going down, the weight of our soaked dresses pulled us down rapidly, almost too rapidly for me, and I fell over onto my face. Ouch. With effort, I sat up, and Lise began feeling for a pulse.

"I got one. He's alive," she pronounced. "He is too. Now what do we do?" Lise asked.

"Start taking off my clothes; we must get out of these wet things and into something warm and more manageable, at least until Hans and Mr. Halvor recover and can aid us."

She began undoing my dress. Wet like this, it was a struggle indeed. At last, I was down to my nickers and corset. Fortunately, by this time, Mia had managed to get back over to us, and she got Lise out of her heavy wet clothes, then Lise freed Mia from hers.

"Okay, Lise, you go get us some dry nightgowns and anything that you can find to dry us off with, please." I suggested.

"Now I can see what I can do for the guys," Mia said. "Golly, I could barely move in that wet dress!" By the time that Lise found dry clothes and had brought them to us, it had begun raining harder, so I had her take them back to the coach. No point in getting our dry clothes all wet.

"Hans is coming around. Hans, are you all right? It's Mia Kallisto!"

He moaned and then sat bolt upright, ready for a fight. His hands went for the back of his head. "Oh my head!"

"Hans, can you see if you can revive the guards? Mia and I will see if we can revive Mr. Halvor." She and I walked slowly back to where his body lay behind us by our carriage. Soon, Mia had Mr. Halvor sitting up; he too held his head, moaning from the pain.

"See if you can get into the coach, Mr. Halvor," I suggested.

"Oh my, you are all naked," he exclaimed.

"Either that or die," I said. This was no time for modesty. Hurting though he was, he still helped Lise into the coach and then lifted me inside as well. By then, Mia and Hans had brought the two guards, and they all climbed inside as well.

Those of us who were wet were now shivering from the cold. Hence, Mr. Halvor and the two guards began to dry us women off, while Hans got out of his wet suit, at least down to his underpants and then began to dry himself off. Of course, Mr. Halvor and the two guards were most embarrassed and very uncomfortable drying three nearly naked women off. There was nothing we could do about the corsets, not until we got into an inn.

Finally, dried off and covered with blankets that the driver guard produced from the topside carriage rack, we finally felt comfortable enough to talk. "What happened to you?" asked Mr. Halvor.

"After they knocked out you two, they knocked out Mr. Halvor and then Hans, who tried to protect us. They then tied our arms behind us and gagged us. They carried us three women and Hans over to the bridge and threw us into the river, hoping that we would drown. One said something about this looking like a drowning accident — hardly with tied hands and gags in our mouths." I explained.

The guards and Mr. Halvor looked incredibly distraught. Crime such as this just did not occur in Annelise. They did not know how to handle it. "My god! In those dresses, you should have sunk like a rock!" exclaimed Mr. Halvor.

"We did sink very fast indeed. I don't recommend that we go swimming in these hoop dresses," I tried to add a bit of humor to this otherwise terrifying incident.

"How, how, who?" Mr. Halvor tried to ask.

"How did we get out? Well, Mr. Halvor, I lifted all four of our bodies up and out of the water and onto the roadway there where the bridge is. Mia got my gag off, and I used my teeth to get her untied. She untied the rest." He looked at us in a complete daze, thankfully not asking how I lifted four bodies out of the river.

"But what was that freaky lightning storm?" asked Lise. "You should have seen it! Five lightning bolts. The first one shattered their coach and the horses — they ran off. Then, the four men came out of the damaged coach. I thought that they were going to come back and finish us off. Four more lightning bolts hit them. I saw their bodies fly up into the air. They have not moved since they landed. I hope that they are good and dead!"

"How can that be? One lightning bolt — that I can understand, because it is now raining. Five and all in the same general area? Why that is unheard of! Guards, you ought to go make sure that they are dead!" Mr. Halvor exclaimed.

"He's right. Come on Frederik. Let's check the bodies." The two guards climbed out into the rain and cautiously approached the fallen bodies. Hans kept an eye on them, just in case. Neither Mia nor I wished to say anything further about our casting of the lightning bolts. It might just be a dead giveaway that we were somehow Santi del Dio members, even though our bodies were Annelise.

A half hour later, the guards returned. All four were dead. All four were not Annelise, and from their clothing and weapons, the only conclusion was that they were from Demokritos. Frederik had confiscated their weapons and had found Demokritos coins on them as well as some gemstones, which he confiscated. After Frederik climbed inside, the driver began rolling us on across the bridge. It was another mile into the outskirts of Genser. For the short ride, keeping us warm became their prime concern. I was glad that they were not asking too many questions just now. How was I to explain how I got us out of the river?

A half hour later, we arrived outside the inn where we had planned to stay. Yes, there was a great hubbub as we three women, covered in blankets, were rushed inside and up to our waiting rooms. Hot food soon followed.

Frederik left to report this hideous crime to the local mayor and city guards. That an attempt on the life of the royal children just outside his town more than upset the mayor!

Later that evening, Mayor Asgar paid us a visit. He reported that the bodies had been found and buried. He assured us that they were from Demokritos and told us that twenty of his guards would constantly watch over us while we were anywhere near his city. In fact, they followed us all the way back to Hodenhagen, ensuring our safety.

Since our traveling dresses were totally ruined, he presented us with new dresses the next day, free of charge. The next morning, we visited the public bathhouse and then on to the clothier. Of course, we spent half the morning getting fittings and adjustments to them. Even Hans' suit was replaced. In fact, the Mayor covered all our expenses while we were in his town. He was most propitiative towards us, sending a message via our treatment after the fact that he was making amends as befitting the King's children. Repeatedly, I told him that it was not his fault, that he and his town had nothing to do with our attempted assassination. Still, he insisted on making amends.

Yes, after that, we did spend three days touring the cobblestone factory and learning our lessons. This kept Mr. Halvor's attention onto the planned field trip and not on the details of our attempted assassination. It was not until two weeks later that we three could be alone back in my room at the palace, where we could discuss the event among ourselves.

"Conclusion is obvious, Bethany," Kallisto said. "Someone or some group within Demokritos definitely does not want you to marry this boy Emperor."

"She's right," Hans added. "There must be some internal strife running through Demokritos. This mission may well be far more dangerous than it seemed at first. I am so thankful that I decided to come down here to be with Kallisto! God, I love you still, you gorgeous woman." They embraced warmly.

Dad was furious when he heard of our near escape. By the time we arrived back at the palace, word had already reached him of the attempted assassination plot. He was beside himself, even to the point of chiding mom for having my arms removed. "She's utterly defenseless. Now she is being thrown into the wild animal den. Lene, we cannot go through with this! I won't have my precious daughter treated like this!"

"It's okay, dad, really it is. With Mia and Hans to protect me, I should be okay. Now we know that the Emperor has some enemies. We will be on our guard from now on. It is okay, really it is, dad." He calmed down somewhat, but now mom was having serious second thoughts about what she had done to me. I needed to console her fast.

"Mom, it is totally worth it. If I can bring peace, it will have been worth all this," I tried to mollify her. Finally, she too calmed down. Both asked us to tell them in detail all about it, which we did, allowing Lise to do quite a bit of the telling, which helped her self-esteem.

Everyone was particularly fuzzy on just how we managed to get out of the river. Lise had no idea how it had been done. "Honestly, it was like some giant hand just lifted me up before my breath gave out. Another second and I would have drowned. You can't hold much breath in these clothes."

"Indeed we cannot," mom said conclusively. "Just how did you four get out of that river? Surely, someone else must have been there; perhaps you didn't see your benefactor? Maybe he left fast. Surely, that is what must have happened." Mom was trying to put our tale into some terms that she could understand.

Lise replied, "Yes Aunt Lene, that must have been it. Maren, there must have been another person there who rescued us. Only he didn't want to stick around to be thanked for saving us. That can be the only explanation."

Mia and Hans looked at me and I nodded. Yes, I decided to let them believe this wild theory because that was plausible to their reality. My lifting four bodies from the river would simply not be believed. It was too farfetched for their notions of the world. From our point of view, this was just as well, since we'd spent thirteen years here not attracting attention to ourselves, well not that kind of attention anyway.

This first evening that we were home, when Cecille returned from her apprenticeship work, she was all over me with worry and concern. "My baby sister! How awful! Are you all right? Let me see." She looked me over and then looked over Mia as well. Satisfied that we really we unharmed by our experience, she hugged us both and began crying.

"You don't know how I cried when I heard that someone tried to kill you, Hans and Lise too. Who would do such a thing to a poor, helpless young woman?" It was not a question, more of a genuine outpouring of her love and worry over us. That someone in Annelise would actually resort to assassination was totally beyond everyone's concepts of the world, I was now quite convinced of that, but not sure how I would use this later on when I was Empress.

Chapter 3 A New Century Begins

January 1, 700 arrived with a bang! Dad had imported a fireworks show from Tashien. All of Hodenhagen celebrated this night, watching the spectacular display of exploding spheres and loud bangs. Dad had opened the evening's festivities with a short speech, "This evening is dedicated to my youngest daughter, Maren Elizabet, who may soon become Empress. This show is for her, a little something to remember her father by when she leaves Annelise." Hans helped set them off, really enjoying lighting the many long fuses.

The half hour aerial display was then followed by an evening of dance music. Because no one knew just how long I would remain in Annelise, many young men asked me for a dance. I've never danced with so many well-wishers. My feet ached, and I came close to fainting several times. I don't recommend lots of slow dancing in these outfits. Yet, I enjoyed all of the attention I was receiving; after all, what young woman coming of age would not?

The next day, mom and dad conducted the Right of Passing ceremony for me, Hans, and Lise. Their excuse was that at any time, this boy Emperor might show up, and they wanted this last official Annelise ceremony done properly. I received a beautiful yellow silk dress with all the trimmings, many bright yellow ribbons adorning it. I was shocked to also receive a small gem encrusted Princess Crown. Dad said that this would identify me as being a Royal Princess, though I was a very long way down the line from inheriting the throne of Annelise.

When Hans was asked what career he wished to follow, I knew what he would reply. "Father, I wish to marry first. King Soren, I wish to marry your beautiful daughter Mia Kallisto. I will then become the lifelong protector of Maren and her handmaiden, Mia. I will travel with them everywhere and protect them both with my life."

This took my parents by surprise. They had not known that Mia and Hans were romantically involved. Both had kept it a secret until now. Dad looked at Mia, "Is this also your wish, Mia?"

"Oh yes, dad, very much so. Hans and I are so in love! Besides, Maren and I will feel much more secure with Hans at our sides when we go to distant lands. Please give us your blessings."

Neither of we three knew exactly how much we needed to say or even to beg to be allowed this request of marriage to be approved. After the assassination attempt, dad was now very willing for Hans to do this, we discovered at once. "Hans, I don't know how to thank you for accepting this most honorable and most dangerous duty. Yes, you have my permission to marry Mia. Thank you for protecting my two youngest daughters. You do not know how relieved I am to have you step forward to do this for us. Be it known, from now on, Hans Ditka, you have the full and complete support of the King of Annelise!" Dad hugged Hans tightly, rather embarrassing him.

Mom, tears streaming down her cheeks, hugged him as well. She whispered, "Thank you for protecting my two babies!"

Finally, Lise received her fancy new dress. She wanted to become a musician. Uncle Gustav got her an apprenticeship with the Collegium Musicum, the finest musicians in Annelise. I knew she would have to work hard and practice day and night, but if she had the talent for music, the time spent would be well rewarded.

Next, Hans and Mia had to decide when they would be married. Dad insisted that they do so as soon as possible. None of us knew when the prophesy would begin to unfold. He wanted them married when it at last began. Thus, on January 7, Hans and Mia were united once more, just as they had been last lifetime. After spending a lifetime together, they were still madly in love with each other, each holding the other with the highest respect and admiration.

Because of my daily needs, the two continued their usual sleeping rooms, Mia with me, and Hans stayed in his boyhood room. We all knew that very soon now that would change. I had secretly ordered them wedding presents from me, having done it six months ago on one of our field trips. I had chatted briefly with one of the Santi captains, whose caravel was being unloaded in Viborg. "I have a present for each of you, but I cannot carry them to you. I am afraid you will have to come to my room and get them yourselves."

"What? How? Have you been doing things behind my back?" teased Kallisto.

"I love presents. Can I have a clue?" Hans teased me as well. Together, we three went to my bedroom. I told them to look under the bed. Hans pulled out a large package, still wrapped the way it had come to me. I certainly could not have undone it to inspect it.

"There is only one package," Hans said, wondering if something had gone wrong.

"They are both in there. I'm sure you will know which is for whom. Now open them please. I'm dying to see how you like them!" I said, unable to contain my own enthusiasm.

Hans began to open it, and then he stopped. "Mia, perhaps we should wait until our wedding day to open this along with the other presents."

"No, no, open them now!" I insisted, knowing that Hans was just teasing me.

Inside, Hans found a short sword and dagger, the finest Highlander blades money could buy. As our official protector, he needed something other than the stupid halberds that were so common here in Annelise. Yes, Hans was very pleased with my gift.

Carefully wrapped in a separate package inside the larger one was a beautiful emerald necklace. Mia was thrilled and tried it on immediately. The large green stone looked fabulous around her neck. The two gave me a very long hug in thanks.

Just then, Linda contacted me from Velona. *Hi Bethany. Linda here. Happy new century. Is this a good time to chat?*

Hi. Same to you. Sure, I just gave Kallisto and Hank their wedding presents. They are off showing them off now, I think. What's news way up north?

I just wanted to let you know about Renzo. His body passed away in his sleep last night. He saw the new century dawn, Bethany. He was very proud of that achievement.

I began to cry. I'd been away from my husband now for fourteen years. Until this second, I didn't realize just how very much I missed him. I had no one with which to really play games or have real fun with down here. Of course, had he been with me, I still couldn't do much, not dressed as I have been. Yet I missed him so.

If it's any consolation to you, Jes Amir, the Guardian of the Anuir, asked him to come to the Red Desert. I took him there last night. I don't know what plans Jes has for him, but it has to be good for him.

Wow. Really? Now I can rest easier! I hope he gets freed like you and Chaucer have. He deserves it; he's worked so hard for us all. That's the best news I've had. Thanks. I miss him terribly though. Life has been particularly boring here; glad it is almost over. I sure would not want to live a lifetime in Annelise!

Any word about the Emperor? We chatted for some time. I realized she would not stop until she was sure that I had recovered from the news about Renzo. I thanked her for that, when I realized what she was doing for me.

Late the next night, Cecille returned home very excited, rushing in to see me. "Maren! I've done it! I've passed! I am a full-fledged dress designer and maker!"

"Terrific!" I leaned over so we could hug, and we danced around the room for a time.

"I'm so excited," she said as she began our nightly ritual, brushing out my hair. "I will get to work for J & H Creations, right here in Hodenhagen! They are one of the most exclusive clothiers, you know!" She gaily chatted away for quite a while. When she had me ready for bed, I sent her off to tell mom and dad about it. Cecille had come to tell me first; what a change in her attitude towards me.

The days slipped way as fall arrived in March. Everyone began wondering just when this Emperor boy would appear to conquer Annelise by marrying me.

Chapter 4 The Boy Emperor

"They're here! They're here!" Lise exclaimed, highly excited. She had just returned from her music practice when a messenger arrived from Viborg with the news. At once, she rushed inside to find me and tell me. It was April 14, 700. "A messenger came just as I was coming inside, Maren. I overheard him telling dad. The Emperor is in Viborg right now! He's actually coming for you! Aren't you excited?"

Scared was more like it! I had a sudden panic attack. What if this man was an absolute dog? What if he was a wife beater? What if he looked awfully ugly? What if his personal hygiene was deplorable? What if he found me disgusting? What if, well, I had so many what if's flying through my head it wasn't funny. Mia Kallisto came in and helped calm me down.

"Dad told me to tell you that the Emperor has landed in Viborg. He is bringing a party here to Hodenhagen by carriage. We expect that will take ten days, so you have ten more days to get things ready for him or to enjoy what little carefree life we have left or whatever you want to do. Mom's already going half nuts, issuing orders to clean the entire palace. I heard her place the most monstrously large food order I've ever heard her request."

"I'm getting nervous, Mia. Hold me a while, will you," I asked. Instead, she ran her hands over my shoulders, back, and chest, which was just as good. I calmed down with her gentle massage.

"I suppose that we ought to be prepared to leave with him," Mia suggested. "Perhaps we ought to start packing our things now, so that we can work out what we are to take while we have the luxury of time."

I laughed. "You realize how silly this sounds? Here I am a maiden who is expected by everyone to run off and marry this man from a foreign country whom no one has even seen. If we weren't on a mission, I'd be petrified no end, and yet here we are cheerily packing away." We laughed.

"Well, at least we are not giving your parents some trauma by making a protest scene — please don't do this to us, mom," she pointed out as we began going through my things. Beyond clothing, I had almost no possessions, save some jewelry. Without the use of arms or my toes, I had not acquired much of anything these past fourteen years.

While we were going through my things, dad came into my room. "You've heard, I see." I grinned. "Daughters, I want to tell you this now before things get crazy around here. Maren, if you don't like this man, if you decide you don't really want to go through with this, let me know. I will not force you to do this, honey. You too, Mia. I feel so awful, the position that your mother and I have put you two into — well, you say the word, and I will refuse your hand in marriage."

I laughed, "Dad, I don't have a hand to give." He looked at my joking face and he roared with laughter, easing his tensions. He hugged me tightly for some time after that. He then went to try to calm mother down, before she ordered the entire city.

"His heart is in the right place, you know," Mia said.

"I know."

Sometimes ten days can seem like a day, while other times, it seems like ten weeks. It was the latter for me; time seemed to drag on slower than a snail crawling across a field. We were packed by the next day, all except for the clothes we wore. The vast majority of our crates contained our dresses and clothing. Even Mia and Hans traveled lightly, both knew this day was coming and had not acquired many personal possessions either.

At last the 24th arrived. Cecille cut work so she could dote over my appearance, as if Mia was not qualified. Well, Cecille was the dressmaker now. She helped me into my finest yellow silk dress, tied up my boots securely, and then brushed out my hair, adjusting it alluringly over my shoulders, hiding what my body was missing. "Golly, you are getting a bust line!" she stated, as if Mia and I didn't already realize that we were growing melons, not breasts. Next, she put just the right amount of black around my eyelids to make my black eyes look haunting. Satisfied, she then walked me down to breakfast.

"My, look at my little baby!" bawled mom. Now that the moment was nearly upon her, she realized that she was losing me and was mentally back when I was indeed a small child.

Dad, however, was not emotionally off the deep end. He looked at me and commented, "Maren Elizabet, I do believe that you have turned out to be the prettiest of all my lovely daughters! Dear, you look stunning this morning. If I wasn't so old and not your father, why, I'd come after you myself." I blushed at his heartfelt compliment. Yes, I had great respect for my father.

This morning, Cecille herself insisted on feeding me, rather awkwardly because she'd only done this a few times in all these fourteen years. Yet, for her, today was special, and she wanted to do her part, knowing that such times were ending, perhaps within days now. I think that everyone here realized that once I left with the Emperor, assuming that I did, mind you, that they would not likely see me for a very long time, if ever again. For these people, Demokritos was a universe away, sea captains, excepted of course, since they traded frequently with the port cities of Demokritos.

During the day, the palace was a bustle of activity. I tried to stay out of everyone's way. Based on the daily messages dad received from the various towns along the cobblestone road between Viborg and Hodenhagen, we could easily estimate just when the Emperor and his party would arrive, around four in the afternoon.

As the time approached, Cecille made last minute adjustments to my appearance and gave me a final hug, not knowing if she would get another chance. "I just want you to know that I was awfully mean to you when I was a child. Please forgive me, Maren. I really do love you, little sister."

"I forgave you a long time ago, honestly Cecille. I will miss your hair brushing. You know just how to make me look really perfect." I complimented her in a manner, which she would understand. In this land, perfect was the key word. She hugged me even tighter.

We stood outside the Royal Palace, our families by the main entrance. Twenty of dad's guards, dressed immaculately in their colorful red and yellow uniforms, halberds in hand, stood at attention. Yes, they were mostly ceremonial in nature. A small musical band was to their left, ready to play a welcoming fanfare. The rest of dad's staff was standing behind us, close to the doors to open them for us or to retrieve any last minute item. At four, we heard the clip clop of many hooves upon the cobblestone road coming our way. Shortly the tops of a dozen carriages appeared over the little hill and then they came riding down the hill into the Royal Palace and its large courtyard. They pulled up before us. I took a deep breath, well as deep as I could anyway, just to calm my nerves. This was it, a moment fourteen years in the making. Gosh, I hoped he didn't look like a pig!

I knew that these men would not appear well dressed to my parents. Riff-raff would be their description. I wasn't wrong. The carriage drivers were our own people, of course. At once, the musicians played a lively fanfare, as the drivers, smartly dressed, hopped down to open the carriage door for them. Out stepped an older man, wearing a heavy fur coat that covered a while linen shirt that looked as if he had slept in it and a pair of cotton pants, equally a shambles. I hoped that mom would not mention this to him. As the man stepped forward, the music ceased.

He looked towards dad and Uncle Gustav. Seeing the crown on dad's head, he faced him. "King Soren Ryker, I am Alekos Tevine, Advisor to the Emperor of Demokritos. Allow me to present your new Emperor, Deimos Gavril. Sire," he said, motioning with his hand that Deimos should climb out. I waited breathlessly.

Out stepped Deimos. He wore a small crown on his head, that's what I saw first, the top of his head, as he seemed to exit in slow motion to me. His brown hair looked like it had been cut by bowl. That is, you put a breakfast bowl over your head and cut away all of the hair you see. It was unkempt at best, ragged looking. His body was tall and thin, a wiry frame. He had brown, piercing eyes; a rage lay behind them. His face spoke volumes. He hated this moment, and yet he was desirous of it. He forced a smile. He too wore clothing that appeared as if he had slept in them, linen shirt and brown pants, badly in need of a pressing. He wore a blue sash around his waist, the one article of clothing I liked at once. It did something for his appearance. Both men wore heavy boots.

By now, twenty-five Centurions had piled out of the other coaches, wearing chain mail and carrying short swords and daggers. They had formed up a line behind Deimos and Alekos, ensuring that nothing ill befall their Emperor, as if it would here in Annelise.

"Sire, this is King Soren Ryker," his advisor said solemnly.

"King Soren," Deimos spoke in a high-pitched voice. I noticed that his voice had not yet changed. Dad held out his hand and the two rulers shook.

Dad said, "This is my lovely wife, Queen Lene. Our eldest daughter Cecille. Our middle daughter, Mia Kallisto. Our very special daughter, Maren Elizabet." One by one, the Emperor moved down the line, shaking hands with each in turn. Each curtsied to him. When he came to face me, I noticed that he was a few inches taller than I was, even in my heels. His face had an outbreak of acne, and I felt a bit sorry for him.

He held out his hand, but before he could become embarrassed, I spoke, "Sorry, no arms. It is customary to greet me with a hug, if you don't mind, Emperor Deimos." For a moment, he stared at me. I do believe he liked what he saw; a real smile replaced his fake one. He awkwardly leaned into me to give me a hug and managed to pull my hair a bit, which I ignored.

"You are actually a very beautiful young woman. I was expecting, well, you know, someone," he was stumbling.

"A hag?" I finished his sentence for him. He grinned.

"Yes, a hag. This will work out just perfectly. I was doubting the prophesy, but not any longer. You, Maren, shall be my Empress and rule over all Tarra. Well, first I have to conquer it, but that is just a trifle."

"Why don't we go inside and have some refreshments before the Grand Feast we have prepared in your honor, Emperor Deimos. I'm sure that you would like to freshen up after your long journey," dad suggested.

"Indeed, Sire, we should take refreshments and discuss these matters of state at once," Alekos stated coldly. I didn't like the way he was ordering Deimos around.

As they began to file into our palace, I said, "Deimos, in this outfit, with these heels, and with no arms, I need some assistance. Will you kindly put your arm around my waist to help me keep my balance? Oh, under my hair please," I added as I felt my hair being pulled again. I noticed that Deimos felt very ill at ease around me, unsure of what to do and how to do it. I surmised that he had very little experience dealing with women.

As we walked inside, I asked, "How was your carriage ride? Long and boring?"

I hit it precisely on target, he smiled, "Yes, very boring, ten days of rolling countryside and nothing at all to do except stare at Alekos. How did you know?"

"You are getting a very wise and observant Empress, though a nearly helpless one, however. Are you sure that you want someone like me to be your Empress? I cannot do anything for myself. I have to have my handmaiden with me at all times."

He grinned, "Absolutely. The only Empress I will tolerate has to be one of the Eighth Degree. I won't have any other woman, period. I am so glad you do not look like a pig. I had nightmares that you would, you know." He was warming up to me, which I found encouraging, though he was dripping hostility and anger. "You speak my language well," he added.

"I was a bit worried myself," I confided. "Yes, pull out the chair for me. Thanks. You best let my sister sit beside me, unless you want to help me sip my tea." I wanted to make him acutely aware of just what he was getting with me, right here at our first meeting.

He sat on my left, Mia, on my right so she could hold my cup. He seemed pleased that she did this and that he did not have to. I figured now would come the hard bargaining. I was not wrong. They wanted everything settled first thing, before any feast.

Alekos said coldly, "Maren will do fine. King Soren, we will take Maren, who is of the Eighth Degree, back with us to be our Empress, thereby uniting our two countries into one for the first time in seven centuries. You will, of course, retain your title and throne, King Soren, just as we allow our seven Kings to rule over their domains, which comprise Demokritos."

Dad cleared his throat. "Not so fast, Advisor Alekos. Before I give up my daughter to become your Empress, we must reach an understanding or I will be forced to refuse her hand, figuratively, that is."

Alekos, who did not tolerate backtalk to his orders, glared at dad. "You do not even have an army to stop us. Our twenty-five men we brought are enough to conquer your entire kingdom. Your guards are a joke, if you think that would hinder us."

"You are absolutely right. We do not have an army, never have had one in seven centuries. Now isn't that something!" Dad replied cheerily. Yes, now that he mentioned it that is an amazing fact. "Yet, if you try to take Maren by force, I am afraid that everyone in Annelise will try to stop you. You would have to kill all seven million of us, after that what would you have? Nothing at all but a wasteland."

"Now then, to business. If you wish Maren to be your Empress, we must have your Emperor's solemn word that she will not be harmed, mistreated in any way, that she will always have her handmaiden, Mia, and their protector, Hans, with her at all times, to assist her. She has no arms and is completely helpless, dependent upon others for everything. Yet, she has a very sharp mind, is very observant, very wise, and well suited to be your Empress. She is kind and loving, a perfect daughter in all ways. She dresses perfectly, knows our customs, laws, and people and can well represent us in your councils. If we ever find out that dear Maren has been mistreated in any way, you may expect seven million people to come marching into Demokritos to seek revenge." Those were the strongest words that I ever heard dad utter!

"We have been studying your own ways — the policies concerning women of the Eighth Degree. If she is mistreated in any way, if Emperor Deimos is unfaithful to her in any way, then by your own rules, he will be cast out, and she will be given everything that he possesses, including the throne of Demokritos, is that not correct?" Dad was playing his trump card.

Alekos replied somewhat taken aback by dad's strong language, "Yes, when a married woman of the Eighth Degree is harmed or mistreated or her husband is found unfaithful, all his property, his wealth, is forfeited to the woman, and he is cast out of our society, coinless. That is correct. You may be assured that Emperor Deimos will be held to that standard as well as any other man who has married a woman of the Eighth Degree. Does that satisfy you?"

"Handmaiden and protector?" dad asked.

"Yes, of course, the Emperor will not always have time to see to her every need, so they will be most welcome to come and assist Maren. She will need help with everything. We have had many women of the Eighth Degree as our Empresses over these many years. In fact, having her own handmaiden greatly assists us, because there are at the present far too few women at our palace. I'm sure that Emperor Deimos will greatly appreciate the efforts of handmaiden Mia and protector Hans." Deimos nodded his agreement.

"Good, that is settled then. Now about the taxes Annelise shall pay," Alekos continued. "We are well aware of the fact that we cannot obtain men for our mighty army as we set out to conquer all known lands of Tarra, forming the vast Holy Empire as foretold in the Prophesies of Demos. By the time that we got your men trained and fit for combat, we will have already conquered the world. Instead, the Emperor asks that you provide monetary support for this global campaign. Shall we say a gold piece per citizen per year?"

"You realize that our taxes here are a silver per person per year?" dad replied. "If we are to donate such humongous funds, my people will need to see something in return. It is criminal to only take and never give, you see. I'm sure that you do not want Demokritos and your Emperor here to be considered nothing more than a common criminal by seven million people. Such a disgrace would be unthinkable by civilized people that we all are, your people and mine. Might I offer a suggestion?"

Since Alekos merely glared at dad, he cheerily continued, "Our country would greatly desire to acquire some of these sleek, new caravels that have been landing at our ports. We know that your brilliant shipwrights have been able to copy them. What say you to giving us back a new caravel each year in return for our taxes? We both know, and I'm sure that my citizens also know, that a caravel certainly does not cost a fraction of the seven million gold coins that you would be receiving from us. Yet, it would be a little exchange of something that we here find valuable and can definitely put to good use."

I think that in that moment, Alekos began to think that he was dealing with a moron. Dad was asking for a thirty thousand gold piece ship in return for seven million. Yet, he didn't know what I knew. Annelise had neither the raw materials, large hardwood trees, nor the shipwright skills to build such ships on our own. The best we could possibly hope for was to purchase them from the Santi up in Velona.

"That sounds more than fair, very reasonable," Alekos replied with a covert grin, thinking he had just gotten a tremendous concession from dad.

Dad then asked, "Surely, you do not want us to ship you seven million gold coins? Maren, what would that weigh?" Dad asked me to do the math as a way of slyly allowing me to demonstrate my skills.

"Dad, that is about two hundred twenty tons. One of our dahabea can carry at most twenty, so that would mean eleven trips from here to there. Considering the sailing distance and our speeds, why, one ship could not transport that much gold if it sailed continuously all year long. We would need to make a fleet just to carry the Emperor his taxes, dad."

Deimos grinned; he evidently enjoyed seeing me in action and Alekos squirming a little.

"Ah, yes, that seems fraught with problems. I assume that you have an alternative?" he nearly sneered at dad.

"Might I suggest precious stones? How about the green jade. Here is a sample. What would you estimate your value for such a stone?" dad asked. I now marveled at dad. Just what was he doing? I had no idea at all.

Alekos examined the raw jade stone, compared its weight against some coins of his in his other hand. "One this large, perhaps one hundred gold coins."

"Excellent," dad said cheerily, "would you accept the raw jade as our tax payments each year? We can send it all in one dahabea trip. Would you like payment for this year as well, even though it is nearly half over?"

Alekos smiled; his greedy eyes sparkled, "Certainly, that would be quite acceptable to us, and I must say unexpectedly kind of you King Soren. Yes, we certainly are starting out our union on the right foot, as they say."

"Excellent, Emperor Deimos. Expect a shipment by the end of spring," dad replied. "Our caravel?"

"Well, we will leave one behind when we sail for home," Deimos answered for Alekos; he was determined to have some little say in these negotiations. Alekos gave him a dark look, but did not countermand his order.

"I believe that is all we need to discuss at this time," Alekos stated flatly.

"I would agree," dad said. "Now our butlers will show you to your rooms. I presume that you will want to bathe and properly attire yourselves for the grand feast in your honor. There is just enough time for you to clean up. You know we are always saying a clean, properly dressed man is a noble man. Proper dress for a proper life; we pride ourselves on always looking perfectly dressed. If perhaps you are in need of better clothing, let me know; we have quite a wardrobe here at the palace, for guests who are in dire need of perfect, proper clothing."

Both men glared at dad, who took this as a no. I took this opportunity to insert myself into the picture a little more. "Deimos, if you like, I can walk with you and show you the guesthouse that dad has for you. It is our finest guesthouse. On the way, I can also show you the public bath as well, in case you wish to bathe first."

Deimos was a little uncertain how to respond; he said hesitatingly, "Sure, why not. Thanks, Maren." He helped me up, and I waited until his arm was around my waist before I began leading him.

"Do you always walk this slowly?" he asked, as we now found ourselves alone for the first time, slowly making our way to the bathhouse.

"It's my boots. Lift up my hoop skirt and you will see why I move so slowly and need your strong arms to help me keep my balance," I said demurely. He did so very awkwardly, as if there was an evil demon just under my skirt.

"Oh, how can you even walk in those boots?" he exclaimed.

"I am very used to them, only it is difficult because of the dress. I have to take small steps, but this dress does not allow me to see where my feet are. Hence, I have to be extra careful. I can't catch myself if I stumble, no arms, you see." I chatted on, making him more and more aware of just what he was getting himself into with a woman of the Eighth Degree. I owed him that much, for his sake and for mine.

On our way at last to the guesthouse, he said, "I liked the way you could do all that math in your head. I have trouble with it myself. I like you, Maren."

"I make up for my lack of arms and dependency on others in other ways. You will see. I do hope that you do not find me ugly or distasteful, what with me having no arms."

"Oh no, Maren. I swore that I would only have a woman of the Eighth Degree as my Empress! I mean it. You are anything but ugly to me."

"Thanks, I hope you don't mind having to do everything more me. I am so completely helpless," I poured it on thick and heavy, testing the waters.

"Well, you will always have your handmaiden and protector with you. I do hope they will see to some of your needs."

"Oh yes, I'm sure they will, Deimos. Yet, when we retire for the night, I will then be dependent upon you. My handmaiden will not be sleeping with us, I hope."

He flushed, and I knew then that he had never slept with a woman before. "No, that's true. I guess you will just have to tell me what you need,

Maren. I will learn quickly," he insisted. I left him at the doorstep, and he wanted to kiss my hand, but realized I didn't have one. I reminded him by leaning forward, and he gave me a hug. He was smiling to himself as he entered the room.

Sometime later, I finally got back to the palace proper and went in search of dad. I found him being ordered out of the kitchen by a worried mom. Evidently, something was not perfect about the coming feast, and dad was just in the way.

"Dad, can we talk a bit, just you and I?" I said.

He was very willing, and he put his arm around me, and we walked into the deserted throne room. "Dad, what is all this about the jade and taxes?"

He chuckled. "I've sold them on accepting boatloads of worthless stones in lieu of gold. The last laugh is on me. Dear, we have tons of those worthless jade rocks up north near the ice fields. The only use we have ever had for them is some women's jewelry. We get a caravel a year, and they get a boatload of worthless stones. Yes, I know that they consider it valuable, but we do not, and that is all that matters. Now our people will not have to pay taxes to this Emperor. I'll just send along boatloads of worthless rocks." I let my dad hug me for some time, but I wanted to hug him. What a brilliant move on his part!

Alone in the guest room with Deimos, Alekos said, "Well, Sire, that went far, far better than I ever expected. We are dealing with complete morons. I've said it before; this entire country is completely batty! They are so hung up on clothing it is ludicrous. We've made the sweetest deal imaginable. Now you have all the funds you could possibly need to finance your coming campaigns. By the way, will she do? Maren, I mean. Is she acceptable to you?"

"Yes, Maren is quite fine. She'll do nicely. She's rather pretty actually. I was expecting to see some ugly woman. I don't know why I thought that, but I did. Maren is rather attractive. She is so helpless, though. Well, she certainly won't cause me any troubles!"

"Excellent. Remember, stick to the plan, Sire. It's your head that is at stake."

"I know, I know. How many times have you gone over this with me?"

"Okay. I suppose that we should bathe and look more presentable. The fools have left us entire suits! It isn't even a subtle hint."

"Well, it wouldn't hurt us to dress up in their suits this once, now would it?" Deimos suggested. "It would make us seem more likeable to these people. It's only this once. Come on. Let's do it. You should see the boots Maren is forced to wear. I don't know how she does it."

An hour later, dressed in a pair of our finest suits, cummerbund and all, the two guests returned to the palace, our butler showing them the way to the large dining hall. Indeed, mom and dad had planned this formal feast well, figuring it might be the last time they had to spend with me and my sister. Musicians played while we dined and then for the dance held afterwards.

I believe that mom and dad were both very impressed that the two took their hint and came dressed properly, well nearly so. Neither wore their bow ties. I suspect they didn't know how to tie them. As before, Mia sat on my right and Deimos, on my left. He watched as she continually looked after me, feeding me while feeding herself. After so many years of doing this, it was second nature to Mia Kallisto.

While we were dining, dad said, "You are welcome to stay here as long as you desire. Deimos can get more familiar with Maren and her daily needs. We can take a tour of our country, if you like. Our cobblestone factory is quite impressive, you know."

That was the wrong thing to have mentioned, because Lise immediately spoke up, "That's where the men from Demokritos attempted to assassinate Maren, Mia, Hans, and me."

"What?" Deimos exclaimed, spilling his ale. Alekos looked sharply up, at strict attention.

"Oh yes, four nasty evil men from Demokritos, wearing masks, stopped our carriage when we were on our way to visit the cobblestone factory. They knocked our two guards out cold, and then knocked out Hans and our teacher. They tied our hands behind our backs and put gags into our mouths so we couldn't yell for help. Then, they picked us up, carried us to the bridge, and threw us into the water to drown. One said that it would look like an accidental drowning."

Deimos looked at me, stark white, "Is this true? Someone tried to kill you?"

"Yes, it happened just as she says," I replied.

"Please, continue, Lise, is it?" Alekos urged her on.

"Well, sir, with these clothes on, why, we women sunk just like a rock. With these corsets, we cannot hold much breath. I was just about to drown when some good Samaritan came along and lifted us four out onto the bridge, just in time too. Maren managed to use her teeth to untie Mia, who then untied the rest of us. We went to help the others. Oh, yes, I almost forgot the important part. It was raining by then, and a lightning bolt struck the coach these evil men were using to escape. After they got out of the wreckage, four more lightning bolts came down from the storm and killed them. We were all okay, but we were awfully frightened by it. I do hope that you are not taking Maren into great danger back in your country."

"This is the first that we have heard of this," Alekos said, a note of worry in his voice. "Are you sure that these men were from Demokritos?"

Hans replied, "Yes sir. We examined their bodies and confiscated their weapons. We have them still. No one uses a sword in this land. Perhaps you might recognize them?" He ran off to fetch them.

"How horrible, Maren! I had no idea that someone would want to harm you," Deimos said, a note of real concern in his voice, which I took as a hopeful sign anyway. He was not behind our attempted assassinations. From the shock on Alekos's face, this was news to him as well. Evidently, there are others in Demokritos who are against this union with me, I thought.

Hans returned with the weapons. Alekos examined them. "No doubt, those came from our land. You are sure these were not some of your people who are dissatisfied with this union?"

"Certainly, their skin was darker than our, like yours," Hans explained. True, their skin was slightly more bronzed than ours is. "The mayor also examined them and buried them; he did not recognize the men. They certainly were not from Annelise. Is Maren going to be in any danger once we return with you to Demokritos?"

"She should be very safe," Alekos attempted to reassure everyone, though he was still pondering the significance of this news. "Perhaps we should leave for home at once, Sire. Maybe there are other assassins afoot who might make an attempt on your life?"

Deimos looked afraid; yes, I spied fear in his eyes. "Sure, let's," he answered.

"I had hoped that we could spend some time together, here, Deimos. I wanted to show you our country," I feigned a bit of a protest. "But if bad men are still after me, I will feel safer when we are at your palace. It is secure, isn't it? I mean I will be safe there?" I pretended to be very worried about my safety.

"Yes, my palace is heavily guarded. There you will be very safe. No one would dare harm my Empress, especially one who is a woman of the Eighth Degree," Deimos answered me.

"It is vital that we return to the palace; only there can we guarantee your safety," Alekos added.

"We didn't know how soon you would want to leave, so we went ahead and packed most of our things. We can be ready to leave as soon as you wish," I explained. "Surely we can stay for the dance tonight? Will you dance with me, Deimos?"

"I don't dance," he said gruffly, but after an icy stare from Alekos, he added, "I don't know how."

As the music started up, I said, "Come on, it is very easy. It has to be for me to do it dressed like this. I'll show you." I stood by him, trying to nudge him into trying. I sensed a cold flash of anger from his eyes, but he stood.

Hans came to my rescue. "Put your arms around her, like this. Two steps forward, two backwards. Make them small steps; remember they are wearing heels." Hans and Mia demonstrated, and Deimos hesitatingly put his arms around my shoulders, as if it might hurt me to have him touch me there. While the guy is supposed to lead, I did it instead. Soon, he caught on; yes, it was a simple dance. In these great hoop skirts and heels, we could not maneuver either well or quickly. Yet, it was enjoyable and fun. Soon, Deimos was smiling, in spite of himself.

The last dance was the lover's dance, in which we would snuggle in close, we women leaning our heads upon our guy's shoulders. I longed for Renzo, but allowed Deimos to be this close. I had to, whether or not I liked it. When the dance finished, I asked Deimos, "Do you want me to sleep in your room with you tonight or can I spend it with my sisters? I don't know either your customs or your preference, especially since we have not yet been married formally."

"Time enough for that later, once you are safe at my palace, Maren. Probably it is best if you spend this last night with your sisters. You may not be able to see them for a long time. I need to discuss some state business with Alekos anyway. We can leave in the morning after breakfast."

"Thank you. Good night, Deimos." I kissed him lightly on his cheek. I just couldn't bring myself to go any further just yet.

"Well, how did it go?" Cecille asked me as she brushed out my hair before bed.

"Well, he is awkward. I don't think he has been around many girls. He has an angry streak in him too. I hope this all works out, Cecille."

"Oh I am sure it will, just give it time. You've only just met him. I wish I could be there for the formal wedding, but I certainly don't want to travel all that way to Demokritos. You understand, don't you?"

"Sure, I wouldn't want to either. Besides, Hans and Mia will be with me. Thank you for everything, Cecille." I leaned for a long hug.

Once ready for bed, all the rest of my family whom I would be leaving behind in the morning came by to wish me well and to thank me for doing this for all Annelise. I worked hard to keep their tears at a minimum. Finally, I crawled into bed, pulling up my covers with my teeth. I wondered if tomorrow night, Deimos would be tucking us in. I would have to sleep with him, whether or not I wanted to, that was for sure. I began to wonder if I could really pull this off.

After Cecille got me dressed and ready for the day, we went down to breakfast together. Meanwhile, dad's staff carried our crates out to the carriages and secured them to the top carriers. I was too nervous to eat very much, though I tried diligently. I dreaded the tearful farewells. It was worse than I had imagined. We cried a lot, before I was at last lifted into the carriage by Hans.

Next came their first decision. Mia and Hans insisted on riding with me so that they could attend to my personal needs. Both Alekos and Deimos considered this necessary. However, Alekos was reluctant to allow Deimos to ride alone with us three, although we did need to become more acquainted with each other. Security overrode privacy. Hence, both of them rode in the same carriage with us. As a result, conversation was minimal at best. Alekos was reluctant to say much of anything, and Deimos was inhibited by the presence of his advisor.

Yes, it was an awkward first day of traveling. I thought about just chatting away about the land and small villages were passing through on our way north to Viborg, but the icy stares from Alekos made me keep mostly silent. Finally, at the inn after our dinner, Alekos left to talk with the Centurion guards, and Hans and Mia went up to arrange our sleeping quarters. I had a few moments to talk with Deimos.

"It's been rather awkward for us today, Deimos."

He sighed, "I know, Maren. It's not what I would want. I think that we should talk and find out about ourselves. I think that is how it should be done. With Alekos there, I just cannot speak, well you know, freely, about us, I mean. He's worrying about my safety. General Alexandr Dros, he's my top general, he was very concerned about my safety. I guess he was right, after someone tried to assassinate you. Now Alekos is very worried. I promise you that when we get to the ship and are safely underway, we will have lots of time to be better acquainted. Can you manage for nine more days?"

"Sure, Deimos. I was beginning to think that you perhaps disliked me, you know, because I'm, well you know, so helpless and all that, needing constant assistance with nearly everything."

"Oh no, no it's not that at all! I mean I honestly don't have any idea of your needs, to be honest with you, but then I will soon learn. I just, well, feel funny talking about such things around Alekos, you know. He's so much older than we are."

"I understand. He's somewhat creepy, I think. Here comes Hans. I think they have our rooms ready. Did you want me to sleep in your room or with Mia? It's probably best if I'm with her, at least until you know what all I will need."

"Sure, I hope that doesn't bother you, I mean, not sleeping with me just yet."

"No, I know that you are going to have to adapt to my special needs, so let's not rush things, give ourselves time to know one another."

"Thanks." He managed a nice smile. Again, I leaned over and gave him a good night kiss on his cheek. He responded by putting his arms around me, giving me a hug.

Nine grueling days passed excruciatingly slowly. I could have cheered for joy when we reached the outskirts of Viborg. Even from this distance, I could see three sets of tall masts, indicating three caravels were docked here. Of all our ports, only Viborg's harbor was deep enough to accommodate the deeper hulls of these ocean-going ships. Probably that would change as Annelise began acquiring caravels of her own.

Soon we reached the docks and pulled up there. Deimos explained,

"We will be taking that one, the Red Dragon. Alekos will be on the other one, the Blue Dragon. Of course, there will be a couple of Centurion guards on the ship with us, though I know that you cannot harm me, probably Mia could not either. Yet, Alekos considers Hans to be a potential threat. Come on; let's get aboard, shall we?"

"Hey, go slower. I cannot go this fast in these boots," I complained as he tried to have me move along with his large strides. I nearly fell over.

"Sorry. I love sailing in the ship. It was my first time, coming here, I mean. Loved it. I cannot wait for longer voyages. I have a cabin just for us and one for your two assistants."

"Can you walk behind me with your hands on my waist so I don't fall off the gangplank, please?" He did so. It was more than a little tricky, especially when my dress completely hid the entire walkway. Worse, I could not tell when I reached the end and needed to step down. At last, he lifted me and sat me down on the deck. I grinned my thanks to him.

The design was very similar to our own caravels. The main stairs to the cabins lay behind the poop deck walls. However, our cabins were the frontmost pair, on opposite sides. Hence, I would only need to go down the stairs into the hold and galley for meals. Unlike our ships, there were only two cabins, one on either side, not four. Hence, our room was rather spacious, which my darn dress managed to fill nicely.

I reached a decision. Now that we were leaving Annelise, we three no longer *had* to dress "perfectly." I looked at Mia as she was valiantly trying to push herself through the doorway into her cabin. We both laughed at how silly we looked. Deimos, who had gone in ahead of me, asked, "What's so funny?"

"These stupid, impractical dresses," I replied. "The Annelise dress in the most impractical way possible."

For once, Deimos grinned an honest grin. "We know all about your absolutely stupid manner of dress. I was forewarned about it, though I had no idea how stupid it really was. I hope I am not offending your customs, Maren."

"Oh not at all. If it was my mom or dad, yes you would have just made enemies of them for life, but not with us. I think you will find us far more practical. Only we just don't have any way out of this mess just yet. I do hope women in your country dress more practical."

"I was so hoping that you would say that! I've brought along some of our dresses. We had no idea of your sizes and all that. If nothing else, you could wear men's shirts and pants, until we get to the palace and can obtain proper clothes that fit."

"Deimos, I could kiss you for this thoughtfulness!" I did so, and he blushed, which I thought was a good start. "Can we change right now?"

"Sure thing. Only wouldn't it be better if Mia helped you? I mean I know nothing about this."

"Well, now is as good a time as any. Undo that tie around my waist, first." Slowly I talked him through the extensive undressing procedure. Partway through it, Mia asked about the clothes she found in her cabin. She was delighted to hear that we could change into more practical clothing. Finally, he had me down to my corset, nickers, and boots.

"Wow, you look, well, better than I imagined you would look. Such a tiny waist. Doesn't that hurt? And I see what you mean about the boots. Should I take them off too?"

"Thanks Deimos. Women in Annelise are obsessed with having tiny waists. However, I don't know if my back is now strong enough to support me without it. Let's leave it in place for now. I know the heels have altered my legs. I can't put my feet flat on the floor anymore. I don't have any real choice but to wear these boots just now."

He then held up each of the three dresses he'd brought with him to see if they had any chance of fitting me. None did, why? My breasts were just too large. "Would you be offended if I wore shirt and pants until we got to your palace?"

"No, it would be far more practical on the ship. Let's see if any will fit you."

One of his loose pullover shirts did fit reasonably well, and his pants were a little big, but otherwise fine. I felt like a new woman as I looked at myself. He gathered up the massive pile of clothing and carried them below deck, while I walked over to see how Mia was faring. She too had donned a man's shirt and pants for the same reason as I had, only more so.

"I hope I never have to wear hoops again," Mia declared.

"What about these corsets? Can we get rid of them too?" I asked hoping against all hope that we could.

"I might be able to, but you've been wearing yours for so long, Bethany, I am thinking perhaps you ought not. Maybe we should ask Linda for advice about this."

I contacted Linda. *Hi, it's me, Bethany. We are on the caravel with the Emperor about to set sail from Viborg. We no longer have to wear those awful hoop dresses. However, Mia wants to know if we dare remove our corsets?*

Loosen them a little each day. I will do what I can for your bodies, but we need to do it gradually.

For the next ten days, at night, I felt Linda entering my body, altering my muscles in my lower body a little each night. By the time that we reached Demokritos, we were finally free from them as well. Linda also arranged for us to get boot replacements, though we did not know that just yet.

By the time that we two were free of our confining dresses, Hans had also changed into more comfortable clothing, similar to what Deimos wore. We four then went on deck to watch the ship set sail. I always did enjoy watching the land slip slowly away as the ship used its spanker sail to clear the dock and harbor. Its crew was efficient and skilled, I noted, based on my many years at sea last lifetime. I could relax about this detail.

Still walking about a heaving ship at sea in these heels proved troublesome for me, far less so for Mia. Deimos kindly began making sure he had his arm around me when I needed to move about. He proudly took us on a tour of the ship. The Red Dragon was his personal ship, we learned. However, compared to our old Sleepy Hollow, this one was filthy. I even heard rats in the bilge area.

Once that was done, Deimos finally said the magic words, "Well, I guess that you'd better start showing me how to properly take care of you, Maren." Yes, he and been putting this off for ten days now. If I was to be his wife and Empress, he had to be able to handle my needs, especially when we were at public gatherings. I believe that he also realized this.

"The main thing to realize, Deimos," Mia explained, "is to imagine that you have no arms. Then see what you suddenly can no longer do, at least not easily. Let's begin with something that's easy, eating. By the way, do you have any tea onboard? We dearly love hot tea."

"Now that I can handle! One second." Deimos found the cook and ordered us a pot. Soon, Mia was showing him the most efficient ways to deal with feeding me. "You must learn to work together as a team, and then it goes very smoothly with no embarrassing moments at the dinner table. You must watch her from the corner of your eyes and take your clues from her. When she leans slightly forward like this, she is ready for another sip, much like you would lean forward to take another sip." Yes, by the time we reached Demokritos, Deimos was doing a fair job of feeding me, though we all agreed that Mia would handle this aspect until he got better at it. None of us wanted to embarrass him at formal dinners.

The embarrassing part was my personal grooming and going to the bathroom. Yet, when we would be retiring for the day, he would need to undress me, brush out my hair, and help me into bed. The first night was a new experience for both of us. He undressed me easily and got my boots off with no problem. I often slept in my corset and nickers, so I tried to have him brush out my hair. That didn't work out at all well. In fact, he got very angry.

"Damn, why can't you brush your own damn hair anyway?" he yelled at me and then flushed, realizing what he'd just said. I began to see the anger side of him.

"Let's leave it til morning, Deimos."

"I'm sorry. I got frustrated Maren. Now what?"

"Can you massage my body for me? I cannot even touch myself and if you can just rub me from my shoulders down, it really helps me relax." One thing led to another. As he began to ease the tension from my shoulders, I noticed the growing bulge in his pants. Soon we were in bed. I discovered very quickly that he had never been with a woman before and had to take the lead. Again, having full recall of my last several lifetimes gave me a very different point of view from Deimos, who was only remembering some ten or so years back. It was awkward. I felt more like a slut, a whore; I did not love or even respect this man. As you might expect, though, he definitely enjoyed this part of his training, but not when I had to go pee afterwards. He got angry and then unwillingly helped me.

In the middle of the night, Linda contacted me. *Hi, Linda here. I see you are on the ship. How is it going with him?*

My body was asleep. I was rather spinning. *Hi. He did it with me tonight. I fell so used, like a whore. I surely don't want to bear his children.*

Leave that to me, Bethany. I promise you that no matter what happens, you will not become with his child. Now, I want you to return to the start of the evening. Go through it and tell me what happened, what you see, what you feel. She was running a therapy session on me again!

Sometime later I was laughing, not my body, which was still asleep down there, but I was. It seems that I had the misfortune to have also been raped some time before I had ever come to Tarra. Now that trauma was gone, and I felt more comfortable in playing my role here. I thanked her and began wondering how she knew just when I needed help. It was like a miracle each time she showed up.

Over breakfast the next day, Deimos began to tell us about his country. This we vitally needed to know. "Demokritos is ruled by me, the Emperor, from my palace in Kefall. However, our country is divided into seven smaller kingdoms; each has their own rulers, the kings. Four of the kingdoms have coastlines and thus port cities and Kefall is located in one of these, the Kingdom of Thrace. We will be docking in the largest port city in the Kingdom of Thrace called Patri."

Their country was founded at least seven centuries ago by two men, Demos and Kritos. Later, the kingdom was divided among their seven sons, becoming modern day the seven kingdoms: Phindos, Alia, Thrace, Theos, Thallyus, Arolas, and Penelopus. Ever warlike in the early years, at last the kings met and chose an Emperor to rule over them, thus ending a century of nearly continuous wars. Yet, to keep the Emperor honest and to limit his powers, a countrywide Senate was created. Their purpose is to create the laws that the Emperor and the Kings enforce. Members of the Senate are elected by popular vote from all the people within their districts. Hence, the people themselves have a say in the making of the laws of the land. Thus, the conflicts of the early years ended. However, over the centuries, the role of the Senate has diminished considerably.

Ever since the two men came to Demokritos, people considered the mountain Aylon Orthos to be a most holy place. In time, a great temple was built there, the Temple of Orthos it is known today. Here the oracles began telling the fortunes of anyone who made the long journey to see these women, who are called orthees, a word meaning Holy Fortune Teller or

Oracle of the Divine, we never were quite sure of the translation.

Deimos related the tale of the Eight Holy Degrees. As we had heard before, a new problem arose in time. Men would often forsake their wives, leaving them destitute to fend on their own. Sometimes the wives broke the sacred marriage covenant. Three hundred years ago, this became a major embarrassment, since half of the entire population of Demokritos was unfaithful to their spouses. The Emperor journeyed to Aylon Orthos, seeking the great wisdom of the Holy Orthee. There he was guided by the oracles to create the Holy Eight Degrees of Matrimonial Binding. This scheme had been in operation some three hundred years now and the broken marriages are at an all-time low. In fact, the only broken marriages to be found are among those of No Degree.

When a couple decided to get married, assuming that they were not extremely poor, they would journey to the Temple of Orthos to sanctify their union. The woman would sacrifice an appendage and the man would thus be bound to her for their lives. Only if they possessed wealth and power, would the orthees allow the woman to become of the Eight Degree, losing both arms at the shoulder. This then ensured her new husband of total fidelity for the duration of their lives, as he would have to assist her with everything in life, providing many servants as well. These were the women who were held in the highest regard by everyone, their sacrifice visible to all. They also wielded great power, but of that in a moment.

The Seventh Degree women sacrificed their arms at the elbows. The Sixth Degree, at their wrists. The Fifth Degree women gave up one entire arm. The Fourth Degree lost one hand. The Third Degree, three fingers of each hand, leaving only the index finger and thumb. The Second and First Degrees, two and one finger on each hand, respectively. Thus, as the degree of sacrifice rose, so did the power, respect, and honor of the union, the women, and the men who were so pledged. The scheme had achieved its goal; couples remained faithful to each other for life. Never in the history of Demokritos had an Eighth Degree couple been unfaithful to each other! The penalties were too great even to consider having an affair outside the marriage. If the man did it, the woman was given everything that the cheating husband had, land, property, money, even his job. Similarly, if the woman was unfaithful, she would be sent out into the world to survive on her own and none dared do this. (Well, none of this was actually true, but most believed it was so.)

Now only the very poor, those who could not afford to even make the trip to Aylon Orthos, had unions of No Degree. Here were found the few unfaithful marriages.

Obviously, women of the Eight Degree were very rare, only the wealthiest and most powerful men could afford such marriages. Further, these women also held great power behind the scenes of normal political life here in Demokritos. While the Senate made the laws of the land, once passed, the women of the Eighth Degree would meet in secret and approve or disapprove the new law. If they disapproved it, the law was void and cancelled! Further, if the Emperor ordered an action that these women disapproved of, they had the right and obligation to cancel his order! Finally, one of these women of the Eighth Degree would preside over trials of those accused of very serious crimes. They would decide guilt or innocence and levy the penalty, including death. Thus, the women of the Eighth Degree were not only highly honored because of their great sacrifice for Holy Matrimony, but also because of the great power that they also wielded.

We three quickly realized that power in Demokritos was illusory. Kings ruled over their kingdoms, yet the Emperor ruled over them. The Senate made the laws, which the Emperor and Kings implemented. Yet, behind the scenes, women of the Eighth Degree acted, perhaps undoing these laws and rulings, even the Emperor's orders.

More than a quarter century ago, the Santi along with Kallisto's aid ended the practice of the Holy Eight Degrees. To our limited knowledge, no new women of Degrees had been created in all these years. Still, it was likely that many still lived. Though likely old by now, they may still hold on to some vestiges of power.

It was a snarled political mess that we would have to unravel, made even more interesting because the Holy Eight Degrees had been reborn up in Megalos, now that that island country had come under the Emperor's control. Couple all this with the Kali band of assassins who made sure that no man mistreated a woman of Degree and the new Santi fortress in Patri and you have a tangled web of control.

Deimos had brought along a large map of Demokritos, guessing that he would need to show his new Empress how his country appeared. It was rather a complex one. We three were extremely glad that he had brought it. Now things became much clearer to us as he continued our education. Demokritos occupied the western third of the continent, bounded on the east by the impassable Katos Mountains. The entire country was a thousand miles long, east-west, while seven hundred wide. All across the extreme southern edge was a giant ice sheet, which Deimos said never melted.

Four of the kingdoms had the ocean as one border. First came Arolas, bounded by the Katos on the east. This was a long and relatively narrow kingdom, whose capital city was called Naxos. The Pinos River ran westward from the Katos across half of its southern border, before veering north to the ocean passing through Naxos. The Dark Forest marked the rest of its border, beginning where the Pinos turned north.

South of Arolas lay the kingdom of Penelopus, which Tinos is its capital city, located a few hundred miles from the Katos. The Illos River ran the length of the country, dividing it in half. Its southern border was the mighty Vardan River, which began at the Ice Sheet, and eventually wound its way through all Demokritos, ending at Patri.

Across the Illos lay the kingdom of Thallyus, whose capital was Thal, located in its center. The massive ice sheet marked its southern border, while the Ice River ran due north, joining with the Vardan just inside Thrace. It also marked its western border.

Across the Ice River lay the kingdom of Theos, whose capital city was called Theolopolis. The Marsha River, flowing north from the ice sheet and joining the Vardan near the imperial city of Kefall, marked the western boundary of the kingdom.

Across the Marsha lay Phindos, whose capital was Pirgos. Its major port city was Filantos, which was two hundred miles north of the ice sheet. The Phindos Mountain range ran east-west and marked its boundary with Alia.

The Crima River ran north from Pirgos through a pass in the mountains and on down to the capital city of Levkas in the kingdom of Alia. From there it continued to the sea, turning westward, emptying into the sea by Alia's port city of Preveza.

The kingdom of Thrace occupied the north-westernmost portion and was shaped like an enormous thumb. The Vardan River ran down its middle. A great road ran from the port city of Patri up to the capital of Axos. It continued following the river up to the imperial city of Kefall and from there on up to the holy mountain of Aylon Orthos and the Temple of Orthos. Thrace bordered with all of the other six kingdoms. Its border with these was very well defined, geographically. A great wall of stone, called the Lonki Basin entirely surrounded the outer edge of Thrace. Here was where the giant marble quarries were located on this lengthy and enormous escarpment.

Similar to Annelise, paved roads connected all the major cities and most smaller towns. Last lifetime, we had also docked in Patri. My memories of that city came back into my mind, as I viewed the large map. I recalled that the countryside was hilly and rocky in many places. Yet, the towns were brilliant and visible from extreme distances. The normal construction material was white marble.

Deimos pointed out, "We have long, tall aqueducts spidering their way across the landscape. They bring fresh water to the towns. Our white paved roads wind through the hills." I remembered them looking like snow paths against the brown earth.

"Mind if I take some notes, Deimos?" Mai asked. "We need to memorize all of this."

"Oh yes, the Empress must know all of the Kings and Queens, you will be expected to host them frequently at our palace. Let's begin with Thrace, since we have more to do with this kingdom than any other, since our palace is in Kefall, Thrace. My cousin has only recently become the king there. King Anatolios Gavril, he is twenty-three. He had only recently returned from Megalos. You see he, like me, insists upon having a wife of the Eighth Degree. Since the Orthee refuse to perform this ceremony any longer, he had to go to Megalos to have this done. He married Amara, who is twenty-two. She has only been of the Eighth Degree for a few months now. My cousin told me that she is having a very hard time adjusting, and I told him that she should come to our palace as soon as we arrive. I offered him your services to help her adjust to your situation. I assumed that you, Maren, would be, well, adjusted by now."

"Yes, I lost mine when I was born. I would be glad to help her all that I can. You were being very thoughtful of your cousin and his new wife, Deimos. Thank you." He smiled. He seldom was thoughtful, unless it served his purposes I was to later learn.

"The King of Arolas is Dimitris Docia, who is twenty-nine, and his wife is Daria, a year younger."

"Has she any Holy Degree?" I asked.

"No, I wish Dimitris the best of luck with her. I think he is very wrong for marrying a woman with arms, like my father. Time will tell though." I sensed a deep resentment in Deimos.

"The King of Penelopus is Eros Eleni. He is an old man of fifty-six. His wife Ariadna, fifty-five, is of the Eighth Degree, as it should be. The King of Theos is Hektor Georgios, the eldest of the kings at sixty. His wife is also proper, Angele of the Eighth Degree. She's fifty-six as I recall. Now the King of Thallyus is Leon Kostas, who is fifty-three. He too is proper, his wife Athena is of the Eighth Degree and is fifty-four."

"You see the problems only develop when the older, proper kings are replaced. In Alia, the King is Petros Homer, twenty-nine. He defies all traditions and has taken Hypathia as his wife; she's twenty-eight, no degree. Also new is the King of Pindos, Manos Kadmos, twenty-eight. His wife is Karis, twenty-six, no degree."

"You may expect all sorts of troubles from Queen Karis, Queen Hypathia, and Queen Daria. They are dead set against following proper tradition and marrying only women of the Eighth Degree. I suspect one of them may have been behind the attempt on your life, Maren. I don't know for sure, but I wouldn't put it past one of them to have tried to kill you. However, you are now safe. Once you are in Kefall as Empress, they cannot touch you, for that would be one of the highest crimes in all Demokritos, the killing of a woman of the Eighth Degree. Soon now, you will be safe. However, expect all manner of treachery from these women with arms; they simply do not know their proper place in our society."

"Well, that's a relief. We were all rather frightened that I would be in danger here in your country. I feel much better about it now. Can I ask what my duties and obligations as Empress will be? I'm afraid that none of us in Annelise has any idea what her responsibilities actually are. Accordingly, I have received a very broad education. What am I supposed to do?"

Deimos got angry again. "You're to do all the things the Empress is supposed to do!" His backflash of anger evaporated quickly. "Ah, well, ah, you manage our whole domestic household, see that we have proper food, and clean beds. Very often I host other Kings and Queens. You will be expected to sit beside me and welcome them. When we men break into talks, you are to entertain the women. You are the hostess for all of Demokritos. When Alekos gets together with us, he can outline them in better detail. He is one of our advisors, you see. I let him handle those details."

I realized that Deimos was just making this all up, what sounded good as he went along. He had no idea what his own Empress was actually to do! He, like me, was only fourteen, so perhaps our youth was to blame. Surely, though, he had seen his mother in action, the previous Empress. Little did I know then.

We contented ourselves to memorizing the map of Demokritos and all of the major cities, the various kings and queens. Knowing at least this, later I could put a face to each name and avoid making a foolish mistake. I certainly didn't want to embarrass Deimos if I could avoid it.

As the days passed and Deimos became somewhat better at helping me with my daily needs, we finally came upon the start of our new country. The Katos Mountains gave way to the hilly countryside of Arolas. Of all the kingdoms, Arolas had the longest coastline, more than double that of Thrace, the next largest coastline.

As we passed some coastal towns and cities, we spied many ocean going ships, many were exact replicas of those found in Megalos, while a few were replicas of Velona caravels. We also spied a few dahabea from Annelise plying the waters as well. Red tiled roofs contrasted with the brilliant white marble of the buildings beneath them, as we watched the ports drift by us. Yes, several times we spotted the characteristic open temples so commonly found in Megalos, great columns of marble supporting a magnificent roof with all sides open to the breezes. However, unlike Megalos, the climate here was much more moderate; the ratio of what we called normal dwellings to the open aired temples was drastically larger than on Megalos.

Several times, we passed so close to port cities, that we could see what the people wore. From a distance, we could see that the men were clean and often wore suits or at least well-fitting shirts and pants. The women commonly wore long dresses, reminiscent of those of Annelise. Instead of tight corsets and huge hoop skirts, their dresses flared out by hidden petticoats, as we remembered from our visit here last lifetime. Kallisto had been born here, so she knew well what we could expect. Dresses of this style would be heaven for Mia and me. One interesting aspect of our new dresses was the arms. While the dresses of Mia had sleeves, my dresses were nearly topless — two small straps went over what was left of my shoulders, baring my "degree" for all to see, as was their custom.

Finally, on the last day of May 700, we began tacking into the large harbor of Patri. Hundreds of smaller fishing boats plied the waters, and seven ships were docked, loading or unloading. The city stretched from the coastline up into the hills, its white paved roads like shining streaks pointing the way to heaven. At the top of one of the most dominating hills of Patri stood an impressive open aired theater, whose seats of white marble were clearly visible from the ship.

However, we did not disembark. Rather, Alekos went ashore and returned later with a number of women and several men carrying several chests. Deimos was also at a loss but recognized the women as they approached our Red Dragon. "Ah, they are the best dress makers in Patri. Now I get it. Alekos knows that many important people in Patri will want at least to see their new Empress. You can't go out in public wearing an old shirt and pants of mine, Maren. I think that they will get you properly dressed. Don't worry; it will be nothing like what your stupid parents forced you to wear. I've never seen such stupidity in clothing before. I really didn't believe all the stories I was told before I came to get you, but now I know that they were not exaggerating. Think of me as having rescued you from all that torture, yes, that's the word, torture."

I couldn't disagree with him. Just now, the party came onboard. "Ah, here is our new Empress and her handmaiden. You will properly attire them at once," Alekos ordered sharply. "Now then, Deimos, we need to talk while they get dressed. Come with me." It was an order, not a request. I felt a bit sorry for Deimos.

For an hour, the four women fussed over Mia and me. Only last night had we finally removed our corsets entirely, following Linda's explicit orders. It felt so wonderful being able to breathe again. Gone was the ever-constant pressure around my middle. I felt fabulous, so did Mia Kallisto. However, our measurements now were anything but the norm around Demokritos. My waist filled out to a whopping fifteen inches around; Mia's was seventeen, extremely tiny for the dresses here. Worse, our busts were already overly large for our height, weight, and age, making the fittings even more complicated for the dressmakers. Their strategy for this emergency dressing was to modify or alter an existing dress to fit. They soon found this not an easy task to fulfill.

Finally, after two hours of constant work, they had us looking quite presentable, though we each wore only one petticoat. My dress had only two thin straps over the shoulders; my ample bust would hold it up securely. Mia's had sleeves and looked gorgeous on her. Both of our dresses were emerald green, which the women said was going to be the official color of this Emperor.

Now looking the part of Empress, we went back onto the main deck. Alekos and Deimos were waiting for us. "Ah, Maren, you look very beautiful," Deimos said, but stifled his enthusiasm when he caught the cold stare from Alekos. I smiled at Deimos.

"Now then, we will depart. As is our custom, all arriving boats must be met by the Harbor Master and granted permission to set foot on our soil. You see, in port cities, the Harbor Master is a man of great importance. In this case, it is just a matter of formality; obviously, the Emperor is always allowed to land. However, many people are going to want to meet and see their new Empress, which is as it should be, especially since Deimos has chosen a woman of the Eighth Degree, bucking the modern trends."

"Here in Patri, the Harbor Master is Helas Dido. His wife is also important, as Melina is of the Sixth Degree. So you, Maren, should treat these two as important people," Alekos said didactically and coldly.

When our Explorers Circle landed here last lifetime, the Harbor Master was a wonderful man, Demetrios, whose wife, Evania, was also of the Sixth Degree. Both were just fabulous people. I wondered if this Helas was any relation to Demetrios. Slowly we walked off the ship and down the long wooden dock toward the throng of people awaiting our formal appearance. Behind them stood a number of carriages, which I assumed would be taking us to Kefall.

As we approached, I could tell Helas and Melina at once, because not only she had no hands, but also Helas was the splitting image of Demetrios. He was in his fifties, as was she. Alekos did the introductions, before Deimos could say a word. "Harbor Master Helas, Melina Dido allow me to present the Emperor Deimos Gavril and your lovely new Empress Maren."

"So very pleased to welcome you to Patri, Deimos and Maren!" Helas said happily, and he shook Deimos' hand and then gave me a hug. Melina followed suit, taking Deimos' hand in her two arms and shaking it. When she came to me, she put her arms around me and gave me a welcoming hug.

"So glad to see you, Maren. You look stunning. I hope you will come to love our country as much as we do. If you are ever in Patri, please stop by our home!"

"Oh I shall do just that!" I replied, although I didn't know if I would be allowed to travel this far from the imperial palace.

"Say, Helas, are you any relation to Demetrios Dido, the Harbor Master of some years ago?" I asked.

He gave me a very surprised look. Beaming, he replied, "Why yes, I am his eldest son. I was most honored to take over his position here a number of years ago. Alas, he and his lovely wife had since passed away. How is it that you know of this?"

"We in Annelise knew of your father. He was a very kind and loving man, a most worthy Harbor Master indeed. As far as we know, he and Evania were something of flower gardeners in their spare hours."

"Why yes, yes they were. Mom just loved her flowerbeds. We are now living there. Melina has continued to keep up the magnificent flower boxes. Please do convince Deimos to allow you to come for a visit. We would be most honored indeed!" He bowed to me, and Melina smiled broadly. I had just become an instant hit with the Harbor Master and his wife. If nothing else, I now had two new friends on Demokritos.

As we took our leave and began walking through the crowd, Deimos waving periodically, Alekos asked, "Well, that was impressive, Empress Maren. I certainly did not expect that. My compliments. Perhaps all of those in Annelise are not ignorant morons after all. Deimos, you may have been right in your choice of Empress. Now let's get going, we have a long way to travel by coach. I need to discuss many things with the Empress along the way."

We climbed in and soon were trotting through the streets of Patri. The buildings tended to be made of white marble, differing only in the colors of the archway stones over the windows and doorways. The streets were wide and filled with people and many shops. Periodically, the street gave way to a huge central plaza, filled with an aqueduct fed water well in the center and open-air markets around the sides. The streets resumed across the square.

Alekos allowed us to watch the city sights as they went by, knowing that we would be distracted by our new surroundings. He could wait until we left the city behind.

"Have you briefed her on our kingdoms and rulers, Deimos?" Alekos asked. I quickly recited our memorized list, which Alekos was very pleased to hear indeed. Again, I thought he was probably saying to himself: she is not an ignorant dummy.

"Excellent. You have no doubt been curious about what your duties as Empress shall be." I nodded. "They lie in several areas. First, you are in charge of all domestic duties of the imperial palace. Just now, we have very few staff, a transition time between emperors, you see. You will be allowed to hire all the domestic staff that you deem necessary to the proper running of the palace. You are to oversee them, giving them guidance and such. In this arena, several other noble women of the Eight Degree have volunteered to assist you in getting this going. It has been several years now since the palace has had any significant domestic staff. You will find things rather like a bachelor's home."

"Secondly, as Empress, you will be expected to host our many guests who come rather frequently for meetings with the Emperor and us advisors. Once more, these noblewomen will be able to assist you and provide guidance. I am afraid we men know none of this; it is women's work, you see. However, it is nonetheless extremely vital, as how you perform directly relates to how others see our Emperor. In these times, it is crucial that Deimos be seen as a wise and strong leader. I'm sure that you will do your part," he said covertly and with a slight sneer.

I decided to play my trump card at this point; after all, it was wise for me to know all of my new duties beforehand. "And how am I to know all the Emperor's plans and orders? As we understand this arrangement, the women of the Eighth Degree, such as I am, are supposed to review the plans and orders, countermanding those we do not feel is right. How am I to do this? Am I supposed to attend the various meetings as well? Is there to be some schedule that I am to follow?" There, I played it. From last lifetime, I knew that here the women of the Eighth Degree operated behind the scenes and wielded great power. Was I going to be accorded that right or was I just a mere puppet figure in Deimos' power grab?

For once, I not only startled Alekos, but also took him by complete surprise. I could tell that he was not intending ever to tell me about this aspect of rule here. Alekos was in a terrible bind! I saw that he most definitely didn't want me in that role, that I shouldn't have known about it, though perhaps I would have learned of it in time from the other women of the Eighth Degree in Kefall.

In a flash of insight, I now saw why Alekos was very hostile to me: I could well be usurping much of his power by countermanding his orders and plans! Deimos spoke first, "Yes, she has that right, you know. All women of the Eighth Degree are given that right, Alekos." Now I saw that Deimos was playing me against Alekos, working to gain some way of being able to override something that Alekos might order.

Alekos stared long at me with his black eyes, before he finally spoke. "Yes, you are much better informed than I anticipated. You are correct, Deimos, by being a woman of the Eighth Degree you are afforded those rights. Will you allow us to work out the optimum means for you to monitor them? At first you will have your hands full getting the palace in working order, I'm afraid. We can go over this detail later. Is that agreeable with you, Maren?" I agreed, very relieved to know that in some small way I might be able to exercise a veto from behind the scenes.

That quieted Alekos down considerably. He said little after that. We were quite content to watch the interesting countryside roll by. Five days later, we arrived in Axos, the capital city of Thrace, where King Anatolios Gavril ruled. His wife, Amara, recently from Megalos, had only just become a woman of the Eight Degree down in Megalos. I was to assist her in adapting to this new way of life. Hence, we stopped briefly to meet them and to bring her with us to the imperial palace. I wondered why the big rush, since from all hints the palace was in shambles.

Our carriages pulled up at his palace. The king's palace in Axos was quite grand, occupying several city blocks, with many buildings and quite a few soldiers present as well. King Anatolios Gavril was a strong man, tall and well-muscled, a leader of soldiers, I thought. His long brown hair and moustache gave him a handsome look.

His wife, Amara, was very pretty, with shoulder length brown hair, light brown eyes, and a well-defined bosom. Mia thought she was positively stunning, which was probably why Anatolios had chosen her to marry. She stood there, however, with a vacant stare. Her eyes were red. I guessed she had been crying just before we arrived.

"Well met, Emperor Deimos! Alekos. Ah, this must be your lovely wife. Empress Maren, I am King Anatolios Gavril, cousin to your young husband and staunch supporter of his."

"Very pleased to meet you, King Anatolios," I leaned forward, the universal signal for a hug greeting.

He was well trained and reacted at once, accepting my offer and gave me a strong hug. "Such a beautiful woman you have here, Deimos! You make many men absolutely jealous!" He turned to me and added, "When he left to visit your country and consolidate Annelise with Demokritos, we thought that he might be getting a, well, a hag, you know. No one had ever heard of you, let alone seen you. Now I see that Deimos was extremely wise in his choice. Is it true that you have been of the Eighth Degree all of your life?"

"Yes."

Now I detected a great sadness, which he had been masking, coming to the forefront. "It is my new, beautiful wife, Amara. I love her so, and she did love me and agreed to become of the Eighth Degree to so honor me and forward our marriage to the greatest of heights. However, since we have returned here, she, well she, she is not doing so well. Deimos has probably already asked you, but I want to ask you myself. Would you be so kind as to take Amara with you, and see if you can in anyway help her adjust to her new life here?"

"Absolutely, King Anatolios. There is nothing more important that I can do than to assist another one of us. I would be honored to help her. I am so very glad that you thought of asking me for help. I know that I can help her a lot." He threw his arms around me and hugged me tightly. When he backed away, I saw tears coming down his cheeks. I knew then that he did indeed deeply love his wife and cared for her a great deal. That was very reassuring to me.

"Thank you. I know that you are all in a hurry, so I have her things packed already." He signaled, and a servant carried a crate to one of our carriages; strong arms hoisted it on top and tied it down. While this was going on, he gave his wife a farewell kiss on her forehead and led her to our coach. After Hans lifted me inside and Mia, he lifted his wife in, and Mia helped her to a seat. Amara said nothing, but continued to stare off into space. I knew that she was traumatized.

Amara's situation silenced all talk as we rode off, continuing our journey to the palace. I had spent much of my last lifetime working with women who had been similarly traumatized by the priests of the Church of Jehosanity of Megalos. Just when we figured that we Santi had finally put an end to their mutilation of women, here some twenty-five years later, it had surfaced again, only it was now being called the Holy Eight Degrees of Matrimony!

As the days passed, Amara either cried uncontrollably or sat silent, gazing at nothing. She spoke not a word in the entire five days we traveled to Kefall. I thought that this would be a very good lesson for both Deimos and Alekos to learn; cutting off women's arms is not a good thing to do! I let them both sit there most uncomfortably for five days.

The imperial city of Kefall was about half way to Aylon Orthos. Spread out as if shining white gemstones across the rocky, brown hills of Thrace lay the grand city of five hundred thousand people. Thriving, bustling, productive described what we saw. The many temples to the Sun God stood taller than other buildings, their white columns standing like fingers pointing to the sun above. Already, I saw the white crosses of the Church of Jehosanity. They had been making steady progress converting the millions of Demokritos over to their religion.

Heavily laden wagons rolled by us coming out of the city, and we passed many heading into the city. The brownstone aqueducts came down from further inland, and at the center of the city, they forked into three others, heading off to the northwest, southwest, and alongside our road, heading west. Engineering feats were commonplace here in Demokritos. As we approached the outskirts of our new home city, we could see the Senate Building. This spectacular building was visible for miles, sitting on top of a hill. An enormous coliseum capable of seating thousands was also on a hilltop. Also clearly visible were the Centurion barracks, where tens of thousands of soldiers were housed and trained. Smoke from armories and blacksmith shops curled into the early morning blue sky above the sprawling city. We passed ten wagons carrying raw white marble stone blocks, one in each wagon. Construction was still ongoing in Kefall, reminding me of my visit here last lifetime.

The imperial palace consisted of large, enclosed marble buildings, occupying ten square city blocks. We pulled up before a huge building with bright yellow stonework over the doorway arches and hundreds of tall, ornate windows. A few people stood awaiting our arrival.

This was incredibly different from when I arrived here last lifetime. At that time, trumpets announced our arrival. The great doors of the throne room were opened as we walked up to them, perfectly orchestrated. Inside, we saw the Emperor and Empress standing before their white marble thrones, throngs of others lined either side of the room, a red carpet led from the door up to the throne. There we met Emperor Alexandr and his wife, Empress Agata, of the Eighth Degree. Evidently, they were the grandparents of Deimos.

In stark contrast, seven people stood waiting us. For the first time, Deimos lifted me out of the carriage. "Ah, here is our staff," he said. Leading me with a hand around my waist, he presented me to them. "This lovely woman is now Empress Maren Elizabet." They all bowed, respectfully. He went down the line introducing each to me personally. I saw that Deimos was proud of what he had done.

First was the second advisor, Darkon Drusus, thirty-three. He was more charming than Alekos and definitely not hostile to me. Next, dressed in his military finery was General Alexandr Dros, a thirty year old veteran fighter, who was in charge of palace security as well as all major campaigns. He gave me a hug in the proper fashion, but I could tell that he really paid me no real attention. I was another useless person in his eyes.

Next, I was introduced to his teacher, Nestor Laos, who was fifty, with greying hair. Then came their butler, Minos Kissos, a young man of twenty-three, who prided himself on dressing properly and being unflappable. "I'm always at your service, ma'am," he said properly.

Pandora Petros was one of the two women here, our portly cook. She was twenty-five and somewhat overweight. She had a jovial personality, and I knew I would enjoy her company. Last was Eirena Therios, who was only a year older than I was. She had long black hair and a pretty smile. She was our maid. "I have your rooms prepared for you Empress." I detected a note of sadness in her voice, however.

"Thanks, Eirena, we have brought a guest with us, Queen Amara. She will be staying with us for some time. Tonight, we will put her in with Mia, until we know better what is going on. Gosh, Deimos, is this all your staff for the whole palace? All ten square blocks?"

He flushed, "Er, yes. I am hoping that you can remedy this in short order, Empress." Eirena smiled.

"Well, I've a hot meal awaiting you," Pandora cheerily said. It's in the small dining room when you are ready."

We entered the main entrance. Here the domed roof over head dwarfed us, one could be thirty feet tall and still have headroom in here. Great tapestries hung from the marble columns, though we did not get a chance to study them just yet. I decided that I would need a road map just to find my way around this huge complex with its many buildings and rooms.

Deimos explained as we walked inside. "This we call the Palace. This entrance room is circular and fifty feet across, designed to show that the Emperor is all-powerful. It dwarfs us. Immediately ahead through those doors is our throne room, where we will hold court."

"Perhaps we should get Amara to her room and let her lie down for a while," Mia suggested. She was supporting the distraught woman.

"Good idea." Deimos turned to the left. "Down this hall is where our rooms are located at the moment. The first one on the left is our room, Maren. The one on the opposite side shall be for your handmaiden and Hans. Put Amara in there please." While Hans and Mia took care of Amara, Deimos continued walking me through the palace.

"Next on the left is where the General is currently staying. Opposite him are the cook and maid. Last one on the left is where my advisors are staying and opposite them, the butler and teacher." We retraced our steps, my heels making quite a racket on this marble stone floor.

"On our left this way is the bathroom. We have installed some new toilets and Bottom Washers, imported from Velona. I'm not sure what the Bottom Washer is for exactly. Opposite that is the coatroom, where we and our visitors can hang up their coats. Next on the left is the bath, yes we have our own bath here. Opposite that is the Small Dining Room, where we normally eat. Next is the food pantry, and opposite that is the Small Kitchen."

We returned to the Small Dining Room, where the others were gathering to eat. Each of these rooms off the long hall was forty foot square, enormous in size, with ten foot ceilings. The entire second floor was vacant right now.

While we dined, Deimos explained that the others who were staying here on the first floor would soon move up to the second floor. "I need a private meeting room," he said. I asked for one for my use as well. Since Mia had not yet come, I had Deimos begin to feed me since the others began supper. I caught several of the staff watching him, when he wasn't looking, just to see how he handled me. I was glad that we had practiced some on our way here. At least I liked the palace that was a start of my new life.

Chapter 5 Getting Organized

We had finished eating when Mia and Hans finally joined us. "She is sleeping now, Bethany," Mia reported. "Have you eaten?" I said I had. It had been a long day of traveling and Deimos suggested that we all turn in early.

"Tomorrow, I promise to show you around the entire palace complex. Then, you can get started on whatever it is that you would be doing." I saw that he really had no idea of what was involved to run a palace. I wondered just how long he had been the Emperor anyway.

I let him undress me, but I conveniently forgot to get my hair brushed out before bed. I didn't want a repeat of his anger outburst. I let him tuck us in and turn out the lantern. At least this bed was very large, soft, and warm. I had just gotten to sleep when everyone was awakened by a high-pitched shrieking, coming from Mia's room. Everyone dashed into their room, only to see Amara standing in the middle of the room screaming wildly.

"You are safe here, Amara. It's safe now. Come, let's lie down," Mia quietly talked the terrified woman down from her screaming. At last, she stopped and allowed Mia to get her back into bed. Everyone else returned to their bedrooms.

As Deimos crawled in beside me, he said shakily, "What was that all about? Is she crazy?"

"No, Deimos. This is a typical reaction that happens very frequently when you cut off some woman's arms. Even though she was unconscious when they cut hers off, the pain is still there. She probably shrieked like that when she awoke from the operation. It is not a nice thing to do to anyone, cutting off their arms."

"I don't believe you. You haven't done that, and you had yours cut off. I don't remember grandmother ever screaming either, or any of the other women I've met who are of the Eighth Degree. I don't believe you; she is just nuts. King Anatolios just married a crazy woman, that's all. Now he has dumped her on us."

"I have had fourteen years to deal with my loss, Deimos. Your grandmother probably had closer to forty years to get used to her loss. Amara has only had a few months; it is still fresh in her mind, shockingly fresh."

"Well, I'm told they used an aesthetic and that she didn't feel it," Deimos defended himself.

"Sure, I was knocked out, lying there totally unconscious, but yet underneath it was the horrible, massive pain. Amara is just now re-experiencing that hidden pain."

"I don't believe it. Let's get some sleep." He ended the discussion. I lay there for a time thinking about Deimos and his total lack of knowledge.

About an hour later, just as I was finally drifting off to sleep, Amara began her intense screaming. Once more, Mia had to quiet her down and get her back to bed. This time, no one rushed into their room. Deimos cursed and put a pillow over his head, trying to silence those screams.

The next morning, I awoke late, only to find Deimos had already risen and had left. I was alone and naked. Worse, the door was shut, and I could not open it easily. Damn. I looked over my options; about all I could do was yell and hope someone would hear me and come in. Yet, that would only draw adverse attention to Deimos' failure, leaving me in this state. I decided to put my ear to the door and listen for footsteps outside.

After a time, I heard someone walking and then called out. "A little help here please. Can you open the door for me and lend me a hand?"

A moment later, the door opened timidly. The head of our maid, Eirena, peered around its edge. "Hi. I need some assistance, Eirena. Can you help me get dressed?"

"Yes, Empress. What should I do?" she said looking at my naked body, deep pity in her eyes, as if I had suffered the most awful thing imaginable. Clearly, she had never been around a woman of the Eighth Degree either.

I made a snap decision. "Help me slip into the dress only and then put my boots on for me. I can't tiptoe around very well. I'm going to begin trying to do more things for myself from now on, Eirena. Oh, yes, from now on, just call me Bethany. It's short for Maren Elizabet."

"Yes, Bethany. Gosh, I had no idea just how awful your life must be like this. You are so helpless. I guess that is why Deimos has chosen you, so he can help you." She began to put my dress on for me. I didn't have the heart to tell her that he had forgotten to either help me get dressed or to send someone to do it.

"What about all of your undergarments?"

"We are forgetting them. Just the dress. This way, with my bottom totally open, I can go to the bathroom by myself, mostly anyway."

"Mia is sleeping in. That sure was awful — with Amara last night. Should I wake her so she can take care of you, Bethany?"

"No, let her sleep. Come on, have you had breakfast yet?" She was on her way there when I had called out. Together, we walked down the hall, stopping at the bathroom on our way.

The breakfast was waiting there for us, a sort of help yourself to what was laid out. "Guess you can poke some food in my mouth for me, Eirena." She giggled. Together we ate our fill.

"You know, today, I am supposed to hire a bunch more staff to get this place going. Eirena, how long have you been here, as a maid?"

"I've been here for three years now, since I was twelve. Why?"

"Good. Then you have some idea of how many staff and what their jobs should be."

"Well, I know some. Minos knows even more than I do. I am just the maid."

"Not any longer. You, Eirena are promoted to Head Maid at least. After breakfast, I want you to figure out how many people we should have here to make this palace run like a child's top." Just then, a sleepy Minos entered and bid me good morning; he was perfectly dressed, though sleep was in his eyes. "Just call me Bethany," I told him. "Today, I am to hire proper staff to run this palace. Eirena and you know the most about how it should be done. You two: make a list of what jobs we need to fill, and then I want you two to split up and go hire us the staff."

"Now I want good, honest, hardworking staff here. Also, let's hire only young people, no one older than you Minos. This is a youthful palace now, so let's keep it that way. Oh and Minos, you are now promoted to Head Butler. I suspect that we need more than one of you to handle the entire palace, right?"

He grinned, "Yes, Your Highness, many more than one. Thank you, Your Highness."

"And no more of this Your Highness, just Bethany, please, just Bethany. Reserve Your Highness for formal occasions when we have outside guests. Is that acceptable?"

"Yes Your . . . Bethany," he chuckled as he corrected himself.

Mia walked in as I was finishing up. "She's awake, Bethany. I am going to take her some food. Hans is watching over her."

"I'll come with you. I need to help her today. None of us can take another night like last night."

Mia Kallisto began gathering up a simple breakfast for Amara. "She is crazy, right?" Eirena asked.

"No, Eirena, she is not crazy. She is experiencing the horrible, awful pain and trauma that she felt when the bastards cut off her arms. The shrieks happened when she woke up from the surgery and discovered what had really happened to her. She is reliving it over and over and over."

"That is so awful! So she is crazy then? Right?"

"No, I will help her erase that trauma and all that pain, and then she will be fine. You will see." I followed Mia out of the dining room. I watched as Mia fed Amara, who was now in her trance-like state. After she was done, I sent them off to get something to eat and keep an eye on things so I would not be disturbed.

The first thing I had to do was to establish a line of communication to Amara. She was in a trance, just sitting on the edge of the bed. I sat down beside her, arranged my body similar to the way she had hers positioned and watched. Every so often, her face twitched and her eyes blinked. I duplicated those motions as exactly as I could. Presently, she awoke and looked at me.

"Hi, I am Bethany."

"I am Amara. Do I know you?"

"I am the new Empress. I only met you yesterday. You are at the imperial palace now. Here's what I want you to do." I explained what I was about to do and then had her close her eyes, knowing that she was still sitting right there in that operation. Off we went, re-experiencing her surgery, which had made her of the Eighth Degree for her husband's sake.

Yes, twice she began screaming as she had done during the night, but Mia and Hans were outside the door, preventing anyone from interrupting me. After two passes through the whole operation, the screams subsided. Five more passes and the trauma began to lighten up, but both of us were getting hungry, since it was lunchtime. I took a short break while Mia and Hans fed both of us. Then, I resumed the session once more. Now Amara began to contact the underlying pain. After a few more passes, she began to yawn heavily, and I knew we were making great progress.

You can easily figure out what had happened to her, so I won't bore you with her lengthy description. Finally, she brightened up, "Now she will be a totally helpless woman. That's what the surgeon said when he finished up. Now she will be a totally helpless woman. That's what it's been like. I've been a totally helpless woman ever since then. I've been acting that out over and over and over!" She began laughing wildly. The more she repeated the phrase "helpless woman," the more she laughed.

Mia and Hans took that as the signal to enter. I quietly ended the session and asked Mia to remove her undergarments. Mia looked at me and then knew why. Still laughing, I said, "Amara, come with me. Let's use the bathroom. I have to go badly; you probably do too."

We walked down to the bathroom. "How can I do this myself? I've no arms," she asked, laughter ending. I demonstrated, and she began to laugh again and duplicated me, going to the bathroom on her own for the first time in months.

Amazing what this tiny bit of self-reliance can do for a person. "I feel so alive, Bethany!"

"I know. I want you to stay with us a while longer. Mia and I can show you how you can do many things for yourself. Once you feel comfortable, you can return to your husband. I know that he really loves you. I met him, and he deeply cares for you. That's why he got you to me the very minute I arrived here. I think that you will find Anatolios a doting husband when you return."

"I loved him so, that's why I went along with this thing. I guess there is no turning back for us, is there? We must learn to make the most of it, I guess. How can I ever thank you Empress Bethany?"

"If you come across others whom I might help as I did you, bring them to me. Okay?" She didn't see how that was thanking me, but agreed anyway. When we left the bathroom, we discovered all of the others had gathered outside. Word of her "cure" spread rapidly. Even Deimos and the two advisors were more than slightly impressed with Amara's miraculous recovery.

Over dinner, I had Amara describe for everyone what had happened to her and how it had affected her. It made for squeamish stomachs, especially with Deimos, but I wanted to drive my point home solidly: cutting off women's arms left them with horrible traumas. I knew better than to come right out and say it should be outlawed.

After we ate, Deimos took me for a long walk around the entire palace complex as he had promised. He explained that some urgent business had come in the early morning, and he had had to leave to handle it. I made him realize what position he had left me in, naked and unable to open the door for help. He realized right then that I had saved him a great embarrassment. Had I yelled for help, everyone would now know that he had blundered badly with my needs. He apologized to me. In the future, he promised to leave the door open a crack if he had to leave.

I discovered that an entire legion of Centurions was spread around the complex, providing daily and nightly security. The treasury building was incredibly solidly built and currently held a rather large fortune in gold and gems. We had the funds to operate the palace.

The next day, the newly hired staff began showing up. In all, she had hired fifty new people, from stable hands, to sweepers, to maid, to cooks, to shoppers, to butlers, on and on. Yes, it was chaos for a few days as we found housing for them all, organized them into day shifts and evening shifts. One entire building was there solely for their living arrangements.

The day after that, reports came up to me on the actual condition of the whole palace complex. It was incredibly filthy! It had been years since any maintenance had been done anywhere. The staff estimated that they'd need three weeks to get everything in top shape once more. Mia, Hans, and I enjoyed seeing all these younger people around.

Next, I sent out request for court musicians and in a week had hired a dozen to play for our evening meals and all sorts of special occasions. Yes, I have a passion for music and wanted as much of it around me as I could reasonably get.

The third day after our arrival here at the palace, the doorman came to find me. "Empress, some guests from Patri have arrived. They wish to address both of you. The Emperor requests your presence in the throne room at once." I thanked him and headed there, just in time.

Deimos had already taken his seat, while both advisors stood in the background, as I hastily sat down. "How do I look, Deimos? My hair ok?" He straightened the fall of my dress a little, but he really felt awkward doing so, I noticed. "We really do need some musicians to announce the arrival of guests."

The doors opened and four Santi del Dio members walked in, their black tunics with red fleur-de-lis crosses boldly displayed across their chests. I didn't recognize any of these four, however, though I suspected they were from the Santi fortress at Patri. They walked up the red carpet and stood before us.

"Hail and well met again, Emperor Deimos Gavril. The Santi del Dio would like to congratulate you on your recent marriage. We've come to honor this auspicious occasion with presents for you and your new Empress."

I watched Deimos closely to see his reaction to the Santi presence. At first, he glared at them, but the mention of presents brought a smile to his childish face. "What have you brought for me?" Deimos replied, totally the wrong opening remarks, self-centered at best.

Instantly, Darkon moved beside him and said, "Well met Santi of Patri, always good friends of the Imperial Court. This is our Empress Maren Elizabet of the Eighth Degree. Empress, these are the official Santi del Dio representatives from Velona, Sea Princes, a country in the far northern realms. They live in that tower that you saw in Patri when you docked."

Facing the four, he said, "Would you be so kind to introduce yourselves to our Empress? Forgive me, but your names are so foreign to us. I do not wish to affront you by mispronouncing them before our Empress." Darkon demonstrated to me at once that he would be handling official meetings, as Deimos only made a mess of things. It was not too encouraging.

"Certainly. Empress Maren, I am the leader, Judger Dag Waterby, my wife, Healer Betsy." He bowed and she curtsied nicely. All four were in their thirties. All four had blonde hair. Betsy wore hers rather short, easy to care for. She and her husband had blue eyes, and I thought that she was rather pretty. He continued adding their Guardian specialties as part of their official names, so that I would know who they really were. "This is my Protector Art Duval and his lovely wife and our Communicator, Sandy." Art was very muscular, while Sandy was rather homely. Worse, she had several dimples on her cheeks that only worsened her appearance. That she was only five feet tall compounded it. Yet, she had a very cheery disposition.

"I'm so glad that you all took the time to come to meet me. I'm sure that you have been of immense help to Emperor Deimos in the past, and I look forward to your kind assistance in the future. Demokritos always needs fine allies." I was testing the waters, Darkon smiled, while Alekos frowned, and Deimos was merely impatient.

"We both thank you for your thoughtfulness. You are the first to honor us with presents. You must forgive us. We've only been back three days, and I'm only now starting to get things presentable around here. You know, the palace needs a woman's touch." I chatted away intentionally to lighten the tensions somewhat.

"Sire, if you will be so kind as to accompany us outside, we can show you what we have brought for you and your Empress," Dag said, motioning for the door. "Betsy, while we are outside, why don't you give the Empress your little gifts and then be sure to bring her outside as well."

Deimos needed no second request, eagerly bolting off his throne to follow Dag and Art. The two advisors followed behind them, leaving Betsy, Sandy, and me in the throne room. Mia and Hans quietly came in as the men left.

"We don't have much time," Betsy said softly. "We wanted you to meet Sandy so you and she can make mental connections later on."

"Thanks, this is Mia Kallisto and Hans, Judgers both, my handmaiden and protector," I hastily introduced them.

"Here, we brought you proper boots, Linda's orders," Betsy said, taking a pair of Alexa's special mantis boots out of the sack she carried.

Quickly, Mia began undoing the laces of my boots. "Wow. My old mantis boots! Thanks, now I can take off my boots and use my feet! I haven't been able to do that since I was five years old! Thank you, thank you!"

"We've also brought along several easy slip on leather dresses. We don't know if those will be allowed here, but we wanted you to have them just in case you might need them. Now we should get outside soon. We've brought you two a pair of fine horses. Yours, Bethany, has been well trained for armless riders. We've brought along your special type bridle as well. We don't know if you will be allowed to ride or not, but if you ever do, you will have the means."

Sandy added, "Just contact me if you need anything, Bethany. There is an awful lot of intrigue going on in Demokritos right now."

Mia had my new boots on, so we headed outside to join the others. Deimos was examining his fine new stallion, all smiles. It was a fine horse indeed. "Ah, there you are Empress Maren," Dag said as I walked up. "We have a very docile, very well trained horse for you to ride. We know how much you love to ride, and we have this mare properly harnessed for you to manage."

"But she cannot ride. She has no arms, you fool," Deimos said rather antagonistically to Dag.

Dag feigned a very startled look, "What? Is this so, Empress? Our information said that you loved to ride in Annelise." This was, of course, a total lie.

I saw that the reins had my familiar wooden block, which I used to hold in my teeth. "Wow, I have not had the opportunity to ride for quite some time now. Oh, do help me into the saddle. Deimos, come let's try out these fine horses! Ride with me, only don't go too fast for me, please." I added demurely, as if I was a helpless woman.

The three men looked at me with shocked looks upon their faces. By now, many others had come outside to see the "presents." Among them was Amara. "Oh, forgive me. Queen Amara Gavril, these are our Santi friends, well, Deimos' anyway. I've only just met them. They have brought us these fine horses as a wedding present. Dag, Betsy, Art, Sandy, this is Queen Amara Gavril; she's staying with me a few days to help me get adjusted to my new home here in Kefall. Isn't that just grand of her to do this for me?" Boy did I ever flip that one around.

Both advisors broke into broad smiles, impressed with what I had just done. Queen Amara had been rather dumped upon us as being crazy or insane, and I had made it look like the Queen was here doing me a service. I'd saved face for both royal courts. Amara didn't quite know what to say, but curtsied appropriately.

"Hans, will you help me up, please? Oh, Queen Amara, Deimos and I are going to try out our new horses. Would you like to watch?" Hans skillfully hoisted me up into the saddle and put the wooden block into my mouth. Deimos mounted up as well. I gave him no choice. I nudged my mare slightly, and she began walking. "Which way, Deimos?" I called out speaking through my teeth.

Slowly Deimos led me around our extensive palace, staying close to my side. "I didn't know you could ride! I didn't think it was possible, Maren. Yet, you are. Amazing. I suppose that we shouldn't go too fast, though, you can't hang on."

"Not on these cobblestones. It's too hard on their feet," I replied. After we rode around the area twice, I thought this was enough, and I came back to Hans. He gently helped me down.

"Oh thank you four ever so much! She is very well trained. She is just perfect! Now Deimos and I can go for rides in the countryside. Thank you so much."

"It is our pleasure, Empress Maren. We are so glad that they meet with your high standards," Dag replied. "We've already taken up so much of your valuable time, Sire. We should be going. Emperor Deimos, if there is ever anything that we can do for you, please send us word."

"Oh yes. Thank you for these excellent horses," Deimos finally remembered his manners. The four left and now everyone was chatting about having seen their Empress riding a horse all by herself.

"That was, well, I don't know what to say," Deimos said to me. "I had no idea you could ride, in your condition I mean."

"Yes, I can ride a little, not like you can, though. Please take me on some rides when you have time, dear." He actually grinned.

As we all headed back inside, Amara came to my side. "How in the world did you manage that? We are so helpless, but then I guess not so helpless. That was amazing."

"We do things in different ways now, Amara. That's why I want you to stay around here with me for a while so you can pick up new ways of doing things."

"I will. Thanks for telling that little fib about me being here. It's rather the opposite. I know that I drove Anatolios out of his mind, and he rather dumped me off on you. I promise you that we will somehow make it up to you."

"Dressmakers!" I suddenly realized what was missing.

"Yes, you should have several here," Amara was quick to pick up my realization.

Eirena, who had been near us, moved closer. "Bethany, I know where we might find two. They are only sixteen and just getting started. They might not be the best though."

"Perfect. Go hire them. I just realized that I've only got this one dress I'm wearing, and it is beginning to be a bit in need of a wash."

"Okay. You are giving them a fantastic opportunity — dressmakers for the Empress and all that!" Eirena added.

She ran off to handle this new request. Amara said, "I do like the way that you are hiring all these younger people. When I get back to Axos, I'm going to do the same. I really didn't like being around all the older people that Anatolios has around, rather like leftovers from his parent's days."

Later on, I found Deimos alone and decided to get his viewpoint on the Santi. "Hi dear. Say, that was awfully nice of the Santi to give us such fine presents, don't you think?"

He grumbled, "Well, I suppose so. They are always trying to find ways to please me, as if that will make me like them any better."

"Oh, I'm sorry. I thought that they were your friends. I'm so new at this, and I really don't know who's who. Do you dislike them? Should I not have been so nice to them?" I pumped him for more information.

I got an outburst for my efforts. "Well damn it. The Santi were partly to blame for getting the Holy Eight Degrees outlawed here in Demokritos! Damn their meddling anyway. I had to go all the way to Annelise to get one like you. I refused to make them force a normal bitchy woman on me as my Empress! Now you take these priests of the Church of Jehosanity — now they are our allies, Maren. They are bringing back the Holy Eight Degrees — at least on Megalos it is accepted practice now. That's why King Anatolios had to go to Megalos with Amara and have it done there."

"Yes, but Deimos, look at how harmful having your arms cut off is to us women."

"I don't care," he snarled at me, "that's the way it's supposed to be. You can't harm me at all. You are just a helpless bitch to look pretty at my side. You can't cause me any trouble this way. Now get out of my sight bitch!"

I quietly headed for the door. Eirena was there with two young women. She was looking for me, having found the dressmakers and had overheard Deimos' tirade against me. I couldn't help but have tears coming; it was such an unexpected, nasty encounter.

As we left the room, Eirena put her arms around me and said, "There, there, Maren. He really didn't mean that. Really he didn't. He just gets angry sometimes. It's probably because of his mother. It's all right. Here, I've found the two dress makers." I pulled myself together, and we four began working out details for Mia, Hans, and me to get new and appropriate outfits.

Later on, I found Alekos alone and decided to get his point of view as well. Expecting the worst I said, "Alekos, I hope I did acceptably well with the Santi. I don't know them or whether they are friends of the court or not. No one alerted me to their status."

"Oh, you did exceptionally well. Deimos nearly blew it. The Santi have always been good for the throne. They helped get rid of the despicable Holy Eight Degrees, so they can't be very bad. Oh, I'm sorry. I don't mean to offend you, Maren. I've nothing against you personally, except you are so damnably helpless without your arms. I tried to get Deimos to see reason and marry a normal woman, one who could really help around here. Oops, not that I am saying you are not helping, Maren."

"That's okay, Alekos. I understand. If I had a choice, I would still have my arms. I agree with you totally. Just look at what it has cost poor Amara. I think Deimos hates the Santi, though."

"Yes, he believes that they are responsible, but the orders came from the Emperor and Empress herself, not the Santi. Deimos is rather blind. Just between you and me, let's try to keep the Santi as our friends. By the way, that was incredibly noble of you today — what you did for Amara, saying she was here to help you. That really saved the Queen. Thank you." I smiled and left. This was the first conversation I had with Alekos that I actually enjoyed. Perhaps he was not the ogre I had originally assumed.

Sometime later, I corralled advisor Darkon and put similar questions to him to see where he stood with the Santi. "I'm sorry, Empress Maren, we should have informed you before they arrived. It's just that there has been so little time, and the darn Santi came unexpectedly too soon. Look out for them. They are not to be trusted. You probably don't know our history. Let me explain, in the olden days, the Holy Eight Degrees of Matrimony were vitally needed here in our country. It was the only thing arresting our moral decay, you see. Men and women were unfaithful in droves. Yes, I suspect that if it wasn't for the Holy Degrees, why, we would be in the same pitiful state as Megalos is in today."

"The Santi were largely responsible for convincing many to outlaw the Degrees. True, it was ordered and signed by the Emperor and Empress and many others of the Eighth Degree, but the Santi were behind it. Tragic loss for Demokritos. We need more powerful women like yourself backing our leaders, Maren. I urged Deimos to go to Megalos where the Degrees are being practiced once again and find a wife there. However, the Prophesies of Demos overruled me. It is just as well, Maren. You are just perfect for Deimos. By the way, very good job with Queen Amara today, excellent indeed. You said just the right thing to save her face. It would have been so embarrassing for the Queen and King of Thrace, had the Santi been told what was actually happening."

"I am so glad that Amara has recovered. Now she, like you, can fully back her husband. She will be another beautiful example of just how perfect and right the Holy Eight Degrees actually are. In the future, Maren, we will make sure that you are briefed whenever possible. Excellent job today." I smiled, and he had to leave. Well, now I had a better picture of the situation here at least. After dinner, I spent an hour with Mia and Hans, telling them all that I had learned.

A week later, Mia and I had the first of our new dresses, the main palace building was cleaned; dust and cobwebs were gone. We were ready to have visitors. Deimos was primed to hold his court, at least according to Alekos. Our first visitor was King Anatolios, who came for his wife. He was astounded and eternally grateful for what I had done for his precious Amara. Two things came from this. One, Amara became totally devoted to me. Two, Anatolios promised to do anything for me if I ever might need help: no questions asked, was the way he put it. The way that things were shaping up, one day, I might just need to call upon that favor.

So happy were both of them that they decided to stay and visit for a few more days. The next day, I had three unexpected visitors. We four were sitting in the throne room chatting, when our doorman announced, "Empress, you have three very special visitors, Kefall's Noble Women of the Eighth Degree. Shall I show them in?"

"Yes," I looked at Deimos, Anatolios, and Amara for guidance.

"We'd best look very presentable," King Anatolios said, and he quickly arranged Amara's dress and fussed slightly with her hair. Deimos, seeing the care he was giving his wife, straightened out my dress and followed my request to arrange my hair over my shoulders to my front side. Just then, the doors opened and the doorman said loudly and formally, "the Ladies Thecia Thanasis, Stefana Tanis, and Phoebe Menes."

Three older women, heads erect, walked into our throne room, followed by three handmaidens. King Anatolios welcomed them, "Welcome indeed. It is so good to see you three again. You've met my wife Amara already. Deimos, would you allow me the honor of presenting the Empress?" Not great on formalities, Deimos nodded, grateful for the king's willingness to do what he ought to have done.

"Our Empress Maren Elizabet of Annelise. These are the most honored noblewomen of Kefall and your confederates in crime," he teased. All three women smiled at his jest. They curtsied before us.

Thecia, the eldest at fifty-nine, spoke for the group. "Greetings Emperor Deimos and Empress Maren. On behalf of the Women of the Eighth Degree of Kefall, we came to welcome you to our city and to chat."

"I'm very pleased to meet you. I apologize, but I was not told that I had companions in crime. Would you care to take tea with me in my private room?"

"That would be perfect," she replied. "Amara, will you please join us?"

"Oh, this is my handmaiden, Mia, and my protector, Hans. Mia, will you have Eirena bring us tea in my room please? Hans will escort us there." Amara and I stepped down and led them to the room I had adopted as my private study. "I'm sorry that it is not all fancied up as yet. We are still cleaning up the place. So many things have been put in storage. As you know, this has been a bachelor pad for some time."

Once in the room, Thecia said, "Maren, allow us to greet you properly, as is our unique way." One by one, they came to me, and we pushed against each other, touching the sides of our heads to each other, first the left and then the right. Then, Hans helped Amara and me into our seats, while their handmaidens did the same for the three. Almost at once, Mia entered and Hans left, followed by Eirena, who brought us a tray. She hastily sat the pot and cups on the tea table and left, closing the door behind her.

Mia poured the tea for us, and the handmaidens assisted us, Mia doing double duty with Amara and me. "I'm so glad that you came to visit. Until now, I thought it was just Amara and me."

Stefana replied with a grin, "Oh no, dear child, yet we are rapidly becoming far too few I am afraid. You are so young, fourteen we heard?" I smiled and nodded. "And Amara, you look positively radiant. We'd heard that you were, well, shall we say, having a good deal of trouble."

Amara could contain her enthusiasm no longer. "I was a basket case! Bethany, here, she worked a miracle with me! I've never felt so alive, so full of energy, so terrific in all my life! I am so happy, and Anatolios is too. I just cannot say enough about Bethany!"

All three women grinned. Phoebe said, "But I thought she was called Maren."

"Maren Elizabet sounds awful," I explained. "I go by either just Maren or Bethany. My close friends call me Bethany, short for Elizabet." I hoped that they would buy this.

"Bethany it shall be then," Thecia replied. "Now has Deimos told you about us?"

"No, I didn't know you even existed, I'm sorry."

"I told you not to trust Alekos!" Phoebe said, disgustedly.

"You as well as Amara are part of our group now, by virtue of being of the Eighth Degree, you see. Have they told you of our special role in leading our country?" Thecia asked.

"Well, no. I heard rumors that I have some duties, but it has not yet been explained. Probably that's because we've only been here so few days, and there has been so much to do to get the palace back into operation," I tried to make it appear acceptable.

"Gracious me, I will have to speak soundly to those men! The very idea — keeping one like us in the dark!" Thecia was more than a little annoyed. She took a sip of tea and continued, "Allow me to fully explain, Bethany. In Demokritos, we women of the Eighth Degree are the most highly honored and respected of all our citizens. Everywhere you go in our country, absolutely everyone will treat you with the utmost kindness and caring. No one, and I do mean no one, is held in higher respect than us, except for the Empress when she is of the Eighth Degree as you are my lovely Bethany."

"Yet, we have perhaps the highest duty to perform of any citizen, to be the final line of defense against bad or ill-conceived or wrong or incorrect orders of officials, laws, and plans. In each kingdom, all laws passed by their Senates must be approved by their Eighth Degree women. All plans and all major orders of their King must likewise be approved by women such as us. Amara, you are the last one of our kind in Axos. As we mentioned before, we are ready and willing to help you out, since you are so new to this. Here in Kefall, we three are the last as well, but now Bethany has been added to our numbers."

"Our proposal is that we five unite and handle the reviews for both Thrace and for the Emperor. Bethany, we can give you the historical guidance that you will need to put any given new law, order, or plan into proper context, that you may weigh its validity."

"Now that is the best news I've heard," I exclaimed. "Amara, is this okay with you? We are both so new to this; we could use all the help we can get."

"Oh yes, please do. I don't know how to thank you all for taking on this extra responsibility." Amara looked very grateful. I realized just how overwhelming this must be for her, so new to being armless. She was fighting learning just how to live. Having to attend to such important matters of state was too much for her alone just now.

"Excellent. We normally meet once a week, on Monday. We meet at Phoebe's home at noon. We will have an excellent lunch and discuss matters over tea, like civilized people. Amara, when you have matters that need review, send word to us and we will come to you. I wish that Axos was not five days away from us," Thecia said.

"Say, what about talking to Sophia Lenois. She was thinking about moving, now that her husband has passed away," Stefana interjected. "Perhaps we could convince her to move to Axos to help Amara and us?" The others though this was a good idea and Stefana agreed to follow up.

Stefana then said, "Bethany, it is so good to see young folks like yourself and Amara here joining us. For many years, we watched helplessly as others of our kind slowly grew old and died. We longed for company, but we could not get the Empress's order abolishing the century's old practice voided. You don't know how good we feel having you two young people joining us! Perhaps there is hope yet with this new Church of Jehosanity.

They have begun using the Holy Degrees in Megalos now. Amara bears witness to it."

"I know quite a bit about this church. They are altogether evil. Amara can tell you the kind of shape that they left her in. If it wasn't for me, Amara would be in deep trouble," I decided to cast my anchor with this church right here with these women.

All three looked shocked and surprised to hear this. Amara explained, "She's right. The real reason I am here is that I had gone crazy. I'd wake up in the middle of the night screaming wildly. It got so bad that poor Anatolios no longer knew what to do with me. I sat around like a zombie all day long. It was horrible. He sent me here to be with Bethany the very day she got here. I mean, when they passed through Axos on their way here, he sent me along. If it wasn't for the incredible help Bethany gave me here, I'd still be a crazy woman. Yet, thanks to Bethany, I have never felt better in my entire life. She has saved me utterly!"

Phoebe looked at me, "Is this true? What she is saying?"

"Every word. That first night we arrived, she woke the entire palace up with her screams in the middle of the night. It was wild. Now, she is doing just fabulous indeed. Look at the color of her face and her smile."

Amara blushed as everyone looked at her. I decided it was now or never, time to drive my point home. "Ladies, we've only just met and I know nothing about you. Yet I bet when you three had the ceremony performed so many years ago, you were not left to live like a zombie, screaming in the nighttime. Right?"

"Heavens no!" exclaimed a concerned Phoebe. "Yes, we had some difficulties in adjusting to life as a woman of the Eighth Degree, but not like that! They must be savages to have left Amara like that!"

"That Church is just using your Holy Eight Degrees as a way for them to control women. When we meet, I can give you a more detailed report, if you like."

"Well, the Santi have been saying ill things about this new Church all along. Perhaps we need to investigate this further," Thecia added. This sounded hopeful.

I added, "Now don't get me wrong. I don't have anything against a woman desiring to have her arms removed. After all, it is her body and her life, her choice. Yet, I am very much against how it was done with Amara, such inhumanity. We of the Eighth Degree deserve far better than Amara was handled."

"On that, we all agree wholeheartedly, Bethany. Indeed we do. We shall discuss this further on Monday afternoon. I know that you have your hands full getting this palace operational once more." We all laughed at her joke — Amara, the most.

"Thanks, it is wonderful to have you backing me. I was feeling awfully alone here," I said, honestly meaning it. With that the tea broke up.

However, the three were not quite finished. They went back to the throne room and summoned Alekos, Darkon, and Deimos there. Thecia spoke for the three women.

"I am terribly ashamed of you three. You did not inform Empress Maren of her most solemn duties as a woman of the Eighth Degree, and you did not inform her of us, her support group. Did you think that we would be ignoring you and your plans and orders? If so, you had best think again! You may have thought the old ways were dying off, but not so. Amara and Maren are testimonies to the fact that it is not. We meet on Mondays, in case you have forgotten. We expect that you will have Maren fully briefed so that she and we can approve or disapprove your orders and plans at that time. Do I make myself perfectly clear?" She glared at the three men.

Darkon apologized profusely. "We meant no insult, Ladies. We have honestly been so busy getting things going here at the palace that we didn't get to it yet. You have my word that she will be so briefed by Monday. Just so you are informed, Lady Thecia, some men from Demokritos attempted to assassinate Maren and her handmaiden before we arrived to get her. We have been attempting to find out who was responsible for that heinous act!"

"What? Our people would dare to harm a Woman of the Eighth Degree?" exclaimed Thecia, indignantly. "Such is unheard of!"

"Well, it has happened. There can be no doubt. The men were from here. We have their weapons and are attempting to trace their manufacture, in hopes that will lead us closer to whoever ordered this attempt."

"Oh Bethany, why didn't you tell us someone tried to kill you?" Stefana exclaimed. "How utterly awful!"

"It happened in Annelise. They told me I would be safe once I got to the palace here," I replied.

Phoebe added, "Well, I should think so. If anyone tried that here in Demokritos, no mercy would be shown to the perpetrators, none whatsoever! Bethany, you should always travel with your protector and perhaps a number of Centurion guards. You will provide her with an escort, will you not, Deimos?"

"Yes, yes of course," the young lad stammered, glad that his advisors were taking the heat and not himself.

Satisfied, the three left. I had five days to learn more about what was going on around here, before I would meet with them again.

That very evening, after supper, I had more visitors. The doorman came to me and said, "Empress, you have another two women here to see you. They request a private meeting. Shall I take them to your room?" I told him to do so, asked Eirena to bring a pot of tea there, while Mia, Hans, and I headed for my private study.

We got there just ahead of our two guests, who wore heavy cloaks that covered their bodies, only their heads were visible. Once inside, they glanced at us, the older woman asked, "Could we speak in private, please?

Your handmaiden can stay." Hans bowed respectfully and left, making sure the door was shut.

"I am Empress Maren Elizabet. My handmaiden, Mia Kallisto. May Mia take your wraps off for you? Eirena will be bringing us tea directly."

"Let us wait until she has gone," the older woman replied. During the awkward silence, Mia continued to stare at this older woman. Shortly, Eirena brought in the tea and left.

"Now Mia, if you would be so kind as to remove our cloaks," the older woman, who looked perhaps sixty years old, grey streaks highlighted her black hair, shoulder length. Somehow, I thought that she looked familiar, but I couldn't place her.

As Mia removed their cloaks, I saw that the older woman had no hands! Her younger companion, who thus far said not a word, was like me. She was in her mid-twenties with shoulder length curly black hair, with piercing black eyes that missed nothing.

The older woman now spoke as the two took a seat across from us and Mia poured the tea. "Thank you for seeing us. I am called Iole Castus." Mia dropped the teapot, shattering it on the floor. Thankfully, she had already filled the cups.

"Iole! Is that really you?" Mia exclaimed.

Iole looked at Mia, but did not recognize her at all. Mia suddenly looked very embarrassed. We all looked at her now. Mia said, "I am or was in my last lifetime, Kallisto, leader of the Kali, before I went to help the Santi and their leader Bethany le'Goeur. When that body died, I took a new baby body in Annelise. Iole, I remember you well. You always looked after me! Gosh, how you've aged. You still look great."

Iole, taken by complete surprise and not at all certain of any of what Mia was saying, challenged her. For several minutes, Iole asked key questions and Mia answered them. Finally, she asked, "We once had two visitors, who wore laced boots. You were serving them tea. What did I do for them and how?" I knew what she was asking now. I was there!

"You used your teeth and arms to undo their boots so that they could join me in drinking their own tea."

"Then it is you; only Kallisto could know that, and Bethany and Linda who were the women," Iole said. "It really is you!"

"Yes, I kept the name Kallisto. Mia Kallisto. Once our mission is done here, I will go back to being just Kallisto once more. Kallisto is not an Annelise name — had a hard time convincing our mother to name me that. How have you been all these years? Oh, perhaps I should let you speak. I don't know what the situation around here is just yet."

"I will speak of that now, that is the purpose of this visit, Kallisto. Is the Empress to be trusted, Kallisto?"

"Absolutely, with my life." Mia didn't want to reveal just who I was just yet. She had perhaps said too much already.

"Empress Maren, I am Iole Castus, second in command of the Kali Assassins. This is our leader, Zenovia Philon, of the Eighth Degree."

At last the young woman spoke, "Very pleased to meet our new Empress and surprised at your youth. You look beautiful, Maren."

"I am very pleased to meet both of you, hug?" I said and we exchanged traditional hugs, though Iole actually was able to give me a hug.

"Mia Kallisto has told me a lot about your organization — well as it was a quarter century ago anyway," I broke the ice, allowing them to know that I knew the real purpose of their organization. "I think that is a very noble purpose indeed."

"Yes and a necessary one at that. I am officially a widow. My late husband, Theo, was caught cheating on me. He'd been frequenting a house of ill repute, shall we say. Yet no men would bring charges against him. Iole handled it for me. He met an accident. Since the Kali needed a leader of the Eighth Degree, I volunteered. I am still a bit new to this, serving as leader for three years now. Iole acts as my teacher and spokesperson."

"I'm sorry for your loss. Men!" I said.

"Thank you. Yes, to give up so much for one you love only to be betrayed, that is almost too much to bear. However, life goes on and I have adapted. Now then to the business at hand, Maren."

"I've come to tell you that we are here for you, should you need us. These are very confused times, a transition period, some say. Lies and treachery abound at all levels of our government. Many are making their moves for power, including your husband, Deimos. Know this, Empress; we will always be watching your back. Should you ever need to contact us, put a small black dot on your main entrance door. One of our many eyes will see it and we will come."

"Thank you, that is comforting to know. Already someone has tried to kill us, Mia and myself." Both women looked very surprised, and Mia related the tale for them.

"This is more serious than we thought at first. There are three main possibilities for those who ordered this attempt on your lives: King Docia of Arolas, King Homer of Alia, or King Kadmos of Phindos. We will look into it further," Zenovia replied.

"Perhaps it is time that we moved, Iole," Zenovia added thoughtfully. "We have been living in Patri, working closely with the Santi there. How did the meeting with the Santi go, by the way?"

"Super. I have boots now that I can take off by myself, so I can at last use my feet and toes when needed, though I have not yet demonstrated that around these here at the palace. I did go for a horse ride, which totally shocked everyone here. I do so love riding."

Iole smiled. "Years ago, I knew another woman of the Eighth Degree who loved to ride like the wind, she always said. She even won the Vladimir horse race, putting men to shame. You remind me much of her. She too was

Santi, the one Kallisto went up north to help."

I smiled, "You are looking at her new body too." I decided to trust these women with my secret. I don't know why, but I felt having the Kali know who I really was may be very useful.

"If you are indeed her, then you can answer this. What did you do for Kallisto that made her so changed?"

"I ran my therapy on her, and she discovered the truth behind the origins of the Eight Degrees, and it was not holy!"

Iole, tears streaming down her cheeks, came over to me and gave me an enormous hug. "It is you. Could I ask a favor of you?"

"Anything, Iole."

"Zenovia, could you help her with your therapy? She has undergone so much."

"Absolutely. I've already done that for Queen Amara of Thrace. She's still staying with us a few more days as she gets more used to doing things different ways. I just don't know whether Deimos would let me go to Patri, though."

"We should move here then for a time," Iole suggested.

"If you did, I am certain that I can get Zenovia into our Ladies Group. We are to meet on Mondays to approve or disapprove laws, orders, and plans. I know that they would be overjoyed to have another younger person join them. They have been feeling so lonely. They welcomed me with open arms, so to speak."

"Well, that would actually be extremely valuable for the Kali to have me on the inside," Zenovia replied. "I don't know what this therapy thing is that Iole is always talking about, mind you, but I'm willing to try it."

"Do we still own the house in Kefall where we used to live?" asked Mia.

"Yes, that's where we would live. I will see to our moving soon," Iole replied. "Now we had better be going. I don't want to draw too much attention to us. None here has seen our Degrees. We'd like to keep it that way. If someone asks about us, say that we were two seamstresses looking for work, but that our ideas were too old fashioned for your dresses." I laughed and agreed. Mia helped them don their cloaks. I realized that these made an excellent disguise; one could not tell they had no hands or arms. They looked perfectly normal. I resolved to have similar cloaks added to my list of clothing to be made. Little did I know how useful this would become.

That night, when Deimos and I retired for the night, he was in an ill humor. I asked him, "Can you help me undress?"

"Take your own damn clothes off, you bitch!"

"What?" I exclaimed rather annoyed at his outburst of anger.

He exploded. "Damn you woman, if you don't stop slapping me, I will beat your brains out! Stop pestering me with your damn lies and innuendos. Take your own clothes off!"

"Just how am I supposed to do that?" I retorted, very annoyed with him.

"Just take the damn clothes off!" he yelled and gave me a powerful shove backwards. I could not keep my balance and fell. Even though I quickly tried to catch the body, its head hit the stone floor, rather hard.

I cried out in pain, "Ouch, my head!" Tears came unbidden; it hurt so.

Deimos stared down at me. His anger vanished as suddenly as it had come. He saw what he had just done and looked pitifully at me. Just as he was about to bend over to help me back up, the door burst open and Alekos, Hans, and Mia came rushing in. They saw me lying sprawled on the floor, crying, Deimos standing over me.

"What the hell have you done this time, Deimos?" Alekos screamed at him.

He didn't answer, but backed away from me. Mia rushed to my side and helped me up. "Gosh, she's got a goose egg growing rapidly on her head. Come with me, Bethany. Let's attend to it before it gets worse." I was a bit disoriented and wobbly, and I leaned heavily on her for support.

Behind me I heard Deimos say, "I, ah, sort of pushed her back too hard and she fell. Honest, I didn't mean to hurt her."

A little later, my head throbbing, I told Mia what had happened. "He sure has an angry streak in him. You had better be careful around him, when you are alone. If this happens again, I am going to speak with Alekos and perhaps insist that I sleep in there with you or that you two sleep in separate rooms!"

Later she helped me back in to my room. In the hallway, Eirena was waiting for me and said, "He really didn't mean to hurt you, Bethany. Honestly he didn't. Sometimes he gets confused." I let it pass and bid her good night. Deimos apologized to me when we entered, but I let Mia undress me, before she left.

The next day, after breakfast, I went in search of Nestor, his teacher. Nestor was the oldest here, and I hoped that he could shed some light on Deimos and his behavior. He was packing. "Are you leaving us?"

"Yes, Deimos claims that I can teach him nothing he doesn't already know. I've had it with him. I'm moving back to my place in Kefall. If he ever comes to his senses or if you have some children of yours, let me know. I've tutored two generations of Gavrils now."

"Before you go, would you take a private tea with me in my room? I would like to ask you some questions."

"Sure. Say, are you all right? I heard about last night."

"Yes, bump on the head is all. Thanks, I'll be waiting for you."

A little later, he and I sat in my room, door closed so that we could not be overheard. "What can you tell me about his childhood, his parents? He seems to be getting me confused with someone else."

Nestor pushed his hands through his hair, eventually resting his chin upon both. "It's a long, sad tale. I knew his grandparents and his parents too. You might as well know, since you are his Empress now."

"Axos and Adelpha, his grandparents and Emperor and Empress back around 670's — now there was a magnificent, competent woman of the Eighth Degree, if ever there was one. She was a wonderful woman indeed. Deimos longs for someone like his grandmother; he has such fond memories of her, kind and loving. Anyway, when they died, the throne came to his son, Alkaios, who was forced to marry a normal woman, because by then the practice of the Degrees had been outlawed. Oh did Alkaios long to find a woman of the Eighth Degree, but he could not. As I said, the practice had been completely outlawed by then."

"He married Ligeia. If ever two people should not have been married, it was those two! They argued day and night over the most trivial of things. At last, though, Alkaios was ready to abandon her, when she realized that he was about to dump her. That's when she finally bore him a child, Deimos. Many of us thought that with the child around, they would make up their differences and raise him properly."

"Rather the opposite. They fought even harder. Poor Alkaios took to drinking, and Ligeia hounded him so badly, that he began to visit all the houses of ill repute as well, coming home drunk and well, you know. That only set her off worse. She would throw things at him and finally began scratching his face so that even the whores would not have anything to do with him. Poor Deimos witnessed their constant fighting, every day as he grew up. It only got worse and worse as the years went on. He got to the point where he was drunk all the time, hitting her as much as she was hitting him. It was really awful."

"Then when the new century celebrations began on January 1, he got even drunker than normal and climbed up on the rooftop to see the fireworks display better. We found him in the morning. Evidently, he had fallen off the roof to his death. Ligeia left the palace that very day and has not been seen since. Some say that she ran off with her boyfriend. If so, god help him. Anyway, Deimos ascended the throne on January 2, though many protested his ascension, saying they'd had enough of the Gavril line ruling Demokritos, that it was high time for a change."

"Poor Alekos and Darkon, they've had a rough time of it, trying to get him presentable as an Emperor. He insisted that he must have a woman of the Eighth Degree for his Empress or he would not take the throne! However, and you may need to forgive me because of this, I was instrumental in convincing all of them to follow the Prophesies of Demos and search Annelise for a woman of the Ryker line, who would be of the Eighth Degree. They took my advice and here you are. I'm sorry now that I got you involved in all this. Look out for him; he has a mean streak in him."

I thanked him and allowed him to leave. I then went to Mia and Hans and told them what all I had learned about out illustrious Emperor. They were not pleased either.

Chapter 6 Fixing Things

"When the shipment of jade arrives later this winter or early spring, they plan to begin to raise the assault army of Centurions. They will be well paid and will be initially barracked at Station Nine, but I do not know where that is at. When spring comes, Deimos will officially begin his fighter training. He is insisting upon leading his mighty army off to conquer all of Tarra, as the prophesies suggest. That is all of their plans. I can get more details if you think that must be done." I explained to our Lady's Support Group on Monday afternoon.

We were at Stefana's grand home in the heart of Kefall. True to his word, Alekos had brought me up to date on their plans, although I had no idea if they were withholding anything from me. "How do I know if they are not telling me everything? What if they also have some secret plans?" I asked.

"If they do and we ever hear of it or find out, they are doomed — fired immediately, no recompense. If it was the Emperor who instigated it, he will likewise be de-throned. The penalties for keeping vital information from us women of the Eighth Degree is too steep a price to pay. Sooner or later, someone will accept a money pouch and spill the tale," Stefana explained.

"As for the current plans, I see nothing wrong with them. The boy does need to learn to fight like a man; perhaps it will do him some good. While we wish that they would not go to war and not build up such an army, while we could veto it, it would do little good. Everyone is following the prophesies now. On this, we should bide our time and pick our battles well," Thecia suggested. We all agreed with her.

"Now then, more tea anyone?" Stefana asked. I took more. I love tea. Mia, of course, assisted me.

"How did Deimos react to our warning message this morning?" Phoebe inquired. Yes, this morning an official letter arrived for Deimos. The Lady's Support Group had heard about his antics, shoving me onto the floor that night. I had not said anything about it, but I suspected someone in our large staff had leaked word to these women on my behalf. Perhaps it had even been Nestor, as a final parting shot.

"His face turned white. Then, he got angry. I know his advisors were extremely upset and dealt harshly with him," I replied.

"Nip it in the bud, I always say," Phoebe replied with a smile. "Men. Think they can get away with everything."

"Say, what would you say to having another addition to our group? I've convinced another woman like us to move from Patri up here to Kefall to help. She is not married; her husband met with a tragic accident some years back. I think the change of city would do wonders for her, so I suggested she move here. She is rather young, twenty-five, I believe."

The three women's eyes lit up! "Wow. She must have been one of the very last to be allowed the ceremony before it was outlawed. Who is she?" asked Stefana, eagerly.

"Zenovia Philon of Patri. She had hers done in Megalos, I believe."

"Zenovia, Zenovia, yes, we heard about her husband, died suddenly and unexpectedly. Tragic loss. She must have been horribly upset you know. After all, she is so young and only been like us for such a short time before losing the one man for whom she gave all. Yes, I say invite her to join us." Stefana said. The others agreed at once. I told them I would relay it to Zenovia as soon as she was moved into her new home.

That evening at supper, Deimos was very quiet. Hans and Mia had accompanied me to the meeting, and we had no idea what had happened during the afternoon. However, we assumed that Deimos had been severely scolded. While we were eating, he said with a scowl, "You didn't have to go reporting that to the Lady's Support Group, did you?"

"Deimos, you have my word that neither I nor Mia or Hans ever said anything about it to anyone. After all, it was only an accidental push. I just lost my balance in these heels, nothing more than that." I attempted to defuse the situation. I had no way of knowing if he believed me or not.

Later when we were retiring for the night, I asked him to help undress me. I'd long given up asking him to brush out my hair. It would just have to wait until mornings, when Mia could do it. He'd gotten my clothes off before he got angry this time. "You can take your own damn boots off. I've seen you do it! Damn it woman, you didn't have to go and blab to the others. You got me into big trouble." Slowly his anger rose.

"Hell, you are always getting me into trouble, you worthless bitch. I ought to get more wine! Slap me around will you? I'll show you; try that on for size!" He actually slapped my face; it stung. "Bitch, don't you dare throw that at me! Damn you, you broke it. I'll teach you a lesson you'll never forget!" He jumped on the bed and lunged at me, intending to tackle me.

This time I was prepared, and I just lifted my body high in the air; he dove at where my body was just at. Of course, it was not there, and he fell hard onto the floor. Screaming, he got up to come after me. "Damn it bitch. Now look what you have done to me! I'm bleeding. I'll beat you to an inch of your life!" He was screaming now. I cleverly kept my distance from him moving about our room. If he had tried to move fast, in my boots I could not elude him and was prepared to pull the body back up in the air if need be.

The door burst open and Alekos, Darkon, Hans, Mia, and Eirena came rushing in. Deimos had a bloody nose, bleeding rather heavily, wildly swinging his arms at imaginary people in the room. "Hell, he's gone off the deep end," Alekos spat on the floor.

"Gang, I have an idea. Hans, you are the strongest, I want you to stay in here with me to protect me. The rest of you, please back out quietly; don't upset him any further," I ordered.

"He really doesn't mean to harm you, Bethany," Eirena pleaded, but Alekos pushed her back outside. It was just Hans, Deimos, and me now.

"Therapy session, Hans. Keep him off me if need be." Hans nodded.

I faced the half-crazed Deimos, who was still flailing away at imaginary people in the room. "Deimos. Go to the beginning of this. Good. Now move thorough the trauma and tell me what is going on, what you see, what you are hearing, and what you are smelling." My voice and intention overpowered him. He complied, much like a baby.

Boy did I ever get an ear full! His parents were having one of their nightly fights. She had thrown a flowerpot, which had broken. Pieces hit Deimos and knocked him out, though he still recorded the rest of the fight. After a few passes through that one, I asked for an earlier time. I groaned as I realized I was about to listen to a lifetime of parents fighting! For two hours, we went through fight after fight, with no relief in the patient.

Then, I reached what had to be the earliest fight, he was only a baby at the time, and the noise scared him half to death. Yet that one did not erase either, so I asked again for something earlier. "I see a man; he's being hanged!" Now this was more interesting, at least the marital fighting had thankfully ended. We proceeded through this trauma.

After ten times through the whole incident became clear to Deimos. He had been a nobleman who had married, and his wife had, at his insistence, become of the Eighth Degree. Later on, she had not adapted at all well, and he had begun to slap her around. It escalated, and he had thrown her to the ground so hard that she cracked her skull, unable to break her fall. He had been summarily hanged for attempted murder of a woman of the Eighth Degree.

However, this one did not erase either, though he did get some relief and many yawns left him more alert. I asked for another earlier one and got it. "I see this woman."

"Go through it and tell me what is happening as you go along. What are you hearing? What are you seeing?"

"I see this man and a woman of the Eighth Degree. They must be married. Yes, they are. They are arguing. She is saying that she knows that he has been sleeping with their maid. She's pointing to the maid's underpants on their bed. He is slapping her around. Ouch, my face is hurting! She is so helpless. I'm getting pushed back, and I cannot keep my balance. I'm swinging my arms, but there are no arms there. I am falling. I hit my head. I pass out. I wake and my head hurts so badly. I vomit and nearly choke to death. I cannot use my hand to help me sit up. Someone helps me. I cough a lot; my throat burns; my head hurts. She cleans me up, and I go to bed. That's all."

"Thank you. Now let's go back to the beginning. Go through it once more. Tell me what you are seeing." He followed my commands. Heavy yawning prevented me from quite understanding all his words. He described the whole incident once more, adding a lot more detail.

"As I lay down at last to sleep, I remembered that awful feeling when I was flailing my arms to try to keep from falling so hard onto the ground and there were no arms there to move. That was the worst feeling I've ever felt. I decided I really was totally helpless, totally useless. I couldn't keep from falling. I had to be helpless." Suddenly, he began to laugh. "I decided that I was helpless, that I couldn't do anything about it. That's the way I have been feeling all my life, as if I was helpless to do anything about it. I couldn't stop my parents from fighting. I was helpless." He roared with laughter. I ended the session. He continued to laugh and we headed off to get a snack. He laughed for over an hour.

Even though the hour was late, the advisors and Eirena drilled me with questions about what had happened to Deimos. Yes, they had listened in at the door; curiosity got the better of them. After a time, Eirena said quietly, "See I told you he didn't mean it. He has a kind heart, really he does."

At last, very sleepy, we all turned in. As Deimos crawled in to bed with me, he said, "I am very sorry for scaring you like that. Thank you for helping me. I feel so free now. I, I think I understand more about how you feel and must live. I mean I really was once as you are now. Do you ever flail your arms only they are not there?"

"Yes, that has happened. It is very scary when that happens, Deimos. I just hope that you listen more to what I have to say from now on. While I might not have arms, I am not ignorant. I know quite a lot. Now give me a kiss and massage my body. It is a little sore." He complied. This was the first time that his hands moved over my body gently and compassionately. Perhaps we were making some progress.

The others and the staff noticed a big change in Deimos in the following days. The constant chip on his shoulder was gone. He treated the various women around the palace with more respect. He no longer was angry with me, though I still didn't ask him to brush my hair before bed.

Two weeks later, Zenovia and Iole arrived in Kefall. A few days later, I received an invitation to come and spend the day with them. I took a coach. Hans drove, while Mia sat with me inside. Her new home was on a hillside not too far from the palace, actually. Of course, the true reason for the visit was to begin her therapy sessions.

I knew that I would have my hands full with this one. She had given all for this man, and he had betrayed her. She was indeed sitting on an enormous pile of raw grief. Imagine having given your spouse the ultimate sacrifice — had your arms removed to bind you two for life — only to later find that he is now sleeping with your maid. Yes, this first day of her therapy, Zenovia shed buckets full of tears! I discovered that the tale of his running off to whore houses had been a fabrication; it was her very own maid.

It was a very long day indeed for me. I had her go through it twenty times before we ended for the day. She was exhausted, but the grief had gone, and she felt much better. I knew we had more to do. I promised to return tomorrow.

When I got back, I learned that Deimos had begun his fighter training. Consequently, he didn't mind my spending several days in a row helping Zenovia get settled into her new home. He actually thanked me for going to her aid, a very nice change in his outlook.

When I arrived late in the morning the next day, I found a rejuvenated Zenovia; she looked years younger. Her youthful face had re-appeared. She was eager to continue our sessions. I had her run through the big betrayal once more, and then I asked for something earlier that was similar. I got what I expected, the actual loss of her arms at the hands of the Orthee. She and her husband had journeyed to Megalos. There, in conjunction with the priest of Jehosanity, a number of dissatisfied Orthee priestess performed the ceremony on the side, for a healthy price, I might add.

We ran through this a number of times, slowly the anesthetic effects wore off, and she contacted the real physical pain that her body had felt. After that, a few more time through the operation and the pain was gone as well. However, she was still sad and not cheerful about it. Again, I asked for something earlier.

"This cannot be real. I see some hideous creature leaning over me doing something to my arms." Here we go again, I thought to myself. I coaxed her to continue going through the trauma.

"My husband and I kiss. I walk away with these women in white robes, Orthee. I am lying on a cold table. They give me something to drink. I fall asleep. I am sitting above my head watching. How can this be? Then this awful looking creature comes into the room. It's huge! It looks like a praying mantis only hundreds of times bigger. It is leaning over my body! I want to flee, but I cannot move my body. God, it is eating my arms off! Then, it is sealing the wounds up. It didn't hurt. It leaves, chewing on what was left of my arms. I am being carried into another room. I lay there a long time. I wake up and try to get up. I can't, my arms don't work. I looked down and there are no arms there. I screamed. I want my arms back. A woman in white robes calms me down. Days later. I go home with my husband, who is being exceptionally kind to me after that. I know that he loves me, but I have this constant feeling that I have been somehow betrayed!"

"Oh god! I kept hounding him, accusing him of sleeping with anyone, not being faithful to me. Yet, he was always totally faithful to me. I just felt I was betrayed somehow, that I was being betrayed. I went psycho on that. Oh god! Eventually, he just couldn't take me continually accusing him of betraying me, and he jumped off the roof, killing himself! I took that as proof that he betrayed me, but he had not! Yet, after that, I calmed down. That awful feeling left me. Wow."

We ran through it a few more times, got some more yawns, and she became completely cheerful. "I just confused the actual betrayal with my husband. I couldn't view the real betrayal, and it sort of got slid over on to my husband. Boy did I ever ruin him. I wonder if I could ever make that up to him somehow some day?"

I ended the session. "Zenovia, my own opinion is that if you continue to help these women in need, taking responsibility for them and their lives as you are now doing, I think that wherever he is at, he will rest in peace and forgive you."

"I certainly shall do that. Say, what was that weird creature thing? That cannot possibly be real, can it?"

I spent the next hour over tea and snacks telling her all about the mantis creatures and what they were doing to us here on Tarra. She was now a true believer of the truth.

"Oh, I nearly forgot. The others asked me to invite you into our circle of Eighth Degree Kefall women, if you want to join us."

"You bet I do. When and where?"

The following Monday, I introduced Zenovia to the other three. I swear I had taken years of age off her; she looked so youthful now, so full of energy and vitality that she impressed the other three women enormously. Now we were six, working behind the scenes for the betterment of Demokritos.

October arrived; spring was in full bloom. The advisors decided it was time to invite the seven Kings and Queens here to meet the Emperor and Empress. It was time for us to meet them and be acquainted.

However, it was also the traditional Spring Council time. Minimally, twice a year the Kings, Queens, and Emperor would meet to conduct the official business of Demokritos. All interested parties were allowed to attend and lobby for their interests as well. While each kingdom had their own Senates, who formulated laws for that kingdom, at these Spring Council meetings, each kingdom would attempt to get the other kingdoms to adopt their new laws, as well as gain the support and backing of the Emperor and ultimately the Empress. If the Emperor so chose, he could unilaterally adopt a law and make it enforceable across all the kingdoms.

At these meetings, the Emperor would outline his plans for the country during the next six months. Of course, the Kings could argue against such plans, sometimes prevailing. If they strongly objected, their Senate could then pass a law against the Emperor's plan. Yes, it was a chaotic political system indeed. All the more so because interested parties, could petition the Senate for a new law or ruling, or petition the Emperor or Empress. Round and round it would go. On top of all this, lay the Lady's

Support Groups in those kingdoms where women of the Eighth Degree still were active, who could veto any of this. However, three of these kingdoms no longer had this "final say women" as a check and balance on their rules, laws, and plans, making those kingdoms now controlled by the kings and political men.

October 7, 700 was the designated day for the start of the Spring Council this year. During the days leading up to this, the two advisors worked with Deimos constantly, attempting to get him prepared to deal with the political situation. I began to see their frustration with Deimos, who could care less about the entire political arena. His only interest seemed to lay in conquering Tarra by force.

Worse, we received notice that the Church of Jehosanity wished to have the opportunity to present their case and suggested new laws to the Emperor. General Alexandr made his request to present his ideas as well. Even the Santi del Dio asked to be allowed to address the council.

To make matters far worse, because Deimos had only been appointed in January in a chaotic mess after his father had apparently fallen off the roof, the Fall Council had not been held. I also learned that these meetings had been brushed off for the last several years before this because the Emperor was mostly drunk all the time. Hence, this council was of major importance to everyone concerned.

Topping everything, this would be the first opportunity everyone had to meet and welcome their new Empress. I was told to expect to receive many gifts. I should expect that some, which might be used by the givers to gain my support. Plus, I had to demonstrate my skills at being a hostess for so many people. All eyes would be on this aspect of the Empress.

Chapter 7 The Spring Grand Council

Even before the seventh arrived, parties began arriving at our palace. Yes, I was now well staffed, and each was properly given appropriate rooms in our many guest rooms. Three separate dormitory buildings lay behind the palace building itself. One would house the various kings, queens, and their party members. Another building would house the official petitioners, whose request for an audience had been granted. The smaller building would house the many other interested parties, who came to watch the proceedings.

I was allowed to have anyone I wished to sit with me as my official observer. While we Eighth Degree women would always have our handmaidens at our sides, the observer could be anyone. Often the advisors told me, it was a dear friend who wished to see how the country was run. I asked Zenovia to be my official observer, even though she was on our Lady's Support Group. While others would see this as having the behind the scenes women in attendance, which some would relish while others would despise, I had another purpose in mind. I wanted the secret leader of the Kali Assassins to be present, so that they would be well informed of what transpired.

Mia observed that now all of the political fractions in Demokritos would be gathered together under one roof. We should expect some fireworks. Indeed we did.

Because it was illegal for guests and petitioners to mingle with the Emperor before the official opening of the council — this would be seen as an attempt to prejudice the Emperor beforehand — our group ate in our small dining room. After breakfast, Mia made her last minute adjustments to make me as presentable as possible, and we took our places in the throne room.

The room had been drastically altered just for these meetings. Yes, Deimos and I sat on our thrones. The two advisors sat just behind him on either side. Mia sat on my right and my guest of honor, Zenovia and her handmaiden, whom I had never met, sat to my left. Hans and two Centurions sat behind all of us, swords at the ready in case of real trouble.

In an arc before us, tables were arranged for the seven kings and queens and their party members. I positioned the table for King Anatolios and Queen Amara of Thrace directly in front of the throne. The three kingdoms, which still supported the Holy Eight Degrees, I placed on my side of the room, just to the left of Amara, from my point of view. That way those of us of the Eighth Degree would be mostly together. The other three kingdoms had their tables to the right, facing Deimos, as far from me as possible.

The petitioners' tables were arranged behind these seven. I had the Santi on my side, behind the kingdoms, which still supported the Holy Eight Degrees, while I had the Church of Jehosanity members on the other side, Deimos' side. I wanted them as far from me as possible, naturally. Finally, many rows of chairs aligned the back wall for all of the other observers and guests.

As we took our seats, Eirena and her staff finished placing water pitchers and mugs on the tables. Her staff, the cooks, the butler and his staff would be very busy. Deimos signaled the doorman, and I nodded to the musicians, off to my far left. They would play a short fanfare as each of the interested parties entered and were officially announced. Yes, there was a good deal of tradition to be followed here at the commencement of the Grand Council. Alekos leaned over to me and whispered, "This promises to be the largest, most well attended council meeting in a quarter of a century!" Great, just what I needed, more stress.

The entrance order was of my choosing. Fanfare. "King Dimitris Docia and Queen Daria of Arolas." The young king with short black hair, wearing a stern countenance masking for a time his antagonistic nature, escorted his lovely and stunning wife, arm in arm. Several of their associates followed them. On their way to their table on my far right and as they reached the center of the room, he bowed to Deimos, while she curtsied. Then, he bowed to me, she, likewise, but sent me an icy stare. They walked gracefully to their assigned table and took their seats.

Fanfare. "King Petros Homer and Queen Hypathia of Alia." The young king with short brown hair and well-muscled body, escorted his young wife, overly dressed in fine clothes, and with more jewelry than I had yet seen anyone wearing, moved into the room. He looked like a man who was used to getting his way. She gave me a forced smile as she curtsied before me. After they were seated next to those from Arolas, fanfare again announced the next group.

"King Manos Kadmos and Queen Karis of Phindos." This young king with his long brown hair and studious eyes, reminded me of a scholar I had once known in Velona. He did not look like a fighter at all; perhaps he used his mind more so than the other two. His young wife was plain, but wore her hair very long indeed, down to her knees. I took an instant liking to her, okay, so I have a fetish for long hair. She couldn't be very bad. As she curtsied before me, I spied her eyes taking in my long, curly black hair draped over my shoulders, reaching my waist. She smiled and I nodded. We had something in common. They sat beside those from Alia.

Fanfare. "King Anatolios Gavril and Queen Amara of the Eighth Degree of Thrace." The youngest of the kings, by five years, he walked proudly in, his arm around his wife's waist. His grin was enormous and sincere. I sensed that he felt he was escorting in the most beautiful woman present. Amara, dressed up for the occasion, looked positively radiant. Her glow was infectious, causing Daria to cringe slightly, but Karis merely smiled sincerely. After he helped her get seated at the middle table, the fanfare announced the next king.

"King Leon Kostas and Queen Athena of the Eighth Degree of Thallyus." This was a study in contrasts, between the old and the new. These last three kings were in their fifties or early sixties, greying hair, seasoned kings who had seen a lot of change in their lifetimes, some good, some they considered bad. He proudly escorted his still beautiful looking wife. Though she was fifty-four, she still had her beauty. In her youth, I imagined that she had been stunning. She wore many jewels — their sparkle competing with that in her eyes. No doubt, this woman was still very much alive. They sat next to Amara.

Fanfare. "King Eros Eleni and Queen Ariadna of the Eighth Degree of Penelopus." He walked with a limp; his greying hair bespoke his age. As usual, his arm was around his wife, who wore her hair straight and long, though it had streaks of grey in it. She, too, wore several pieces of jewelry. Her eyes told me that she stood for no nonsense. She struck me as a businesswoman. After seating beside Manos, the fanfare sounded once more.

"King Hektor Georgios and Queen Angele of the Eighth Degree of Theos." He was the eldest of the kings. His hair was all grey, and he sported a full, bushy grey beard, neatly trimmed. His wife, whom he carefully escorted, was quite similar to Ariadna. She wore her hair long and had similar tastes in jewelry. Likewise, she struck me as a practical woman, no nonsense. They sat on my far left.

Fanfare. "Cardinal Rax Ciros of the Church of Jehosanity of Kefall, Cardinal Lethos Theo of Patri, Prelate Kel Dios, Prelate Brutus Felios." The cardinals were youthful, dressed in red flowing robes of office. Stern was both their countenances. They smiled covertly at me. I believe that they thought I was on their side at this moment. The two Mano del Dio security men, assassins really, looked strong and able — the sober kind of men that you should always avoid.

Fanfare. "The Santi del Dio delegation from Velona, Sea Princes. Dag and Betsy Waterby, Art and Sandy Duval." After they took their seats, the doorman allowed the others to enter; at least twenty-five men and women came to observe. Once they were seated, Alekos rose and the fanfare sounded one final time.

He spoke. "It is with great pride that I present to you Emperor Deimos Gavril and his lovely Empress Maren Elizabet of the Eighth Degree of Annelise and her charming guest, Zenovia Philon of the Eighth Degree." We received a round of applause and foot stomping.

He continued, "It is my understanding that many of you wish to give our imperial couple some welcoming presents, as well as meet her personally. At this time, you may do so, please do so in the order that you entered, so that our new Empress may better associate your names, which she knows by heart, with your faces. We will begin the official business in one hour's time."

Dimitris and Daria came up to me first. I stood aside my throne chair, near a small table on which presents could be laid. Mia was at my left side, ready to assist me. "Good to meet you at last. I hope that you will not regret having left Annelise," King Dimitris said, a hint of antagonism in his voice.

"So good to see you, Maren. I can call you that?" Daria said bitingly. I nodded, she continued. "We've brought you a set of very fine china, though I don't see how you will be able actually to use them. Your handmaiden can deal with them for you." She dug her barbs in deeply. "Have you been this helpless for long? I mean when did you lose them?"

"The day after I was born, Queen Daria. I've lived my life like this. Thank you so much for the china. I found this to be mostly a bachelor's pad when we came, so your gift will help add a woman's touch to the palace." She took my reply gracefully, and the two moved back so others could greet me.

King Petros and Queen Hypathia came up to me next. "Well met, my Empress," he said formally, hugging me in the proper manner. "I do hope that you do not find being our Empress entirely too challenging for you. Being of the Eighth Degree, it can often be more than any woman could handle. If you find it so, let me know. There are ways." He winked as if he knew some secret that I did not.

"You are so pretty and so young. I do love the way you have your hair; it hides your malady so well. One would not see it at first," Hypathia greeted me. "We've brought you a present of some very ornate silverware, though I'm sure you will at least enjoy looking at them if nothing else." Again, she was cleverly reminding me of my condition, rubbing it in, I wagered.

Next, King Manos and Queen Karis moved forward to greet me. "You are indeed a lovely flower for the palace," he said, giving me the traditional hug greeting. "Pleased to make your acquaintance. If you need anything, please don't hesitate to call upon us. Phindos is always at your service. I would like to extend an invitation for you to visit our fine kingdom this summer, if Deimos will let you travel. He ought to, by the way. He should not be allowed to keep you locked away in this palace."

"Dear, we've brought you a present of some very colorful flower bulbs. I know that you cannot plant them yourself," Karis said sympathetically, "but your staff can. We've noticed that the palace has become so drab these past years. I thought you might like some help making it more, well womanly. I do like you hair. It is so long. Is it naturally this curly? Mine is so straight."

"Thanks ever so much for the flowers. Yes, the palace is very lacking in such simple things of nature. I will definitely oversee their planting. Perhaps the next time you visit here, you can see the rewards of your present, Karis. I do love your hair too. I just love long hair, don't you?" We began to chat about our hair preferences. I liked this woman, unlike the other two, Karis, plain though she was, had a heart of gold. She did not hold my situation against me as the other two women had.

"Oops, Amara is getting impatient with us, Karis. We can chat more later. I would love to spend more time with you and your husband and get to know you both." They smiled and backed out of the way for the Thrace royalty.

Amara and I hugged our special way, while Anatolios gave me a strong loving hug. "Dear, show her what we've brought for her. I do hope you like it. I know that you favor yellow," she said. He opened a small box to reveal an exquisite necklace with many yellowish stones in it. I had Mia fasten it around my neck.

"How do I look?"

"Really beautiful!"

We chatted a bit longer, before they had to yield to Leon and Athena of Thallyus. He gave me a good, warm hug. "So glad that you are our new Empress, Maren. I'm sure you will do well," he said. "If you ever need anything, just let us know. The Kingdom of Thallyus is here to serve you."

Athena then hugged me in our special way. A tear formed in her eye. "It so gratifying to find our new Empress belongs to our Old Ways. You look fabulous! Don't ever let anyone tell you differently. You are going to be a powerful force for good in Demokritos — I just know it. From all of us of the Eighth Degree, thank you for accepting the sometimes trying position of Empress." They presented me with a pair of gorgeous diamond earrings.

Eros and Ariadna came up next. He gave me a strong, but gentle welcome hug, as only an experience husband of one of us can do. "It does the throne good to have one as pretty as you sitting upon it. You are a true beauty," he complimented me.

My first impressions of Ariadna were not wrong. "Welcome to Demokritos, my lovely Maren. So young and so keen. We've already heard a lot about how you are managing this palace. We've also heard about the slight mistreatment by Deimos. Maren, do not tolerate that kind of conduct, not for even an instant. We have firm rules concerning the mistreatment of honored women as ourselves. Listen, there is much going on in the kingdoms at this time. I would like the opportunity to chat with you about it."

"I'd love to, Ariadna. Let's get together as soon as possible. Don't worry about Deimos. I have already handled it totally. There will not be any recurrence, I assure you."

"Good girl. I like that about you, a take-charge woman. You go get them! If you need anything, just send word to us. We will stand by you. Oh yes, we've brought you a number of yellow dresses, knowing that you love yellow. Of course, you will need to have your dressmakers alter them to better fit. My, but your bust line is impressive for one so young." We chatted a bit more before they had to back away as well.

Hektor and Angele of Theos came up next. These were the oldest reigning monarchs. He too knew just how to give me a hug that could only come from one who had been around one of us for a very long time. "It is good to see our new Empress at long last. You are indeed a flower in this wasteland. Maren, I've been in power going on a half century now. I've seen it all. Times are in a great flux. I wish to speak with you to give you advice that none of these younger men can." I agreed to meet with him as well.

Angele hugged me in our special way. "I am so glad that you also love long hair, as much as I do. When I heard, I just knew what we had to get you. Dear, show her. We've collected a number of jeweled hair bands and ties. I know that sometimes it is awkward when you lean over and your hair gets in the way. Use these; they work well for me. Now Hektor is right; there are all manner of ill things in the wind for Demokritos. It will take all of us working together to eliminate them. Let's do get together and discuss things."

I was surprised to see Cardinal Rax Ciros waiting next in line. "Greetings from the Church of Jehosanity, Empress Maren Elizabet. It is so wonderful that a woman of your stature should accept the challenging task of Empress of all Demokritos. Many Good Marks shall be your goal; I'm sure. Since we know you come to us from Annelise and we have not yet established our churches there, allow me to present you with the Holy Gospels, our holy book. As you know, the previous Emperors have decreed that the official religion of Demokritos shall be the worship of the one God, Lord Jehosa. If you will study these gospels, you will begin to understand our most holy religion. I would dearly love to have you begin attending our High Mass on Sundays. You would be given a position of high honor there. Being a woman of the Eighth Degree, you are setting an example for all women of Demokritos."

I wanted to tell him that his book was nothing but total lies and fabrications, and that none of it bore any resemblance to the truth, but I dare not. Pick my battles, I kept telling myself, smiling at the Cardinal.

Immediately behind him, Dag came to say hello and he said, "Don't believe a word in the Cardinal's holy book. Here is a copy of the True Holy Gospels, from Velona. We Santi have the real, original gospels as written by the ten disciples of the Son of God. Compare the two and you will see the awful lies and untruths exposed."

As he stepped back, the Cardinal glared at him so hard, that I thought they might start a fight! If looks could kill, Cardinal Rax would have slain Dag on the spot! Meanwhile, Mia had Eirena and her staff moved all the presents out of the throne room. On their return trip, they brought in pots of steaming tea, a variety of cheeses and a wide sampling of baked goods. From the looks of the older women, I had timed this perfectly. Athena gave me a big smile and nod of reassurance; I'd done just the right action at the right time.

Now came the opening session. As coached, Deimos stood and began his summary. "Kings, Queens, and guests, I'm supposed to bring you up to date." He wasn't supposed to say it that way. Alekos cringed. "I am proud to announce that Annelise is now a part of greater Demokritos!" A round of clapping validated this good news.

"I do hope that their king and queen will not be attending our councils," King Hektor said. "Otherwise, we will all end up being forced to be way overdressed!" A bit of stifled laughter followed. I laughed along with them, breaking the perceived awkwardness of the remark.

I called out, "You don't know how glad I am to be your Empress. I would have done anything to get out of wearing those enormous hoop skirts!" My levity was appreciated, and the group roared with laughter. I didn't want them to think that they were somehow affronting me.

"No, and we will not be conscripting their men for our legions either. Rather, I have made a rather stupendous deal with King Soren. He will be supplying yearly funds for us to use to finance our global conquest. Already he has sent an entire year's taxes to us. The ship has arrived in Patri two weeks ago. Expect seven million gold coins worth each year from our Annelise!"

Now he did receive a loud round of applause. Everyone was very impressed that my homeland would be so generous. Deimos had fulfilled the prophesy without drawing a sword. Annelise was now part of greater Demokritos, and more importantly, their taxes would take a great financial burden for the coming conquests off these kingdoms, which I suspected were already bearing a heavy load.

Alekos whispered, "Your plan, tell them your plan next."

"Oh yes, for this coming season, it is the Emperor's plan to begin raising the Assault Centurions. We plan to raise, train, and equip, ah. . ."

"Twenty legions." Alekos whispered, grimacing.

"Twenty full legions this season. We will house them in Kefall at the unused, old Barracks Number Nine. Is there any discussion?" He sat down relieved that he had somehow gotten through this speech.

"Sire, why only twenty legions?" asked King Dimitris.

Helplessly, Deimos turned to General Alexandr, who had been sitting quietly in the back. "If the Emperor will allow me to answer that?" he said. Deimos readily nodded that he should. Dimitris scowled; the Emperor evidently knew little about his own army! This was not a good signal to be sending these kings; even I knew that.

"Slow build up is the answer. We do not want to show our intentions to the world until we are fully ready to strike. Strike from surprise is always the wise move." Alexandr sat down.

King Manos then said, "Ah, thank you General Alexandr. You are to the point as always. I am then led to assume that you, General, will be leading the assaults, while Emperor Deimos sits here in Kefall, safely on his throne?" It was a slam, veiled in a question. Although Deimos did not see the put down, he did react, but for a different reason.

"No, King Manos. I will be out there in the field, leading my mighty army to glorious victories. I am in training. I began my fighter training a short while ago. Please, give me time to master the art of combat. Then, I shall lead our mighty army to victory after victory, until all Tarra is under the control of Demokritos!"

Again, there was the appropriate applause, although I saw the younger kings scowl. King Hektor frowned and shook his head, evidently disapproving of some part of Deimos' declaration.

King Anatolios spoke, "Is there any other discussion of the Emperor's plan? Hearing none, I move that we accept his plan. All those in favor say yes." All seven kings did so. "The Emperor's plan has the acceptance of the kingdoms. It is now to be reviewed by the Lady's Support Group, as is our long standing tradition." This, of course, meant that my group of Eighth Degree women must approve it before it would be implemented.

King Dimitris spoke up loudly, "Why should we continue to allow these women, who know nothing of such matters, be allowed to veto our well made plans? Surely, their time has come and gone. In Arolas, Alia, and Phindos, we have abolished completely such silliness. The Lady's Support Group in our kingdoms no longer exists. Those honored women have all died. We now are free of such meddlesome interference with state business. I move that we officially abolish the use of the Lady's Support Group countrywide, especially here at the Imperial Palace. After all, think of poor Maren, who comes to us from Annelise, where she spent her entire life dealing only with how to move around in giant hoop skirts, not on such vitally important matters that would now face her here in Demokritos. Let us show her some pity, abolish this ancient and no longer needed or useful tradition. I say down with the Lady's Support Group!"

As you might expect, the meeting instantly turned into utter chaos! Yelling, screaming, fists pounding on the tables, even threats flew around the room! Dimitris, Petros, and Manos were red faced as they screamed and argued their case, while Anatolios, Eros, Hektor, and Leon yelled wildly back at them.

The women of the Eighth Degrees were just as livid as their husbands. The proposal would strip them of their mighty power of veto. Their voices were shrill and heard above those of the men. I noticed that Daria, Hypathia, and Karis said nothing, but smiled. They were enjoying this immensely. As it stood, they had no power at all, while their counterparts, those of the Eighth Degree had immense power. I could tell that they wanted to strip these women of their power completely, leveling the field. Actually, it would then totally escalate their power, because they were not helpless women; they had arms and could fend for themselves.

Alekos yelled over the chaos to Deimos, telling him it was his responsibility to regain order. Deimos shrugged his shoulders, saying he couldn't yell loud enough. I decided this fiasco had to end.

I stood up, faced the whole arguing bunch and put my full attention on them. I spoke softly, but with total intention. "Stop! Thank you. Gentlemen, ladies." Instantly, a hush fell in the room. They were shocked by me into silence. "It is obvious that this issue cannot pass at this time. There are four kingdoms that yet have women of the Eighth Degree, and they wish their honored women to continue as they always have. I'm sorry, King Dimitris; your suggestion has no chance of being passed at this time. Would you be so kind as to bring it up for a vote sometime later on when you have at least four kingdoms to back you? I'm sure that it will stand a good chance of being passed at that time. Now it is close to lunchtime, and I am starving. So let's adjourn briefly for lunch. My cooks tell me that the roast duck is deliciously made. Please indulge your palettes."

King Anatolios began slowly clapping for me, a big grin on his face. I had turned utter chaos into an acceptable solution, had cleverly shunted the anger off until later, and given everyone a chance to calm down over lunch. Soon, many others clapped and began leaving for the Royal Dining Hall. Alekos whispered to me, "Fantastic, Empress, absolutely fantastic job!" I smiled at him. His respect for me was growing; I wanted him on my side.

As slow as Mia and I had to walk in our boots, the others quickly left us behind as they headed off to the lunchroom, including Deimos, who didn't think to stay with me. However, Zenovia stayed by my side. She said, "That was brilliant, Bethany. I am amazed with your skills. Isn't this disgusting? Those who no longer have women like us now want us to give up the last thing of value that we can contribute to our society! If we did, we'd have nothing left to contribute, except being a sex slave for men. The balance of power hangs on a thin thread at this time in Demokritos. I've found out something interesting about King Anatolios. When he came to power, Dimitris, Petros, and Manos urged him to take a normal wife. Had he done so, they could have passed that ruling today. Then, only the thing standing in the way of its implementation would be the certain veto of the Eighth Degree women here in Kefall. Laws or no laws, if that had happened I wouldn't give a hoot for how long we would remain alive!"

"Amara had arms when they married. What changed his mind?" I asked.

"His cousin, Deimos. Both knew the prophesy, and Deimos told him no matter what he did, Deimos was only going to marry one of us. Yet, I think that there must be something else that caused Anatolios to go to Megalos and have it done there, but I don't know what. Perhaps we may find out from Amara, if she knows. At the time, this did not seem important, yet now it may well be. I will make some inquiries."

As we finally entered the large dining hall, already everyone was seated and beginning their lunch. As we walked by, Queen Angele said, "Oh Maren, everyone has started without you. Please would you and your guest please dine here with me. Hektor is off talking to Deimos. I long for some honest company."

"Sure, why not. You know Zenovia?" Mia helped me into my chair, while Zenovia's handmaiden helped her. Both of our handmaidens sat on our right sides, so that they could more easily feed us and themselves. Quickly, we four were brought our plates. I sat directly across from Angele, while her handmaiden was helping her as expected.

"Sorry about being so slow. It's these heels. Customs in our country had us wearing them since we were children. Our legs adapted, but now we can only walk on our tiptoes or in these heels. Small steps."

"Yes, we once took a vacation trip to Annelise. Honestly, Bethany, I just don't know how you could have possibly managed wearing their tight clothing and those enormous hoops. I mean as we are, it must have been so very hard for you. I can see why you feel in heaven wearing our style of dress." We chatted away for a time.

She then said, "You know going to war is often a risky proposition. Have you given any thought to what you might do should Deimos somehow be killed on the battlefield? I mean you are one of us. It would be pure torture for you to go back to your country and wear their awful clothing once more."

"Well, no. I've only just arrived here and am trying to catch on to what is needed as the Empress. Yes, Deimos is not yet a fighter. You are right, if he does as he says, leads the fight, then he may well get himself killed. I'm afraid that no one has told me what happens to me, the Empress, if the Emperor dies."

"Isn't that just like these men not to fully inform you of your rights?" Angele said snidely. "It's simple. A new Emperor is chosen. An Empress is never in line for succession. The only way you could still be Empress, when Deimos dies, is if you should somehow marry the new man chosen to be Emperor. You would be given a home and a living expense stipend for your services to the empire, nothing more. However, as a woman of the Eighth Degree, you would still be part of the Lady's Support Group and have veto power, as long as we all keep that right, which might not be all that long, if some have their way."

"We came perilously close to losing that a few years ago when King Anatolios ascended the throne. He was not married, and his choice would swing the pendulum either way. I know that Hektor was terribly worried about this; he's fanatical about us women, who have made the ultimate sacrifice for our husbands. He insists that we will retain our veto rights or else. He's quite vocal and vehement on that issue. I know that he paid Anatolios a visit after he announced his marital plans. We all were very worried that we would lose our right of veto; Amara had arms you see. Boy did we ever celebrate when we heard that the two had gone to Megalos to have it done!"

"Yes, but, Queen Angele," Zenovia asked, "won't we all be facing this same crisis within the next decade? You, Athena, and Ariadna are getting along in years now. Ten years from now, it may be only poor Amara and Maren here against everyone else."

Angele sighed, "Yes, we are acutely aware of this, Zenovia. Honestly, Maren, I will do everything in my power to see that doesn't happen to you, to be suddenly robbed of the only real contribution a woman such as us can give to our country, veto power. I so swear. Our only real hope lies with this new religion that is sweeping across Demokritos. They are bringing back the Holy Eight Degrees of Matrimony, only from a religious viewpoint. Mind you, I personally don't believe much of their silly rants about heaven and hell, Good Marks and Bad Marks. Yet, through them, those of us who wish to make the ultimate sacrifice for our marriages can do so again. In them lies our only hope."

"In who lies our only hope, dear?" Hektor had just come up to join us and overhead that last.

"Oh, dear, I was just explaining to Maren that we must support this new church because they are bringing the Degrees with them."

"Yes, yes, we must, Maren," he replied. "Say, perhaps one day you can come to visit us in Theolopolis. I would be most honored if you would speak to our son and his wife about this very thing. You see, Angele and I are getting old. If we could, we would be retiring from the throne this year. However, we have had the misfortune of having three daughters in a row. Finally, when we both thought we would not begat a direct heir to our throne, then along comes Maximus. He is now twenty-five and happily married to Lyris. For the last five years now, we have been trying desperately to convince them to undergo the Holy Eight Degrees of Matrimony. However, Lyris continues to defy Maximus and refuses to make the ultimate sacrifice of the Eighth Degree that she knows darn well she ought to do. If you could come and talk with her about it, alleviate her fears, whether or not you are successful, we both would be eternally grateful. This balance of power is so tenuous right now. I couldn't live with myself if you, Maren, were suddenly stripped of the most important right due to you because of your ultimate sacrifice. It would be utter sacrilege suddenly to usurp that veto power from you. You've all given us so much!"

"If I can get to Theolopolis, I will certainly be glad to speak with Lyris and see what her point of view actually is. Mind you, I do not think that cutting off a woman's arms is right. I am seeking to find other ways that women of Demokritos can have a say in the laws of the land, much like we of the Eighth Degree currently have. Yet, I will speak with her. It may be that she greatly desires to do this for all the right reasons, of her own volition, but that fear of pain is stopping her. While I find this mutilation of women deplorable in and of itself, I will fight to the death to guarantee that each of us had the right to the disposition of our own bodies. If she wants to do it, okay, she should have that right, as long as it does not harm more than it helps. I will speak with her."

"Thank you, Maren. Thank you. By the way, Deimos sure made a complete fool of himself this morning. Yet, you have shone like the evening star! It is quickly becoming clear to all of us who wields the wisdom and power behind this throne. Very well done, Maren. We, Angele and I, are very pleased to have you as our Empress."

I thanked him for his compliment. Now the others were beginning to head back to the throne room for the afternoon session. I had to hurry up. I certainly didn't want them all waiting on slow me. Mia and I just barely made it in time, without causing any disruption. They were just getting ready to begin again as we took our seats.

Deimos called the session to order. King Petros rose. "I would like to ask a question, if I may. We all are familiar with the Prophesies of Demos. We've watched as our previous Emperors have retaken Acropolis and Megalos just as foretold. We've now bear witness to Emperor Deimos and his remarkable feat of rejoining Annelise with us, as well as finding an Empress of the Old Ways." He cleared his throat. I wondered what his question was.

"Well, actually it's two questions. First, the prophesy says that we are to leave the yellow for last. Does the Emperor have the factual meaning of that worked out at this time?"

Deimos looked blankly at Alekos, holding his hand in front of his face, as if this would hide him, he whispered to Alekos, "What's he talking about?"

Alekos whispered back, "Tashien."

"Oh yes, King Petros. We have that one worked out fine. The prophesy is referring to the country called Tashien. I understand that the people there, from whom we get much of our fine silk these days, have very yellow skin, though I have never seen one, mind you. If the Santi are to be believed, they say that there are many tens of millions of people in this country of Tashien. Hence, prudence suggests that we conquer the rest of Tarra first. Conscript many of these conquered men into our legions, before we invade and take over this Tashien. Yes, the Emperor will be leaving Tashien for last."

"Ah, very good, Emperor Deimos. That does make sense. Many of us had arrived at the same conclusion. It is good that we all see eye to eye on this matter. Yes, indeed. Now, my other question has to do with the timing of our conquest of these other lands. The prophesies do not indicate a specific year, only that it occurs after this one, the turn of the century. Can you enlighten us on just when you hope to begin our glorious conquest of the rest of Tarra?"

"When I am ready," Deimos replied haughtily. Of course, this was not an answer at all!

At once, General Alexandr jumped up. "Allow me to reply, King Petros. It will begin when Deimos here is ready, that is, when he has been fully trained in combat and the art of war. He wishes to lead forth our conquering army, so we must prepare him for that role."

"Yes, that is all well and good and as it should be, General, but are you talking one year, two years, five years, ten years?" Petros insisted on a firmer answer.

"We will not commit to a specific year at this point in time. Besides, the Lady's Support Group must first approve our plans. However, I will say that it most likely lies somewhere between two to five years hence. Will that suffice?" It did, he appeared satisfied for the moment. I wondered why he needed this time frame. Had he his own plans to bring to fruition?

King Dimitris rose, "May I ask why we cannot at least get the invasion started sooner? We already have seventy legions of our finest troops sitting idly on Megalos, doing nothing, but getting fat on the local food. Why not move them onto the Southlands, move them up north to the enemy border? There is really nothing in the Southlands to actually conquer; it already is part of the Megalos empire. Perhaps if our young Emperor must be seen leading our Centurions, he could go there and lead them north. You could certainly continue his training as a fighter there just as well as here. Then, we would be that much closer to achieving what the prophesies have foretold."

General Alexandr began to reply. "As I said earlier, we wish to take them by surprise. If we move ahead now, long before we are ready, before we have built up our mighty conquering army, we lose that element of surprise."

I desperately needed the viewpoint of a Protector. This made no sense to me. I made contact with Art Duval, the Santi Protector, who was trained in warfare concepts. *Art, it's me, Bethany. This doesn't make sense to me. What element of surprise is he talking about? I don't get what Dimitris is suggesting.*

There is not any element of surprise. Just we being here in this country know that they plan eventually to attack us. Seventy legions might be enough to conquer most of the Sea Princes, but not Velona. If they did attack with this force, they would have two problems. One, they would have to leave behind a substantial security force to hold on to the conquered lands. Two, if they move all seventy legions out of Megalos, then that allows the Holy Paladins to retake control of Megalos once more. I think Alexandr is more worried about the possibility of losing control of Megalos. That would utterly cripple their entire war machine — no lines of supply. Besides, Bethany, we both know that it takes years of planning to provide the material support for a large army in the field. The food supplies alone are daunting to deal with. I think Alexandr is aware of these, but does not want to speak of them aloud before both the Church and us.

Now I began to see what might lie behind Dimitris's thinking. If they lost control of Megalos, they would lose the Holy Eight Degrees of Matrimony, exactly what Dimitris, Petros, and Manos greatly desired to have happen. No more women of the Eighth Degree.

"I accept your opinion, General Alexandr. I wish to go on record as favoring using our seventy legions in Megalos to advance up the Southlands just as soon as possible. Thank you." Dimitris sat down, a satisfied look on his face. Petros nodded to him.

King Petros rose. "Emperor, I wish to revisit the conscription law passed two years ago — the law that is being used to form up the Assault Legions for our mighty conquest of Tarra. As you are well aware, we do not have the option of resorting to using the Lady's Support Group in Alia any longer to veto this law. I therefore wish to revisit this law, and I specifically request that Empress Maren and her Lady's Support Group pay particular attention, that they may find that it should be vetoed at once." Several men groaned, but it was his right to so request, I learned.

"Because Maren is new to our land, I will present some crucial background information for her benefit. Per the conscription law of 625, Demokritos is to field a standing army of four hundred ninety legions, of which three hundred legions are on supply duty, one hundred ninety legions are active duty. Of these active duty legions, seventy are in Megalos as I speak, ten legions are on security duties in the kingdoms without costal access, twenty, in those with coasts, and an additional ten here in Kefall to protect our Emperor. To support this buildup, plans were passed to build a fleet of one hundred caravel copies, the last of which was launched last summer. The plan called for two caravels to support each active legion in the field."

"Your point King Petros," King Hektor attempted to force him to get to the plan he wanted to call into question.

"Patience Old One, our lovely Empress does not know this. Now, the current plan, which I wished reviewed, calls for the buildup of three thousand legions, of which one thousand will actually take the field to conquer new lands; the two thousand are supporting troops. The plan calls for each kingdom to conscript fifty thousand additional men, beyond the current levels, which we are already providing. To field these troops, the plan calls for an additional six thousand new caravels to be built. Only four kingdoms can build the ships, unless King Hektor has some plan to move a caravel overland magically. That is to be fifteen hundred caravels per each of the four coastal kingdoms."

"My point is this. If we are to build this staggering number of caravels, we cannot provide this many men for the army! Already, we are taking the first-born son from nearly all families, creating many hardships, since some of these lads are shipwrights! If we must meet these new levels, then ship construction will be nearly halted! Plus, many families will lose two sons to the army, leaving them unable to plant crops and carry on the vital commerce necessary to keep our kingdoms surviving. Empress, this plan must be vetoed at once and a more equitable plan created. We four coastal kingdoms simply cannot comply." Petros sat down satisfied he'd raised a perfect objection.

"Might I add some additional details for your consideration? They tie in with King Petros's objections," King Manos of Phindos said as he stood up. No one objected. He continued. "In so far as the plan calls for an additional fifteen hundred caravels to be built in each of our four coastal kingdoms, the court is lacking some vital information. We four kingdoms are out of suitable hardwood trees for lumber. Only at great expense in time and manpower can we extract the vital hardwood from deep within our kingdoms, hauling it to the shipyards. Even if the other three landlocked kingdoms offer their lumber, the problem remains: how to transport such volumes to the coastal shipyards. I request that this issue be also readdressed along with the conscription numbers."

This was a gloomy setback to the assembled kings, who had been anxiously awaiting the start of the foretold conquest of the known world. I realized that the level of coordinated planning in Demokritos was sadly lacking, something which greatly benefitted the Santi, giving us much more time to prepare for this enormous army, intent upon sacking Velona and the other Sea Prince countries.

For quite some time the men discussed the situation. I suspected that the landlocked kingdoms had desired to weaken substantially the coastal kingdoms. Why? Except for Thrace, the coastal kingdoms had outlawed the Holy Degrees, while the landlocked kingdoms retained them. If the coastal kingdoms were substantially weakened, the landlocked kingdoms may make a takeover move. Their discussions suggested this may well be the case and further, the coastal kingdoms were aware of this ploy.

Now it was the Emperor's job to moderate the discussion and to offer suggestions on the stalemates. However, Deimos was not up to the task. Disappointed that he would not be getting his huge army rather quickly and that the needed ships would not likely even be built, he began to dope off. Twice, Alekos had to nudge him to his senses.

I decided to take action of my own. "Excuse me, but am I allowed to make suggestions?" abruptly the discussion, which was going nowhere, stopped. Silence.

"Certainly, Empress, you may speak freely," King Anatolios replied kindly.

"Thank you. It is obvious to me that taking so many men from so many families all at once is going to be terribly disruptive. We have already heard that the three thousand legions are not needed at this time; General Alexandr has requested only two thousand men. That is only about two hundred eighty-five men per kingdom. Why don't we just agree to supply those men for now and veto the original plan? Next, why don't we have the coastal kingdoms study their unique shipbuilding situations? I have not yet had the pleasure of visiting any of our kingdoms, only driven up here from Patri. I do not know what the true situations are. I would dearly love to visit each of your kingdoms, see our incredible country, and meet with you personally. Then, I would have a better understanding of our true situation. I don't know when our next council is to meet here, but why not have the coastal kings be prepared to present to the council at that time just how many ships they realistically could make with what little resources remain to them. That way, we would know our precise current situation and could then make more realistic plans."

As I sat down, I heard King Hektor whisper, "She's a sharp one!"

King Anatolios rose and said determinedly, "I move that we do as our wise Empress suggests. I move that the original conscription plan be vetoed, that the orders for new ships be vetoed, that we continue to provide the twenty legions the General Alexandr has requested this year, and that we four coastal kingdoms do as she says, be prepared to present a complete report on our ship building potentials at our fall council meeting."

These were passed unanimously! Alekos gave me a big smile of relief. I could see that he saw Deimos as a big disappointment. Each of the kings asked me to come and visit any time I desired, to which Alekos was forced to agree with them, whether or not he wanted me traveling about the country.

Prompted by Alekos, Deimos said, "Would the Church of Jehosanity like the opportunity to address the council at this time?"

Cardinal Rax rose in a holy, stately manner. "As you know, our Holy Church has now two gorgeous cathedrals finished, one in Patri and one here in Kefall. As those of you who regularly attend High Mass can vouch, church attendance is demanding that we build more churches. Cardinal Lethos will be handing you our plans to build more churches here in Thrace. Our mother churches in Penelopus, Theos, and Thallyus are nearing completion and will be operational in another month. The document shows our plans for more churches in those kingdoms as well."

"I know that what I am going to report next is a controversial subject for three kingdoms, yet it is my responsibility to do so. Our physicians are now fully trained and apprenticed by the Holy Orthee themselves and have arrived from Megalos only two weeks ago. No longer will those who wish to partake of the Holy Eight Degrees of Matrimony have to journey all the way to Megalos to participate in this most sacred ceremony. From now on, the ceremony of the Holy Eight Degrees of Matrimony can be performed in Thrace at any time. By fall, it will also be available in Penelopus, Theos, and

Thallyus. Currently the delay is the completion of the churches and proper facilities there. I would like to take this opportunity to urge those of you who approve of this most holy ceremony to begin to encourage more couples to partake of our services. Remember, it does not cost the participants anything. The Church of Jehosanity bears the full cost of the ceremony, doing our part to assist all souls to earn the Good Marks that will allow the souls into Heaven, Jehosa's Holy Realm."

Cardinal Lethos placed a copy of the document before Deimos, after glancing at me, giving me a look that said mountains: "You cannot even hold the document." I contented myself to looking over Deimos' shoulder.

"I move that the expansion plans be approved," King Anatolios volunteered. It passed four to three, with the Emperor, Deimos granting his approval, much to the consternation of the other three kings. I would have loved to veto it right here and now, but decided now was not the time to tackle the Church of Jehosanity.

Next, the four kings who supported the Holy Eight Degrees of Matrimony rose and in turn made short speeches praising the ceremony, thanking the Cardinal for persevering and bringing the ceremony back to Demokritos. Each told how wonderful it was being married to such devoted, beautiful wives. Interestingly enough, the wives did not speak on their own behalf. I wondered what all this was leading up to, but I soon found out. It was a well-orchestrated move on their part.

Cardinal Rax then said, "Thank you for speaking so freely and spontaneously of the great merits of the Holy Eight Degrees of Matrimony. As you all know, by the treaty signed by the late Emperor Axos Gavril, the Church of Jehosanity was to be allowed to construct churches in all the kingdoms, to administer to those who wished to convert to Jehosanity from the pagan Sun God beliefs. In return, we are under the obligation to bring the Holy Eight Degrees of Matrimony ceremony to each of the kingdoms, all per the signed treaty, which gives Demokritos sovereign control over Megalos."

"As you know, we are diligently attempting to fulfill our responsibilities of said treaty. Megalos has completely complied in all ways, even to the performing of the Holy Eight Degrees of Matrimony ceremony on our island for you. However, I hate to bring this up to the council once again, but the treaty leaves me no choice." Several people moaned in mock protest. Evidently, this argument had been aired here before.

"Arolas, Alia, and Phindos still refuse to allow us to either build our churches in their kingdoms or to conduct the ceremony of the Holy Eight Degrees of Matrimony in their lands. Again, I point out that this is in strict violation of the treaty signed by Emperor Axos Gavril. The Holy Pope in Megalos, who runs our vast church, has said that we can no longer sit idly by while certain people actively break said treaty, signed in good faith by the Pope himself."

"He has asked me to once more petition the council to take firm action on this violation of our treaty. He stated to me clearly two factors: no one in said kingdoms shall be forced or coerced into converting to Jehosanity and that the Holy Eight Degrees of Matrimony ceremony is strictly voluntary on the part of the loving couple. The Church will not stand for nor tolerate any woman being forced or coerced in any way into participating in this most holy and sacred ceremony. Hence, the Pope asks what possible reason can this council therefore have for not enforcing said treaty?"

"In conclusion, I once more plead with this council to honor the treaty and to allow the Church of Jehosanity to begin constructing churches in Arolas, Alia, and Phindos and to begin conducting the Holy Eight Degrees of Matrimony ceremony for those loving couples who desire to bind themselves for the greater good of their own souls."

I expected fireworks and was not disappointed. King Dimitris bellowed, "We've been over this before. Arolas does not want this church nor its ceremony anywhere on its soil! Already, we have passed five kingdom laws outlawing this church. Must we do it yet again? We don't want them on our land, period. We don't want their mutilations of women on our consciences. Mind you, we have not stood in the way of those kingdoms who desire to further mutilate their women, so I ask that you allow us to choose not to do this!"

King Petros of Alia yelled, "How many times do we have to tell you: *no*, we don't want you or your religion or your butchery of women in our kingdom?

"But the treaty must be honored!" King Leon yelled back.

"A treaty we vetoed!" yelled Petros.

Soon the talk got very ugly indeed. Once more, it was the job of Deimos to moderate, yet he sat there completely overwhelmed by the arguing and yelling.

King Hektor yelled even louder, "The treaty has been passed and must be enforced! It has not been vetoed by the Lady's Support Group of the imperial court, so it stands as a valid treaty!"

Now all seven kings were standing at the same time, yelling so loudly at each other that none of us could understand a word they were saying. I had to step in once more. Deimos was unable to do so.

Again, I faced them and with no doubts or reservations said, "Stop! Thank you." The room was instantly quiet. "Gentlemen, if you will take your seats, I would like to say a few words at this time on this matter."

"I wish to fully understand the situation. Please correct any misunderstandings I might have here. First, King Axos made this binding treaty, correct? And it is valid?" Someone yelled out that it was. "It has not been vetoed by those who hold the veto power?" Again, I received confirmation of that. "Am I correct in then assuming that this treaty is therefore binding upon all seven kingdoms?" Begrudgingly, this was also correct.

Oh, I had a clever idea in mind. "Then, the Empress sees no reason why the kingdoms of Arolas, Alia, and Phindos should not comply with the wishes of the church." I expected a sudden outburst from these three kings, but I added very quickly before they could react. "However, it is one thing to allow these so called holy men to build a church on your soil, and quite another to guarantee their priest's safety." I shut up and sat down, hoping the three kings would notice my not so subtle hint.

All three kings stared at me, straight into my eyes. At first, they thought I was their enemy, by agreeing that the treaty should be enforced in their kingdoms, over their protests of course. Realistically, they had no choice in the matter; they could continue to pass laws outlawing the church, and each time said laws would be vetoed higher up the command lines accompanied by yet another order to comply with the treaty. I just suggested another option, a nasty one at that, one that would not put me on the good side of the Cardinals!

All three stared at me to make sure that they had heard what they thought. I winked at them and smiled, convincing them that I intended what I had said. A smile spread over the face of King Manos, as he realized just what I was proposing.

King Manos rose and answered me, "Yes, Empress Maren, there is no law and cannot ever be a law that guarantees the safety of someone who is hated by an entire population. Perhaps we should allow these priests to come and build their churches, if they can stay alive long enough to do it. Who can control the actions of irate citizens who feel that their concerns are being totally overlooked, eh? No one. Not even our loyal Centurions who are there to protect our people. Even they are against this wicked mutilation of women and wild lies of this so called religion."

He paused and then smiled, "Petros, Dimitris, I say let these priests come and try. I just hope that they already have earned enough of their own Good Marks so that their souls go to wherever they desire to go." Boy, if I had ever heard covert hostility in a speech this one took the cake. While smiling, he delivered a death threat to the Cardinals, almost daring them to enter their kingdoms!

I know, I had just set into motion a brutal conflict between the Church of Jehosanity and the people of these three kingdoms. Men would surely perish as a result, but this would hinder the church here and also buy the Santi more time to prepare or find other ways around this threat of war.

King Anatolios stood, "Cardinal Rax, your plan has been passed by this council. You may begin to build your churches in these three kingdoms, and you may conduct your ceremonies, by the permission of the Grand Council. I do not believe that the Lady's Support Group here will be vetoing said ruling. I for one am getting hungry. I suggest that we adjourn for supper. I know that the Empress has planned a royal feast for us all tonight, complete with music and a dance for us all afterwards."

The meeting adjourned. Cardinal Rax came up to me right away. "Cardinal, I hope that I have been able to at last assist you and your church." Yes, I was lying through my teeth.

"Empress Maren, I want to personally thank you for at long last making these three kings see reason. We have been trying for over a decade now to be allowed to begin our holy work in their kingdoms. Thank you very much. I do hope that I will see you at the High Mass on Sunday." He bowed and left.

Kings Dimitris, Petros, and Manos came up to me, as Mia and I were about to leave the throne room. Their wives were waiting for them at the doorway. Because we walked so slowly, we were waiting for the others to leave. Hence, it was just we three and the three kings who remained in the room. Zenovia listened in carefully.

Dimitris said softly, "Thank you Maren for giving us that idea. You are right; we have been fighting a legal battle without any hope of ever winning, stalling for time, you might say."

"Yes, I realized that you were on ill ground, Dimitris. I hope I wasn't too blatant in my suggestion. Construction accidents happen all the time, you know. Religious fever has cost many a man their lives. Who can say what a man might do late at night that he might not otherwise do in the light of day? Who can say what a man might do to protect his religion?"

All three men grinned. Dimitris said, "You are a very wise Empress, perhaps the wisest Emperor Demokritos has ever had. We thank you. I must admit to you that at first, I thought that you would be our enemy, you being of the Eighth Degree, that you would be totally against our position of not desiring this to ever be done to our women."

"I may be of the Eighth Degree, Dimitris, but I certainly am against doing this to others, though as I have often said, I still will fight to the death to protect a person's power of choice over the disposition of their own bodies. I just do not want this to spread widely; being of the Eighth Degree is dismal to say the very least. Take my dear friend here, Zenovia. She did it out of love for her husband, to bind them solidly for life. Yet, he died a few years ago after a few years of marriage, leaving her like this, helpless and unable to fend for herself. No one apparently thinks this far ahead when they are planning doing the ceremony."

"Precisely the point. Please accept my apologies, Zenovia; we are trying our very best to see that this barbaric practice is halted," King Manos said kindly. She thanked him.

Together, we headed off to the feast. After joining up with their wives, they all walked at my speed to the dining hall, chatting about the events of the afternoon. King Dimitris made a comment that got me thinking. "Empress Maren, I have been completely wrong about you all this time. You are indeed a very wise and able woman." What did he mean about "all this time?"

The dance was a big hit. I had planned this one perfectly. Deimos, who was all left feet, was more than happy to have me dance with others. One by one, various people danced with me. It was a perfect time to socialize and to have a private word with me. Hans danced with me first.

"You nearly crossed the line there suggesting assassinations to those kings. Yet, there aren't many other options for them to use to keep the priests out of their kingdoms," Hans pointed out.

"I'm surprised that they had not already thought of that."

Hektor cut in on us, his hands were very gentle, for he was very used to handling one of us. He was also a good dancer. "Thank you for your support today, Maren. You are more the Emperor than your husband."

"Hogging our Empress, I see," King Eros said, as he cut in on us. "I just wanted the opportunity to tell you that I thought that you did a fabulous job on the council today. If you ever need anything, let me know. I am always here for you women. Do you think that Petros will actually harm the priests who come to his kingdom?"

"Expect trouble whenever two religions clash. I've always found it so." He nodded his understanding.

King Anatolios cut in next. "You were stupendous today, my dear, just fabulous. Somehow, you have gotten all seven kings on your side. I don't know how you did that one!" His kissed my cheek.

"Ah, kissing our Empress, are we, Anatolios," teased King Leon, who cut in next for a word with me. "Excellent handling of the conscription mess, though I would still like to see these coastal kingdoms weakened. Then, we might be able to force them to see reason and better adopt Jehosanity and the Degrees. You did very well, Empress, very well indeed, especially for one so young! You have demonstrated for all just how able women of the Eighth Degree can be. Well done."

"The Empress should dance with someone her own age, Leon," Manos teased, as he cut in on us. "Permit me to escort you across the dance floor." A bit later, he said, "You know, we were wrong about you. Before we met you, we believed that you would be saying just what you were told to say. I like a woman who speaks her own mind, especially as well as you did today. My compliments, Maren. Sometime I would like to talk with you more about the lies put forth by this evil church." I promised we would.

Later, Petros danced with me and said, "Maren, good job today. I would very much like to meet with you and find out what you know about this vile church that is pervading our country like a plague. Your views seem to be parallel to those of the Santi." Again, I promised that I would do so.

Much later on, after Dimitris had danced with me, Alekos took me onto the dance floor. "Maren, I have completely underestimated you, in fact, mostly ignored you. My only defense is that we were trying so hard to get

Deimos up to being able to handle things."

"I hope that I have not made things harder for him by jumping in as I did," I said demurely.

"No, not at all. You show a depth of maturity and wisdom seldom found in one so young."

"Well, just give Deimos some time; he'll grow up." I wanted to give Deimos a safe way out of his mess.

"I promise you that from now on until he does grow up, I will spend my efforts with you, keeping you apprised of everything first. You have become the real power behind this throne, my dear." I smiled.

He went on, "I will speak to Darkon about this as well. He was furious with Deimos' performance today."

"I should really tour all of the kingdoms, if I am to have a good grasp of what's really what. Is this permitted of an Empress?" I asked, batting my eyes, flirtatiously.

"Yes, yes. You should do so fairly soon at that. Summer is nearly here. That would the best time to visit, especially those kingdoms to the south. Winters there can be nasty, cold and a lot of snow. I will begin to make some arrangements. Would you be affronted if Deimos stayed here? He really does need to learn how to fight if he continues to insist on leading this new army."

"Not at all. I suppose the smaller the party, the better?"

"Perhaps so. After today, I am no longer worried about your safety. Somehow you have gained the support of the three kings whom I thought wanted you dead!" I smiled, for that was part of my intention.

The musician's called out, "Last dance."

I found Deimos, "Come on, dear. You should be seen dancing this one, above all others, with me."

He was clumsy, but we managed. He said, "Thanks for bailing me out today. I get so frustrated with those kings, worrying over silly stuff. I heard that you are going to visit all of them later on. Thanks for not insisting that I come, I really need to learn to fight, you know."

"I know. Just don't get yourself hurt, Deimos."

Deimos and his advisors went into a private room. I presumed they were trying to prepare him for the morning's session. Me, I went in search of a cup of tea. Mia took Zenovia to her room, assisting her handmaiden in bathing and getting her ready for bed. Eirena fixed me a pot of tea and poured my cup. She glanced around, but we were alone in the small dining room. "Guess you will need me to assist you this time," she said rather embarrassed. "I'm not used to this, my lady."

"Maren, just Maren. Oh, we have company," I looked up to see Kings Hektor, Eros, and Leon glancing about rather secretively. "Eirena, would you excuse us for a while? Thanks for making my tea for me." She glanced at the kings and beat a hasty exit.

"Could we have a word or two with you, privately?" asked Hektor. He seemed worried or perhaps concerned that they might be discovered completely alone with the Empress. I didn't know if their protocols allowed such a visit.

"Certainly. Come in. I was having a cup of tea. Would you care for some?"

"No thanks. I'm sorry that we've just run your helper out. Would you want one of us to help you?" Eros asked kindly.

"No, I can manage. I hope you don't mind if I take off my boots, though." They smiled, but had no idea what I was about to do, use my feet and toes to sip my tea. This startled them, never having seen this done. "We can do many things that you might not believe that we can, just differently. Now then gentlemen, what did you wish to ask?"

"We've decided that you are the real power behind this throne. We wish to let you know where we stand on several issues, and we would like your position on them as well, truthful answers. Things are in a great flux in Demokritos at this time, and none of us can afford the slightest mistake," Hektor said very seriously.

"Yes, I would agree with that synopsis. I've only been here a short while, but it is very plain that is the case. I will be honest with you," I replied, taking a sip of tea. I was very grateful for my cup; I always think better with my tea.

"Go ahead, Hektor, you are the eldest," Eros suggested.

He hesitated a moment, and cleared his throat before beginning. "We three kingdoms, our people, we believe in the old ways. The supreme sacrifice that our wives willingly did for us must not be allowed to die with us. Until this Jehosanity religion appeared, we were nearly without hope. For years, we watch the older ones die off, helpless to renew their commitments. Verily, I say unto you, none of us has ever taken the commitment our wives have given us for granted, never."

"So when this new church offered us a renewal of the Holy Eight Degrees of Matrimony, we saw this as our salvation. Thus, we have been loyal supporters of this new church, just so that we can renew our commitments. Yet, we are beginning to understand the Santi del Dio cautions and warnings that they have repeatedly given us about the true motives of these priests, who used to control Megalos. They say wisdom grows with age. We are all greying, so we must be wise." It was a slight tease and I grinned.

"We can see where this church may end up leading us years down the road, and frankly we are in a quandary. Do you foresee this church attempting to dominate and control Demokritos as their ultimate goal here?"

"Absolutely, that was their goal, which they achieved by lies, deceit, treachery, assassinations, you name it, they've done it. Why?"

"She sounds like a Santi," Eros commented, though he meant it as a joke. I flushed slightly.

"Then Empress, we four see this alike. Yet, can you see our great problem? We need the church so that we can continue the Holy Eight Degrees, binding contracts of love between us and our wives, proudly displayed for the whole world to see. In obtaining what we desire most, we then are sacrificing our country's freedom, something which we likewise cannot afford to do," Hektor said sadly.

"Yes, you are in, as we say, the pickle barrel on this one. You heard the Cardinal urging Deimos to deploy the seventy legions now based in Megalos. If that is done, the Pope's Holy Paladins will be back in control of the island nation once more. You lose. We must not deploy those legions until more can replace them." I thought this summed up my viewpoint nicely.

"Yes, that is just what we three have concluded ourselves. Rest assured we will do everything we can to prevent their deployment."

"You know why it is the Megalos wants you to go to war, don't you?" I tossed this one out there to see where they stood.

"To fulfill the ancient prophesy," declared Eros.

"Wrong. They and the Santi del Dio are long standing bitter enemies. The Santi have continued throughout history to thwart their nefarious schemes to enslave other countries and to halt their brutal mistreatment of women. The Pope is using you to destroy the Santi for them, since they have failed repeatedly to do it themselves. You should listen more to what the Santi say. After all, it was the Santi who opened up all of Tarra, brought your country into the known wider world. I believe that you would find the Santi strong allies."

"Yes, but they were the ones who convinced the Orthee and the Emperor and Empress to order the abolition of the Holy Eight Degrees," protested Eros.

He had a valid point. In my haste to abolish their mutilation of women, I failed to replace that system with another workable system. In a way, I was responsible for the mess these kings were in today! "Perhaps that was an error in judgment on their part. Suppose that the Santi would support a version of the Holy Eight Degrees ceremony that was humane to the woman, not leaving her as was done with King Anatolios and Amara. She was in an awful state because of the way that the priests handle it. Would that help you to change your minds?"

"Well, yes, if it was indeed as you say, more humane," Eros spoke for the three.

"Then, let me speak privately with the Santi representatives as soon as I can."

"That would resolve the issue. We would no longer support this religion," Hektor stated.

"Tell her about the war," Leon whispered.

He cleared his throat. "Again, we speak from the wisdom of our years and that of our devoted wives. We three do not want to see the Emperor go off conquering Tarra. Wars are destructive. We have all that we need right here. We can see no point in enslaving other lands. As much as we, our wives desire only to live in peace. Yet, there are the Prophesies of Demos to consider. I swear they are driving three-quarters of our people, who believe that we are destined to rule all Tarra. We've tried to push forward plans that will slow this war machine of the Emperor down, but we are too few to stop it, especially because it is backed by the Prophesies. Where do you stand on this coming war?"

"I want peace just as much as you men do. It is folly to go to war just because some paper written seven centuries ago says you should. Let us work together to find ways to avoid this terrible war." I couldn't come right out with what all I knew, and I needed a more acceptable way to put this. "In Annelise, while we do wear stupid clothing, highly impractical, that does not mean that we do not know what is going on in the world. If Demokritos actually goes to war against the Santi del Dio, the amount of blood spilled by our men will be utterly sickening. While I do not doubt that we will eventually be victorious, the cost will be staggering, beyond imagination. I fear then that in our hour of tremendous weakness, the sleeping yellow giant will awaken, as it once did with Megalos. Tashien can field an army far larger than we can field, unless I am mistaken. I really do need to visit all our country to know better our strengths. Alekos has given me permission to do so this summer. Does this answer your question on where I stand?"

"Indeed, more so than we ever imagined, Empress Maren. We will work together on this, we promise you," Eros answered me. I believe the men were impressed with my little impromptu speech.

Leon said, "Hektor, go ahead, you owe it to her."

He fidgeted with his cloak. "Maren, have you given any thought to what you shall do should Deimos die prematurely? I mean he is insisting on leading the war. Unless some miraculous learning occurs, he is not going to be an impressive fighter. If he should die, you should have some plans in the wings. I will say this. Many in Demokritos are more than completely fed up with the line of Gavril rulers. We've have nothing but poor quality leaders of late. Deimos' father was an utter disgrace. I mean you no affront, Empress, but Deimos is not seen by many, many citizens as fit to rule us. His conduct or lack of it today will become widely known as we kings return to our kingdoms." He fidgeted with his cloak once more. I knew that he was withholding something from me.

"Are you saying that some disconcerted citizen of Demokritos might harm him?" I asked what I suspected he was withholding from me.

"You are an astute observer. Yes, that may well happen, pity the day. However, I owe it to you to forewarn you that you, a noble woman of the

Eighth Degree may be prepared. If you should ever need sanctuary, our three kingdoms would treasure your coming to our lands."

"Thank you. I will remember your offer, should I need it."

"We should be going, I hear someone coming. Thank you for hearing us, Empress." The three kings stole out of the dining room on their tiptoes, doing all that they could to avoid detection.

"Hi, Bethany. We've got Zenovia handled. Tea still hot?" Mia reported. I related what had just happened to her, as we finished off the pot. Of course, now I was anything but sleepy. Mia suggested we go for a walk around the grounds. I slipped on my boots, and we set off, heels breaking the silence of the halls. We passed the night guardsman and went outside.

The air was a little chilly, but refreshingly spring. Slowly we wandered around the wide grounds. We noticed a number of other younger couples out for a stroll as well. After a time, we ran into Manos and Karis, who were also out enjoying the lovely spring evening. "Well good evening Empress," Karis said, she had been resting her head on his shoulders, perhaps even kissing. It was dark, only the quarter moon illuminated the cobblestones.

She straightened up her long straight hair, as the two separated slightly. "Say, Manos, may I have a private word with you?" I asked, inspiration striking.

Mia moved over to Karis's side, while King Manos moved with me a ways from the two. "Am I correct in assuming that you, Petros, and Dimitris are dead against the Church of Jehosanity and want to get rid of it here in Demokritos?"

"That should be plainly obvious after today, Empress," he replied flatly.

"What would you say if I could bring Hektor, Leon, and Eros onto your side, the removal of this church from our country?"

He laughed, "I'd say that you are dreaming, Empress. We've been fighting those old codgers for over a score of years. They'll never change their ways."

"I've may have just done that. I need some time to see what can be done, but I am hopeful that by next council, those three kings will be backing you to get rid of these meddling priests once and for all."

"Not likely, Empress, they are hung up on having a way to mutilate their wives, as you are. I am so sorry that you were mutilated in the name of love. We just cannot tolerate the mutilation of women in Demokritos any longer, but these priests are giving them what they want. You'll never get them to turn against this foul religion, not ever."

"I may already have, Manos. You see, I am totally against the mutilation of women against their will just as much as you are, maybe more so."

"That is plain, but you are now completely helpless for the rest of your life, and for what? That adolescent ignorant boy who desires to be Emperor? Sorry, Empress, I did not mean to speak so harshly against your husband, for which you have given away your arms and your life."

"No, you speak truthfully. He has much to learn and quickly, if he is to remain Emperor. Yet, I also support fully the right of any person on Tarra to do what they will with their own bodies. Their body is their body. I only draw the line if what they chose to do with it harms others more broadly than it helps, you see."

"What are you getting at, Empress?"

"A compromise, Manos. If some way can be found for those wives, who desire to do such things to their bodies, of their own free will, without coercion, without duress, without suppression, and if a way can be found that does not involve this despicable religion and is done in a much more humane manner, would you allow those that so desire to do this to do it? After all, look at the horrible mess these priests left poor Amara in when they were done with her! That I cannot stand for at all. If a humane way can be found, would you compromise on this point and allow those who wished to do so?"

"Does that mean that we cannot attempt to persuade them from doing this horrible thing to their bodies?"

"No, I would like each woman who is contemplating it to know completely what she is getting herself into, not like poor Zenovia, who gave all for a couple years of marriage and now has the majority of her life ahead of her with no arms. This should be made very clear to those contemplating doing it. However, I will not stand for coercion of said women, no traumatizing them further over it. Informed yes, coercion no."

"I see. You believe if we compromise on this, the old ones will join us in trying to find ways to remove this vile religion from our shores?"

"Yes, I do. I just need some time to work it out, say until the fall council? Will you give me that chance?"

"Yes, after today, it is plain that you are the throne, not Deimos and his advisors. I will speak to the other kings. We will give you until the fall council, but we would like a hand in working out how these mutilations are done. We cannot understand why any woman in their right mind would even consider such a thing."

"Stranger things have been done for love, my fair Manos. Thank you. We should join the others. I do love the way your wife does her hair. I wish mine were not so curly, but straight like hers. It would be so much more manageable."

"Ah, we both love her hair."

"What's this, you are talking about me and my hair?" Karis teased, having overheard our light conversation.

"I was telling Manos that I love yours. Mine is so hard to handle. Want to swap hair?" We women chuckled over this.

"Mia does such a great job with yours," Karis complimented us. We four strolled for a time, before I yawned and Mia and I headed off to bed.

The next day, the Santi del Dio had their turn to address the Grand Council. Dag stood and spoke. "The Santi would like to extend an open invitation for any of you to come to Velona for a visit. You can see the wondrous sights of Velona, visit with other women of the Eighth Degree who now reside in Velona, and sample our culture and arts. This trip is open to all who wish to come. The Santi will provide all expenses and transportation. Naturally, you will be treated as royalty, staying in the very best accommodations, finest dining. You will get a chance to attend our music recitals and dance recitals. Of course, you may bring whatever security forces you deem appropriate. If you wish, some of us can accompany you and act as your guides and translators. Thank you."

There was a good deal of discussion about the offer, was it really at no cost to us, how long would it take to get there, how long would they stay, and so on. I also saw the military minds kicking in as well; it would be an opportunity to size up the enemy's strength firsthand. Yet, I understood Linda's plan: get these kings to see that Velona was cultured, civilized people just as they were. Perhaps the war would not then occur. She was making every effort to avoid this potential war.

After much discussion, King Eros and Queen Ariadna decided they would go, along with General Alexandr, and advisor Darkon Drusus. Several others sent along their sons to represent them. It was decided that the trip should take place after the fall council meeting; they would be gone most of the winter, from April to September 701.

The rest of the day was taken up with mundane decisions, how much grain was in excess from the winter season, what was the crop forecast for the coming season, such things as these. I found this aspect extremely boring, quite a difference from the previous day. At last, the meeting ended, on the morrow, they would all head back to their homes. As expected of me, I hosted another large feast.

I had left word for the Santi to have a private meeting with me later that night, once the festivities died down. Around ten, I sat in our small dining room, with Mia and Hans, awaiting the foursome to arrive.

"Well, what is all this cloak and dagger meeting all about?" Dag teased, as the four of them, Dag, Betsy, Art, and Sandy entered alone and shut the door so that we would not be overheard.

"I need to correct a huge mistake that I made a long time ago," I began. "When we first came to Demokritos, we found that the origin of the Holy Eight Degrees was indeed the mantis creature staying at Aylon Orthos. It was using the Orthee seers to do its dirty work. Naturally, I was instrumental in getting this practice abolished. As you know the order was signed by both the Emperor and Empress herself. In other words, I assisted the abolishment of a many centuries old tradition here in Demokritos. My error in judgment was that I put nothing in its place. Hence, a natural vacuum was created, which pulled in the mess that the country is in today."

"Yes, but that was a horrible practice you eliminated," Betsy replied.

"True, yet my failure to put something in its place created the vacuum, which has pulled in Megalos and their filling of that emptiness. I need to correct my error in judgment, my mistake here. I believe I have found a way this may be done, humanely. I have gotten tacit agreement from the three kings, who are supporting the Church of Jehosanity solely because it is offering them a way to continue their tradition, to dump their support of the church. They too see this church as a severe threat to Demokritos, yet nevertheless are supporting it only because of the ceremony."

"I still believe that each person's body is their own to do with as they choose, as long as that action does not harm more of the Seven Aspects of Life than it helps. I want the Santi to now offer the Holy Eight Degrees of Matrimony for those that desire it here in Demokritos."

"But that's awful!" Betsy, the Healer protested, as I knew she would.

"Yes, it is awful. You think I enjoy being like this? Yet, many of these people view this entirely differently than we do. Betsy, as a Healer, you can perform such surgeries safely with minimal physical risks to the patient. I would insist that someone who can perform the Jenna Rose therapy sessions to follow up and erase the trauma that is there and the pain that the anesthesia is masking. That way, the patient recovers best, and the side effects are drastically reduced, unlike what happened with Amara."

"However, from our point of view, this is not enough. We must make certain that the woman desiring this is not being coerced in any way, is not being pressured, is doing this of her own free will and choice. Still, I don't think this is enough, personally. I've another idea. Let's make the two who desire this surgery to undergo a one month trial experience with it."

"Huh? What do you mean? I can't take off limbs and put them back on," an annoyed Betsy exclaimed.

"No, it is permanent. I want them to experience what life might be like, if they were that way. For example, a woman wants to be of the Eighth Degree, fine, then she and her husband must live that way for a month's trial. We bind her arms such that it simulates no longer having their use at all. Now the two of them can get used to it and see if this is something that they really desire to do. Only if they both are still desirous of the operation after this month trial would it be done. What do you think? I am sure that I can sell the three kings on this."

"Well, I should think that any woman going around like that for a month would see that it is not a good thing at all," Betsy said. "Okay, if they underwent that, then I would feel comfortable in doing it for real, though I would hate doing it, mind you."

"I know, but remember these people have different customs and values than we do. They see it as something vitally important and very significant. We see it as mutilations. Different viewpoints. I will leave it to you to pass this along up the lines. It will need Linda's approval in the end. I have until the fall council to get it Okayed. If we can get this working, we would now have nearly all the kings behind the ousting of the Church of Jehosanity from Demokritos."

They agreed to pass my request formally up the command lines and they departed. Hans said, "Well, you may have just done the impossible, the removal of this vile church."

"It's not gone yet," I cautioned.

A week later, I received word via Sandy that my proposal had been approved. Further, it would be another three months before the written approval arrived here along with the needed anesthesia and other supplies. Betsy could not go into operation until at least January 701.

Chapter 8 A Tour of Demokritos

In December, I began my grand tour of our country. Deimos stayed in Kefall, practicing his fighter training. Alekos decided to accompany me so that he was there to assist me with any policy decisions or political moves. Ever since the spring council, Alekos spent far more time coaching me than he did Deimos. Darkon would watch over Deimos while we were gone.

We took two coaches. Mia and Hans accompanied me in one coach, while Alekos and his wife Zena rode in the second coach. Also, a half legion of Centurions rode in some wagons, seeing to our security on the trip.

Our path was to be a simple one, essentially. From Kefall, a great paved road ran northeastward to Naros, Arolas. From there it continued in an enormous circle touching all of the capitals of all the kingdoms, before arriving back in Kefall. Only Axos in Thrace was not directly on this road. Of course, there were many other paved roads as well, but this one allowed us to tour the entire country in a most efficient manner, without any backtracking.

The first thing that really attracted my attention was climbing up and over the edge of the Lonki Basin. A huge marble escarpment rose sharply up. In many places, it could not be traversed. Where the road went up to the top, the engineers had made a giant cut, making a smooth grade to the top. Here was where all of the marble was mined, easily accessible and all that anyone could ever want.

From here, we crossed the rolling hills and valleys of Arolas. However, King Dimitris and Daria Docia met us at one of the smaller towns and rode with us into Naxos, giving us time to get better acquainted with each other. Daria was one of those lucky women, who can crawl out of bed and, without even fixing her hair, look positively stunning! However, she also was both stern and bitingly covertly hostile towards me.

"Oh my dear, Maren, you positively must try on some of these cooler summer dresses. Oh, I'm sorry. Mia can help you try them on to see how you fit. I'm afraid that our dressmakers may not be able to remove the arm sleeves for you; it has been so long since they were called upon to do that. Did you bring one of your dressmakers with you who could do it for you?"

On it went. However, I sensed a lot of her hostility came more from being very ill at ease around a woman of the Eighth Degree. I suspected that she didn't know how to react or respond to us. I tried to make her as comfortable as possible and didn't react to her hostilities towards me.

We took a detour from Naxos due north to the main port of Andros, where their largest shipyards were located. Two ships were under construction there. "Dimitris, I certainly can tell that your kingdom has been overworked. Just look at all the time, labor, and precious materials that have gone into all these ships that your kingdom has made, to say nothing of the cost. I do feel that the balance is more than a little lopsided. I will speak with the Emperor about a fairer equalization of the load that you bear."

This, of course, pleased the king immensely, swinging him slightly closer to my side in this chaotic political mess. I relayed that there should be a very significant development with the other kingdoms regarding their position with the Church of Jehosanity at the next council. This surprised him and once more tended to increase his liking of me. I began to see this more as a good will tour.

As we were leaving, we heard that the priests of Jehosanity, who had recently arrived to build their new church in Naxos, had been attacked by hooligans or so it was concluded and were brutally killed. Naturally, King Dimitris asked my opinion on the matter, testing me.

"Well, they took it upon themselves to enter a kingdom where they were hated and not wanted. It doesn't surprise me that they were killed. However, one ought to attempt to find those responsible. Murder is a crime; running them out of town might have served better. I suspect that the Cardinals will be screaming for justice or compensation or protection at the next council meeting."

He laughed. "That, we will not give them. If as you are hinting the other three kingdoms will now support us, they may have something worse to handle." I smiled and hoped that they did.

From here, we headed southward and into the kingdom of Penelopus, arriving in several weeks at their capital city, Tinos, on the banks of the Illos River. I rather liked this city of quaint stone homes. It definitely gave one the feel of older times. In Naxos, the emphasis was on being as modern as possible, due in part to the youthful leaders. Here, King Eros and Ariadna Eleni preferred the old ways. It was as if time slowed down in this land.

I explained in detail to Eros and Ariadna just how the new Santi procedure would operate, including the one-month simulated trial. "Well, that is a brilliant idea, Maren," Ariadna said. "It will give them both more of an understanding just how deep the commitment must be."

"And less surprises, my dear," Eros added.

Since they were going to travel to Velona in a few more months, I spent a lot of time telling them just what sights to see. I explained that I had heard a lot from the Santi in Annelise. Well, we didn't exactly have a Santi post in Annelise, so it was a small exaggeration. Both were quite excited about the visit. I really enjoyed the time spent in Penelopus.

From there it was on southwestward to Thal, Thallyus. After we crossed the Vardan River into Thallyus, King Leon and Queen Athena Kostas met up with us to show us the sights of their kingdom. Again, it was a laid-back land, I discovered. Often around two in the afternoon, everyone would close up shop and take a long relaxing lunch break, lasting until nearly four in the afternoon. Suppers, therefore, came more like at eight o'clock. I had a relaxing time here.

Then, it was on westward on this huge circle of a road. As we crossed the Ile River into Theos, King Hektor and Queen Angele Georgios met us and gave us a guided tour of their lands. Nearly the smallest of the seven kingdoms, life was again very laid back, quaint, and peaceful here. I began to see a pattern. Bereft of the hustle and bustle of the ports, bringing in exotic trade goods and new people, these rural kingdoms moved along at a much slower pace, one that I enjoyed.

As promised, I met with his son and daughter-in-law, Maximus and Lyris about the Holy Eight Degrees of Matrimony. Maximus was twenty-five, tall, thin, and handsome, with long brown hair and eyes to match. Lyris was twenty and very pretty indeed, with the most perfect cheeks and lips I'd seen yet. She wore her reddish brown hair long, down to her waist, proudly telling me that it had never been cut. We sat in their tearoom of Hektor's palace. Tea had just been served.

"Okay, Hektor, Angele, Mia, Hans, would you please take your tea and give us three some privacy?" I know that Hektor dearly wanted to hear this whole conversation, probably Angele even more. Yet, this was a very personal matter that in fact did not involve them.

"Why did you shoo mom and dad out? They have been pressuring us to do this ever since we got married last year," Maximus asked.

"Frankly, because what you two decide to do is none of their business. This is your marriage, not theirs, though I suspect at times, Lyris, you believe that you are also married to Hektor and Angele," I teased, but was spot on.

She chuckled, "Yes, how did you know? Oh, now you don't have your handmaiden with you. Am I supposed to be helping you? I have to do that sometimes for Angele, but I'm not very experienced with it."

"Thanks, but I can manage nicely," I slid off my boots and demonstrated taking a sip from my teacup.

"That's incredible! Mom cannot do that," Maximus exclaimed.

"I am rather an independent sort of person, preferring to do those things that I can do for myself. Yes, there are some things that I simply cannot easily do or that take forever to accomplish, like wiping myself after going to the bathroom, awkward indeed. Taking tea is quite manageable as is feeding myself. Cooking, no way, I let others handle that, it takes me far too long to prepare a meal. Yet, I love to ride horses."

"What, ride? But you have no arms! How is that possible?" Lyris said shocked by my statement.

"I need a horse that is gentle and well trained to take neck reining commands easily. I take the reins in my teeth and away I go. Riding a horse is all about balance and legs, since it's your legs that hold you on to the horse, you see, not your arms."

"I suspect that you two have been badgered to death about Lyris becoming of the Eighth Degree, correct? Nothing less will do?" I asked.

"True, we thought about a lesser degree, but that only infuriated my parents and many others. If you are going to bind yourselves, then do it right, dad says," Maximus replied.

"Okay. What are your own personal opinions of doing this?" I asked.

"Well, I will become king within a few years. I want to set a very good example for our people, keep their faith and trust in me. For over three hundred years now, the queen has always been of the Eighth Degree here in Thallyus. Our people come to expect that from our queen. While my mom and dad are insistent on this, I pride myself on being my own man, making my own council, but including Lyris of course. I've more or less allowed dad's continual harping to go in one ear and out the other; not so with Lyris, however. I am being pulled in two directions at the same time. I feel a deep obligation to my countrymen not to break with tradition, and yet Lyris doesn't want to do it. I am, as they say, stuck smack in the middle."

"How about you, Lyris?"

"They have pestered me day and night about it. Sometimes I have cried myself to sleep over it. I'm scared of it. I don't want to be utterly helpless for the rest of my life. Yet, I deeply love Maximus. I know I will be queen one day soon, and I know our people expect that I be of the Eighth Degree. I've heard so many common people talking about it when they didn't think I could hear them. Yet it frightens me to be so helpless. I won't be able to do anything at all. I would be so totally dependent upon others and that's not like me. I am always doing things to help. If I went through with this, I couldn't even make up our bed! I know that I ought to go through with this; I should do it and soon, but I am terrified of it and being worthless afterwards." She began to cry.

I leaned over and gave her my shoulder to cry upon, and she put her arms around me for a minute. I allowed her to calm down, before I spoke again. "You both are displaying the classical symptoms of a problem."

"Huh?" they said in unison.

"You are being pulled in opposite directions by two forces that are equal and balanced. Hence, the problem remains solidly around you."

"That's an understatement," he replied. "I will never force her to do it, though."

"Noble of you and extremely wise at the same time. No, the way to handle a problem is to make one side bigger than the other and the problem vanishes." I decided I needed to drive this home a bit more, so I purposely used my feet to pour more tea into my cup. Both watched me — their eyes staring in disbelief.

"I will say this, Lyris, having no arms is not a fun way to live life. I lost mine the day after I was born, so I really haven't been in the position that you are facing. You've grown up using arms as a person is supposed to use them. Now you are facing the possibility of losing them. Worse, the only role models I suspect that either of you have ever seen is your mom. I don't know her well, mind you, but I will wager that she does next to nothing for herself. She has others dress her, brush her hair, put her clothes on, make her food, feed her, handle her bathroom duties, make her bed, and so on. She probably does do an awful lot of talking though."

Both laughed at that last. "Yes, mom's certainly the talker."

I continued, "Yes, that is one way to deal with no arms. Yet, there are other ways, as I have been showing you. We have feet and teeth. You can adapt and find other ways to do things. I've already said that I can ride a horse very well. I often make my own bed by using my teeth, you see. If really pressed, I can even light our stove and make my own tea, but I prefer not to do so, since it takes me interminably long to do it. The Santi in Velona are experts at training women of the Eighth Degree to be able to do nearly everything for themselves. I hear that many have become painters of renown, engineers, dancers, musicians. The only thing that can stop you from achieving what you desire is yourself, but I freely admit, sometimes it takes a darn long time to get something simple done. Take sewing for example, though I never have liked it, it would take me a year to make one crude dress. Hence, I let the dressmakers do this for me."

"Now you may have heard from your father that I have been working out a humane way for the Holy Ceremony to be performed. The Church of Jehosanity is butchering women, and we want them stopped from ever harming a woman again."

"Yes, we heard what happened with Amara. That scared both of us!" Lyris added.

"Part of the new process will involve a one month experiment involving both of you, a sort of trial situation. Let me explain how I believe this will work. Say she desires to become of the Eighth Degree. Then, they will secure her arms behind her such that she has absolutely no use of them at all. You and she would then live one month together like this. Both on you would get a reasonable feel for just what life is going to be like for you, if she actually went through with the ceremony."

"I like that, Maximus. I could see how it would be, though I would be terribly frightened of being so helpless."

"Who would not be scared? Further, if one then decides that this is still something she wants to do to her body, then once the operation is completed, the Healers will then perform therapy to erase the trauma she has undergone, much like I did for Amara. You heard about that too, I expect?"

"Yes, from the way dad explained it, you saved her life!"

"Yes, she was near crazy as a result of the horrible way that the Church had performed her ceremony. What I am telling you is that this new Santi method will give her the best possible chance for success in life. Yet, there is one more detail that I wish Lyris to consider. Talk with your Santi about how the women of the Eighth Degree are helped by the Laird Foundation in Velona. In her case, she wants to be as independent as possible, not as helpless as your mother is. Both you and she ought to take an extended trip to Velona and stay at the Laird Foundation for as long as she needs to learn new ways of handling life. Your stay there is free; helping women such as she would then be is their main purpose, so it is completely free. Maximus, you owe it to Lyris to do this if she decides to go through with the ceremony. If you don't, I will attack you myself."

He laughed, "You cannot attack me, Maren. You have no arms."

I jumped up and threw my body into his, knocking him over. Of course, I then fell down on top of him. We both began laughing hysterically. Lyris helped me up off him, chuckling as well.

"Okay, point taken, Maren," he said. "I promise you, Lyris, that if you go through the ceremony, I'll take you to this Laird Foundation for as long as you need." She felt better about it.

"In the final analysis, you two, I cannot tell you what Lyris should do. It is her own body, and she should be in control of what she wants to do with it. I just want to do everything I can so that she can make an educated choice, knowing in advance how life will become for her afterwards. Me personally, I'd take my arms back in a second, if I had that choice, but then I did not give them up out of love for another. I am not in the situation you two are in nor am I from your culture. I am from Annelise, you see."

Both thanked me profusely for this long, frank, and honest talk. Indeed, Lyris looked much better now. The color returned to her cheeks. "Say, I've heard that you have actual ice sheets further south. Is this true? I've never seen an ice sheet. I've heard that we have them in Annelise, though my father never allowed me to go there to see them."

"Yes, in the summertime, it is a popular resort area — nice and cool walking on the ice sheet. However, there is no road that your carriage could travel. It is reached by horseback," Maximus explained. "It's about one hundred seventy-five miles south of here. Would you like to see it?"

"You bet, if they will let me."

A little later, Hektor pleaded, "But Empress, the only way to get there is by horseback. That would be so terribly difficult for you. I once led Angele there many years ago. We had to go so very slowly, I led her horse, and she tried so hard to stay on it. We had an awful time. It was so hard for her, camping out in the rough. There are no towns within fifty miles of the ice sheet."

"I can ride by myself, Hektor. Why don't you let us younger ones make the trip this time? It will be good for Maximus and Lyris to get away for a while. I can talk with them further." I hinted at what I hoped was a trump card with him.

"Maren, if anything should happen to our Empress, it would be on my head," he pleaded.

"Alekos, I want it clearly understood that I am ordering Maximus and Lyris to take me to see this ice sheet. I am assuming full responsibility for the trip."

"But Empress Maren, you need arms to do this thing!" Alekos tried to make me see reason.

Two days later, Mia, Hans, and I stood beside the horses. Maximus and Lyris walked theirs up to ours. Four younger Centurions were still saddling up their horses and all of the six packhorses, which carried our tents and camping supplies. "Last chance to turn back," Max said, sincerely meaning it. He still didn't believe that we were actually going to go to the ice sheet.

In these heels, mounting would be more difficult, so I let Hans help me into the saddle. He carefully got the reins into my mouth, and I bit down securely. The others mounted and off we went, though half of the king's staff turned out to watch me as we rode off, heading down the south road. Hektor just could not believe that we were doing this, but Alekos assured him that his Centurions would look after us. Both expected to see us return, possibly by nightfall, certainly by tomorrow.

I felt a sense of freedom that I had not had this lifetime. For once, I was doing something I truly wanted to do, a little adventure, a little fun. If nothing else, Lyris would see that I was not entirely a helpless woman. I had only one little problem, the same one that Mia also had. Our growing melons continually bounced, very annoyingly.

Nearly a week later we arrived at the ice sheet. During our evening camps, I helped, doing as much as possible, even assisting Mia doing the dishes. It felt so good to just be myself and do these things for myself once again. I was very sick of being tended to for everything in life. Okay, I was rebelling a little.

We met a dozen others who were also at the ice sheet. The ice stretched on south as far as the eye could see. While the weather was warm and sunny, the evenings were chilly. A little ways out onto the ice and the temperature dropped quickly, a pleasant change from the summer's heat. Some of the others had brought along a homemade sled that could seat five or six people. Although I did not tell them who I was, they invited us to come sledding with them. For two days, we all had a ball. The tricky part for Mia and me was actually walking on the ice in our heels. Hans got a work out keeping us two on our feet. Yet, all of us were laughing and enjoying ourselves, particularly Max and Lyris. I hated to have to return.

On the ride back, Lyris commented, "Maren, you are just incredible! You do nearly everything that we do. It is simply amazing. I've watched Angele for a couple of years, and she never did anything remotely like the things you do for yourself. I am seeing this in a whole new light."

"Yes, but it is an awkward light. I'd just as soon have my arms, if you please," I jested and everyone laughed. We arrived safely back in Thal, having taken a two week leave from the grand tour. I felt alive and very refreshed when we said farewell and continued down this grand circle of a road, now heading west towards Pirgos, Phindos.

As expected, when we crossed the Marsha River into Phindos, King Manos and Queen Karis Kadmos were waiting for us. Again, the pace of life picked up noticeably. Once more, we took a detour to visit their large port of Filantos. I repeated my observations about Manos having born more than his fair share of the burden, and he was very pleased with my statement.

Then, we headed north toward Alia. Crossing the Phindos Mountains was spectacular. Their still snow-capped peaks stood ruggedly against the summer's blue sky. I marveled at the engineering that went into the making of this paved road, which cut through this formidable range. Manos talked at length about the construction of the road, and I enjoyed hearing about it. He loved to chat.

Once at the top pass, we said our farewells and rode down into Alia proper. Soon King Petros and Queen Hypathia Homer met up with us to give us a tour of their kingdom. The pace of life in this kingdom was again quite brisk, and we took a fast detour to visit his largest port, Preveza. He was also very pleased to hear that I thought that he was making a much larger contribution to the effort than his fair share. Yes, I was working to build up their approval of me. One day I would need their support.

From here, the road angled to the northeast and at last, we reached the southern portion the great bowl, the Lonki Basin. At once, we saw marble stonecutters at work, preparing to break loose what would eventually become another great pillar. We stopped to watch them for the rest of the afternoon so that I could see the fruits of their efforts — the fifty-foot long square column come free.

Late December, we arrived back in Axos to meet with King Anatolios and Queen Amara Gavril. For several days, they took us on a grand tour of Axos. Then, we went on down to Patri, primarily because I had heard that there were super public beaches there, and I longed for a swim. I had not been swimming at all this lifetime.

Amara said, "But Maren, we cannot swim! Are you forgetting, as I sometimes do, that we do not have any arms?" She looked very worried.

"Well, we sure can splash around a lot, Amara. However, we can swim if we lay on our backs and use our feet. Speed records are not going to be broken, but we ought to be able to do it. I've never been swimming before. In Hodenhagen, there are no lakes and it is hundreds of miles to the coasts. Mom and dad never let me swim. So Anatolios, take us swimming. That's an imperial order!" We all laughed.

Five days later, we all were relaxing on the whitest sandy beach I've ever seen. The waters were warm and here quite shallow for nearly a half mile out. Yes, eventually both Amara and I got the hang of swimming around on our backs. It was so great to see her smile when she actually did it, a true sense of accomplishment. Anatolios beamed like a peacock at his beautiful wife. The next day, it was back into the coaches for the return trip to Axos.

On December 31, 700 we arrived back at his palace. Alekos wanted us to leave for Kefall the next day. I begged him to allow us one more day in Axos. Amara and I wanted to go shopping, and she wanted to take me to the finest diner in her city. Thankfully, Alekos consented. I had Zena, his wife, to thank for this stay of execution, she wanted him to take her shopping for baby clothes, she was expecting. Surprised by the news, the proud father-to-be promised to take her shopping.

Never let two women, okay, three women, Mia was with us, go shopping with an unlimited budget. We brought back half the stores, or so Anatolios claimed, laughing at the voluminous packages we had carried into his palace. I'd bought souvenirs for my staff and a nice looking new suit for Deimos, along with a magnificently made dagger. After a lovely evening dinner, we all turned in early. Tomorrow, January 2, 701, we would head up the road to Kefall and back to being Empress again.

Around midnight, Amara began screaming as loudly as she could, a terrified, panicked scream! Something was horribly wrong. Everyone dashed out of bed and raced to their giant bedroom. Ten guards beat us to the door and opened it. Nothing could have prepared us for the sight we saw.

Amara, screaming wildly, lay on her bed, nightgown covered in blood. She was trying in vain to stop the massive bleeding of Anatolios. I saw at once that his throat had been cut, slashing the key arteries. He was already dead, but Amara, screaming wildly, continued to try to save her husband.

The Captain of the Guards tried to get Amara to tell him what had happened, but she was completely in shock, terrified. At last, we got one word from her, "Window." At once, the guards raced there and found a grappling hook still attached. They raced out of the room and sounded the alarm. I figured it was already too late to catch the assassin. Her handmaiden passed out. His advisor slumped on to the floor and began crying like a little kid.

I took charge. Mia, you are with me. Let's get her away from him and get her cleaned up. Hans, Alekos, you take charge of the body. Zena, will you lend us a hand with Amara?"

"It's okay, Amara, you are safe with us. Let's get you cleaned up," I said soothingly to her.

"I have to save him! I have to save him! You don't understand I have to save him!" she screamed, as Mia and Zena pulled her off her dead husband. It took some doing, but we three managed to get her into their bathroom and out of her soiled gown. While Mia and I began to bathe her, I sent Zena to find her handmaiden and get her to bring us some clean clothing for Amara.

Poor Amara, her long hair was drenched in blood as was her face.

Lacking hands, she had tried to stop the massive blood flow with her head. We worked for an hour on the sobbing woman to clean her up. I was grateful for Zena's assistance, as she took over for me and began to wash out Amara's hair, which I was having a devil of a time managing using only my teeth. Finally, dressed in some clean clothes, a towel around her head, Amara had finally calmed down and was only crying to herself now.

Her handmaiden had finally recovered and had some warm tea waiting for us, as we led her into their small, personal dining room. "Ma'am, here let me give you something warm," the young girl said, helping Amara take a sip.

Funny thing about tea, it has many uses. It was just what I and Amara needed at the moment. "Can you tell us what happened?" I asked her. Unfortunately for me, Amara actually began to run the traumatic event, as if we were in a therapy session!

"We just made love and I am rolling over to go to sleep. Anatolios is now snoring. I hear this strange noise and try to roll over to look. It is so hard to roll over without my arms. I am struggling. I get turned over and see this man wearing a mask over his face coming through the window. He shoves me over, and without arms, I roll over. 'Out of the way, helpless one,' he says to me, and he cuts Anatolios. I hear the sword cutting. I have to roll over. I struggle and struggle and make it. I see blood coming out of his neck. I have to save him. I try putting my hands onto his neck to stop the blood. I kept trying and trying, but my hands are not there! I panic. I have to save him. I use my head and put pressure on the wound. I begin to scream and scream and scream. I feel so helpless. I cannot save my own dear husband. I am totally worthless." She began crying a lot. "Then the door opens, and everyone comes in and sees just how worthless I really am." Now she bawled uncontrollably.

Mia, get this detailed account to the guys. I have to continue to run my therapy session on her; she's trying to run it out somehow. Mia took off in a flash.

Zena watched me carefully. "Okay, Amara, let's go back to the beginning and go through it again. Tell me everything that you are seeing, all that you smell."

Zena started to say something, but I mouthed a "sh" message and mouthed the word "listen." She did so. We ran through it several more times. Each time, Amara got a little more of the actual details of what exactly had happened. She had smelled olive oil on the man's breath and a whiff of incense. The blade was curved, unlike the blades normally found in Demokritos. He had no distinguishing marks on him, unfortunately. However, Amara now became utterly convinced that she was completely worthless, saying this over and over and over.

Then, the next couple passes produced no change at all, so I asked her if there was something earlier that was similar to this. I knew that there had to be something else here, something which was convincing her that she was worthless.

"I see a blue thing," Amara said. We began to go through this earlier one. "I'm a young woman. I kiss my loving husband. These women in white robes are leading me away into another room. They give me something to drink. I feel strange. I feel so weak, so helpless. I am falling. Arms catch me. I am on a table. God! They are cutting my arms off! Oh, these are the Orthee. Now I get it. I'm getting the Holy Eighth Degree ceremony. It's up at Aylon Orthos. I don't feel a thing. I am sleeping. Now it is later. I try to get up, but my arms don't work. I look down and they are gone. I scream. Now I know that I am utterly worthless. My husband holds me tightly, but I am telling him that I am utterly worthless. He takes me home and is feeding me. See, I am utterly worthless. He says it takes time to adjust. Days go by, I keep seeing just how utterly worthless I really am. I cannot take this any longer. I walk to the barbican of our tower and I jump off. I am falling, knowing that I am worthless. I am flailing my arms like mad because I am falling, but they do not work anymore. I hit something hard. There is my grotesque body lying down there. I leave, knowing I am utterly worthless now."

Zena was absolutely fascinated by this, yet she kept still. I had Amara go through it several more times. Then, a period of heavy yawning ensued, and I knew we were coming down home stretch with this one. She had uncovered what was happening while her body was drugged unconscious. The woman is cutting around the sides of my arm. Now she is peeling it back like an apple. Oh, that hurts! She's cutting it out of its socket. Now she is doing the same to the other side. Two others are pinching off the arteries. Now she is sewing it all up, like a dressmaker. Oh, she says, 'There, finished. Now she is utterly worthless. She won't be able to do anything anymore, another utterly worthless woman. Take her to the recovery table and wash off the blood off this worthless woman.' They did so."

"Oh!" Amara opened her eyes and looked at me; a grin began forming. "Oh! She said that. I didn't. I was following her orders! So that's why I felt like I was utterly worthless. She said I was! That's why I felt so utterly worthless when I couldn't save Anatolios!" She began laughing at the silliness of the whole thing. I ended the session.

"Thank you, Bethany. I feel so much better! I am not utterly worthless after all. Honestly, even if I had arms, there was nothing I could have done to save my dear husband, was there, Maren?"

"No, he was dead almost in an instant. There was nothing anyone of us could do. I wish the man had not worn that mask though; it would make finding him easier to do."

"God! Anatolios is dead! Whatever will happen to me now? This wasn't supposed to happen, not for years and years! We are so happy together. I gave up my arms for him. Now what will I do? Maren?"

"Simple, Amara, you are going to come and live with me at the imperial palace, that's what. No way am I going to leave you here alone. Are you hungry?"

"I'm famished. We need to bury Anatolios. I need to let his family know. I . . ."

"It can wait until morning," I said.

"Zena and your handmaiden here will look after you for a bit. I want to go and see what news the others may have for us. Back in a while, Amara."

First, I went to my room and put on my boots. Up until now, I was walking on my tiptoes. I could not put my feet out flat any more, not for years. Next, I went in search of the others.

I found them in the throne room. Alekos had taken charge as the Emperor's advisor. This was an assassination, and Alekos had declared this an imperial crime, whether it was or was not. He reported, "Empress, the assassin was well trained. He got away cleanly. No one saw anything. The guard who was on duty in that section outside was found with his neck cut, just like Anatolios. Very professionally done."

"Any clues?" I asked.

"Nothing at all. As I said, a professional hit."

"Mind if I have a look? Perhaps some detail has been overlooked."

"Sure, but from now on, one of us must accompany you wherever you go. I'll take you. How's Amara doing? Probably going to be hysterical for days after this."

"I gave her my therapy, and she is recovering. Zena's with her. She can tell you all about it." He opened the door to the king's bedroom. His body still lay on the bed, though now it was covered with a sheet.

"According to Amara, the assassin came thorough that window. She heard a noise, probably the hook hitting the stone. It's warm out, so naturally the window would be open." I walked over to the grappling hook and turned to face the scene, much as the assassin had. Slowly, I began to walk the path he must have taken. Then, I noticed something on the floor.

"Alekso, come here. Look at this." He came to my side. Two tiny drops of blood were on the floor. "Bring the lantern here very close to the floor, please." Now we could see that these were two very tiny blood drips. "Ah, here are two more. And here."

Alekos said, "Here by the bed, look there are quite a few on the floor. Could it be that his sword made these?"

"Well, Alekos, let's find out. Dip your sword in Anatolios's blood and see if you can get a drip to fall to the floor near here." He drew his sword and with a little effort managed to get enough blood to cause a drop to fall onto the floor. "Good. Now bring your lantern close and let's compare the drops from your sword to these tiny ones."

"Maren, they are very different. See how mine splashes outward.

These others do not."

"You are right; they did not come from a blade dripping blood. Now try it again, only let the sword be almost touching the floor." He did so and we again compare them. This time they looked remarkably the same.

"What does this mean? That the assassin was himself bleeding from his ankles?"

"Not likely. Blood was probably dripping down his legs and landed here. There is more when he was likely standing for a longer period doing his dirty work there. See, more drops here by the bed."

"But how did you see all this? We missed this entirely."

"I am forced to take tiny steps, but you probably moved around here very quickly; you do have a big stride," I grinned. It was a slight distortion of the truth. I am a trained observer of the obvious. Besides, I had a good idea who may have been behind this assassination, one of the dreaded Mano del Dio, the assassins of the Church of Jehosanity, their "Security Personnel" as the church calls them.

"At first light tomorrow, I want you to begin your search directly below here. Look very carefully. I predict that you will find more of these tiny blood drops out there. If you are very lucky, you may even have a clear trail to follow."

"Yes, Empress, I will follow your orders," he said. I looked at him. This was the first time that he had ever said that to me!

I went back to check on Amara. By now, she was exhausted, but we all were, for it had been a very long day, and it was very late at night. "Amara, come with me. Tonight, you will sleep in my bed alongside of me." She didn't hesitate but followed me, Mia hot on our tails. After she climbed in and Mia helped her lie down, I crawled in beside her, but insisted on pulling up the light sheet myself, using my teeth of course in an awkward motion. Mia left us, turning out the lantern as she left. In the darkness, Amara rolled over to lean against me for comfort.

"Whatever will happen to me now that my love is gone? How am I to survive? Where will I go? How will I live? They will elect a new king, and he will have his own queen. I must move out."

"I've already said that you are coming to live with me, Amara. Until you feel comfortable sleeping alone, you are going to sleep at my side. Deimos can just sleep by himself a while, that's all." I kissed her on her forehead, much as if she was my child. In a way, she was, although she was several years older than me, five to be exact.

I awoke to many bells tolling, a cacophony of sounds echoing throughout the city of Axos. Mia told me that someone told her that they were announcing the death of the king to the city. She helped we two get dressed, but I put on my own boots. We three went off in search of breakfast. Alekos and Zena were already there.

He said, "Maren, as soon as you have eaten, I want you to come outside with me. You were correct about your prediction last night." He said no more, afraid to upset the women. A little while later, Hans, Mia, and I accompanied him outside the palace, we walked around to the spot below their window, some twenty feet above us. Alekos pointed out the telltale blood drips. Here where he climbed up, there were over a dozen of them.

More importantly, Alekos had found a trail of them, though he could not tell if they were coming or going from the scene of the crime. "I followed the path, Maren. See, let's verify my findings." Heads lowered, we followed the tiny droplets trail across the courtyard, past where the guard had been slain, a large pool of drying blood marked the spot. His body had already been moved. Then on went the trail, until at last we were standing in a secluded location, just outside the palace grounds, a spot from where the king's window as clearly visible.

"He must have waited here for some time. See how many tiny drops there are here?" Dozens of them littered the ground, very tiny drops. "The trial leads off on down the street. However, with all of the traffic that has already passed by, I have lost the trail there. Now what does this mean? I have learned enough about you by now, Empress, to know that you already have some ideas about the assassin."

"Yes, the signs are very telling, if you know what has made these signs. You may know the answer too, though you might not yet have realized that you know the answer. Let me ask you some leading questions, if I may, Alekos. If you were going to assassinate the king, would you cut yourself first and allow yourself to bleed down your legs the whole time you were on the assignment?"

"Hell no. That is stupid. No one would do that intentionally."

"What do you know of the Mano del Dio?" I asked the leading question, wondering if he knew as much about them as I did.

"Damn! You are right again, Empress! Those security men — they wear circlets of thorns to give them pain. I've seen some of them. They bleed down their legs, just as we have seen here! Incredible, Empress. I am impressed beyond words with your keen powers of observation. The assassin was a Mano del Dio security man; there is no doubt. Yet, which one and how do we prove it was one of them?"

"I am afraid that I do not have all of the answers, Alekos. I have no idea how you are going to prove which of them did this vile deed, though circumstantial evidence points to them. Will you be able to even prove this much?"

He sighed. "I don't know, Maren, I surely don't know. I will, of course, share all of these observations with the Captain of the Guards, who will see that . . . Well, I don't honestly know what will be done about it, to be truthful. We'd better get back inside. I have much to discuss with you. This assassination is going to cause enormous repercussions throughout all of Demokritos. I am so thankful that you are taking in poor Amara. Zena told me what happened last night. I would like to speak with you about that later on when we have time." He opened the door for me and we went inside.

We found all of the staff gathered in the throne room. Amara was doing her last duty for her husband, working out the manner that his funeral would take with her staff. She had finished when we joined her. "I guess that is all for now." Many hastened off to follow out her requests.

"I've arranged for his funeral tomorrow. He always told me that when he died he wanted to be cremated soon after his death, though he never said why. Have you found out anything?"

Alekos replied, "Queen Amara, we have solid evidence that the assassin of your husband was one of the Mano del Dio members. Unfortunately, there is no way that I can see of determining which one did the deed. There are other matters, which we should discuss, if you feel up to them just now. It can wait if you need more time to grieve, Your Highness."

She let out a fake laugh, "Time to grieve — I will be grieving the rest of my life! I gave him everything including my arms; now I can only sit and grieve. Now is as good as any time, Alekos."

"It is the official disposition. Per our laws, in a situation such as this, the woman of the Eighth Degree is awarded the complete personal wealth of her husband so that she may be provided for as befitting one of her highest stature. Queen Amara,"

"Oh do stop calling me that, Alekos," she acidly cut him off. "You know as well as I do that I am Queen no longer. How soon must I vacate the premises?"

"As I was saying, I must be proper and official about this, Amara. I will meet with his advisors next, and we will arrange a transfer of funds to Kefall for you. I will give you a full accounting as soon as I have the figures. We should be returning to Kefall as soon as the funeral is over, Amara. Shall I have the staff begin to pack for you?"

"Yes, please do that for me, will you? I'm sorry I snapped at you, Alekos. You are doing your very best on my behalf. I want to leave this place as soon as I possibly can. I cannot bear to spend another night in here. His family will be arriving shortly. I should dress formally, out of respect for them."

Mia and I followed her to lend her what assistance we could. I was leery of allowing her out of my sight so soon after such a tragic loss. She held up remarkably well, probably because of our therapy session last night.

The day was a whirlwind of activities. His mother, brother, and two sisters arrived; grief was shared by all, along with many curses. At nightfall, his funeral was held, and I stood by her side throughout it, lending such moral support as I could. She bravely did all that was expected of her. I was with her when she whispered, "Goodbye my one and only true love; I will miss you more than you can ever know." I had her lean her head on my shoulders for a time as we watched the flames consume his fleshly body.

Throughout the day, her staff had been busily packing into all available sacks and crates the possessions that she would take with her. Much of those which belonged to Anatolios, she left for his family so that they would have remembrances as well. During the late evening, her staff packed the sacks and crates into the carriages, which we would use in the morning.

When we were in bed, she snuggled up beside me for comfort, "Maren, I will be leaving behind all the staff here in Axos. I cannot even take my handmaiden with me; she is in love and hopes to be married in two months. I cannot bear to take her away from that. Will you help me find someone to care for my needs when we get to your palace?"

"Certainly, Amara, and until we find her, Mia will help us both. You were very brave today. I'm sure that Anatolios would have been very proud of the way you handled everything for him."

"You are kind. He was my whole world, Maren. I chose to share my life with only him. Now he's gone. I've no arms and no goals. I feel so lost right now."

"I know, Amara, I know. I want you to be with me until you have made some new goals and have created a new world for yourself, however long that may be. Snuggle with me."

At dawn, we rose, dressed, and ate quickly. An hour after dawn, six carriages pulled out of the palace in Axos, heading southeastward toward Kefall. Amara rode with me, along with Mia and Hans. It was a very silent ride for the next few days, pulling in to our palace on January 7, 701. Gone was a lot of my enthusiasm from the long trip — assassinations tend to do that to one.

When we arrived, my staff was waiting to greet me, solemn faced as well. I half expected Deimos to come rushing out and hold on to me. Instead, he welcomed me and said, "Glad you are back safely. Terrible thing, Amara. I have ordered a full investigation, and I will not rest until we find the assassin, you have my word."

"She's going to stay with me now, Deimos. Can we use our bedroom or should she and I take another one?"

"It might be simpler if you take the one next to ours, Maren; it's not occupied at the moment. That way, I will not have to move all my things, taking time away from my training. I can see that I need to improve my fighting skills or the assassin might get me next time."

I ordered the staff to take Amara's things into that room and to move some of my things in there as well. Actually, this would be a simpler arrangement, because Amara really needed the support during the next weeks. Eirena apologized for him though, "Maren, he was really upset when he heard about the assassination. He was terribly worried that you might have been hurt too."

After we had Amara settled in, Alekos asked me to join him for tea in our small dining room; just he and I were there. He poured my cup; I removed my boots to drink it myself. "We need to discuss the political ramifications of this assassination, Empress." Indeed, his death could well become extremely pivotal, depending upon whom was selected by Thrace to be their next king.

"What happens next? How is this done?"

"If Amara and Anatolios had a son, a regent would be chosen to safeguard the throne until he became of age. I did this for Deimos for a couple of months until he had his fourteenth birthday. A daughter does not count. Since they have not been married long enough to have children, the Gavril line ends with Anatolios."

"What happens to Amara? She gave everything for him."

"She gets his fortune, which should be enough for her to live comfortably for the rest of her life."

"She's only twenty-two with her whole life ahead of her like this," I sighed and shrugged my shoulders.

"Point taken, I don't think these Holy Degrees should be done. I'll not let my Zena even consider it. I leave Amara in your care, Maren. I have no answers for her. What happens next in Thrace is critical. Because the line is ended, the noblemen of Thrace will have to meet and decide whom they wish to be their next king. First though, they will have to decide on just which men are currently the noblemen. I mean they have not met for this reason in nearly a century. During that time, some men have made their fortunes and are now in the nobleman category. I suspect there will be considerable power plays made before they meet for the first time."

"Once they meet, they must choose a man to be king. He could be married, he could be single, he could be powerful, he could be weak, he could be young, or he could be old. He could be a supporter of the Holy Degrees, he might not be. Whoever is chosen may well tip the balance of power here in Demokritos. All of the other kings will know this, just as soon as the word of his death reaches them. You may be assured that these other kings will be making their influence felt with the nobles. A hefty bribe goes a long way toward getting the new king that you desire. I'm sure that the supporters of the Holy Degrees will be passing out money pouches like mad to ensure the next king likewise supports the Degrees. Yet, the three kings who are opposed to the Degrees will be handing out just as many favors, in hopes of getting a new king who is opposed to the Degrees."

"If this is not enough pull, then there are those who are pushing for this global war of conquest and those who are not. Then, there will be those seeking support for the Church of Jehosanity and those who want it opposed. Some want to have the Santi play a more dominate role; others do not. Some want a youthful king, while others desire an older man, a wiser man. Even now, there is another smaller factor. While most favor following the Prophesies of Demos, some are pushing to choose our own destiny."

"In the coming days, much will be promised these men and much will change hands. Above all, the Emperor and Empress must be publically seen as having no direct influence on their choice."

"Well, you don't have to worry on my account. I don't know any of them. Does this whole process bother Deimos? After all Kefall is in Thrace and we will have to get along with whoever is chosen as King," I replied.

"Honestly, the Emperor is more interesting in honing his fighting skills at the moment. I think he was upset about his cousin's death for a few minutes. He was more worried about your safety, but today, he is out there on the practice field. Probably this is a good thing, since keeps his attention off of other things."

"How fast do you think they will act? I mean should I expect a new king by the fall Grand Council meeting?"

"I'd place my money pouch on that, Empress. Thrace knows that it must be represented by then." Just then, we were interrupted by the arrival of an accountant with the figures for Amara. Alekos excused himself to deal with this, while I went to check up on Amara.

I found Zenovia looking after Amara. Zenovia was nearly twenty-six now and had lost her husband after less than a year of marriage, though not for the same reason as had Amara, who was approaching twenty-three now. Hers had been unfaithful, sleeping with her handmaiden. Still, both had a lot in common, and Zenovia was the right person for Amara to be with right now.

"Hi Maren," Amara managed a stiff countenance as I walked in, her eyes were red; I knew she had been crying some. "Zenovia lost hers early too. We have been talking about my future. We both agree. We will never be able to find another loving, kind man again, not while we are like this. She's told me to be on the lookout for men who will come courting me, but are really after what little money I have. Honestly, I didn't think men would be like that to us, Maren. I guess I have a whole lot more to learn."

"Amara, you are holding up exceptionally well. Both of you are under my care now, I insist. Where I go, you go. Is that clear?" She smiled.

"Any word on who was behind the assassination, Maren," Zenovia asked, cold steel in her eyes. I knew why she was asking about this; she wanted to get word to her Kali associates.

"Yes, without a doubt, the assassin was one of the Church of Jehosanity's Mano del Dio security men. I doubt that we will ever be able to find out his identity, though. Alekos also doubts that we will be able to prove conclusively beyond any doubts that it was the Mano del Dio, either." I described what I had found and what Alekos had discovered.

"There can be only the one answer, Maren. We've seen similar things," she was choosing her words carefully. Amara had no idea that Zenovia was the leader of the Kali in Thrace.

"Even though we might not be able to conclusively prove it, I think that I have now drummed up enough support from the kings that they will all six demand action be taken against the Church," I said sounding as hopeful as I might for Amara's sake.

"Maren, will you watch over Amara for a spell, I have something I need to do in town for an hour or so," Zenovia asked. I knew what she was going to do, however. I said I would and she left.

"More tea, Amara?" I asked, clumsily pouring us another cup.

"That's pretty cool how you can do that with your feet. I suppose that I ought to learn how to care for myself now that I am alone."

"Yes, you should, but you are not alone. You have Zenovia and me to look after you."

"Thanks." I showed her how to drink from her cup herself. She found it awkward, but she did get a sip.

"Now I'll never be able to have any children, Maren. I can't even find another man, while I am like this. Only noblemen can afford to have a woman of the Eighth Degree. What nobleman would desire one who already is this way? It proves nothing about the new marriage. I am doomed utterly to sit around until I am an old maid, doing nothing."

I longed to take her off to Velona, where there were good men who might fall in love with her in time. I knew I couldn't do that, yet I ached to give her some hope for the future. I wanted at least to tell her about the possibilities of finding someone to love in Velona. Still, I could not even do that without blowing my cover. "I know that I am only fifteen to your twenty-three years, Amara, but I promise you that there are plenty of kind, loving men out there in the world who would love you for yourself. Amara, I will make this bargain with you. If you will work hard on becoming as independent as you can, I will work hard of finding you just the right man for you. Promise?"

She grinned sheepishly. Only a tiny thread of real hope was there; yet she said, "I will do so, Maren, if only so that I am not hindering you and Mia."

"That's the spirit. Come on; let's get your hair brushed out. It's rather a mess this morning." To her surprise, I did not summon Mia. I knew she was busy. Using the brush in my teeth and sometimes in my foot, I did a half way decent job of it. It took us a long time, but right now, we had the time.

Chapter 9 The Fall Council

In middle February 701, I wanted to have a surprise birthday party for Deimos. Since I realized I didn't even know what kind of cake was his favorite, I went in search of Eirena, who I figured would know, since she had been the maid around here for so long. I found her watching Deimos on the practice field. "He's getting better isn't he?" she said as I came up to her. She often came out to watch him battle away with the wooden swords.

"There is a huge difference between a wooden sword and a real one. Say, I am going to throw him a surprise birthday party, but I don't know what kind of cake is his favorite. By chance do you have any idea?"

Without any hesitation, she replied, "Chocolate, he loves chocolate."

I found it interesting that she would know that immediately. I thanked her and headed to the cooks. Yes, he was surprised by the party and pleased as well.

In March of 701, the fall Grand Council convened here at the imperial palace. By all speculations, this one promised to be full of fireworks. Alekos did his best to brief me on all the latest news. It seems that during January, the six Mano del Dio members in Axos had themselves been assassinated during the night. All six had their throats cut in the same manner as had Amara's husband. Of course, the Church was in a furor over this lawlessness, demanding the culprits be found and executed. On each body was left a black rose, that is, a rose dipped in black paint, the signature of a Kali assassination.

Of course, Cardinal Rax Ciros knew this as well as everyone else. Still he had demanded action. The only remaining Mano del Dio member in Axos was the Prelate Kel Dios, who had been in Patri the night of the slayings. I was certain that the Church would raise this issue at the council.

During the past few months, Alekos was right; an enormous amount of lobbying had been done. Some was very visible, such as the visits of several kings to noblemen of Thrace, while I suspected even more was going on hidden from view. Only last week had they finally elected a new king of Thrace. Milo Kourgos was the new King of Thrace, he was twenty-one, a fighter trained man, well-muscled. His wife, Maria, was twenty and expecting their first child. She was a quiet person, seldom speaking much, though pretty however.

Alekos hastily briefed me on what little was known about the new king. Milo was very vocal about starting this war of global conquest as soon as possible. He certainly was against the Holy Eight Degrees; his wife still had her arms, and they had been married two years now. After some inquiries, Alekos determined that Milo was probably for the Church of Jehosanity, since reports said he and his wife attended weekly High Mass.

Beyond this basic information, we knew little else about him.

March 7 finally came. I sat at my usual spot in the throne room. Only this time, Alekos sat close to me, not Deimos. He had taken my advice and arranged for the Santi to make their presentation first, before the expected fireworks occurred. At last, everyone was seated. Deimos made his rehearsed opening speech, welcoming everyone and announcing formally the new king and queen of Thrace, who got a round of applause.

Alekos said, "First, we will hear from the Santi del Dio." This, of course, rattled a few feathers. Many kings wished to go first, for they had a lot to debate. Further, the Church of Jehosanity had always spoken before the Santi del Dio were allowed to speak. A commotion arose.

I took control immediately. "I have asked them to speak first, because what they are about to say may well modify what you have to say. Dag?" That shut them all up. My presence allowed for no backtalk and they knew it. They could get away with it, if Deimos was running the meeting, but now it was quite clear that I was running it.

Dag rose and began, "With the recent horrible dishonor done to poor Amara Gavril, the Santi can no longer sit idly by with this Holy Eight Degrees of Matrimony as conducted by the Church of Jehosanity."

"She deserves it — stupid woman for cutting her arms off," someone yelled out. I couldn't see who said it, however. They were sitting in the back guest row. Immediately, the three older kings stood up in protest. Even Deimos rose with them, surprising me.

Deimos spoke loudly, "Guards, find whoever said that and remove them. Kick them out of my palace!" He sat down and the three kings, smiling, also sat down. For once, Deimos took immediate action on his own volition. I smiled at him and he, me.

Dag then outlined the new Santi procedure, a vastly more humane handling of the entire ceremony. When he had finished, one by one, the three older kings rose and praised him and the Santi for their great understanding and kindness. All swore that from now on, their kingdoms would make exclusive use of the Santi for this ceremony, effectively blocking out the Church of Jehosanity from having any more couples coming to them for the deed. Cardinal Rax was livid, but was not allowed to speak at this time.

I kept my eyes focused alternately on the other three younger kings of Alia, Phindos, and Arolas. I needed to see their reactions to this. I sensed that they realized that there had just been a subtle shift in the balance on this issue of the Church of Jehosanity, a shifting into their favor, the removal of the church!

I rose again. "Next on the agenda, I call upon the Captain of the Guards of Axos for a detailed report on the assassination of King Anatolios Gavril. Please pay particular attention to what was found."

The young captain began to outline the events, as we were able to piece them together, beginning with the assassin's long wait just outside the palace grounds, his slaying of the guard near the king's window, the grappling hook, and the slaying itself. He repeated what the assassin had said to Amara at the time, how he had treated her. Finally, he outlined the tiny blood drop trail. "Our best conclusion is that one of the Mano del Dio men did this deed. However, we cannot prove anything beyond this."

Everyone began talking and yelling at once. The Cardinal feverishly denied everything, while many others vehemently accused him of having the king assassinated. For months Hans, Mia, Alekos, and I had speculated on why the Church of Jehosanity had done this particular assassination. The king had been a supporter of the church and had them perform the Holy Eight Degrees ceremony for them, that is, the removal of Amara's arms. Why would the Cardinal kill one of its own supporters? We had not ever been able to come up with an obvious reason.

Now the new king was dead against the Holy Eight Degrees, although he supported the Church of Jehosanity. It seemed that the Church had only worsened its position with this assassination. I knew that we had to be missing some very critical information. Something else was in play here, something hidden, and something about which we knew nothing. Consequently, Hans, Mia, Alekos, and I were watching very carefully with whom the Cardinal made direct eye contact. So far, in the chaos, I'd seen nothing illuminating. He was defending himself from everyone.

Since I could see nothing more forth coming, I abruptly ended the chaos. "Thank you. With these preliminaries out of the way, the Imperial Court opens the floor up to you kings."

King Hektor rose immediately. "In light of these two singular events, I would like to suggest that we make a law outlawing the Church of Jehosanity from Demokritos." He sat down at once. Had he said this at the spring council, three kings would have immediately risen to the defense of the Church, including Hektor himself. Indeed, last spring, he would never have made such a motion!

This was the bombshell that I was expecting and had been working for during the summer trip around the country. King Hektor lived up to his word. Having established a more humane method for his traditions, he was at last willing to abandon his support of the Church. Not unexpectedly, King Eros and King Leon also rose and supported Hektor's motion, demonstrating to King Petros, King Dimitris, and King Manos that they too had changed sides, and all six were now against having the Church of Jehosanity in their kingdoms.

We four continued to watch Cardinal Rax like a hawk. We noticed that his eyes darted to King Dimitris, and fixed on him. King Dimitris looked at the Cardinal and rose to speak. "What is happening here, kings? For years, we have been arguing this very point, and you three have fought us tooth and nail all this time. Now you are ready to join our side? And just when I was about to make a motion that we should try to get along with this Church. As they have been arguing for years now, our Emperor did make that treaty with the Pope, guaranteeing the Church the right to come here to Demokritos and build their churches."

"I think that perhaps we are all too quick to jump to conclusions that cannot be proven. You, yourselves, just heard the Captain of the Guards say that there was no way these deductions could be used in court to prove that a member of the Mano del Dio committed this heinous crime against the king and poor Amara, although we in Arolas do not have much sympathy for a woman who would so mutilate her own body."

"While I have never been a supporter of this church, I do not want to rush to judgment, to accuse them without proper proof. That goes against all that Demokritos stands for, rule by law. I would hope that the rest of you have calmed your passions by now and realize that we cannot condemn anyone without proper legal proof of their guilt. King Hektor, I request that you withdraw your motion." He sat down; the Cardinal looked very relieved at this point.

My suspicions began to grow. The only king now supporting the Church was Dimitris of Arolas, who last council was vehemently against this very same Church. Why was he now the only supporter? True, he raised a valid issue, rush to judgment on no concrete proof. Yet so far, the Cardinal had made solid eye contact only with his eyes. Could King Dimitris somehow be involved with the assassination of the King of Thrace? If so why? What would he gain?

King Hektor rose, "King Dimitris, please note that in no way did I accuse the Church of Jehosanity of the assassination of the King of Thrace. My motion stands as is."

"Here, here, I agree with Hektor," King Eros added.

"Yes, I do too," added King Petros.

"I say call for a vote," put in King Manos, eager finally to get such a motion passed by the council.

The motion passed, only King Milo and King Dimitris voted against it, Dimitris still insisting on a rush to judgment was clouding their wisdom.

Cardinal Rax rose, "I demand to be heard in full at this time!" He was livid with anger; evidently, this council was going in an entirely different direction than he had carefully planned. I allowed him the floor.

"First, I would like to point out that these assassinations of our priests in Naxos, Arolas have still not been solved. Now here in Axos, six of our security men have likewise been assassinated. Demokritos has become a lawless country. I demand that the Emperor do something to guarantee the safety of our holy priests and our security men."

"Second, as King Dimitris, who until today has always been opposed to our church — our priests were assassinated in his city, mind you — as King Dimitris has said, you are rushing to judgment. How can you so suddenly change sides, Hektor, Eros, Leon? Haven't the Church and your kingdoms gotten along well all these years? While you may have passed this motion, it matters nothing. I have a signed treaty by your own Emperor that allows us to be here. Your simple motions cannot overturn the treaty. Hence, I am totally ignoring the motion you just passed. I demand the Emperor do something to ensure the safety of our priests and security forces." He sat down and glared at Deimos.

Poor Deimos, he was once again in the hot seat. He looked to Alekos for assistance. "Sire, allow me to address the assemblage," Alekos requested. Deimos nodded, grateful for the bail out.

"I think that it is in everyone's best interests, especially with Milo so new to all of this, that I point out some details about the treaty that Cardinal Rax brings up. Yes, he holds a valid treaty. He is correct that new laws and motions cannot replace or supplant that treaty. The treaty can only be broken in one of three ways. First, if the Church fails to live up to its obligations, the treaty becomes null and void. Second, if Demokritos fails to live up to its obligations spelled out in the treaty, it likewise becomes null and void. Third, if the Lady's Support Group for the Imperial Court declares that it is not in the best interests of all Demokritos, it is null and void. However, the Lady's Support Group has long ago given the treaty its okay. Hence, the third option is gone."

Alekos continued. "Cardinal Rax, are not our legions stationed on Megalos and have we not been receiving yearly taxes from Megalos?"

"Yes they are and yes you have been receiving them," he replied, sensing where Alekos was heading with this line of questioning.

"Good. The first way out of the treaty is not applicable either; the Church is upholding its side of the treaty. Cardinal, have you not been allowed to build churches here in Demokritos? Even in those kingdoms where you were being prohibited from doing so until last spring?"

"Yes, we have begun building our first churches there."

"Good. Then Demokritos is upholding its side of the treaty. Hence, it is obvious that the treaty is still actively in force. The recently passed motion of King Hektor is merely to serve notice that the kings do not wish the Church here in Demokritos. Wishing is one thing, Cardinal, and the doing is quite another matter. You are free to continue your ministries here on Demokritos."

"But what about the assassinations? The killing of our holy priests?" Cardinal Rax asked, very upset.

"Cardinal, re-read your treaty. It says nothing in there about the Emperor or anyone else providing for your security. That is your problem, not ours. A wise man, seeing that he is not wanted in an enemy's house, leaves that house." Still livid, the Cardinal could not respond. Alekos had the last word. The Emperor would be doing nothing at all. Deimos liked that result.

I rose, "That being clarified and settled, let's move on. Milo, you wished to address the council?" I saw that he wanted to say something, and I was curious to hear his views, knowing so little about him.

"I apologize if I am out of turn. I've only had a week's worth of advisement. However, at this time, I would like to inquire of General Alexandr and Emperor Deimos about just how his fighter training is progressing. We in Thrace would like to begin fulfilling the prophesies as soon as possible, as soon as our illustrious Emperor is ready to lead our Centurions to victory." Deimos puffed up proudly, unable to see that Milo was egging him on.

"He progresses well, King Milo. Shortly, he will be taking up an actual blade. If all goes as it has, I would expect our Emperor would be ready by next spring." Deimos looked very pleased with the general's evaluation of his progress.

Now the meeting settled down. Since I had pointed out the inequities in the coastal countries contributions to the war effort to their kings and since at the last council a study had been ordered, we now sat through a very lengthy briefing from all of the kings on this topic. It lasted beyond lunch. I had to halt them for a needed lunch break.

During the lunch break, I overheard a short conversation between King Hektor and King Dimitris. Dimitris said, "We ought to get together old man. Here I was being prepared to compromise with your side finally to break the stalemate, only to be blind-sided by all three of you shifting your position to ours."

"Yes, your surprised me, Dimitris. I thank you for your compromise. I believe that we will be assisting you and the other coastal kingdoms with this inequity situation. So take that as my apology." Both men smiled at each other for a welcome change.

The afternoon session dragged on endlessly, figures presented, accepted, argued, and queried. I thought it would never end. It didn't. I had to call a break for supper, continuing this boring discussion at tomorrow's session. As before, I hosted a grand feast and had even more musicians playing than last time.

Again, I had the chance to dance with each of the kings, Hektor first. "I want to personally thank you from the bottom of my heart, Maren! Your talks with Lyris have done it. She is willing to take that first step. They will be going off to the Santi fortress in Patri just as soon as Angele and I return from our trip to Velona. We have decided to take up the Santi's offer for a visit. We leave right after this council. I believe that they will be living somehow as if she were already as you are, a woman of the Eighth Degree during that month. I hope that Maximus does not mess up this golden chance to prove to her that he is up to the tasks she will be setting for him. Thank you, Maren, thank you. If she decides to honor him and us and does the ceremony, I have offered to pay all of their expenses so that she can take that trip to Velona that you so encouraged her to do once the ceremony is competed. I am amazed with your skills. Thank you. I owe you a very big favor; call on me whenever you need it."

When dancing with Dimitris, he said, "Maren, I should have listened to you and believed you. I sure made a fool of myself today, coming out with weak support for the Church. Ah well, water over the dam as they say." I felt like he was trying to smooth out what he had done this morning. I no longer trusted him.

Later that night, Mia, Hans, Alekos, and I met privately to discuss the events of the day. One thing bothered us all. "Did you see the look that Cardinal Rax gave King Dimitris today?" I asked.

"Yes, somehow, I get the feeling that something is or was going on between those two men," Mia added.

"I am beginning to suspect that Dimitris made a bargain with the Cardinal to have Anatolios assassinated," Alekos suggested. "That would explain his sudden and unexpected defense of the Cardinal today, although it was a weak defense at that. I just don't see what Dimitris would get out of having Anatolios killed. Milo supports the Church and Dimitris is or was vehemently against the Church. Milo at least is against the Eight Degrees, where Anatolios was for it. Surely, that was not enough reason to want him dead."

I added, "I agree that alone is not enough. I told him all about the Santi proposal when I visited him on my trip. He knew months ago that the other three older kings would very likely now be on his side, the removal of the Church. Thus far, nothing has been said about the validity of the Eight Degrees by any of the kings. There must be something else that Dimitris greatly values so highly that he would join with this vile Church, which I know he hates."

Hans interrupted, "It's as plain as the nose on your face, Maren. Milo already told us the reason. Milo wants this war to begin as soon as possible. Anatolios did not. Now there are four kings ready to go to war just as soon as Deimos is ready to take command. I think that is what Dimitris had in mind with the removal of Anatolios." Now it all began to make sense.

The next morning's session continued with the discussions from yesterday. After lunch, I finally decided I'd heard enough. "May your Empress make a suggestion?" I interrupted them.

"For this coming year, why don't we limit the four coastal kingdoms to the delivery of ten more caravels and let the three landlocked kingdoms provide the twenty legions of Centurions that General Alexandr has asked for? That seems more than fair to me."

At last, they agreed with me. A motion was made and passed. Mid-afternoon came and no more business was forthcoming. We had finished a few hours earlier than the last conference. I decided to sew some seeds with these men.

"Before we adjourn until the spring session, your Empress would like to give you something to think about during the ensuing months. Why are you slavishly following someone else's grand plans for your own future? The Prophesies of Demos. A free man is a man who creates his own goals, follows his own purposes, and takes his own independent actions. He creates his own future, not slavishly working to bring about a future that someone, dead seven hundred years, is dictating that he must create. Yet, I am only an armless woman from Annelise, the land of stupid clothes. What do I know of these things? The feast and dance begins at five."

On his way out, Hektor whispered to me, "Mighty powerful words, Maren. Well done. You have three backers, even if we are old!"

Now I needed more backers. Deimos, who usually ran out with the first to leave, stayed behind this time, coming up to me. Mia and I always brought up the rear, as always our heels made us slow. "Maren, I liked that, what you said. Men should make their own destinies. I like that." He gave me a kiss on my forehead. He walked me to the dining room this time. Interesting, I thought, however, he was not the ones that I was trying to reach.

Chapter 10 All According to Plan

Holding the dispatch from Cardinal Rax to his bosom as if it were extremely valuable, Pope Aison headed to his private study. He remembered the day when he signed the treaty with Demokritos. Emperor Axos Gavril and his stunningly beautiful, but armless wife, Adelpha — yes, he remembered them. The man knew how to treat women, a man after his own heart. Adelpha needed help with everything; she could never cause problems for her husband, perfect. Now he had outlived not only Axos, but his son as well. His grandson, Deimos, still but a lad, was on the throne at this most pivotal time in history. Pope Aison smiled to himself; he could not have planned this any better, if he had the ability to pick their Emperor. That Deimos also took an armless woman was all the better.

Secure in his private study, Pope Aison carefully unwrapped the outer waterproof packaging. Inside was a sealed package, he carefully inspected the Cardinal's seal. It was untouched. Satisfied, he opened it and found the rather lengthy letter from Cardinal Rax. It was written, as he had ordered, in the Arad language. Pope Aison was cautious, bordering on paranoid some might say. If their dispatches were intercepted, rare indeed would be the person who could read it in the modern world of today.

It was the Cardinal's official report on the Fall Grand Council meeting. As he read the letter, parts of it he read aloud to himself.

> Your Holiness, again I am humbled at your great wisdom. All has gone according to your plan, though I did not believe that it would. During this past season, I sent a small detachment of missionaries into Arolas, there to establish our first church in that kingdom. As you will recall, Arolas is one of the three kingdoms that has stood steadfast on not allowing us into their land. At the Spring Council, they were ordered to allow us in, just as you predicted they would. As instructed, their numbers were few and no Mano del Dio went with them.
>
> It is with a sad heart that I must report to you the deaths of these brave missionaries, who perished attempting to spread the Holy Word of Lord Jehosa to these heathens. Yet, it was as you predicted, Your Holiness.
>
> Again, as you suggested would happen, one of these younger kings did come to me, the very king of Arolas! With the council deadlocked on beginning their great war of conquest early, the

young King Dimitris was very anxious to find a way to break down that last remaining barrier to an early start of the war. Prelate Kel Dios was superb in action; all praises must be sung to his great skill. The deed was done. The King of Thrace was slain in his bed. I must admit that I felt some pity for his poor wife, who only recently underwent the Holy Eighth Degree for her husband, but it was only a fleeting feeling. I said my penance tenfold, Your Holiness.

Just as you predicted, their new King Milo Kourgos is a young and brash king, eager to get on with their prophesied great war of conquest. Now the council is no longer divided on this issue. Five to three, they go to war as soon as this Emperor is fit. Expect some action to begin perhaps as early as next year.

I can report that they have spent their resources on building caravels, yet as you said they will not have remotely enough to support fielding an army of four thousand legions. Expect only ten more caravels to be built in the coming year. I believe that they will be sending at most another ten to twenty legions to begin their war of conquest.

Concerning the Santi del Dio, Your Grace, just as you predicted, they once more interfered with our Holy Eight Degrees Ceremony. However, I was shocked by what they have indeed done! They are now going to be performing that very ceremony for those who desire it in Demokritos! I could not believe my ears when their leader Dag rose to explain it to the council! How can this be, our own enemy who had fought us every inch of the way on this has now begun doing that very same thing? While I humbly submit that I do not have the wisdom to understand how this could be, it has had exactly the effect that you foretold.

Yes, all kingdoms have united now and wish to throw the Church out of their country! Amazing. I was able to get the Emperor, via his advisor, to explain fully and make public the only ways that treaty could be invalidated. One by one, he demonstrated that the treaty remains in full force and cannot be undone as long as we continue to hold to our side.

As per your orders, I made a valiant plea for the Emperor to provide security for our humble priests and the church. He, of course, refused, saying that was not in the treaty. Magnificent. At that moment, I wanted to sing high praises to Lord Jehosa, but managed to restrain my exuberance at his ruling. I am very, very pleased to announce to you, at this time, Demokritos is ready for you to send in our security forces en mass!

If they press toward war within a year, it would be wise to have our people in place here when they move their army to the north.

He skipped over some lines outlining the desired forces and where they ought to be placed within Demokritos.

There is one other minor matter, Your Holiness. This Empress woman of the Eight Degree is becoming something of a problem. In fact, the advisors are making no secret of the fact that she is the brains of this union. Deimos is but a figurehead. What troubles me were her parting words, which I will repeat here for you to ponder.

She said: Your Empress would like to give you something to think about during the ensuing months. Why are you slavishly following someone else's grand plans for your own future? The Prophesies of Demos. A free man is a man who creates his own goals, follows his own purposes, takes his own independent actions. He creates his own future, not slavishly working to bring about a future that someone, dead seven hundred years, is dictating that he must create. Yet, I am only an armless woman from Annelise, the land of stupid clothes. What do I know of these things?

This troubles me, Your Grace. It is as though she is seeing through our grand plans. I doubt that she will be able to sway them; however, it is worrisome. Ought she to meet with an accident?

Speaking of accidents, King Hektor of Theos has a son who will succeed him to the throne. As you know, the King is very old now, and will not live much longer. His son is now about to make his wife into one of the Eighth Degree. Evidently, the Santi have convinced her to do this. This is not according to your plans. Should he meet with an accident as well?

There was more, but Pope Aison sat back and pondered this strange, unexpected twist, that the Empress, of all people, should be so intelligent. He had not anticipated that someone from Annelise, the land where everyone was docile, living only to wear the most outlandishly impractical clothing imaginable, could actually be so bright, intelligent, and wise to have said this. Yet, she, too, was a helpless woman, locked into an armless body, for which others had constantly to care. Pope Aison said to himself, "No, I would never pay such a woman any mind. Those young kings and the Emperor will not pay her any heed either."

He then summoned the Supreme Prelate Anatol, who was in charge of security for the church. "The time has at last come for our next move. Here, read the latest from Cardinal Rax of Kefall." The head of the Mano del Dio read the entire letter, smiling all the while.

"Then it is time we began our mobilization, Your Grace," he said.

"Precisely. Is all prepared?"

"Yes, Your Grace."

"Excellent. Deploy them, but remember, exercise extreme caution. We do not want the Centurions on Megalos to get wind of this move. It must be done in secret, a few at a time."

"Yes, leave that to me. Our men are fully briefed, fully trained, and eager to deploy. It shall begin tomorrow night. Allow for a month before all are underway. Yet it is a lengthy journey down to Demokritos."

"Yes, and one day they will come to appreciate just how long that supply line actually is. Thank you, Supreme Prelate. Your work is excellent, as always."

"I must say that the Cardinal Conclave that opted to put a youthful Pope in place this time chose wisely. Do you realize we both have outlasted three Emperors? Well, Deimos will not last long, once he is up here in the field. Amazing, we have had such continuity of planning all these years."

Pope Aison smiled, "Yes, Lord Jehosa works in mysterious ways for our betterment."

He sat down to write Cardinal an answer to his questions. He pondered long on the situation in Theos before his quill touched the paper.

Chapter 11 A Long Winter

Winter of 701 came long and cold. Deimos was constantly in the practice room, hacking and slashing away. His body was definitely growing more and more well-muscled; he was growing into manhood at a rapid rate now. Occasionally, I would stop by the practice room to watch his progress. True, his skill was far below that of one of our Protectors or even one of our seasoned Santi fighters. Still, he was improving, a fact that Eirena constantly reminded me.

Yes, I saw her there watching nearly every time that I dropped by. She was even cheering him on a couple of times. "He's getting good, isn't he Empress. One day, he will be out there on the battlefield conquering all of Tarra for us. Isn't that exciting? I wish I could be there to see him win the world for us."

I smiled, remembering the many battlefields I had seen over these centuries. Bloodied bodies, rotting flesh where limbs once grew, death and decay, people's lives ruined utterly. Husbands who would never return home to their wives and children — no I had seen enough of war. It was not exciting to me, anyway. I had half a notion to bring her along and let her witness the stark reality of war and its aftermath.

Taking tea one day with Mia and Hans, I lamented, "God how I miss playing games. I miss Renzo so badly that sometimes I could scream! I sit here day after day, how many years has it been now?"

"Nearly sixteen," Mia reminded me.

"Sixteen years of pretending, of not allowing myself to play and enjoy life, to have fun. God, will I ever be glad when this assignment is over!"

"We know, Maren Bethany, we know. At least I have Hans, and he, me. We are managing very well together. You seem so distant from Deimos."

"Well, we have not been sleeping in the same bed since we brought Amara back here to stay. It has given me an excuse not to sleep in his bed. He stinks so badly after those daily workouts, and I cannot get him to bathe but once a week at most. Amara smells better." We all laughed at that jest.

"Well he is making good progress, especially considering he did not start as we did, when we were very young. He has to pick it up all at once in the space of a couple years," Hans came to his defense. "I'll give the lad that; he is really working hard at it."

"Well, at least he has something to do, while I sit here and sip tea, day after day. Come on; let's play cards again. No, that is just too damnably hard for me to mess with — more trouble than its worth. God, I miss Renzo and our games!"

Time passed, the dead of winter was upon us now, late July 701. Via the Santi Communicator, Sandy, I learned that King Hektor and Queen

Angele were due to arrive back in Patri from their long trip to Velona within ten days. A month earlier, his son Maximus and his wife Lyris, came through here, stopping for a day's visit. They were on their way to the Santi fortress in Patri to begin their month's trial period. If all went well for them and if she decided to undergo the Holy Ceremony, then they planned to do it just before Hektor and Angele arrived.

"Come on, gang, we are going to visit Patri and meet up with King Hektor, Queen Angele, Maximus, and Lyris. If she decides to go through with it, I owe it to her to be there for her. After all, I feel some responsibility for the situation."

Alekos gave us permission, but sent along two dozen Centurion Imperial Guards to protect our safety. Since all we women were bored out of our minds, I suggested that Amara and Zenovia come along with Mia, Hans, and me. We would all fit in one coach; our bags rode topside. Amara protested slightly, saying, "Who will help us and feed us? There's only Mia and there are three of us."

"Don't forget me," Hans admonished her playfully.

That settled, we packed up and headed down to Patri. During the ten-day journey, we stayed in some of the finest inns, ate some fabulous meals, and enjoyed a relief from our intense cabin fever boredom. When we arrived on the outskirts of Patri, a small Santi force met us. Dag was with them, and he rode beside our carriage.

"Empress, we are so honored by your presence. You are the first Empress to set foot in our fortress. You do us a great honor. Lyris has become a most honored woman of the Eighth Degree and has had our therapy already. It is amazing, Empress! You will have to see for yourselves. In just two weeks, her body has completely healed, not the six weeks or more that I would have expected. This therapy works miracles of healing. Yes, she and Maximus are both doing splendidly."

"King Hektor and Queen Angele have just arrived, put in at suppertime. Yes, he was overjoyed with everything. She is too. Both are speaking very highly of our Velona. It was very good for them to have made the trip that we suggested the leaders here take. I do wish that you and the Emperor would also visit our homeland and see for yourselves."

I hated all this pretending, this acting as if I was a dope. "Yes, I suppose it must be a fine place to see. I am so glad that the king enjoyed it. I am more pleased that all is well with Lyris. I was so worried about her. Will there be enough room at your fortress for all of us, or should we make arrangements to stay at the finest inn?" I acted the role of Empress.

"It might be unseemly for the Empress to be staying within our walls. I have taken the liberty of obtaining fine quarters within a short walking distance of the fortress for you. King Hektor and Queen Angele are also staying there. There will be space for your Royal Guards there as well. I do hope this meets with the Empress's approval."

"Oh yes, we love to stay at fine inns. It is good that we can just walk to visit your fortress. Is Lyris still there?"

"She is due to be released from our care tomorrow. I know that they all plan to spend a few days here in Patri, a family reunion, I was told by Angele. I am sure that you all will be invited to join them."

Sometime later, we pulled up at a very fancy inn, the last one of quality before the docks. The Santi fortress rose high, dominating the view toward the ocean, a white marble tower six stories tall. Beautiful and impressive was its design, but then all the more important buildings in Demokritos were built from polished white marble.

We found that between our two parties, we had the inn exclusively to ourselves. The staff here went out of their way to make us feel comfortable and at home. Yes, they were hosting the Empress and a king. After this, the stature and reputation of the Red Dragon Inn would rise far above all other inns in Patri. Hosting the Empress had that effect on others.

Once we were settled in and had cleaned up from the day's journey, we headed off to visit the Santi fortress and meet up with the Georgios family. It was a long walk for Mia and me wearing our heels, but we enjoyed the sea air and the chilly, but fresh air. Amara and Zenovia also greatly enjoyed this outing; we all had cabin fever badly.

Dag met us and escorted us on a short tour of their fortress, ending up in their large meeting room, where we found all the others awaiting our arrival. I've never seen four people so happy. Hektor was a beaming a most youthful smile, while Angele was incredibly cheerful. Maximus stood like a proud peacock beside his lovely wife, Lyris, who looked lovelier than ever. As I suspected the therapy sessions had taken years of worry out of her mind and her body responded, looking radiant and healthy.

Our first action was for Lyris. I went to her and we exchanged welcoming hugs, the kind that only we women of the Eighth Degree can do. She whispered, "Thank you ever so much." Amara and Zenovia were right behind me, welcoming Lyris to our fold, so to speak. We then greeted the others and took seats with Betsy pouring our tea for us. Cleverly, Betsy held the cup for me, Sally, for Zenovia, and Mia, for Amara. So smoothly did they do this that Amara hardly noticed.

"Maren, I am so happy!" Lyris began. "I don't know how to thank you. Maximus is the greatest husband on Tarra. Now I am living, visible proof of our undying love for each other, proudly displayed for all to see and emulate." She was most proud of her transformation; I will give her that. "Maximus and I will go to Velona in the spring, after the council. Hektor, do you want to tell her why?" she radiated happiness towards him. This was now a whole family indeed.

He cleared his throat, "I am so proud of my daughter-in-law! In honor of their ceremony, I am retiring from the throne of Theos. When we return there in a few weeks, I will formally transfer the kingdom to

Maximus. I give you King Maximus and Queen Lyris!" We cheered and stomped our feet, Mia and Hans, clapped, of course.

"You see, everything has worked out better than perfectly!" Lyris declared. We all are so happy. Hektor and Angele have been telling us such wonderful things about Velona; we cannot wait to see it for ourselves.

Angele exclaimed, "Maren, I actually saw a woman of the Eighth Degree painting, yes oil painting, with her feet and toes. I don't know how she could possibly do that! Her paintings are, well just fabulous! We bought one. Hektor show them the painting when we return to the inn tonight, will you dear?"

We chatted a long time. All of us, even Amara, felt uplifted, so great was the happiness within this family at this time. Even the four Santi, who sat with us, were beaming proudly as well. We had achieved a victory of magnitude, one family at a time.

At last, my stomach was growling, and we left to get dinner at the inn. Maximus and Lyris stayed behind, she would be released from their care in the morning. We all promised to be here for that. Our small group walked slowly back to the inn, chatting all the way. Yes, our guards were all around us, but they said nothing, but kept alert for trouble. There was none.

The Red Dragon spared nothing for our evening meal. All had a wonderful time. Hektor and Angele talked on and on about the wonders of Velona. I only got more and more homesick! God, did I ever want this assignment to be over with, so Mia, Hans, and I could return home to Velona or even Zargarb, anywhere but here. They too felt the same way, but we hid it well from the others.

As we three crawled into the very large bed, Amara spoke for both Zenovia and herself. "Maren, we two have decided that somehow, someway, we want to visit this Velona ourselves!"

"Ladies, one day I promise you, that if you stick by me, I will take you there myself. Might be a while, but I will do so!" We three crawled into bed, struggled to get situated, and snuggled together, three happy women, longing for the future to arrive, but for different reasons.

After a fine breakfast the next morning, we again formed into a group and walked slowly to the Santi fortress. The streets were crowded with people, bustling with activity. The guards had a devil of a time keeping us secure within their lines. At the fortress, their Healer, Betsy, had already carefully inspected Lyris. Her wounds had completely healed, something Betsy still marveled over; the therapy session had worked more wonders than she had expected. Of course, Lyris was very excited finally to be released to show herself beside her husband for the whole world to see the enormous magnitude of their love for one another.

With enormous pride, the young couple stepped out onto the streets of Patri. We formed ranks around them and began the walk back to the inn. Once at the inn, we would pack our things and leave for home after lunch.

That was the plan at least.

The streets were crowded with people. Once more, our guards had a difficult time making a clear path for us to follow. We, well we were all chatting gaily about the future as we walked along. Then out of the corner of my eye, I spied something amiss. I saw a man, a mask pulled over his face; he had an arrow notched. I yelled a warning, but I was too late. I didn't have time to react. As if out of nowhere and dripping a black liquid, an arrow came flying into our midst. I heard the awful sound of the arrow hitting a body. Maximus stopped and slowly dropped to the ground. The arrow had entered his forehead, just above the eyes, a perfect shot indeed, done by a marksman.

I watched the chaos erupt, but in slow motion. My eyes never left the assassin. I was so angry that I completely forgot about my disguise. I floated over to the assassin, who was turning to flee, and lifted him high up into the air. My voice sounded terribly distant to me — yes I believe that it was actually screaming, "Guards! Seize that assassin!" Of course, I soon discovered that I had to lower this man's body; twenty guards had their swords out, but couldn't reach him until I lowered his body down to them. I heard the assassin screaming all the while that I held on to him. Once the guards got him, he screamed even louder and was then quiet.

Around my body, Lyris was screaming hysterically, jumping all around in a complete panic. Amara was crying wildly and shaking. Angele and Hektor were screaming wildly telling the air around them to do something — that this cannot be happening. Zenovia raced over to the assassin, while Mia and Hans worked on saving the life of Maximus. I moved into my body and bent over the two.

"Died instantly," Hans reported as soon as he saw me leaning. "Poisoned as well, but he died from the arrow. Did you get the assassin?"

"Yes, I lifted him and dropped him into the arms of the guards. What's Zenovia doing over there? Come on; let's see who this assassin was." We three, ignoring the utter chaos around us, walked the short distance to the collection of guards.

Already Zenovia had them carefully undoing his robes, cautioning them against touching nothing of his with their flesh, "Beware, this man uses poison. Careful, don't let that robe touch you." We arrived just as the robe was removed. Everyone stared at the rope of thorns tightly wrapped around his waist; small blood drops left tiny trails down his chest and legs. Around his neck was the cross of the Church of Jehosanity. His arms, legs, and neck had been thoroughly hacked by their many swords; he was more than dead five times over. "Remove his mask," Zenovia said sternly but commandingly. "Careful, don't touch him with your fingers, poison!"

They cut the mask off to avoid touching the body. "I recognize his face," Zenovia said. "He is one of the Mano del Dio men stationed here in Patri."

Hektor, finally regaining some semblance of sanity, came over to see the assassin. Zenovia repeated his identity to Hektor. I thought that Hektor would burst a blood vessel, so great were they pounding in his anger. "Cut off his head and dump it on the Church of Jehosanity's door step!" Eagerly, the guards obeyed; it was gruesome to watch, but Zenovia had seen much worse things. Soon six carried the head of the assassin away.

"He's dripping poison, Hektor," Zenovia said sternly. "His body should be carried to the ocean and dumped. Otherwise others may become accidentally poisoned."

"See to it!" Hektor ordered, his anger subsiding. More guards confiscated a blanket from a nearby stall and used it to dispose of the body safely; all were most concerned about the poison. We walked back to the others and the body of Maximus.

Lyris had finally collapsed of exhaustion. Angele had fainted as well. Amara now sat beside Lyris, while Mia kept everyone away from the black poison on the body. Zenovia took charge, "Get some water, and wash the poison off before we remove the arrow." Quickly, one of the remaining guards dashed off and came back quickly with a water skin. While he was washing off the poison, the four Santi and six fighters raced up to us.

"Oh dear god!" Betsy exclaimed, seeing the arrow in his head.

"Okay, the poison is mostly gone. Carefully, pull the arrow out will you?" Zenovia ordered the guard who had washed Maximus off. It took a good deal of strength to pull it out. "Pour more water over the wound and over the arrow. We want all the poison removed before we touch Maximus. Thank you. Good job, soldier."

Dag said, "Let's get you all to the inn at once. There is a huge crowd around watching, and there could be more trouble. I'll carry Lyris. Art, you get Angele." Because Mia and I moved so slowly, Hans picked up Mia and carried her, while a guard carried me. Okay, it was nice being carried swiftly through the streets. Indeed, I saw that thousands had gathered to witness this assassination. This would be the talk of the town for weeks now. The repercussions would be enormous, I wagered.

Soon we were all in the dining room, and the two unconscious women were placed on tables so that Betsy could examine them. The mood had gone from intense, joyful happiness, to incredible depths of grief in that split second. Hektor cried like a small child, "A father should not out live his own son!"

Recognizing that they were all in deep shock over this sudden and traumatic loss, we Santi kept as quiet as we could. The focus of our attention was on the two unconscious women. Betsy got Angele awakened. She began crying uncontrollably, and we put her into Hektor's arms, allowing them to grieve together.

Lyris was more of a problem. She had gone into hysterics and then into a deep shock, a life threatening shock at that. "Her pulse is very, very weak. This enormous a shock so soon after the major surgery may well take her life," Betsy whispered to those of us gathered around her.

She moved us away from the unconscious body so that Lyris could not hear us. Betsy explained, "We have two equally bad choices. One, we can leave her alone and see if she comes out of this naturally. She may die before that happens, however. Two, I can force her to consciousness; however she will be right there in the horrific loss and may well go into hysterics once more, also killing her weakened body. Your call, Empress."

She deferred the life and death call to me. Hektor was in no mental position to make such a decision; she was only his daughter-in-law. Obviously, the Santi could not make this call. It was thus mine to make. I felt sick, really sick. In many ways, I had made it possible for her to conquer her fears and have the surgery. Now she was a widow and armless at the same time. I guessed that Lyris had lost her will to live. I noticed Zenovia and Amara watching me very closely, waiting for my pronouncement.

"Mia, I may need some food before this is over. Keep watch over my body. Betsy, revive her. I will deal with her. I owe her that much at the very, very least. Hans, you watch over the others. Go ahead, Betsy."

We two moved over to the table. Betsy put a foul smelling stick under her nose. I watched as she rolled her head from side to side trying to escape the awful smell. Her eyes opened; I saw the stark terror, the horrible grief in them, and the loss of will even to live. "I want you to go to the beginning where he was shot. Yes, now go through it and tell me what you are seeing, what you are feeling, and what you are smelling." I had no choice but to run this emergency therapy session. I didn't know if she had the physical strength to survive this, but I had to try. If I did nothing, she would very likely die as well.

She began whispering about walking along side Maximus, his arm around her waist. Naturally, she began to shriek as she had done when it happened. It took Hans and the Santi to keep the others quiet and from interfering with me. After some time, she made it one time through. I had her go over it once more, but by then I was starving, and figured she was too. I had to take a food break, whether or not it was a good therapy move. Mia force-fed her body; she was in no mood to eat unless it was forced into her mouth.

After I was full and satisfied that Lyris had gotten enough nourishment as well, I had her go back over it once more. This time, her hysterics were more subdued, much to the relief of everyone else. I saw Hektor and Hans leave the room; some men had come, but I paid them no mind. I concentrated fully on Lyris. All that afternoon, we ran over this horrible, tragic assassination. By suppertime, she was up to being in a deep apathy, a long ways from dying — at least that was some small progress.

Again, I had Mia and Hans stuff food in her mouth as well as mine. It was a short, fast supper. I was not about to stop and leave her where she was at, if she and I could avoid it. Back over the loss, we went once more. Finally, by dark, she was in a heavy grief, bawling her head off over the loss of her husband. Now I had no choice but to end for the night. We both were utterly exhausted. I had to go to the bathroom in the worst way; she probably did too, but could care less about it.

I left her sitting there sobbing quietly to herself. Whispering, I said, "Okay, take her to the bathroom and get her ready for bed. She will sleep with me tonight. Don't let anyone talk to her. We are right in the middle of it all. In the morning, bring us some food, and I will continue right where we are leaving off. Got it?" Mai and Hans nodded.

I knew that the others may want to talk with me about things, but I was too tired, and I had to remain with Lyris. She was in critical shape just now. I had her at least up to an outpouring of grief, but she could very easily slide back down into a deep apathy or even lower into death. We'd come this far, and I was not about to have her succumb.

Sometime later, Hans lifted her into bed beside me. Lyris rolled over onto me and continued to cry. By morning, my nightgown was very soaked, but she had slept a good deal, which her weakened body desperately needed. Mia and Hans came in like two well-oiled machines, "pottying" us and feeding us. With food in her, I continued right where we had left off last night.

"Soon, she came up to anger. If she still had arms, she would have been pounding the bed. Instead, she kicked our pillows relentlessly. A little later, she reached a wicked antagonism, virile and cutting she was. I pressed on until she was bored, but then we had to stop for lunch. Once more Mia and Hans came in and fed us rapidly and silently. After "pottying" us, they left, and I had Lyris go through it once more. Finally, she became somewhat cheerful.

At this point, I had a decision to make. I expected that there would be earlier material here; such wild hysterics should not result from the assassination of your husband, at least not the wild reaction she had. Yet, she was finally doing well over it, at least for the short haul. I knew that the others wanted either to talk to me or to get us all safely back to Kefall. Then, there were the funeral arrangements, which could not be made while I was tied up like this.

"Lyris, we are not yet fully finished with the therapy. However, we probably have a number of things that we really must attend to right now. If it is acceptable to you, I am going to end the therapy session for now. I want you to come back to the imperial palace and stay with me for some time so that we can continue with this. Is this all right with you?"

"Yes, thank you Maren. I, I would like to see him, to say goodbye. We need to bury him, but where?"

"The others probably will have that all worked out. Come on; let's go see, shall we? From now on, I will be looking after you as if you are my sister. Okay?" She gave me a big grin. Boy was I ever glad to see that grin!

We found everyone snacking in the dining room, the only place big enough to hold all of us at one time. I learned that the guards were now patrolling the perimeter, joined by a hundred city guards. Many officials had come and gone.

Hektor and Angele looked a hundred years older when I saw them. Only days ago they had looked twenty years younger, now they looked like they were ready for the grave that they were preparing for their only son. He looked up at me and asked, "How is she doing?"

"I'm feeling better now," Lyris answered for herself, a very good sign I thought. "I cannot believe this is happening to me. It is so surreal. Can I see him? Maximus?"

Mia led her to a side room where his body lay. Meanwhile, I said to Hektor, "She is doing remarkably well, all things considered. I believe she is out of the woods. Touchy there for a while, we almost lost her as well. I want her to come with me to the imperial palace for more therapy. Funeral arrangements?"

"Good. Good. Yes, that would be best for all concerned. Thank you Empress. Tomorrow, Angele and I have decided to lay him to rest here in Patri. It is many weeks of travel to our home. We think it best that he lay here."

"That makes good sense," I said.

"Maren, can we talk now? I've some questions that need answering."

"Sure, Mia, please something to eat and drink?" She smiled and left to fetch me something.

"Hans and Mia have helped us understand much of what happened. It all happened so very fast! You sounded the alarm, am I not correct?"

"Yes, I spied the archer from the corner of my eye just as he fired the arrow. I am so sorry that I could not react any faster. If I only had one more second, maybe Maximus would still be alive. I take the blame for not acting fast enough, Hektor."

"Good god woman! You are not to blame. In my youth, I might have reacted as fast as you did. No one could act faster than you did. I'll not hear another word like that. Now then, after that things got so confused. I seem to remember seeing the assassin sort of, well floating in the air, before he was hacked to pieces by the guards. I know that is not possible, but Angele also seems to recall it that way too."

I had a decision to make. I felt that I owed them at least a partial explanation for what they saw. "In Velona you saw many things that would never dream women of the Eighth Degree could do, correct?"

Both nodded. "That is an understatement," he muttered.

"Let us just say that, although I come from Annelise and have lived my whole life this way, I have learned or developed other skills. I was very, very angry, and I did lift him up to keep him from escaping. I wanted him held accountable so badly that somehow I held him. I am not as helpless as many would think, probably because I was born without any arms — you know, making up for that lack in other ways. I have never said anything about it for my own safety. I came from Annelise to here nearly all by myself, excepting for Mia and Hans. Who is going to look out for me? Please don't tell others about this. I may need this skill to save my own life in the future."

"Ah, then we were not hallucinating. Thank you for being honest with us. I give you my solemn word that we will say nothing about this to anyone. I must say that I was incredibly impressed with the four of you, Zenovia, Mia, Hans, and you. While the rest of us were in shock and hysteria, you four kept alert and took decisive actions. Incredible. Zenovia has explained that her husband once taught her a bit about poisons so she was able to recognize it at once. I have thanked her repeatedly for her timely assistance or others may have died from the poisoned arrow."

"Empress Maren, the debt that I owe you has grown so enormously that I may never be able to repay you enough. As far as Lyris is concerned, it is best that she stay with you. Her parents are both dead, three years now. He died in combat and she, in a tragic accident. I know that she has an aunt and uncle somewhere, but you will have to ask her about them. I feel that she will be very uncomfortable living in our palace without Maximus around, you know, a constant reminder of her horrid loss."

"As far as retribution is concerned, I've met with the mayor of Patri and sent word on to Milo. I told him that he is to run all of these vile priests and their assassins out of Thrace or I will bring my entire army down here and do it for him. At the next council I will get these wicked men cast out of Demokritos or do it myself. One way or another, their days in Demokritos are numbered, thus speaks King Hektor Georgios of Theos."

Just then, Mia arrived with some food for me, so our conversation ended. Lyris came back, her eyes red. Yet, she joined me and ate well, another good sign I thought.

The next day was a sad one, Maximus, son of Hektor was laid to rest just outside of Patri. Later a large marble monument would be erected on this grave, marking his resting place for centuries to come. Shortly after the burial, we climbed into our carriages and began the long trip back to the imperial palace.

Five days later, King Hektor made a brief stop in Axos, where King Milo, quite pale, offered his condolences. He had already received Hektor's ultimatum, but had no idea actually what to do about it. Milo promised action, but was not specific about what action. Even from this distance — I was in the carriage — they were standing some feet away — I could tell that Milo had no idea what he could do about this incredibly awful event that happened in his kingdom.

Five days later, we arrived at the imperial palace, where everyone rushed out to meet us, as if something bad had happened to us. Alekos was terribly sympathetic to Hektor, while Deimos made all sorts of veiled threats against the Church, none of which he could actually carry out. Me? I just got Lyris inside and into my room as quietly and quickly as possible.

Hektor left before I had a chance to say goodbye, but Hans reported that the king said that they would send along her things just as soon as they got home. I had Mia go around to all our staff and explain that we had a woman who had just undergone the Holy Eight Degrees ceremony and who had lost her husband as well. She was in the very first stages of learning how to live this way. I wanted everyone to be extra careful around Lyris, just about anything might set off her despair right now. Normally, the woman would spend considerable time quietly learning to adjust to her new way of life with her husband aiding with everything. For Lyris, this would not be the case. Worse, all her hopes, plans, and goals for her future had been destroyed by that single arrow from the Mano del Dio.

Only now, did I ask why. Alekos answered, "I have no idea why they would openly assassinate Maximus. It makes no sense."

"There has to be a very good reason," Hans said, "for them to risk so much. Surely, they knew that they could not get away with killing the son of the king?"

"We know that he was going to retire and let Maximus take over," Mia thought aloud. "Perhaps we should be asking what would have changed had he been allowed to be the king of Theos instead of his father?"

"Well both men were staunch supporters of the Holy Degrees," Hans followed through on his wife's suggestion. "Both men are not supporters any longer of the Church. About the only difference I can see is Maximus might have wanted to go to war sooner than his father. That's about all I can see. What if, Mia, this was payback to Hektor? He openly changed from actively supporting the Church to being against it. Worse yet, what if it was payback for using the Santi instead of their Church for the ceremony?"

"Ah, both of those seem more plausible," Alekos replied, finally seeing some reasonable reasons for the assassination.

Mia asked me, "Bethany, you saw the assassin first and best. Can you say absolutely that he was aiming for Maximus and not Hektor or perhaps yourself?"

I recalled that image into my mind, made contact with her and with Hans, replayed that split second of action. Then, for Alekos's benefit, I said, "Yes, very sure that his aim was on Maximus."

"Well, that certainly rules out an accidental hit. Maximus was the intended victim," Mia concluded, giving me a wink.

"Well, there is one other possible explanation," Alekos said, swiping his hands through his hair. We looked at him. "It is doubtful that Milo, so new to the throne, is actually going to attack the Church there in Thrace. The Church now has deep roots there, more so than any other kingdom. It's where they first landed years ago and began their works. Could it be that the Church wishes to foment inner-kingdom warfare? I am sure that Hektor will march a huge army into Thrace if Milo does nothing. Will Milo then allow this army in there? Highly unlikely. His people will be demanding that he stop Hektor's army. Are we looking at a war between the kingdoms as a result?"

"That's scary," I said, suddenly seeing these kingdoms at war with one another. "Only the Church would stand to gain from that."

"Well, at least now we have three workable theories, and that is better than I had before," Alekos replied. "We can keep a sharp watch on things. If it was merely payback, one way, or the other, this should be an isolated event. If the Church is trying to incite wars between kingdoms, we should see other events, which may lead other kingdoms to fight against each other. Time will tell. Such a shame though, I liked Maximus. He would have made a fine king. Well, I'd better see to Deimos now. Excuse me."

"I'd better see how Lyris is coming along." I went to my room. She was sitting on our bed looking hopelessly around the room.

"How am I ever going to survive like this? I've lost everything. Maximus is supposed to be here to help me with everything. I cannot even go pee by myself any longer."

"Sure you can. Use your feet to slide the chamber pot out there a ways. Good girl, that's the way. Now wiggle your dress up, yes use the bed. Mia didn't put any under garments on you for this very reason. Yes, that's good; now slide down over the pot. Here, I'll slide it just right. Have at it."

A little later she stood up, a half smile on her face. "We just have to learn a whole new way to do things. It will be harder for you than it was for me, because you have lived all your life with them and now suddenly don't have them. Me, I never had them. It just takes time, Lyris, and we have plenty of that to spare."

For the next while, I continued to run therapy sessions on her. Each time she had a major slump, I gave her a boost. Finally, she became somewhat stable and began to try to learn how to do things. Yes, we definitely were not bored any longer. Amara, Zenovia, and I worked with her daily, a crash course in how to survive as we four were. Additionally, with time on my hands, I gave Amara and Zenovia more therapy sessions as well.

At night, we four slept in the same very large bed. This way, Mia could easily help anyone of us during the night. Further, I began to work with these three trying to get us to work together as a team. I recalled how in Velona we had worked out that four of us armless women working together had been the ideal number to get things done. Slowly but surely, we four began to bond with each other, to be there to help the other with simple things like brushing our hair, putting on our clothes, and even wiping our butts.

As winter ended, Mia pointed out to me that all three women were now routinely positioned just behind their heads. They were no longer stuck inside their heads. I had to educate them further. We had a long talk about spiritual beings, and they finally realized many things that they had long forgotten about themselves. I desperately wanted these three to get somehow to Velona for training, though I had no idea how this could be done, especially since soon their country might launch a war against Velona.

Chapter 12 Coming to a Head

The Spring 701 Grand Council was a week away now. Tempers were broiling, of that I was certain. Already reports came in to the Emperor from Theos. King Hektor had taken action against the Church of Jehosanity in his kingdom. None of us knew the precise facts, speculation ran wild. At the very least a dozen churches had been destroyed and twenty priests and thirty security forces had been hanged in public squares. Numbers varied from report to report. Some even said the King Hektor had formed up a sizeable army and was marching on Thrace already. That, we chalked up to wild speculation.

What was certain, however, was that their Pope Aison was coming to the Grand Council! He had requested that he personally address the Emperor and assembled kings. This promised to be the most interesting council yet.

What I found more disturbing were the reports I periodically received from the Santi Communicator, Sally. Nearly every day all winter long, a slow Megalos merchant ship had docked in Patri. While supplies were unloaded, they each also brought around twenty Holy Paladins and their horses. These men discretely left the docks, disappearing into the large church complex in Patri. After that, they were not seen again. I had Mia keep a running tally, though the Santi were obviously doing the same. Already twenty legions had arrived, a sizeable force of cavalry. Their purpose we could only guess. Alekos suggested they were coming to protect the Church interests, since the council made it perfectly clear last time that the Church could expect no assistance from Demokritos. Another possibility he suggested was to provide protection for the Pope. If that were the case, we should see them leaving after the Pope returned to Megalos.

One by one, the various groups began arriving at the imperial palace. I kept my eyes peeled for sight of Hektor and Angele. I wanted to see how they were doing and to tell the about the progress that their daughter-in-law, Lyris, had been making. By supper of the night before the spring council meeting, he still had not shown up, and I began to worry.

Taking tea with Mia later that night, we were both chatting about what was delaying Hektor. "Surely he would not miss the council," I said.

"Who would not miss the council?" the tired voice of a man I recognized spoke from behind me. Hektor had quietly come into our small dining room. I got up and turned to greet him, a big smile on my face. I had come to like this old man. Shocked, yes that is a good description of what I felt as I looked into his friendly face. He look old, very old, the loss of his son had aged him enormously. "Do you have time to take a final tea with an old friend?"

171

I moved up to him and gave him a welcoming hug, after our fashion, kissing him on his forehead. Mia hugged him as well, and then poured his tea. Slowly, he sat down, took a measured sip, and sighed.

"I'm late. I had a very important duty to perform, Maren. Please don't say anything until I am done. I might not be able to get up the courage to continue." I looked surprised, what was he up to anyway?

"Tomorrow, I will be giving up my throne to my nephew, Lysander Georgios, a young lad, not married, but full of ambition. You will get along well with him, I'm sure." I started to say something, but he put his finger to my lips, urging me to be silent.

"Angele is gone now. The loss of our son took the very life out of her. I am now a shell of a man. Yet, before I too turn to the dust from which I came, I have two duties yet to perform. The first concerns you, Maren, my ever faithful, constant, dear Maren. I often now think of you as the daughter I never had. Ah well. Now listen very carefully to what I have to say. This war is coming as sure as the spring follows the winter. I am taking a gamble on the outcome. Maren, when the war is over, I want you by any means possible to journey to Velona. There you are to meet a lady known as Linda d'Grange. She will have something from me for you. Promise me that you will do this. Don't speak, just nod." I did so. Evidently, he had met my dearest friend from last lifetime and more. She was my chosen leader of the Santi to replace me when I left for Zargarb. What was he talking about anyway? Now I was curious indeed.

"There, the first duty is finished. Of the second duty, I cannot tell you at this time. In the years to come, you will know what that second duty was." He took another sip of tea and sighed heavily.

"Maren, I have an admission to make to you. I must clear my conscience. I only hope that you can forgive an old man for the follies of his judgment. Maren, I am responsible for Anatolios's assassination." I gasped. This did not make any sense! Why would Hektor want Anatolios dead, leaving Amara in such plight?

"Indirectly, so. You see, I had, well, I was, I mean — this is so hard for me, Maren. I promised to put Anatolios on the throne of Demokritos after I had Deimos slain. It was to happen when he takes the field, leading our army to war, a war that I still am totally against. I know that I would have made you a widow, a horrid thing to do to a woman of the Eighth Degree, deplorable, but then I could see no other way to stop this war machine. Somehow, Dimitris discovered my plot, and he arranged with the Church to have Anatolios assassinated in return for his support of the Church. I dug deeper. I still have a few old friends in Arolas. It was Dimitris who sent those men to Annelise to assassinate you, before Deimos could come for you. I believe that he was trying to force Deimos not to make an Eighth Degree woman Empress. Maren, be extremely careful around Dimitris; he is not to be trusted with anything."

"It may well be that the assassination of my son was his payment for my attempt to kill Deimos and put Anatolios on the throne. It may not be so just as easily. His death remains a mystery. After tomorrow morning, we will not meet again in this life." Again, I started to say something, but once more, he put his finger on my lips.

"I am not through, Maren. I know the war is inevitable now. Nothing I can do will halt it. Yet, you may still have a chance to alter its outcome for the sake of the entire world. When Deimos takes the field to lead his army forth, I urge you in the strongest possible terms to go with him and be at his side. With your guidance, he may well come to his senses before it is too late. When you go, it is of the utmost importance that you take Amara, Zenovia, and, most of all, Lyris with you. Under no circumstances whatsoever are you to leave them here in Demokritos. If you do, they will undoubtedly perish long before you return. Keep my daughter, Lyris, safe so that she may yet have a life, though I cannot see how she will ever manage. How is my daughter, Maren? Oh, you may speak now. The old man, whom you have every right to hate, is finished, finished in many, many ways."

While I had much I wanted to say, I took pity on him. "Lyris is doing extremely well, all things considered. I, and the others here, have worked with her constantly, and she is learning to adapt to life as a most honored woman, Sire. Mia, go get her out of bed will you please?" Mia ran off to fetch Lyris. "She longs to see you and Angele. We did not hear of her death. I am so sorry for both of you, Hektor. And I do not hate you for plotting against Deimos. You had your reasons. We are both working to save Demokritos from destruction.

Lyris came running into the room, wearing only her nightgown. The glow on her face and in her eyes told me how anxious she was to see Hektor again. "Lyris, my dear, dear daughter! Come let an old man hug you tightly!" She flew into his open arms and sobbed for joy on his shoulder. He whispered, "Angele has passed away."

Lyris pulled back slightly. "Oh dad, what happened?" Now the tears turned to grief again.

"The loss was too much for her heart to bear. Let me look at you my child, my daughter. You look so fabulous, so very much alive!"

"Yes, but Angele, I am so sorry. Did she suffer?"

"No, died peacefully in bed with me, but enough talk of death. You look so beautiful, Lyris, so incredibly alive and radiant. Let me hug you, our time together is very short now." They hugged for a long time before he pulled away.

"Daughter, in the morning I will be turning over my throne to my nephew, Lysander, and I will be leaving. We will not meet again in this life, though I will treasure this time with you now, dearest daughter, forever. War is coming, Lyris, ugly, nasty, uncaring war. I have made Maren promise me two things. One, she will accompany Deimos into the field when he goes off to make war. Two, she absolutely must take you with her, as awkward and as difficult as that may be for you to manage as a woman of the Eighth Degree. If you remain in Demokritos while the war rages, you will most certainly become a casualty of the conflicts. More than anything in the world, I want you, my dearest daughter Lyris, to live, to able to have and enjoy the life that is within you. Now give me a kiss, daughter, for I must go now to prepare Lysander for the morning. Maren will explain more fully. I simply cannot face you with the bitter truth of what I have done in the past."

Tears flowing, she obeyed, kissing him lovingly on his forehead. He gave her one last hug and then left us alone. I let her finish crying before I spoke.

At last, she asked, "What did he mean by not facing me?" I explained what he had admitted to us, that he felt that the assassination of her husband might have been in retaliation for his attempt to secure the throne for Anatolios, after having Deimos slain.

"I don't think that is the reason Maximus was assassinated, Lyris, but he does."

She thought for a moment and said, "You know, Maren, he had never ever called me his daughter, much less my 'dearest daughter.' He has changed somehow."

"I believe that he is making closure on his life, Lyris. Perhaps he knows that his body is dying and wants to put his affairs in order. However, I do not detect that his body is dying. I saw no signs of any illness, but then I am not a Healer."

The next morning, the throne room was packed; more had come this time than at any previous council. An extra row of chairs had to be hastily brought in for the many guests as well. I honored Hektor's request to speak first, primarily because he would be announcing the change in kings. Lysander deserved to be introduced fully before the main council began discussing the many issues.

Deimos called the meeting to order. I rose and said, "The council will first hear a few words from King Hektor of Theos. You will understand why momentarily." More than a few protests began, but were quickly silenced as the old man rose.

"I have only two things to say to this council today. One is a question. The first and only question is directed to King Milo Kourgos of Thrace. Sire, what action have you taken against the Church of Jehosanity for the assassination of my son and heir, on the very day he brought Lyris, newly of the Eighth Degree, out into the world?"

Milo hemmed and hawed a bit. He'd conducted an investigation. The Cardinal had said that the assassin had acted alone and without the Church's direction or consent. In short, he'd done nothing.

Milo was quite surprised when Hektor then said, "So be it, Milo. Second, I am announcing to you all today that I am retiring as King of

Theos. My nephew Lysander is now the official King of Theos. Treat him with the respect that you have shown me all these years. Lysander, please stand so that they may recognize you. I hereby hand you the crown of Thrace." He handed the young lad his small crown. As soon as Lysander took it from him, he walked out of the room without saying another word, though many tried to say a few words to him.

Lysander was twenty, tall, and well-muscled. He had a youthful face, but stern eyes. He then took Hektor's seat, sitting beside Hektor's old advisor. He was unmarried. For several minutes, the room buzzed with chat over this unexpected event. I knew several of the kings were re-evaluating the overall political situation.

I rose, "The Emperor wishes to allow our special guest to address us next. Pope Aison of the Church of Jehosanity has come here to personally speak to the council."

Resplendent in his purple robes with the white cross, the portly older man rose to speak. He had a nicely trimmed beard and wore a purple skullcap. I noticed that Cardinal Lethos Theo was absent this time. Cardinal Rax Ciros was on his right and another man wearing the red cardinal robes sat on his left.

"Distinguished Kings, Queens, Emperor Deimos, Empress Maren, I am Pope Aison, holy leader of the Church of Jehosanity. It is with the saddest of hearts that I was forced to come here today to address you. When I learned of the despicable, heinous action taken by a zealot within the Mano del Dio security forces, the wanton slaying of Maximus Gregorios, I was deeply troubled and appalled that such zealots could exist within our holiest of churches. I knew then that I had no choice but to come to Demokritos and apologize to King Hektor and all you other kings as well as the mighty Emperor and Empress. Please, accept the sincere apologies of the entire Church. I have withdrawn the Cardinal in charge here in Thrace and will take him back to Megalos with me, there to receive his just rewards for having allowed such a crime to occur on his watch. In his place, I give you Cardinal Myron Morpheus."

"I want to personally let you know that such dereliction of duty will not be tolerated by the Church. While these actions cannot undo the life so disgracefully taken, I want you to know that we too do not tolerate such criminality."

"I prayed to Lord Jehosa for guidance on how the Church could make amends for our lack of vigilance, not having discovered the zealot and dealt with him before he could carry out his vicious crime. My prayers were answered. Our church is always ready to minister to the needs of our people. Thus, I came here today to announce to the Emperor personally that the Church of Jehosanity will be backing his coming glorious conquest of Tarra, and the elimination of the abominations, the Santi del Dio. We will be providing one thousand field nurses to look after the wounded, to help prepare nourishing meals needed by the brave fighters in their quest. The Church will provide one thousand wagons to ferry your supplies up through the Southlands to the battlefront. Even as I speak to you today, they are already prepared to go into action. I took the liberty of mobilizing them now, not knowing just how soon the Emperor would begin his conquest. I hope this will demonstrate that the Church is and always will be your close ally. So yes, all is prepared, you can send forth your mighty legions from Megalos today, knowing that they will be supplied and have the medical support, as needed in battles. Thank you."

The room filled with buzzing chatter, as many whispered over this surprise assistance. Alekos leaned over to me, "What do you make of that?"

"All I get is a sense that he wants to hurry this war along, get it started sooner."

"Same here. I will caution Deimos about depending upon this so-called offer of supply wagons. I do not trust the man."

I rose, "Now it is time for the reports from the kingdoms. Lysander, do you wish to go first? I see you are anxious to do this. Don't worry, we don't bite." He gave me a sheepish grin.

"I wish to report that the legions requested at the last council meeting have been formed and are in Axos as I speak, on their way to the barracks in Patri, awaiting deployment. I must honor a request by my uncle. He wished me to report that unless the Pope can raise the dead, his apology is insufficient. All the priests of Jehosanity and their assassin companions either have fled Theos or have been publically hanged. I share his sentiments, Pope. In the strongest possible terms I say unto you, do not send other priests into the kingdom of Theos. Finally, I wish to say that Theos is ready to fight this glorious war of total conquest!"

This last brought cheers from many others here, who wanted this prophesy to get on its way to being fulfilled. One by one, the other kings reported either that the legions had been raised or that the caravels were ready to sail. General Alexandr proudly announced that Deimos was now acceptably trained and ready to lead their army forth.

I was shocked; the much anticipated fireworks did not materialize. In their eagerness to fulfill the promised prophesies, everyone overlooked the assassination. Was no one going to put a damper on their enthusiasm for war? Had none listened to my parting words at the last council?

I rose again and a hush fell over the group. At least I had their attention. I figured that this was my last chance to dissuade them from this war. "At the end of our last council, I asked you to ponder this. I said then, 'Why are you slavishly following someone else's grand plans for your own future? The Prophesies of Demos. A free man is a man who creates his own goals, follows his own purposes, and takes his own independent actions. He creates his own future, not slavishly working to bring about a future that someone, dead seven hundred years, is dictating that he must create.' Yet, still you desire to go to war."

"I would be remiss in my duties to you as your Empress if I did not bring this to your attention. The Prophecies of Demos states, 'Now the Emperor, with his Empress of the Old Way at his side, will move north, reclaiming the northern lands, forming a Unified Empire of wealth and beauty that has never been seen before on Tarra.' Certainly, I know that I must accompany my Emperor when he goes forth; it is so written. Yet, there are three key words in that prophesy that, to my way of thinking, you are all misunderstanding."

"The first word, and perhaps the most important one, is reclaiming. Reclaim has two meanings. One is to demand as one's property; this is the meaning you seem to be accepting. Knowing that you cannot walk into another country and demand they hand it over to you, you take it by force of arms. Yet, I call your attention to another meaning of reclaim: to assert that something is the case."

"How are we to choose the correct meaning? By examining the other two key words: wealth and beauty. If you go to war, destroy, and conquer these northern lands, then you can pillage to your hearts content and thus get their wealth that is true. But what about beauty? Wars destroy all things of beauty. Thus, I say unto you, going to war to conquer these northern lands is not and will not fulfill this prophesy written down that you are slavishly following to make it come true. In fact, the Prophesies of Demos are saying that you must follow an entirely different course than conquest by war and force of arms."

"Thus, you have been forewarned by your Empress." I sat down. I had ranted a bit more than I intended. The four Santi, alone, smiled and gave me their support, secretly of course. They knew that I was right.

Unfortunately, only two kings supported my views. Quickly, Dimitris moved that we go to war at once. The motion passed with two dissenting votes. I also knew that my Lady's Support Group would not veto this motion, for too many of them firmly believed in the prophesies, and I had been unable to convince them otherwise.

The motion having passed, I had to tell them that it would not be vetoed by our support group. I hated to have to say that, but I was honor bound to do so. Now, everything fell into the hands of Deimos and General Alexandr. By lunchtime, the entire council business was finished! Not only were there no arguments, but this was also the shortest council meeting in nearly a century, according to Alekos.

The rest of the day was more like a party than a deadly serious meeting! Even the Pope mingled with the kings and Emperor, offering his blessings for glorious victory on the battlefield. Yes, I played hostess, but forsook the dance. I was in no mood to celebrate.

Before the Santi left, I held a private meeting with them, perhaps my last chance to talk openly with them. "I have one more chance to turn this around," I began. "There will be a number of planning meetings; maybe I will have better luck then. In case we leave, I am very worried about what will happen here while the army and the Emperor are gone. I need your eyes and ears, Sally. Help me take off my boot, the right one."

Sally made a funny face over the seemingly out of place request, but did so. Some papers fell out on to the floor. "I snatched them earlier this afternoon. Darkon will be in charge of the country in the absence of the Emperor. His signature is on that paper. I wanted you to have it, just in case we needed a "dispatch" to mysteriously arrive where we are located."

"Ah, court intrigue," she said with a wry smile. "His signature may well come in handy. What happened to Hektor?"

"No one knows. I suspect Lysander knows, but he isn't saying. I will be telling the General and Deimos many things about the Santi and its defenses. I will attribute them to either you folks or to Hektor from his visit there. Back me up when needed."

"You got it. We all want to wish you the very best of luck, Maren Bethany. You are going to be facing tough times indeed, especially as you are now." We hugged and they left for the return trip to their fortress in Patri.

That evening while I was avoiding the dance, Alekos found me sitting with my group, taking tea. We looked very somber, according to him. "Maren, I just wanted to let you know that I have been studying the Prophesies again, in light of what you said this morning. I believe that you have the correct interpretation. This proposed war of conquest is not what is foretold at all. Are we doomed?"

"Alekos, well done. At least one other in power sees my point!" Amara, Zenovia, and Lyris already had agreed with me. Of course, Mia and Hans did. "To be utterly blunt and frank with you, Alekos, yes, doomed is the right choice of words." I decided that this might be the opportune time to get one of the three key people onto my side — the three being Alekos, Alexandr, and Deimos.

"I will level with you. We've known about this proposed war of conquest for years now, and I have been doing a little investigating of my own. Do you think that Hektor's trip to Velona was all pleasure? No sir. In part, he was on a mission for me. Let me explain just how we are doomed."

"First, if we fielded the originally planned four thousand legions, we would easily succeed. However, we are not, only some seventy or so. Now we are in for a hard fight as soon as we reach Santi protected countries. Their fighters wear plate mail, making them terribly difficult to slay. The Holy Paladins already discovered that, which is why they are now armoring themselves similarly. The Santi have many stone fortresses, which will have to be taken by siege warfare. This will prove our undoing. As our forces approach, they will unleash a devastating barrage. I expect entire legions to succumb with each barrage, maybe more. I do not have too many details about this weapon of theirs, only that we will be devastated by it. It is doubtful that we will be able to take even one of their fortresses without losing half our army right there."

"It gets worse. Hektor verified that the Santi have a mutual defense treaty with the Emperor of Tashien, the yellow giant. He reports that if the Santi are attacked, the mighty army of Tashien will come to their defense. Now we are talking in terms of thousands of legions under their command. If they come, as they once did with only a few legions, taking over half of Megalos, what then remains of our army will be completely destroyed, outnumbered more than ten to one, maybe even a hundred to one."

"This whole thing reeks of the Church of Jehosanity treachery, Alekos. With our legions gone from their soil, they are back in control. What is to keep them from cutting off our supply wagons? Worse, do you know that already there are twenty legions of their Holy Paladin cavalry housed in secret in Patri?"

He muttered, "I remember you telling me, and my reply was security for the Pope's visit. If they do not leave, this spells trouble."

"I've asked the Santi to let me know if they do leave or if more continue to arrive. Alekos, while we are away, there could well be startling developments here at home! We might return home only to find the Church is in control, not Deimos!"

Alekos had not thought of this possibility, and he pushed his hands through his hair. I wished I could do that too. "I'll give that some serious thought. I'll get back to you later."

"Say, any ideas what happened to Hektor?"

"None, my Empress. I know he left the palace grounds in a carriage, but that's all. Sad to see him leave."

Alekos left and King Leon and Queen Athena came in to see me. "Ah here you are hiding. We missed you at the dance, beautiful Maren," old Leon jested with me. He hugged me, and then Athena and I shared our special kind of hug. They went on down the line, greeting Amara, Zenovia, and Lyris in a like manner. "Ah, the four most beautiful young women are hiding out in here away from all the young men, tisk, tisk."

"I can't say that I blame you, though," Leon became serious. "We both wanted you to know that we believe as you do, that they have the wrong meaning of the prophesy." I thanked him for his support.

"It is so terribly sad what has happened to you, Lyris, and to Hektor," Athena said consolingly. "All these years, golly I do not know how I could have possible spent them if it had not been for dear Leon here. Lyris, I am so sorry for you. I wish that there was something that I could do for you, but we both know there is nothing that can take the place of Maximus. He was a fine man, and I know that he was in heaven with you for those two weeks that you spent together as a woman of the Eighth Degree. Always remember that, you gave him the happiest, best two weeks of his life. That is something to console you." Lyris had not thought of it that way.

"You know, he was happier and brighter than I can ever recall seeing him, during those two weeks. He really was. I had not thought of that," Lyris replied, realizing that all this time she had been focused on herself and her desperate plight.

"Lyris, somewhere out there in the big, wide world is another man who will treasure you. I know that one day you will find another to love. It won't be the same as with Maximus, but it will be good. I know that I would come calling today, if only I were thirty years younger," he looked at Athena, and quickly added, "and did not know Athena here."

"Hey, monopolizing the women again, are you Leon," the teasing voice of King Eros distracted us. He and Ariadna were just entering the small dining room. Both of them hugged us all and gave us their well wishes.

"As long as we are here, Leon, let's ask Maren," Eros said. Looking at me, he asked, "Do you know what is going on with Hektor? That took us by surprise. He never told us or sent word that Angele had died. We would have made it to her funeral if we had known. Now he's given up his throne. Where has he gone? Is he really retiring? If so, where?"

"I was as surprised as you, only he told me late last night when he finally arrived. I know that he left in his coach shortly after he left the throne room. I was hoping that one of you might have some ideas?"

Leon replied, "I know that he was going to give the throne to Maximus and Lyris when they returned from Patri, only he was, well, you know." He didn't come out and say it for fear of upsetting Lyris. "You were days from being the queen."

"You know, Hektor has always been a man of his word. Maren, can you recall what he may have said while you were still in Patri?" asked Eros.

"I was handling Lyris most of the time, but I do remember him saying this much: 'I've met with the mayor of Patri and sent word on to Milo. I told him that he is to run all of these vile priests and their assassins out of Thrace or I will bring my entire army down here and do it for him. At the next council I will get these wicked men cast out of Demokritos or do it myself. One way or another, their days in Demokritos are numbered, thus speaks King Hektor Georgios of Theos.' Does this help? Does he have an army?"

"Not any more, Lysander has control of the official legions," Leon answered.

Eros pondered my words. "Hektor meant what he said, especially if Angele also died as a result. That man knows an awful lot of people; many owe him favors. We kings get owed lots of favors by the time that we get this old," he jested.

Leon added, "He could not, as King, take an official Centurion army and march through Milo's Thrace. The Grand Council would be forced to take stern countermeasures. It is against our laws for one kingdom's army to invade and attack anything within another's kingdom. Those rules have been upheld for six and a half centuries now. No, as king and with his official army, he knew as well as I, that he could not do it."

"He must have had another idea. Hektor always said what he meant. If he said he was bringing an army to wipe them out, then he is, Leon," Eros countered.

"If that's the case," Mia concluded, "there is only one other answer." We all looked at her. I realized the Judger in her was on display, for she was quick to grasp situations.

Hans added, "Mia, you are right."

"What? What?" both men pleaded with Mia and then Hans.

"He is or has already formed up his own militia, his own private army. He is now not a king and is not using official legions. He has his own men, his own legions. Since he encouraged everyone to go to war quickly, my guess is that as soon as the Emperor and the rest of the legions set sail, he will begin his march to the sea from somewhere in Theos," Mia stated, satisfied that she had at last figured out this riddle of Hektor.

"That's why he said that we would probably never see him again," Lyris added. "He thinks that he will probably be killed while driving these wicked priests into the sea."

"Why that old fox! Mia, I could kiss you. Look out, Hans. I am going to do just that!" Eros exclaimed and planted a big one on her forehead.

"With all the main legions off to war, there will only be guard legions scattered about the kingdoms. He would not need a huge army to accomplish his task," Leon concluded.

I began to fear for Hektor. "Yes, yes he will! The Church had been sneaking in their Holy Paladins all winter. There are nearly twenty legions of their heavy cavalry here now, down in Patri, hiding out in the large church complex there. If he doesn't have a lot of men, he'll be massacred."

"Now don't you boys be thinking of retiring too," Athena teased them, but also half-serious. "I planned on being queen a few more years yet."

"You are not as young as you used to be," Ariadna added, staring at Eros.

"Ah, we are so loved," Leon teased, and hugged his wife. Eros did the same. In their fifties, their love was still going strong. This was not missed by Lyris, who bravely kept a tear from falling. She had so wanted such love.

"No such thoughts, my dear Athena," Leon stated. "We too are owed many favors. What say we call in some of those, Eros? Join the favors together, eh?" The two men shook hands. I knew very well what they were planning to do. Somehow, someway, they were going to form up militias of their own, somehow sending them along to help Hektor's bunch.

"Thanks guys." I leaned in to each of them for a hug. Lyris offered them some tea, and we shared more relaxed conversations for a time.

As we six walked towards my bedroom to turn in, we came across Deimos and Eirena, our head maid, taking animatedly in the hallway, just outside the room in which he had been sleeping by himself, while I had Lyris with me these past months.

He was saying, "But my dear Eirena, it will be very dangerous. We will be camping out on the cold hard ground. It would be so awful for you. I do want so much better for you. I would feel just horrible if anything bad happened to you."

"I will be just fine, Deimos, really I will." She saw us and came to me pleading her case. "Empress Maren, you will be going with Deimos when he leads our armies, the prophesies say so. I heard you today. You must take me with you, please. I have looked after Deimos' needs ever since I was a little girl. He must have someone there to make up his bed each night. You must take me along. You will need me too. I know it. I will not be left behind this way."

"But Eirena, you could get badly hurt, even killed. Arrows will be flying. What if some men get by our lines, you could be captured or even raped. I care way too much to see anything bad happen to you," Deimos continued to plead. I noticed that he had genuine feelings for her, real ones, not as he had for me. Interesting, I thought.

"Well, Deimos, as long as we are discussing what staff comes along with us, I will be bringing these with me. Yes, Lyris, Zenovia, and Amara, besides Mia and Hans. Just because you want to go fight a battle does not mean that I am going to stop helping these poor women learn how to adjust. We need another set of hands at dinnertime. Eirena, if you will agree to help us, then I say she comes with us. We will need our camp made up for us, since we don't have the arms for it." I lied a bit there. I knew darn well that we four could manage completely without the help of Mia and Hans, though with three sets of arms, things would be infinitely easier.

Deimos looked at me pitifully. "But I would die if anything bad happened to her, Maren."

"So don't let anything bad happen, then, Deimos. What about me? Okay if I get knocked on the head?" I teased him; boy did he ever blush. Bingo. Now I had a certainty on what had up to now been speculation.

"No, I mean I don't want anything to happen to you either, but the prophesies say you have to come along. They don't say she does. Okay, okay, you win. Eirena you can come, but you must help our Maren and the others with whatever. I need to turn in, big day tomorrow. We begin the great plans of conquest!" He hastily ducked into his room, mostly to get away from me, I wagered. I had discovered a little secret of his, one that he certainly didn't want me knowing.

"Oh thank you, thank you, Maren! I'll do anything you ask," she was greatly relieved, that's for sure.

"We'll talk more tomorrow about what we need to bring along." We six entered my large bedroom, with Mia and Hans helping us four quickly change for bed. I wondered if Mia had picked up what I had sensed. I resolved to ask her the next time that we were completely alone.

Chapter 13 Plans Are Made

November 1, 701 brought with it daily meetings between Deimos, Alekos, General Alexandr, Darkon, and me. The general laid out an enormous map of the northern continents, placing toy soldiers, representing a legion each, onto the map. For my benefit, he had the map on the floor, so I could view it better and point out things with my spiked heel, lacking the hands otherwise to do so.

Mia, Hans, Alekos, and I had already decided that the best strategy on our part would be to let Deimos and Alexandr work out their complete battle plans first, before we spoke up with objections or suggestions.

Deimos was like a little kid playing with the toy soldiers, no reality on what it would really mean in the field. "See, Maren, first we will move these ten caravels with the ten new legions and us from here to Sud. That's where we start, Sud."

"Where are the other seventy-five caravels, Deimos?" I asked.

"These sticks here around Megalos represent them. They are currently at anchor off Megalos. Now where was I? Oh, yes, Alexandr will issue the orders to have seventy-four legions cross over into Sud ahead of us, moving out in a glorious line, heading north. They have a paved road there, you see. We leave this one legion in Galantas, just for security's sake, Alexandr says."

"Now we move north up to here, where the desert of Juda Arad begins. There is nothing at all in the desert land, so we ignore it. There is nothing out there in the middle of the Southlands either; we just pass it by. This huge area here is the Red Desert, which is deadly to cross; you get some kind of disease and die. We will definitely avoid that place."

"Now up here is New Barq. No one seems to know why it's called New Barq, though. Where's Old Barq? Ah well. There is a Santi del Dio fortress there, outside the city. It used to be a Megalos port city, until the Santi took it over during some war. Megalos wishes it back."

"Now what we are trying to work out is just what this here means," he handed me a letter that had just come to him. He suddenly realized I had no hands to take it from him, let alone unfold it so I could read it. Alekos fumed, even the General was a bit miffed at Deimos' apparent insensitivity to me. Alekos took the offered letter, opened it, and read it aloud.

Emperor Deimos Gavril,

This is to inform you that as of the first of the new year, 702, the port and city of New Barq is once more a free city, open to whomever desires to visit or live here. The Santi Fortress is and will remain outside the city walls. We only provide security for the free city when they desire it.

Sincerely,
Chaucer d'Grange
Santi del Dio Headquarters

"What the devil does this mean?" Deimos asked, very frustrated with the information.

"Do you really want to know the history of that place, Deimos? We studied it in our history lessons, didn't we, Mia?" She nodded, playing along with my outright lie.

"Please, Maren. If you know, please tell me. I'm sorry about embarrassing you with the letter."

"Originally, Al Barq was a port city belonging to the original followers of Lord Jehosa, they lived in Juda Arad. The Centurions of Megalos captured their city and their country and brutalized them. When the governor of Al Barq heard that the Great Messiah of Lord Jehosa was born, he had all of the newborn babies in Al Barq murdered during the night. After that, all remaining original Arad people abandoned the city to the Centurions."

"Later, during an uprising in Juda Arad, the city was captured and burned to the ground, revenge for the baby murders. Later, it was retaken by the Centurions and they built a new city just beyond the ruins of the old city, called New Barq. From here, they could supply their legions, who tried to conquer the world, just as you are. During the First Crusade for Religious Freedom, the crusaders with some help from the Santi del Dio, captured New Barq, sending the Centurions there back home."

"The Santi built a tall stone fortress on the ruins of the old city and until this letter, controlled the city. Now it has been turned into a free city, which means, Deimos, you do not have to attack it; you can walk through the gates. No one is going to fight you here."

"Ah, thank you for the history lesson," Alexandr commented stiffly. "Sire, there is no point in laying siege to that fortress; it is of no military importance any longer. I would suggest that you leave a legion there to watch over it, however."

"Okay. You mean these Megalos Centurions murdered new born babies, Maren?" Deimos asked.

"Yes, by the hundreds. He even killed his own newborn son, if my history lesson is correct. These people from Megalos are vile indeed, not like you or I, Deimos." I had made my point, and it had reached him. Plus one for me.

"Then, we move my mighty legions on northward up to this place, Zargarb. Here is where we begin our glorious conquering, right, General?"

"Yes, they have a line of defensive fortresses all along their border.

We must stop and eliminate at least two of these, preferably the two closest to the coast and the huge city of Zargarb," he replied. "We will bring up our siege towers and climb in over their walls, taking them out by our sheer force of numbers."

"Wrong!" I feigned annoyance with them. "Haven't either of you paid any attention at all to what Hektor reported to us on their defenses there? Honestly!" I huffed, as if I was annoyed.

"Okay, Empress, what do you say will happen here?" General Alexandr taunted me.

I slid the first toy soldier towards the fortress. "When your legions get close enough, the Santi will open fire with their massive dragon weapon. According to Hektor, one blast from the dragon weapon and one entire legion is gone, dead or badly wounded. By the time you actually reach the tower, you won't have any legions left to attack them with. Golly, I do wish you two would have paid attention to what Hektor and Angele reported to us about the Santi defenses. What good is it if we send up spies, if you don't listen to them?" I feigned being mortally offended.

"Damn! I didn't realize old Hektor had that in mind. Where's he gone? Can we summon him here?" Alexandr asked.

Darkon replied, "No, general, he retired and left. No one, not even his new king knows where he is. Probably off getting drunk at some inn somewhere. He's had two terrific shocks in so short a time, you know, losing his son and heir, and then his wife."

Deimos wasn't listening. "Hey, we can just sit there and starve them out!"

"No silly, they are the Sea Princes. They will just bring in all the food and water they need by sea. Didn't you pay any attention to your history lessons? Alekos, didn't his teacher, what was his name, oh yes, Nestor, didn't he teach Deimos anything about geography?"

"We didn't know much about this part of the world then, Maren." I acted as if I was mollified.

"Perhaps we should come by sea to Zargarb," suggested Alexandr.

As the two moved the sticks representing our caravels around, I said, "That's much better, guys. Now you only have to wait a while and face four thousand legions coming at your rear. Have you forgotten what else Hektor told us and what the prophesies said? Leave the yellow to last? The people in Tashien have yellow skin, spooky I hear. They have armies larger than ours. Hektor was shown the mutual defense treaty signed by the Santi and the Empress of Tashien. Hektor said that if the Santi are seriously threatened, just like what you are now doing, then Tashien would sent four thousand legions to help them. They would be coming from way over here, guys. That means they would come marching up the paved road behind you. Now your army is cut off and outnumbered badly."

"Well, if we have all our caravels here by New Barq, then we can all escape by sea," Deimos smartly countered this move. Darn.

"Ah, sire. Let me make another suggestion. Perhaps the Empress is right. We must know well in advance if the Tashien armies are coming. We should leave heliograph men all along the road from Sud to where our army is located. Then, if our men spy this mighty yellow army coming, they can signal us, and we will know that very same day!"

"Oh, I like that, General. I had not thought of doing that! We would have several weeks warning at least! We could circle around the Southlands and hit them in their rear. No, I forgot they greatly outnumber us. I see why the prophesy said to leave the yellow for last. I will need to raise four times as large an army as we now have, that will take us a few years to manage." He completely ignored the number of boats it would take to move that many men this far north.

"Haven't you two realized that you are not doing what the prophesy says to do?" I acted childlike.

"Don't be silly, Maren. I am supposed to conquer the world, right General?"

"Right, Emperor."

Alekos, Mia, and I left them to work out new plans. We took tea in the small dining room. "Deimos idolizes the General. He's like the father the boy never had. His was nothing but a womanizing drunkard," Alekos explained away Deimos' faults.

"Nevertheless, did you see that they are planning to only leave one legion of older guardsmen in each of the kingdoms while they are off conquering the world?" I asked him.

"Yes, that has me very worried! I have not heard from our Santi friends about the Holy Paladins having left yet," Alekos stated soberly.

Hans came in with a short dispatch. "Hey, another boat load of Holy Paladins has landed in Patri. Santi dispatch just came, must have landed ten days ago now. They are building up, not leaving."

"Damn, and they can simply say that we are forcing them to bring in support troops to protect them, since we are not going to do so," Alekos replied angrily.

"Honestly, Maren, sometimes I wonder why I spend all my time trying to keep Demokritos going. Zena accuses me of spending more time with the Emperor than I do her."

"Well you must. If you leave her behind, she might be harmed by the events here," I suggested. "I sometimes wonder the same thing, Alekos. I mean what have I gotten out of being the Empress and worrying so about everything? Nothing. Well, that's not entirely true," I looked at Mia. "I got out of having to wear that awful corset and that impossible hoop dress." That made the advisor chuckle.

While the boys were playing with their toys on the floor, we worked out how we would travel along with the army. I knew that I would have to ride my horse alongside Deimos, as much as possible, though I drew the line at going into combat with him. If he chose to be on the front line, I would not be at his side. However, the other three like me could not ride yet, though I hoped one day that they might be brave enough to try. A carriage would do fine since we would travel by paved road much of the way, according to current plans anyway. Mia and Hans would ride with Amara, Zenovia, and Lyris, handling their needs. Eirena would also ride with them, helping.

When we would make camp for the night, we would need a tent to sleep the six of us. I included Eirena with our group, again helping with us four, who were going to need assistance. I understood their point of view; all this was very scary for them. They still felt extremely helpless, especially Lyris and to a lesser extent, Amara. However, every mile of northern progress we made, the closer I would have them to Velona.

Not knowing our exact departure date, I had our staff begin to pack up what we thought that we would need, spare clothes, blankets. I made sure that we had several chamber pots ready for use in the coach. Hans kept reminding us to travel light. Well, to we women, traveling light means something different from a guy doing so. We spent a week adjusting and discarding items, until our gear met with Hans's approval of light.

Finally, Deimos made the pronouncement over dinner. "We have everything worked out now. We leave on January 1, 702! Yes at long last!" That was two days from now. He suddenly realized that and asked me, "Can you be ready that soon? I rather forgot that you might need time to pack and all that."

"Dear, we are all set to go. One carriage for them and our gear, one horse for me, so I can be by your side, as the prophesy says I must be. I warn you Deimos Gavril, if you go charging off into the actual fighting, I am not riding in there with you!" I was teasing him of course, and he laughed along with me.

On the first, we mounted up. I let Hans lift me up and get the reins into my mouth; once I had a good grip, I was ready to go. Deimos mounted like he as an old hand at riding. Together, the Emperor with his Empress at his side rode out from the imperial palace in Kefall. The legion assigned to protect us followed behind us, the carriage bringing up the rear. Half of the city turned out, lining the streets to watch this minor spectacle, cheering Deimos on, as if he needed any encouragement. I heard many gasps and whispered comments about me riding a horse. I ignored them.

Once we were outside of the city, it became an ordinary ride. I had an excellent view of the countryside, the aqueducts, which occasionally crossed the landscape, and the picturesque hills. For several hours, I enjoyed the ride. After that, it became a little boring, and my jaws began to ache from constantly biting down on the reins. This was the longest I had ridden in this lifetime. Yet, I knew I had to get used to this and that my legs would be sore for several days, as they toughened up.

We stayed in very nice inns along the way each night. Deimos enjoyed the parade as we entered or left each of the smaller towns. The turnout in Axos was huge, the capital of Thrace. King Milo stood and waved to us as we rode through his city. Ten days passed quickly, and the port of Patri appeared on the horizon. I spied sea birds in the distance and smelled the good old salt air, refreshing.

At the docks, we boarded the Royal Arc, the Emperor's private caravel. It had just been thoroughly cleaned and de-ratted, before the many provisions were loaded for our trip. While we stood around watching the dockhands load the carriage and horses into the cargo hold, the Santi Healer, Betsy, came up to us.

"Empress, I have brought you some herbs to help counteract seasickness. I hope you have a good trip."

"Oh thank you very much. I was just now thinking that I ought to have brought some along. I don't know who will get sick, but this will surely help. Thank you." Hans took the pouch from her.

At last, we were allowed to board. On the poop deck, one enormous cabin was reserved for the Emperor and Empress. In this case, Deimos suggested that we stay in it because there was more room. He and the General shared an adjoining smaller cabin. Ten others took the remaining beds. The rest of our legion of protectors was coming on a separate caravel.

None of my three companions had ever been on a ship, let alone on a long ocean voyage. I remembered how I loved to watch the ship tacking out to sea, and I made sure that we all were on deck as the lines were cast off. Hans, Mia, and Eirena stood beside us to assist us. I knew that Mia and I were in for a rough time, trying to keep our balance on a rolling, pitching ship in these boots. Worse, my three companions would have just as hard a time keeping their balance, though from experience last lifetime, I knew that they would soon get the hang of it.

"When we are in motion, remember to keep your feet far apart, wide. It is much easier to keep your balance that way. Mia and I are in for a hard time in these boots, so Eirena and Hans, you need to keep a close watch on us. Good, we are about to set sail. Watch, this is so great, moving out to sea, watching the city slip away! I love it, my favorite part of sailing. I really enjoyed it when Deimos came to get me, and we sailed all the way to here from home." I added that last to make it more acceptable.

Yes, the three were very impressed with the sight. An hour later, under full sail, the coast now barely visible, and the boat rolling and pitching, we began to adjust to moving around on the ship. Hans, Eirena, and Mia had their hands full caring for us for the first few days. Hans brewed pots of the herbal tea to prevent seasickness. The other three were quite scared of walking at first, very wobbly on their feet. I worked hard to adjust, because I knew my situation would be the most difficult of all.

Yet a week later, the three were more confident, and we settled down to enjoy the warm summer weather. That's when I discovered that not everyone enjoys sailing on long ocean voyages. My three companions and Eirena became very bored with it after two weeks, constantly asking how soon we would make landfall. I estimated probably two months to Megalos. They groaned and complained.

I remembered all the wonderful times I had last lifetime with all my dear friends in the Explorers Circle. Renzo, oh how I now missed him! My husband back then. He and I would spend hours playing games either on deck or in the cargo hold. Just now, I missed him so badly it wasn't funny! I had to find something to do to get my mind off Renzo and the others, plus somehow help the boredom of the others.

I had a brilliant idea. What could four armless women actually do? We could sing. Lyris had an alto voice, mine was somewhere in the middle. I wish that I had paid more attention to the choral music that Bard Tal conducted back in Velona. I sprang my idea on the threesome. At first, they groaned, but they at least tried. Soon, we four began to enjoy singing together. Our voices were at four different ranges. Amara's was the highest, Lyris's was the lowest. We had a good sounding quartet.

Hans and Mia alternated leading us and helping us get coordinated, ironing out our rough spots. Now we had something to help pass the endless hours at sea. Our singing also helped Deimos and the others, who began to listen in on us.

He, on the other hand, was not bored. It seemed he was really enjoying every minute. I concluded that he, like Renzo and me, loved to sail. I also saw the Eirena often watched him while he gazed out at the sea. Other times, I saw him gazing at her as well.

Days passed. Then, we heard the sound of "Land Ho" coming from the crow's nest. We put in on the island of Acropolis for fresh water and a restock of fresh fruits and vegetables. Two days later, we were back at sea. Everyone was more cheerful now, after I told them that Sud was only weeks away, not months.

Sud, Southlands, was vastly different than I remembered it from my last visit here. Okay, so what if that was one and a half centuries ago, when as Elizabeth Stanton with my Lightning Circle, was here. Now, Sud had quintupled in size! Commerce flowed in all directions as we walked from the large docks to many waiting carriages, which would take us to the inn where we would join our forces. Our own carriage would be unloaded and brought to us.

"Please, smaller steps, Deimos. I cannot keep up with you, these heels," I whispered. We were walking as Emperor and Empress, passing the large welcoming crowd that had turned out to welcome us. Musicians had even played a fanfare as we walked off the gangplank.

"Sorry, I'm a bit excited. They love me, Maren. You too," he said.

"No, they don't know you. They've never seen you or me. They are just being respectful to their supreme leader," I whispered back, all the while smiling, nodding to those around us. I was never more grateful to be lifted into a waiting carriage.

"There, how's that?" Deimos said, proud that he had actually helped me manage as he was supposed to as the husband of a Woman of the Eighth Degree.

"Perfect, Deimos, thank you." I watched as the others came along behind us and got into the next carriage. For once, it was just he and I in the carriage. "Deimos, can I ask you something personal, just between you and me?"

"Sure, Maren. I know I haven't spent much time with you these last few months. I had to learn to fight, and you had to help poor Lyris and Amara. I have never told you this, Maren, but I was really, really glad that you were able to help Lyris. Seeing how you, Mia, and Hans have been working with her, how you are always right there when she needs something, even something as simple as getting her hair out of her eyes, made me realize how awful I have been towards you, Maren. I've not treated you at all as you deserve. I will try to do better."

"I've been fine, Deimos; we were both terribly young when you came for me. Besides, it's not like Lyris, who just had it done. I've been like this all my life."

"Oh, what did you want to ask me? I got distracted," he smiled at me.

I wondered now if this was the right time to ask. "I promise you that what we say in here right now will never be heard beyond here, not even by my handmaiden. "Deimos, do you really love me? I mean really love me?"

"You are my Empress. Am I supposed to love you? I suppose that I am, Hektor loved Angele, I could see that. Even Anatolios, he was crazy about Amara. Like that, you mean?" I nodded. He hung his head downward and muttered, "No. I'm sorry, I don't."

"There is nothing to be sorry about, Deimos. Thank you for being honest with me. I will be so with you too. I am not in love with you either, but I think I know someone who is." His face crimsoned.

"It's that obvious?"

"No, you two are being very discrete. I think that I am the only one who suspects. She ought to be your Empress, not me."

"But she can't. You are. She can never be so, though I think that nothing would make me happier, except perhaps somehow fulfilling the great prophesy."

"Deimos, here is something for you to ponder. The woman who is your wife is by definition the Empress. You and I, we have never been married. You just came and got me. We were never married. No priest, no ceremony. I just jumped right in there and became the Empress. I thought that was a bit strange at first, but I forgot all about it until I saw you two looking at each other. So technically, I am not the Empress. Let's keep this between you and me for now. Perhaps one day, we can use this to make each other very happy." I put a tiny ray of hope into his mind and heart.

On March 5, 702, we met the field generals here at the inn. General Alexandr had taken over the entire main dining room area and had his large map on display. Deimos, head held high, began to outline the grand plan to these men who would be carrying it out. A dozen Holy Paladins, who were leading the massive supply wagon convoys, were here just as the Pope had promised. With these men from Megalos were a large number of nuns, who would tend to the wounded.

"We move our mighty legions up the road all the way to New Barq, where the Santi have already surrendered the city to us. From there, we move on Zargarb, striking the first two fortresses here on its border. Once we have taken those two, we press on to the actual city and take it." On paper and ignoring any Santi action, it looked like a good plan.

"Now Legion 45, your task is vital to our success. We suspect that the yellow giant, Tashien, will attempt to come to the aid of the Santi in Zargarb. The only way that they can come is here through the Sud area and up the very road that we travel. Consequently, you have been given a large number of heliographs. Four times each day, signals are sent northward to us. This way, you will give us advance warning of their army, and we can prepare to deal with them."

I didn't point out that they could even more easily get to us by the same route that we had followed last lifetime, when Renzo and gang had come to rescue us in the Desert of Desolation. If they landed way north where the mountains reached the sea, they would be but two weeks travel from New Barq, not months from Sud. However, I knew that Linda had not and would not call upon aid from Tashien. Our objective was to keep Tarra quiet so that the Guardian of the Anuir, Jes Amir, could continue his work of freeing spiritual beings. Bringing in hordes of Tashien soldiers would turn this into a global war, something we were trying desperately to avoid at all costs.

I learned that already most of the legions had been moving northward in long lines. Each legion was followed by numerous supply wagons with several nuns aboard. Essentially, we would be bringing up the rear of the mighty army.

The men discussed the plans for quite some time, while I rather dozed in my chair. Later, we ate our last fine meal at the inn. From now on, it would be trail food for us all. We spent our last night in a soft comfortable bed, here at the inn.

Chapter 14 On the Trail

I sat tall in my saddle, holding the reins between my teeth. I felt like Empress on parade. All the Centurions and thousands of onlookers watched the official launching of the mighty army of Demokritos on its prophesied war of global conquest. The streets were packed with cheering people. At least I didn't have to have a fake smile plastered on my face, I concentrated on not screwing up, keeping my horse beside that of the waving Emperor. Deimos was exuberant, naturally with such a scene. I hoped it didn't go to his head; doom lay before us, though I wasn't sure just whose doom it was.

Finally, we left the last traces of the city of Sud behind us. Open countryside lay on either side. The cheering crowds were gone. "That was some send off, Maren!" Deimos said happily.

"Don't let it go to your head, Deimos," I muttered through my teeth. He smiled, he was not about to let me destroy his elated feelings of the moment.

We rode until noon, at which time we paused for a break. "You are going to have to help me down, Deimos," I said after dropping the reins and wiggling the soreness from my jaws.

He looked at me and saw that there was no one else but him to do this. "Er, what do I do? How?"

"You put your arms out to catch me. I will lean over and drop into you." I did so, but he nearly dropped me. Ah well. I walked back to the carriage, if only to work the stiffness out of them. Deimos had the luxury of using his hands.

"That was some send off," Zenovia said to me, as Hans helped her step out of the coach. "I wonder what the reception will be on the return trip?"

"Or if there is a return trip," Amara added as she joined us. Hans next helped Lyris down.

"Maren, we are so useless," Lyris said as she came up to me.

"Yes, not much to do but sit and ride. It will be boring. Just remember each day brings us closer to Velona. I wish that you three would not have to see the battlefield after the combat is finished. If it is too gruesome, have Hans shut the blinds on the carriage. Come on, let's get someone to get us a drink and then some food, I'm starving." I knew that this portion of the trip would be the worst part for these three women — nothing to do but sit in a carriage all day long, mile after mile. At least at night there would be more activity.

Indeed there was. Late in the afternoon, the army stopped for the night. A bustle of activity arose at once. Tents were pitched, cooking fires lighted, horses unsaddled, watered and fed. Hans took charge of setting up our tent. Mia and Eirena took care of setting up the rest of the camp. I took the three others off to gather some firewood.

"Honestly, Maren, how are we to get the firewood?" Lyris said rather annoyed with me. "We have no arms to carry even one stick."

"Hold it between your head and shoulder. Come on, I'll show you. We will have to make a number of trips, but it will give us something to do." Yes, we had many stares from the nearby soldiers who watched us dragging small deadwood awkwardly back to Mia. It did give them something to do anyway.

By the time that we accomplished this task, Eirena had the beds ready, and Mia was all set to cook our dinner. Later, Deimos and Alekos joined us. "Maren, I have assigned one of the supply wagons to travel with you. A Holy Paladin and a nun will handle the cooking and firewood gathering for you," Deimos said, sitting down to eat with us. Rats, he just took one simple thing we could do away from us. Ah well, he meant well by it. My three companions, however, were overjoyed with his gift.

During the next few days, I began toobserve this army closely and the tactics being employed during the massive troop movement. I was grateful that they had none of those war chariots with the scything blades that cut enemy bodies to shreds. Evidently, those were unique to Megalos. Two lifetimes ago, as Ket Bethany, I had commanded the Santi Strike Force. Now I compared my field movement tactics to those of General Alexandr.

What a difference between our tactics. He marched legion after legion straight up the road. Each legion's supply wagons and nun nurses followed along behind the men that they supplied. No scouts were out flanking our lines on either side, as I would have done immediately. He had no scouts at all, for that matter. All told, there were seventy-five legions on the move, but one more was being broken down into heliograph signal men, pairs left behind at key locations. At these locations, such as at the top of a tall hill, they would be able to see the reflected sunlight signals from further down south, relaying the messages up to the General.

His tactic was simply this: with such a large force, who would dare interfere in any way? Now I also realized that this supreme general was not very competent at warfare other than those he had studied: one line versus another line. He had no concept of guerilla warfare. Considering the hundreds of miles to cover, had the Santi been interested in attacking this army, they would have suffered significant casualties long before they ever arrived at New Barq. This deficiency worried me, though I didn't yet know why.

The third day out from Sud, the early afternoon sun scorched down relentlessly. I was on the right side of Deimos. General Alexandr rode in front of him; Alekos rode behind us. Fifty of our protection legion walked in front of the general; fifty walked behind Alekos. Behind them came our carriage and bringing up the rear were the many supply wagons for us and our legion. Far behind them walked the heliograph legion, which stopped periodically to establish another outpost. Seventy-four more legions were stretched out for miles in front of us.

Having to hold my reins in my teeth forced me to keep my head up and eyes open. Just then, I spied a sudden flash of light reflection off something in the small woods off to our left, some two hundred feet. I moved up above my body for a better look. As I watched, ten men with bows in their hands moved into firing position. Without warning, ten arrows came flew at our left flank. Five of these were aimed at Deimos; the others were slightly ahead and behind his position. I reacted instantly, deflecting each of the five coming towards Deimos downward. They shattered harmlessly onto the road just at his horse's feet.

Deimos screamed in panic and shock at suddenly finding himself a target. I heard two arrows impacting something, one ahead of me and one behind me. I didn't have time to bother looking; I was still watching the archers, who were notching another flight of arrows. One man seemed to be giving orders to the others, I noticed. Again, I had to react lightning fast, to deflect another five headed at Deimos. Yet, I heard another impact something ahead of me. I latched onto the man who I though was giving the orders, lifted him up into the air a ways, perhaps five feet off the ground, and held him there.

Seeing their leader somehow magically held, wiggling and screaming for help, unnerved the other ambushers, who turned and retreated into the woods. I saw a hundred Centurions now breaking into an all-out run towards the position of the archers. Only when they reached the wildly struggling man, did I slowly lower him to the ground and move back towards my head.

Now I picked up the complete chaos of our forces. Ahead of me, I saw Alexandr had an arrow in his left arm and one in the left flank of his horse. I whirled around to see how Alekos had fared. His horse had taken a hit as well. Both men were struggling to maintain control of their panicking horses. A number of Centurions ran up and formed a protective human shell around Deimos and us. People were shouting conflicting orders in all directions.

"Deimos, are you hurt?" I asked, trying to get him out of his panic. His hands were white, gripping his reins like a vice. "Deimos, help me dismount, please."

He turned towards me, fear in his eyes. Yet, he began to act. He dismounted, but his knees nearly gave out as he touched the ground. I leaned over for him to catch me, but I was prepared to catch my own body, should he lose grip of me. He very nearly did. "Thanks. I'm okay too."

We turned to look at the action on our left flank at the start of the woods. I noticed that the bottom of his pants were quite wet. I grinned to myself, recognizing what had happened. "Hold Alekos's horse for him,

Deimos," I ordered, seeing the advisor nearing a panic level, unable to control is horse. Deimos took the reins, and Alekos dismounted as fast as he could, he lost his footing and sat down hard on the ground. Still he was relieved to be off the horse.

At least Deimos had a calming effect on the horse, which now began to stand still. Hans came running up to us. "You all okay?" he yelled as he approached.

"Alexandr took an arrow to his shoulder, Hans. Two in the horses. See what you can do for them," I suggested.

"You got it. Good work on the arrows and capturing the leader of these ambushers," he said.

He went to assist Alexandr, who had dismounted and was holding his arm, watching his Centurions bringing the captured man over towards him. "Hold a minute Hans," the general grimaced. He wanted to interrogate this assassin himself. I moved quietly closer so that I could hear, Deimos did likewise.

"What is your name? Who ordered you to attack the Emperor of Demokritos? Out with it man, before I take this arrow and stuff it down your throat!" Alexandr was angry.

"Ain't say'n 'nothen," the man replied.

Several Centurions twisted his arms, causing him to cry out in pain. "Lots more where that came from! Talk, if you want to live." Alexandr was losing his temper rapidly, understandably because of the arrow in his shoulder had to be hurting like the devil about now.

"Shall we beat it out of him, Sir?" a Centurion suggested.

"Yes, have at him. Okay, Hans. Do you know what you are doing or should I wait for the nuns?"

"Relax, I know something about healing. This is going to hurt. Got to pull it out." Hans gave a strong, sharp pull. Alexandr groaned, but didn't yell out. He had to set a good example for his men, I figured. By the time the nuns arrived, Hans had the wound bled and ready for bandaging, which he allowed the nuns to handle.

He turned to me, "They are not going to beat it out of him, Maren."

"I know. Let's see what we can tell just by observing, shall we? Steady me; this ground around here is a little rough." Hans out an arm around my waist, steading me, and we slowly walked over to where they were beating him with their fists. By the time we arrived, he was unconscious and the beating had stopped. The Centurions began strip-searching him, looking for concealed weapons and such. This gave Hans and me time to examine him for ourselves.

"Megalos, Holy Paladin?" Hans suggested. I agreed, for we had both seen many of these men. The skin coloration was right; his muscles looked like those of a fighter. His legs were slightly bowed, a sure sign that he spent long hours in the saddle. "He'll die before he speaks," Hans concluded. I didn't doubt him, but an idea began to percolate in the back of my mind, as we returned to check on Deimos and Alexandr.

"Your men have beaten him unconscious," I said flatly. "Yet Hans and I believe that he is from Megalos. See his skin coloration for yourself. It's darker than yours is. Second, look at his arm muscles and then his legs. We believe that he is a Holy Paladin of the Church of Jehosanity. You are never going to get him to say that though."

"Damn that Pope anyway," Alexandr was in an ill humor.

"I have an idea you might try when the prisoner regains consciousness. Watch him closely and tell him something like, 'You don't need to speak; we already have found out that you are one of the Pope's Holy Paladins.' You should see some visible confirmation from him, like surprise that you found out." Alexandr nodded.

A while later, after water thrown on the man, he was awake once more. Alexandr yelled at him. "You don't need to talk now. We have already figured out that you are one of the Pope's Holy Paladins. Take him away." I saw the telltale reaction on his face that gave him away; Alexandr also saw that. He added, "And execute him for high treason."

By now the foot soldiers who had given chase to the other archers returned with the news that they got away on horseback. Alexandr had to be satisfied that he only got the one man. With the horses patched up, fresh mounts were brought for Alekos and the general. I noticed that Deimos had snuck off to his supply wagon to change his pants. He returned now asking what had been discovered.

As we prepared to continue on our way, Deimos asked, "Maren, what did Hans mean about those arrows coming at me? The man must have been a terrible shot; they all fell just short of me."

"I stopped all ten of them, rather just pushed them out of the way, silly. Otherwise, you would look like a dressmaker's pincushion right now. I grabbed a hold of the one that appeared to be their leader and held him until the Centurions had him. You owe me one or is it ten that you owe me, one for each arrow?" I teased him a little. The time to hide all my skills had gone. I needed Deimos alive, if I were to yet find a way to stop this war from happening.

"But how? How could you do all that? You don't even have any arms to catch them?" he asked.

"So you have noticed that I don't?" I teased him with a big grin. "Alright, call it my 'magic' then if you will. I kept those ten from hitting you or your horse. Let's leave it at that. After all, the prophesy does say that I need to be at your side, only no one bothered to ask why that is so." After this, he looked at me somewhat differently. I could tell that a gulf between he and me was growing. I exceeded anything in his worldview.

In our tent that night, Hans said, "You'd think they would learn from that, yet they continued on their way as if nothing had happened!"

"Rather stupid of them, Hans. Their idea of warfare may be good when you get two armies lined up to clash with each other, but it is failing miserably in the current situation. Expect more ambushes ahead."

"What about us? We're defenseless!" Lyris asked, a note of fear in her voice.

"You are not defenseless, only you don't know it. We should level a bit more with you three. Hans is trained to be my protector, Mia, also. Both of them are very capable of protecting you. They will not let any harm come to you." She seemed a bit relieved hearing this and looked at both of their smiling faces.

Not two days later, we were ambushed in precisely the same way. Once more, I kept Deimos from being hit on the first volley. This time, Alexandr had placed a row of archers on the outer flanks. They returned fire at once, preventing a second volley of arrows. Four of the ambushers were killed, while the rest escaped on horseback as before.

"You are living a charmed life, my Emperor," Alexandr said to Deimos, as we mounted up to continue on our way. The four dead also appeared to be Holy Paladins, less their distinctive tunics and heavy armor of course. Deimos thought about telling the general that it was the Empress who was protecting him, but decided against it. He couldn't explain how I could have possibly have done such a thing. He didn't want to appear a fool before his mighty general.

At camp that night, Eirena was all over Deimos, urging him to be extra careful, telling how lucky he was not to have been shot, how glad she was that he wasn't harmed, and how brave he was sitting up there leading his army. At first, he greatly enjoyed her kind words, but then he admitted to her, "Eirena, I'm not brave; at least I don't feel that way. I'm quite scared. I wet my pants the first time. Maren had me go change before anyone noticed. I hope I fare better when we get to the actual battles."

"Deimos, Eirena, there is nothing nice and pretty about a battlefield. Wait until you see dead bodies, mutilated bodies, men with their arms hacked off, men dying of chest wounds, blood flowing out of their mouths. That lies ahead if you continue on this course, which is not what the prophesy is telling you. It will be the most horrid thing you could ever witness. A couple months more and you can vomit your stomachs out after the battle is over."

"But we will win, won't we?" Eirena asked, very concerned now about the safety of Deimos.

"Who can say? You are going against the prophesy. None of us may survive this battle." I left it at that, doom and gloom. I just had to reach Deimos and get him to reconsider before it was too late.

A week later, while I was just about to fall asleep in our tent, Sally contacted me from Patri. *Sally here, Maren, you were right. The Holy Paladins have come out of hiding and are now trying to enforce a new law: that everyone must go to church on Sunday or be arrested. King Milo is helpless to stop it, what with only one legion against some thirty Holy Paladin legions that are here now.*

Any word on Hektor?

None yet. Rumors have him fielding an army, have him vacationing on some island, and have him off fishing in a lake. We are constrained to stay here in Patri, so we cannot tell for sure. Dag is going to start going to this new Cardinal's High Mass. Perhaps he will get some overall feel where this is all headed. How's everything with you?

Twice the Emperor has been ambushed by disguised Holy Paladins. I've kept him from harm thus far. Alexandr knows little about how to run an actual field operation, I can tell you that. Keep me posted.

Weeks later, we came to Oldavai Pass. Here sheer rock walls rose a hundred feet on either side of the canyon floor, where the road wound along. The land was very hilly here on the southern entrance. I tried to recall how long this pass was and what lay on the other side, but I couldn't. Already seventy-four legions had passed through this pass without incident. Me, the hairs on my neck bristled. If I were laying a trap, this would be the perfect spot for it.

I tried to tell Deimos, but he couldn't understand my words well, talking through my teeth. I didn't dare use my telepathy on him yet. *Hans, I don't like the looks of this. You be alert back there.*

As we rode along, actually our horses were merely walking along so as not to outpace the Centurions on foot ahead of us, I saw the first group of fifty enter the pass. So far, nothing, perhaps I was just being paranoid after all.

Several things happened nearly simultaneously. Ahead, I saw two huge boulders begin to fall down from the top of the cliffs, one on either side. In yelling to Deimos, I dropped the reins from my teeth, rats, but he saw the boulders falling now. While our attention was directed forward, over the hills on either side, mounted riders came charging at us. I watched the developing scene carefully, trying to ascertain just what would likely be happening in a minute or so. One large group rode on a line to cut off the fifty Centurions who were behind the carriage and the supply wagons. A second wave made a direct line towards our front Centurions, those that were not going to be cut off by the boulders, which I now heard crashing thunderously on the road. Yet a third line, though far fewer, were headed straight for us, Deimos and myself. Damn. I needed help dismounting. Worse, in these boots, I could not even dodge or move quickly, if on foot. This attack may well force me to reveal what I had been carefully hiding, all my Santi spells!

Alexandr spun around on his horse, sizing up the situation. He began yelling orders to form up a battle line near the rear of those Centurions who had yet to enter the pass. I saw Deimos following him, a petrified look on his face. No one was looking at me, so I lifted my body off my horse and onto the ground. I was about fifty feet from the carriage and saw Hans at one of the doors, his sword at the ready, and Mia at the other door. She had a dagger, but I knew she would be using her Judger spells in preference. I was clearly in the open now. At the dismal pace I could walk, I'd never get to them before I was overtaken by the riders. I lifted my body an inch off the ground and moved it rapidly to the carriage. The driver had climbed down and drawn his sword, but couldn't figure out where exactly to position himself.

"To Hans," I ordered the driver and moved over to the other side to assist Mia. She, seeing me standing along outside the carriage, opened the door and stepped out to protect me. Like a speeding Tashien rocket, the three waves hit us. Sword upon steel shields and swords echoed from behind the carriage, battle had been joined. We could not expect help from the rear. Ahead, the second wave had engaged the general and his forces. I saw that Deimos had been moved to the rear, where the boulders now lay. That was the safest place for him. I gave the general a point for that move. The third, but smaller group descended upon the coach.

Seeing only women, the riders reined in and began to dismount. That gave us some time. "Out, everyone out. Hans, you and the driver, on this side. We stand a better chance of holding them off if we are together." Mia hastily began lifting the three women out, while I had them move beside me, our backs against the coach. At last, Hans and the driver came racing around the back of the coach, taking up a position just in front of us six women. I was on the left side of the women, Mia, on the far right.

I heard Mia say something in a language that I did not understand! Zenovia replied, using the same language. Although I wondered what that was all about, I had no time to dwell on it, as ten men with swords drawn began to move towards us. On either side of us, the sounds of battle raged, yet here things went at a slower pace. One man called out to Hans, "Surrender the women and we won't kill you." Hans said nothing, but studied their movements. The leader made a hand signal, and the ten closed upon us. The driver and Hans engaged several of these enemy fighters.

Two men closed upon Mia; I heard her chant. I concentrated on the three who were coming towards me, flanking the engaged men. I picked up a lose boulder and threw it at the one nearest me, hitting him squarely in the head. He dropped as fast as the boulder did. Out of throwing material already, I picked up one of the men and gave him a pitch, his body arced into the air and landed a good distance away. Now the third man was so close to my body that I could smell his breath. "Gotcha," he said.

I latched on to his head and threw it back as hard as I could. Oops, it was a little too hard, his neck snapped, and his body dropped like a sack at my feet.

On the other side, as the first man drew close to Mia, she took control of his mind and forced his body to turn around and walk back the way he came. This caused two others with him some initial confusion, but they saw that she was concentrating on their buddy and moved to get her. Mia dropped her connection to the original one and sent an illusion into the mind of the one so close to her. The man saw that his face was on fire, dropped his sword, slapping the flames with his hands to put them out, and ran screaming away from her. The third she had no time to handle.

Just as that man reached out to grab hold of Mia, Zenovia acted. Swinging her foot upwards, she timed it perfectly, delivering a solid punch to the man's privates. He doubled over, howling in pain. She then did a circle swing with her left leg, connecting with the man's neck. Using that for leverage, she swung her other leg up and locked both together, twisting her body sharply at the same time. Zenovia achieved the desired effect; she heard a loud snap from the man's neck at the same time as she hit the ground hard with her butt. Now she had to awkwardly untangle herself from the dead man and get to her feet, no small feat for her. Eirena jumped to side and helped her regain her feet, giving the dead man a kick as well. Yet, this had given Mia enough time; both of the original two men were now running away from the area, believing they were on fire.

The noise of combat in front of us ceased, our driver slumped to the ground, badly wounded. Hans was bleeding from a slice on his arm, but the other men lay in worse shape than he upon the ground before his feet. "You all right?" he called out.

"Mia, get to his arm, I'll keep guard with Eirena," I ordered. One of the wounded men tried valiantly to take a stab at Mia as she was fastening a makeshift bandage on Hans. I acted without thinking. I kicked at his head. My steel spike on my right boot went into his left eye, burying itself deep in his head. I nearly fell over trying to get it out. Zenovia moved over to me and leaned against me, followed at once by Eirena. Their help allowed me to keep my balance, and it came out. "Thanks. Death by heels," I joked.

Zenovia grinned and nodding her head towards the man she had eliminated, replied "Death by legs."

I looked at the frightened Amara and Lyris. "You two, go over to those fallen men and stomp on their necks. Make sure that they will not stab at Mia, while she is tending to Hans." Realizing at last that there was something that they could do, that they were not useless and helpless, they each moved over to a fallen enemy and stomped hard on the necks. Albeit the men were already dead, but neither they nor I cared about that. With abandon, they now stomped on the eight fallen enemy men.

"There, I feel lots better, Maren," Lyris declared.

"Me too, foul men! Who ever heard of attacking a woman of the Eighth Degree?" Amara stated angrily.

"What happened to Deimos?" Eirena asked, suddenly remembering him.

"Last I saw, Alexandr moved him back to the boulders, where he will be safest. He'll probably be just fine." She looked incredibly relieved to hear this.

Slowly, the noise of the battle died down. I cautioned everyone to stay put, they would come for us when it was safe. I had visions of a wounded enemy stabbing at anything that move by him. I saw some of the men ride off, back the way that they came, a sure sign that we outlasted them on this sortie.

A little while later, we saw Deimos making his way towards us. As he approached, his face was white as a sheet. I thought for a second that he had been wounded. "Are, are, are you all right?" he said, slightly in shock.

"Deimos over here. Eirena, you look after him. Sit down, Deimos before you collapse. Don't let him pass out; keep him talking, Eirena." That gave her something useful and positive to do. He did as I asked.

Mia was now working on our driver, who had sustained several serious wounds. "I don't think he will make it, Maren," she whispered to me.

"Okay we did our best. Since the battle is over, get Hans into the carriage and get him properly fixed up. I don't want these nuns touching him."

"You got it. Holler if you need anything." Hans willingly climbed into the coach, followed by Mia. I knew that she would soon be stitching up his cut and properly bandaging it. Best not to have these others see that, I thought.

"Say, can you ladies roll those dead men way away from us?" I thought that would give them something else useful to do. With abandon, Zenovia, Amara, and Lyris began working together to roll each of the eight dead men far away from our carriage. I continued to keep a sharp lookout.

A bloodied General Alexandr came limping up to us, "Everyone okay back here?"

"Yes, Hans took a wound, but our brave driver died protecting us, sir," I replied. "Good job on protecting the Emperor." He managed a slight grin. Militarily, this was a disaster! He had been caught in a significant ambush that ought to have killed his lieges. That we were mostly unharmed seemed a miracle to him. At this point, many nuns came up from the rear, and began caring for the wounded, beginning with Alexandr. I had not heard how Alekos had fared and went in search of him. I found him sitting on one of the two boulders, head buried in his hands.

"Folly, tis but folly," he said when he heard me approach; heels upon the stone roadway could only mean me. "I figured you all were goners. How bad is it?"

"Hans took a wound, and our driver is dead. The rest of us are unharmed. How about you?"

"I did as best I could to keep Deimos safe. We lost way too many men today, just look at them." I saw a dozen wounded men, looking after each other. Another twenty lay motionless on the ground, dead presumably.

"Nice thinking. I wanted to make sure you were all right. I'll go back to the others now, come with?" He rose and slid his arm around my waist, steading me. I smiled at him. I had not even asked for this minor kindness.

Indeed, death toll hit sixty-three, with twenty-two wounded. Alexandr had no choice but to pull another legion off the assault list and reassign them to protecting us. Because of the boulders, we were delayed here nearly a week. So hard had the boulders hit, that the pavement was shattered and had to be repaired before we could continue.

That night after supper, Eirena and Deimos went for a walk, supposedly to visit the wounded. She was bringing them some hot tea for them. We five had our tea in our tent, where we could talk. Hans had dozed off, his arm hurting like the devil now.

Amara asked, "Mia, when they came at us, you said something to Zenovia, but I didn't recognize the language. Is that Annelise?"

Mia looked at Zenovia, then spoke, "As Maren Bethany has said, we are all immortal spiritual beings and have had many of these bodies over time."

"We know that now, Mia, but what has that to do with this?" asked Amara, who felt that her question was not being answered.

"I'm getting to it. Last lifetime, I came from Demokritos, Kefall, to be precise. I was one of you, a woman of the Eighth Degree. Unfortunately, my husband ended up having an affair with my very own handmaiden, blatantly rubbing my nose in it."

"But that is never supposed to happen," Amara replied, very upset that such could ever occur.

"Oh, yes it happens, happens very frequently as a matter of fact. However, you never, ever hear about unfaithful husbands. You want to know why?"

"They ought to be hanged for that! We gave them the ultimate sacrifice, and they betrayed that!" declared Lyris.

"That is the sole purpose of the Kali," Mia said softly, allowing her pronouncement to register.

"What? The Kali Assassins?" Amara said in disbelief.

"Yes, you see, they have always been against the Holy Degrees and worked hard to ensure that those of us who sacrificed herself for her husband were not then later betrayed. My husband met with an 'accident.' The Kali gives everyone else the impression that they are evil assassins, but that is just their cover."

"Are you saying that the Kali are really protecting us?" asked Lyris.

"You bet, that is their sole purpose now, to make sure that you are treated with dignity and great honor. When the Kali suspect a husband is slipping, they send him a 'reminder' as the first step. Sometimes, that has been enough to get the husband back to being honest with his wife."

"Well, I sure didn't know that! I think that is wonderful, but have there really been that many unfaithful ones?" asked Amara. "Gosh, that must have been devastating to you, Mia, when you saw him with your handmaiden, who is supposed to be helping you with nearly everything in life. Too awful for words even!"

"It was. For a time, I felt so helpless, so hopeless. I cried for weeks. Then, I did something about it. I joined the Kali myself. I worked my way up the command ladder and ended up being the leader of the Kali in Kefall. That's when I met the Santi Explorers Circle and Bethany Rose Wilkins le'Goeur; she changed my life forever. She did her therapy on me, much as Maren has done for you three. I went with her to Velona, learned their ways, and became one of their most trusted Guardians. When my body died, I came down here and got a new one in Hodenhagen, Annelise. More important, I have not forgotten anything that I knew last lifetime, only now I am even more powerful because I still have my arms, you see." That was a tease, and we all grinned, as if having arms had anything to do with our spells.

Zenovia decided to level with them as well. "When Mia spoke to me, she used the secret language spoken only by the Kali." She paused for a minute, watching the two women's reaction. Both realized what she had to be implying.

"You?" Lyris said.

"You're Kali?" Amara added.

"Yes, my husband betrayed me as well. I caught him in bed with one of my younger servants. I cannot begin to tell you how I felt seeing him with her, naked, going at it. I gave him everything. I vomited even. I let the Kali know, but they already had their suspicions. He met with an 'accident' too. Later, I too decided to do something about this and am the Kali leader in Kefall, well, not at this moment. I've left another in charge while I am gone. Mia told me to use my assassin skills if any men got by her. You saw what happened to the one that did. I broke his neck. Never mess with a Kali trained woman. I may not have arms, but that does not make me any less dangerous."

"Thank you for the assist, Zenovia. I was in deep trouble, more than I could handle," Mia said.

"Say, why did the two men run away, flapping their heads? It looked weird," Lyris asked, remembering that strange scene.

"In their minds they saw that their heads were all aflame. They totally believed my little illusion and fled as if their heads were on fire," Mia explained.

Amara, astute Amara, asked, "Did you learn how to do this in Velona with the Santi, Mia?"

She smiled, "You bet. That and a whole lot more. Now do you see why Maren is so keen on getting you three safely to Velona?"

"Maren, will we actually be able to learn these things?" asked Amara.

"You three are sitting behinds your heads now, right?" I asked. All three nodded. "The simple answer is the sky is the limit to what you can learn. However, I caution you, it may take you ten years to master the type of illusions that Mia can create. She is a master at that."

All three were impressed with my reply. After a pause, Lyris asked, "Where does Hans fit in? He's your husband, right?"

"After I became a woman of the Eighth Degree and was so horribly betrayed by the one man that I loved and gave all for, I swore that I would never be with a man ever again. I didn't either, not until I was in Velona getting my advanced training. That's when I met Hank; he was my advanced studies teacher. He turned out to be my heartthrob! He's the greatest man alive! We got married and had a bunch of children. Those were such happy years — it was what this Holy Eight Degrees was supposed to be all about. Anyway, we loved each other so much that we are continuing our marriage this lifetime too. Hans, there, is my Hank."

Zenovia asked curiously, "Say, Mia, what was your name when you were in Kefall?"

"Kallisto."

"Not *the* Kallisto.

"Yes, *the* Kallisto.

"The Kallisto who?" asked Lyris.

"A famous leader of the Kali in Kefall — my mentor spoke very highly of her," Zenovia replied.

I noticed that these women were highly intelligent. I wondered how long it would take them to derive the conclusion, with respect to me. Not long, I'm afraid.

Amara thought aloud, "Well, if you were this Kallisto last lifetime and you remembered everything and are using that now, as we saw you doing, what about Maren here? This therapy, is it not the same kind of therapy that you have been saying is done in Velona? I remember someone saying a woman named Jenna Rose Weston invented it and her daughter Bethany used to do a lot of it as well on women like us. How is it that Maren knows how to do this incredible therapy? She comes from Annelise too. You and she look an awfully lot alike, including your large bosoms. Do they teach how to do this therapy in Hogenhagen?"

"Amara, Lyris, Zenovia, can you keep a secret? What I am going to tell you must never be heard by another around here. Promise?" All three did. From the eager looks in their eyes, I knew they expected something earth shaking.

"I'll tell you my name last lifetime, first." I paused and watched their faces, until they were about to force it out of me. "Bethany Rose Wilkins le'Goeur." I sat there quietly while they absorbed this key datum.

"Well now it makes sense. I mean how you could work those miracles on us! You saved Lyris's life, I know that!" Amara said.

"No wonder you can do so many, well strange things, like with those arrows," Lyris added.

Zenovia made the vital deduction. "She was the Santi del Dio leader last lifetime! Now she is the Empress whose husband is heading there to conquer the Santi held lands!"

"Yes, that's right. I want you to know that I have not betrayed Deimos. I know now that he and everyone else, including the Santi, have badly misunderstood the prophesy. I am trying my best to get him to re-evaluate the prophesy before it is too late. While I don't know what the Santi will do — I haven't been in Zargarb for nearly sixteen years now — what I have been saying is indeed a reality, especially that dragon cannon thing. I saw it in operation. Who knows what else they have developed for their defense since then?"

"Why don't you just kill Deimos and be done with it?" asked Lyris.

"I will not betray him, just as you would never dream of betraying your Maximus, nor he, you. Secondly, if I did, that would not stop the prophesy, another Emperor would be chosen, and he would pick up right here where Deimos left off. No, I must get Deimos to somehow see that he and many others are completely misunderstanding the prophesy and get him on the right path. The path to glory is not through war, but through trade. Yet, if I cannot do so, I feel that we may all perish in the attempt. However, you three will be still taken to Velona. I have made Mia and Hans promise that if anything happens to me, they will see that you get safely there and helped. I want you three to have a chance at a wonderful life. I love you three too much not to do so."

"Can I ask you something, Maren?" Lyris asked, a curious look on her face.

"Sure, just don't ask me or Mia how big our bosoms are supposed to get; we don't want to know!" Everyone laughed at that, already Mia's were larger than the other women we had around us; mine were right behind hers now.

"Will we be able to remember everything from this life when we have our next one? Does that even make sense?" Lyris asked.

"Who can say? Yet, if you do get the training I want you to get, there is a strong likelihood that you will, especially after all the therapy I've given you. When we are safe in Velona, I will try to give you all some more of it as well."

"That is interesting. Thanks. Say will we be at a big disadvantage learning all these things in Velona, since we are like this, I mean, women of the Eighth Degree?" asked Zenovia.

"Bethany Rose was also of the Eighth Degree," I replied.

"What? You mean you were like us last lifetime? And you did all that?" Lyris said flabbergasted.

"Arms have nothing to do with the abilities you have potentially available. Yes, no arms makes daily life most troublesome at times, perhaps unbearable at others, but the things that I do I am doing, not my body. Yes, I would like my body to be able to pick up my own teacup. I just learned other ways of doing it, my feet. You will be utterly amazed just what is possible. King Hektor also discovered that himself when he visited Velona last year."

Of course, that reminded Lyris of Maximus. "I wonder what has become of Hektor? Do you suppose that he is trying to get revenge for my Maximus?"

"Honestly, Lyris, I do not know what his plans are or where he disappeared to after he left. He is a fine man," I replied honestly.

"I am not a fine man; I hurt badly," Hans muttered half-awake; pain had awakened him. Mia went to tend to him.

Zenovia looked at me and said, "Maren, I don't know if I should say this or not. All this talk of unfaithful husbands and all, well I remembered something I've seen. It's about Deimos. Maybe I should keep my mouth shut, Maren."

"Out with it, Zenovia, what have you seen?"

"Well, I've noticed that Deimos has been gazing an awful lot at your maid, Eirena. She positively dotes on him. She watches him every chance she gets. I just wanted to give you a heads up warning. I've not seen them doing anything unfaithful, mind you, just looks."

"I've never been good at telling when others are in love or even when I am in love. Yet, I do know that those two are very likely so. Please don't worry about it, Zenovia." I looked at three shocked faces, however. Here was yet another man about to be unfaithful to a woman of the Eighth Degree.

"Can you promise to never say a word of this to anyone, especially Eirena?" They did so.

I lowered my voice, "Deimos and I were never officially married. Alekos had a hand in that, I suspect. I think that he reasoned that if I did not work out as Empress, Deimos would be free to get rid of me — we not being officially married. Please, do not say anything about this to anyone. Yes, Deimos knows this; we've talked about it." If these women were going to be successful in Velona, they would have to keep their integrity intact. This was a little test of that. Would they keep quiet? I believed that they would or I would not have said what I had said.

The next day, I had a chat with Deimos. "Can I give you a little piece of tactical advice, Mr. Emperor?" He was willing to listen, so I explained. "From now on, you should sent out scouts on either flank, probably out at least a mile on either side. Let's not be taken by surprise again. Yesterday, we got very, very lucky. Either you or I could have easily been killed. Alexandr will not listen to me, but maybe he will listen to you, Deimos. It is about time that you started making decisions around here, before Alexandr gets us all killed." He promised that he would do so. It worked, when we started back up a week later, the remains of the legion that had been protecting us were sent out wide on either flank. Now we might have some advanced warning of ambushes.

Later on, I had plenty of time for further chats with Deimos. Alexandr was in his tent, recovering from his many wounds. "Are you starting to believe me when I say that this Church of Jehosanity is not to be trusted, that they are out to kill you? This is the third attempt that they have made on your life."

"It does look that way. I don't see why they want me dead though."

"You don't have any male children, do you? If you are gone, they have to choose a new Emperor. Now who back home might be desirous of your throne, eh? I can name quite a few youthful kings. You are right, it makes no sense for this Church to want you out of the way, since after all, you are going to try to eliminate the Santi, the Church's archenemy."

"Yes, that's what I have been saying, it makes no sense."

"Ah, but what if, pick a king, say, Dimitris is desirous of becoming the next Emperor. He makes a bargain with the Pope. The Pope has you killed; Dimitris becomes Emperor, and he, with his superior fighting skills, goes after the Santi for the Church. Nice and tidy package. Just substitute any one of the coastal kingdom's kings for Dimitris. We both know that the three older kings were dead set against this assault against the Santi. One of those four kings may well be behind all this, Deimos. As long as you continue to follow this wrong interpretation of the prophesy, you are playing into their hands."

"Let me think about this, Maren," he said. After a pause, he lamented, "I wish I knew what was happening back home, if anything." I wanted to tell him, but decided against revealing I had telepathic skills.

That night, I asked Mia to come take a stroll with me, to help me keep my balance I said to the others. When we were alone, I asked her, "Mia, can you create an illusion of a rider coming up to us, handing Hans a document, and then leaving. It needs to be very believable."

"That's a tough one, if we need a fair number to believe that they are seeing it at the same time. If you give me enough time to prepare and we are not being threatened, I think so. Why?"

"The time is rapidly approaching when I need to present more convincing data to Deimos, information about what's going on back home. I cannot reveal our telepathic connections, especially with the Santi. It must look as if Darkon sent us a message. Hans will forge it, of course. We've a sample of his signature and seal."

"Okay, I will prepare myself. Let me know when you need it." We continued our little stroll. I noticed that many of the Centurion soldiers lying around their campfires were noticing us — well, these heels do attract men's attention.

We began to move once more. Unable to deter Deimos from this catastrophe, slowly I became discouraged and then down right depressed. Here I was going into a war on the front lines once more, in a body that had no arms and could barely walk on the uneven ground. What in the world was I doing? Who could come to my rescue this time? No one. Worse, if I didn't succeed, there might not be anyone left, no Velona as I knew it.

Chapter 15 Morpheus Makes His Move

April 1, 702, Cardinal Myron Morpheus called his Prelate, Brutus Felios, to his study. "It is time. By now, the Emperor is either dead or halfway to New Barq. Fall is upon us and soon the snows will come. Now is the time that we begin the Holy Work as requested by Pope Aison. How many Holy Paladins do we now have here to protect our Church?"

"Three thousand five hundred and fifty-nine, Your Eminence. That is nearly forty times what King Milo could possibly throw against us. His legion is scatted around Thrace."

"Excellent. Pope Aison is a man of his word. More than enough. As you know, I have been preparing the way with my many masses. Daily our flock of believers grows. Soon, we will not need our Paladins; the people of Thrace will work willingly for us. We will not make the blunders that we made in the Sea Princes. We have learned from history, my son." The Prelate nodded his agreement.

"Are the lists compiled?" asked the Cardinal.

"Yes, Your Eminence. As you have requested, we have discretely observed the Patri women. All those who have or would likely cause trouble for acceptance of the Church and our ways have been identified. The list is ready for consolidation," Prelate Myron, proud of his secret accomplishment, replied.

"Is the list lengthy?"

"Aye, some three hundred at this date. The Axos list contains one hundred fifty. Kefall, even less."

"Yes, we must narrow the list down to the most critical women; those will be first. Perhaps lesser women will see the errors of their ways and change their behavior after seeing how these critical ones are handled."

"Will we be taking only those from Patri first or the most critical ones from all Thrace?"

"Let us not be too hasty and overstep our growing power. The first should come from Patri, say fifty. That should be enough to get our message of earning only Good Marks across to some of these women who are lower in priority. After all, we are only doing this so that they can stop, cease, and desist the earning of Bad Marks. We only want their precious souls to go to heaven, Jehosa's Holy Realm. Let us look over these three hundred and chose our first fifty. I know our nuns are ready as are our physicians. I'm told that they can handle at least three each day. In two weeks' time, all fifty can be put on the Righteous Path to earning only Good Marks for the rest of their time on Tarra."

An hour later, the two men had made their selections. A list containing some fifty women had been culled from the lengthier list. "When will we actually begin, Your Eminence?" greedily asked the Prelate.

"After High Mass tomorrow. I will present to each of the six masses what it is that we are about to do. After all, we do not want to cause any undo alarm. We must see to it that our brethren fully support us."

"Your Eminence, may I ask a question of you?"

"Certainly my son."

"Suppose that the Emperor somehow manages to avoid the ambushes our Pope has planned for him. Suppose further that he is actually successful at conquering the Sea Princes and eliminating our archenemy the Santi. What happens when he returns home here to Thrace with his many legions? If he does not agree with what the Church is doing, could we be in jeopardy? I need to know if I am to provide the security that we need here."

"My son. While he may elude the ambushes, think about what history has taught us my son. How many legions were needed to take a walled city? Now they have many stone fortresses lining their borders, some of which must also be taken or they could easily cut off valuable lines of supply for the fighting legions. How many legions faced the Santi who wore chain mail? Now the Santi wear plate mail, making each one nearly impenetrable. How many of the Emperor's legions wear plate mail? How many of the Santi are cavalry? How many of the Emperor's army are cavalry? Now, my son, how few legions has the Emperor with him to command, this I ask you?"

"Yes, had he brought four thousand legions upon his road to conquest, nothing would stand in his way. Yet, he has but seventy-five, ill equipped and ill armed for the fight that they are walking towards, on foot, no less. If by some unforeseen miracle the Emperor could take the Sea Princes, gaining their riches, his return would be accompanied by a handful of legions at the very best. Already we have thirty here, with more slowly arriving. You need not concern yourself overly on the matter of his return, if he returns at all."

"You are wise, Your Eminence, I had not though this through so logically. You are right, should he return, so few legions would remain that he would not be able to challenge our mighty Church, even if he desired to do so. Forgive my worry."

"You are forgiven, my son. Now, let us prepare the way for the first fifty women that they may finally begin to earn only Good Marks. Come, we have work to do."

On Sunday, Dag once more forced himself to attend the Cardinal's High Mass, along with a thousand other devote worshipers. The hymns sung beforehand, he had to admit, were angelic, creating a great peace in one's mind. Perhaps, this was their intent, so that the mass was more readily accepted? At the beginning, Cardinal Morpheus spoke in his usual dreary voice, tediously outlining the basic tenants of Jehosanity.

Part way into the mass, the tone began to change. Fire came into his voice and words. "I say unto you, we must not let these precious souls, given unto us by Lord Jehosa himself, go into purgatory, the depths of fiery Hell, the realm of Lucifer himself. Nay, it is our duty, our obligation, by our will and by our faith in the Lord Jehosa that we strife, each and every one of us to earn our soul's passage to the wondrous realm of Heaven, where Jehosa doth dwell. Lord Jehosa has not given us this precious soul to waste, to squander. It is our duty, each and every one of us to do everything in our earthly power to earn our soul's right, upon our fleshly body's death, to enter that most Holy Realm."

"How is this done you say, just how doth one obtain your own soul's right to pass unto Jehosa's Realm? You have heard the Holy Decalogue. Use that as your starting guide. Earn those Good Marks each and every day. Remember, the Holy Ledger has your very name written in it. Whether or not you are even a believer in Jehosa, your name is written there upon the birth of your fleshly body, at which time Jehosa places your precious soul into the care of your physical hands. You must not earn more Bad Marks. Strive to earn Good Marks, each hour of every day."

"Now we all know some of our neighbors who have sinned, who are sinning even as we speak. Some may call them recalcitrant, others may call them liars, and others may call then temptresses. Their words may sound like honey unto thy ears. Hear them not; close thy ears to their pleadings, which would lead you to gain so many more Bad Marks. Precious life is short, brethren. What is a mere sixty years compared to all eternity that your soul has to rot in eternal damnation in the pits of Hell? A trifle at best. I say unto you, close thy ears to these temptresses that seek to lead you down the path of Bad Marks."

"Yea, I challenge you to achieve even greater Good Marks. Work to make those who do not believe, as you once did, in the Lord Jehosa. Work to make those who would tempt you to earn Bad Marks to cease and to begin to earn Good Marks. Yes, work with them, work to help them achieve nothing but Good Marks, for then you yourself gain many Good Marks on your soul's ledger. Thus when the time comes for our bodies to die, as it comes for all of us, even my humble self, and your dear, precious soul goes up to those pearly gates, the Holy Ledge entry for you allows your soul to enter Heaven for all eternity."

"As the Holy Scriptures have told us, woman created the first sin, the first fall from Holy Grace. We know that every woman born on Tarra begins with her ledger filled with the Bad Marks born from the Original Sin of Woman. Thus, all you men realize that, unlike yourselves whose ledger is balanced at birth, women have a major obstacle so often barring the road for their soul to reach Heaven, a ledger full of Bad Marks. Hence, no woman can afford to continue to earn any Bad Marks. Yes, we men, we can occasionally sin and stray from the Holy Path, costing us a Bad Mark. Yet if we take Holy Confession and do our penance, a Good Mark is added, balancing the ledger once more."

"But woman, who is born with a ledger full of Bad Marks, cannot afford any new Bad Marks, for her soul would certainly be sent to purgatory." He paused and changed his tone, "How would heaven be, men, if there were no women it for us? I ask you that? How would heaven seem to you if there were no women there, because they were all cast into Hell, burning in the eternal fires for all eternity?"

Now he turned up the volume once more. "Nay, men we must do everything we possibly can to get women to earn only Good Marks. I realize that for many of you this seems a most difficult task indeed. Yet there are two paths you may follow to assist a woman to earn only Good Marks. Your esteemed Emperor and the Grand Council has opened that path for those of you who are married. Go to the Santi and partake of the Holy Eight Degrees of Matrimony. Do it today, help her earn those Good Marks each and every day. Today, the Church of Jehosanity is offering you a second path, one for those women and girls in your lives whom you love dearly and want to help them obtain the right of their soul to enter the gates of heaven. We will perform at no cost to you or to them the appropriate Holy Degree, one chosen to assist them in achieving Good Marks. If they are straying but a little, though earning Bad Marks still, we will assist them in becoming of the Sixth Degree so that they can no longer earn these Bad Marks, but will have no choice but the earning of Good Marks. If they have strayed significantly from the Holy Path, we will assist them in becoming of the Seventh Degree. If you feel that they are so very far from redemption, that their ledger is so full of Bad Marks already, then we will assist them in becoming of the Eighth Degree that they have no choice but to earn nothing but Good Marks each and every day after, that their Holy Ledger entry will weigh in on the good column and their souls be allowed to enter heaven."

"We will begin to help these women tomorrow. Yet, if you are married, you owe it to your loving wife to go to the Santi and partake of the Blessed ceremony, as your Emperor has shown you by setting the highest example. Yet still, if you have a loved one whom is in need of earning Good Marks, bring her here unto our Church that we may assist you in helping her soul, her very precious soul, enter heaven above. I look forward to seeing so very many of you women in the future coming here to High Mass, showing for all to see, just how you are truly earning your soul's passage into Lord Jehosa's Realm of Heaven. Now let us pray for all of the souls on Tarra."

Dag's mind blocked off the quiet prayers being whispered all around him. He wanted to scream and puke at the same time. As the High Mass ended, he exited as quickly as possible, jogging through the streets of Patri to his fortress tower.

"Good god! The Cardinal has gone absolutely insane!" angrily cursed Betsy, their Healer. "How the devil are we going to deal with this? We can't handle hundreds of request for the amputations! What are we going to do for all those women who they are about to mutilate? I'm going to be inundated with botched hack jobs, traumatized women. Good lord, I never thought I'd see a day such as this, Dag." His wife was upset; he was too for that matter.

Sandy, quietly said, "I'll contact Linda for advice; we are going to need it." A little later, she reported to the others. "Linda says hello. Sometimes, I think her messages are very cryptic. She said for us to hang in there and cope. She is sending a medical caravel here today, whatever that is. Have you all heard of a medical caravel?" None had. "Well, I haven't either, but then maybe that is one of the recent developments. After all, we've been stuck down here for over a dozen years. Anyway, she says that there are yet invisible forces at work here in Patri and that we will get help from an unexpected source, whatever that means. Dag, any ideas what she is talking about? What invisible sources?"

"Dear, if we could see them, then they wouldn't be invisible, now would they?" her husband, Art attempted a stab at levity, falling a bit short.

"If there were time, I would go to King Milo and urge him to put a stop to this," Dag commented.

"Dear, there isn't time; you would be gone twenty days. I am afraid we will have more than we can handle before you could get back," Betsy countered.

"They are going to cut off the hands and arms of innocent young women!" Dag continued to protest. "While we just sit here and do nothing?"

"What can a mere three hundred of us do against nearly four thousand of them, dear? We must sit tight, hold the fortress, help as we can, and pray that Linda is right," Betsy consoled her husband. She had finally calmed down herself. "I'd better check on our supplies. We ought to try to purchase as much as we can ahead of time. How about lending me a hand, Dag?" The two went into their small infirmary and began a quick inventory.

On Monday morning, three groups of Holy Paladins, wearing their sky blue tunics with white crosses on their front and back sides, rode up to three homes in Patri At the first house, one asked, "We have come for Akanta." Her mother attempted to slam the door in his face, but his boot prevented it. They barged in and wrestled a screaming girl of thirteen to the floor, gagged her, and tied her arms behind her. "Ma'am, we will return her when she is capable of only earing Good Marks. You, as we, only want what is best for her precious soul. Right?" The poor mother had to agree, fearing to be taken herself!

At the second home, their woman was outside preparing to herd her flock of sheep to a winter shelter. "Agele, you must come with us."

"Sirs, I have to move dad's sheep. Can't it wait a while?" They overpowered the girl of fourteen, tying her hands and gagging her, before lifting her up behind one of their men. They rode straight for the church complex.

At the third home of the wealthy Philon Gavril, an uncle of Deimos, the men had to bash down the front door. "Where is Eleni? We've come to take her. She must be taught to earn only Good Marks that her soul may go to heaven." Philon refused to say. Hence, the men quickly searched the spacious home and found her hiding under her bed. Again, they gagged her to keep her from screaming, tied her up, and carried her back to the complex. The sat her on a chair next to the two other young women. Eleni was fourteen. She looked at her two terrified companions beside her, and they, her.

Cardinal Morpheus, resplendent in his new robes purchased just to celebrate this very day, walked in and stood before the three women. "You three have been doing everything possible to earn Bad Marks each and every day. With you Holy Ledgers so full of Bad Marks, your precious soul has no chance of gaining entry into Jehosa's Holy Realm, unless we assist you. After today, you will be unable to continue to earn Bad Marks and can only earn Good Marks to get your ledgers back in balance. However, I warn you three, if by some means unknown to me this day you continue to earn Bad Marks, then we will have no choice but to increase your Holy Degree. As soon as you are healed, we will send you back to your homes, there to earn only Good Marks so that your precious souls can enter heaven."

They made all sorts of protest sounds, but he merely turned sharply, his robes flaring out in a graceful arc behind him. He'd practiced that motion often to get it perfectly right. His physicians entered and led the struggling women into another room.

It was dark outside, but a nun sat patiently on a chair in the recovery room. A dim oil lantern allowed her to watch the three women. Suddenly Eleni woke up. Her arms hurt horribly, she tried to sit up, but her arms didn't respond right. She looked down at the heavy bandages wrapped around her arms where her elbows used to be. Nothing of her lovely arms remained below there. She screamed as loudly as she could. The nun, used to the women's wake up reactions, took it in stride, moving to her side.

"There, there, Eleni. It will be all right. The pain will go away in a few days. You will only be able to earn Good Marks for yourself now." When her voice was hoarse, she finally stopped screaming. It had awakened her two companions, who struggled to sit up and see how Eleni fared. Both of their arms were heavily bandaged where their wrists had been. Eleni raised what was left of her arms, while Agele and Akanta raised their arms. Both realized Eleni was in far worse shape than they were.

Earlier that afternoon, Drusus Laslos called upon Cardinal Morpheus, who granted him an audience, though he did not recognize the name. "How may I be of service, Drusus?" he used his most pious manner.

"Your Great Holiness, I have listened to you most Holy Words on Sunday. They have moved me greatly, for I have a wife and two daughters to care for. I truly want their souls to go to heaven, though I know that their ledgers began with so many Bad Marks, as you have explained to us. Would it be possible for my three dear women to partake of your appropriate Holy Degree? I would be ever so thankful if they could. Then, I can sleep at night, knowing that my three most precious women's souls will be able to enter Jehosa's Realm."

"Certainly my son. You are most wise and most caring husband and father. I so wish other fathers cared as much as you do for the souls of their loved ones. Tell me a bit about them, that I may ascertain the correct Holy Degree for each."

"My wife, Daphna, she is thirty-two, she works hard keeping our house. Cynthia is my eldest daughter who has just turned sixteen. She is to be married in three months. Then, there is my baby Charessa, who is thirteen. She, like her sister Cynthia, is very pretty. I do worry so that their beauty may yet lead them down the path to Bad Marks."

"Ah, that tells me all that I need to know, Drusus. I will see that they are given the most appropriate Holy Degree. When would you like us to perform this Holy Ceremony?"

"As soon as possible. Let us waste not a day longer. Bad Marks continue to mount up, as you tell us."

"I understand your sense of urgency. Bring them in tomorrow."

"I know that they will not come and I am only one and they, three. Could I perhaps beg you to send me some assistance?"

The Cardinal smiled, "Of course, our Holy Paladins will come tomorrow morning, while you are at work. Is this acceptable?"

"Oh yes, yes, Your Holiness, thank you, thank you. All praises to Lord Jehosa."

The next morning, a dozen Holy Paladins arrived at the home of Drusus Laslos. Once more, they tied up the three women and gagged them, before bringing them to the church complex.

Cardinal Morpheus gave his speech to the three women, who were sitting on the same three chairs the others had sat upon yesterday. "Your loving husband and father has requested that we perform the Holy Degrees upon you. He wishes to make very sure that your souls will be able to enter Lord Jehosa's Realm. This shows you the depths of his love and caring for you, his wife, and you, his lovely daughters. If only all husbands and fathers cared so deeply for their wives and daughters, heaven would be filled with you women."

Much later that day, the three awoke from the surgery, screaming as expected from the pain and heavy shock. His wife no longer had her hands. Cynthia, who was about to be married, was given the highest honor; she was of the Eighth Degree, while the younger daughter was only of the Seventh Degree, as was Eleni.

A week later, when they had recovered from the shock and the intense pain subsided, Daphna said, "Wait til I get my hands on your father! I will kill him!" She was intensely angry at what her fool of a husband had done.

Charessa managed to point out, "But mom, you no longer have any hands. How will you kill him?" She looked down at her own arms, which now ended at her elbows and cried.

Cynthia sobbed, "Mom, he won't marry me like this. You know he is totally opposed to these Holy Degrees. Now I will never be able to marry anyone. I wish I was dead, and I can't even do that anymore." She wailed for some time.

Indeed, two weeks later, when they were recovered sufficiently to have visitors, her fiancé came to visit her. One look at her pathetic body and he said, "Cynthia, the wedding is off. I don't want to marry a woman who is totally helpless. What were you thinking of?" She couldn't speak, just sobbed to herself.

Charessa stood up for her older sister, "She didn't. Dad did this to us. Kill him for us, will you. Mom wants to, but she doesn't have hands any more. Please, kill our father for us." He said nothing, quietly leaving.

Soon Drusus stopped coming to visit them. Why? Whenever he entered their room, all three cursed him, swore to kill him, and screamed for his death. As the nun escorted him out, she explained, "You must give them time to adjust to the Holy Degree. You are seeing the Devil that resides in their bodies coming out now. In a little while, the Devil will finally leave their bodies for good, and then they will be capable of only earning Good Marks. You will see. Just have faith in our lord and savior. Drusus was satisfied and asked her to send him word when the Devil had left his three dear women.

Two weeks after that first Monday, fifty-three women were now in various stages of recovery in their infirmary. That kept the nuns exceedingly busy, caring for all of these women's needs. Yet, in their minds, they were certain that they were earning themselves mountains of Good Marks by so doing. Cardinal Morpheus halted further ceremonies for a few days so that these women could be healed enough to be sent home.

While he and his Prelate were working on the next list of fifty women, King Milo Kourgos stormed into their room, pushing aside the Holy Paladins who stood guard. "What is the meaning of this, this mutilation of unwilling women? I'm up to my ears in protests."

"Calm down, King Milo. It is good to see you again. Come, take wine with me in my chambers, and I'll fill you in, this way, please." He used his most soothing, comforting voice tones. Over wine, he explained what the Church of Jehosanity was now doing to the women who refused to earn Good Marks here in Patri, saying mostly what he had said in his Holy Masses.

Milo, who supported the Church, detested the harming of women. The Cardinal quietly pointed out the key datum. He had thirty legions of Holy Paladins, while Milo had but one. Milo quietly left the Church, fuming, but unable to do anything about the situation, but send his protest on up the line to Darkon, who was acting as regent while Deimos was gone. Of course, Darkon could do little more than curse.

At his secret camp in the deserted mountains of Phindos, near the Lonki Basin, Hektor stood and stretched his old muscles. He was far too old for camping in the rough, especially on this rocky ground. He surveyed the many men milling around their tents. Hektor had called in every favor owed to him over his forty-five year reign as King of Theos.

He had just awakened from the recurring nightmare that plagued him every night. He saw the pleading look from his son's eyes, the arrow sticking out between them, he saw the begging, the pleading from his dear Angele, who stood by helpless to do anything, not even cradle his son in her arms. She had none. He felt her helplessness, and yet it was the last images that always woke him up in a cold sweat: the cries, the shrieks from Lyris, who newly armless herself, stood panic-stricken jumping up and down beside her husband, unable to respond in any way to help her dying husband. He wiped the last of his sweat from his forehead. The cooler fall temperatures had arrived, and his excess heat quickly vanished.

After breakfast, he addressed his men. "Today, we march on Patri. First stop, Kefall. Leave none of these vile men alive. Five days to Axos, then we repeat it. Five more to Patri. Only in Patri can we find relief. Are you with me?" Hundreds cheered and waved their swords.

They packed their camp, loading everything into several dozen wagons, which would follow along behind them. They mounted their horses and carefully picked their way down the steep escarpment known as Lonki Basin. Seven days later, avoiding all major towns and as many villages as they could, the Hektor Revenge Militia halted atop the last hill before entering the imperial city of Kefall. Here they waited until full dark.

Each man donned a black mask, hiding their faces. Each checked their many weapons. At last, Hektor gave the order to move out. One by one, his men rode down from the hill and into the streets of Kefall. In this city, the Cardinal had built five great churches and lived in the large rectory building, which housed their infirmary and the nun's quarters. Expecting the most resistance at the main church where Cardinal Rax Ciros dwelled, Hektor sent the majority of his forces there.

As they approached, the militia spied six Holy Paladins on guard duty around the four-foot high fence that surrounded the church, the rectory, and the infirmary. Crossbow men took their positions. Hektor gave a hand signal. The guards died before sounding the alarm. Hundreds of black clothed men leaped over the fence, scattering about the grounds. Surprise on their side, the men systematically went through the buildings, room by room, killing without hesitation anyone they found, man or woman. Occasionally, they had to fight it out with Holy Paladins rushing from their rooms, responding to the cries and sounds of battle.

When they found the sleeping Cardinal, he was dragged outside before Hektor. "This is for my son and the many other sons," the old man spoke, just before he cut the Cardinal's neck open. "Burn it to the ground," he ordered.

An hour after they had entered the city, the men left, and the hue and cry of fire began echoing through the imperial city. By morning, the Church of Jehosanity in Kefall was naught but ashes and burned stone. The Hektor Revenge Militia was thorough.

Five nights later, they repeated their actions in Axos, burning down six churches throughout the city. Low on supplies, Hektor sent dozens into Axos the next morning to buy food supplies, sending each to different quarters of the city. These men brought back far more than food.

"I am not kidding. Milo has just returned from Patri. He saw dozens and dozens of mutilated women in their recovery room. He is not going to do anything about it," the man reported.

"I think I shall pay a visit to Milo myself," Hektor replied, thinking over this horrendous and surprising news. Late that afternoon, Hektor requested an audience with King Milo and received it.

"Ah so good to see you again. How are you holding up? I am so sorry about the loss of Angele; she was fine Queen," Milo attempted to put on a friendly face. After all, it was in his kingdom that Maximus was so brutally slain.

"That's not what I am here about, Milo. What's going on down in Patri?" Milo squirmed in his seat, as if his throne had suddenly become terribly uncomfortable. He looked into the steeled eyes of old Hektor; he knew he had to fess up to the ex-king. After all, what harm was there in that? He outlined all that he had learned, heard, and seen firsthand.

"At this point, I am powerless to do anything about it. Thirty-three legions. I'll just have to wait until the Emperor and his seventy-five legions return. Then, we will set matters right," Milo explained his decision to do nothing.

Hektor slowly walked to the door, he turned and said in a soft voice, "Milo, if I was you, I would abdicate your throne and leave Axos before midnight tonight."

"Why? Come back here! I order you, come explain yourself! Hektor!" The old man ignored him and walked out of the palace, mounted his horse, and rode out of town into the hills just south of the capital city, where his camp was located.

He felt so sick that he could not eat his supper. While the campfires burned, Hektor explained what had happened and what was likely to happen down in Patri. "Thirty-three legions! Fifty women every two weeks! Criminal! Milo did nothing when they assassinated my son. Now he does nothing when fifty of his own citizens are mutilated for life. This man has failed his people."

"Sir, let us take care of it tonight," one of his aides suggested.

Hektor sighed, "Yes, thank you. Wait until midnight. If he has not left, do what is right. I feel sick. I need to lie down." He entered his tent, collapsing onto his bedroll and cried. Later, he fell into a fitful sleep. This time the nightmares increased in severity tenfold.

The next morning, he was informed that Thrace would need to choose a new king. He thanked his men, but the death of Milo brought him no relief, but he had not expected that it would. Milo was a mere pawn, and pawns are sacrificed all the time. No, this Cardinal Morpheus had to die, only then could he be satisfied his sole remaining mission in life would be complete. This was the only thing keeping him alive. They broke camp and headed for Patri, knowing that they were greatly outnumbered, with little hope of ultimate success.

That same night down in Patri, Karis K. — no one knew her actual last name — called her leaders together. "Kali, I have the saddest news that I have ever heard. This is beyond anything we've ever seen before." She wiped back her long black hair, which had slipped over her face, with what remained of her arms. Karis was of the Seventh Degree, leader of the Patri Kali. She outlined the sad tale of Drusus Laslos and what he had had done to his wife and two daughters.

As she expected, their outrage exceeded hers. "How could a man do this to his own family?" one man asked. "It is inconceivable."

Karis waved her arms, slicing the air as if her stumps were blades, "Killing is too good for this vile, wicked man. No, my friends, I have a better idea. We need to send a different message than we usually do to the unfaithful husbands of Holy Degree women, a very, very different message indeed. Tonight, go to his home and bring him hither to our hidden chamber. We will make him of the Seventh Degree and remove his tongue so that he may never utter words that may harm other women ever again. We will burn a black 'K' upon his forehead so that everyone who sees him knows that we took revenge for his wife and daughters. I will burn him myself! Go now. I foresee that we will be very busy here in Patri for days to come. Kleo, stay a while, I have something else to ask of you."

The dozen men, dressed all in black, donned their black hooded masks, and departed quietly. Kleo, one of Karis's most trusted eyes, a young woman in her twenties, a washerwoman by day, very homely and unmarried, helped Karis take another sip of her tea. "Yes, Karis, what task have you set for me?"

"I need the precise layout of their main church complex. I need also the city sewer plans. The dangerous part, dear Kleo: I need to know if this Cardinal is accessible to us at some point in time. Careful of their assassins, the Mano del Dio."

"I will do my very best, Karis," she whispered.

"I know you will. You are the very best," Karis whispered back. She rose, standing before Kleo, smiling. "Pleasure me before you go." Kleo smiled, and the two began kissing. Kleo knew that ever since the betrayal of Karis by her husband, Karis trusted no man, rightly so, Kleo thought. She was very pleased that Karis chose her to pleasure her; certainly, no man ever would touch her; Kleo was too ugly for that. Karis, however, treated her as she always dreamed a handsome man would, though she knew that day would never come. An hour later, Kleo slipped out into the dark of night. Hers would be a most dangerous mission.

Karis picked up the teacup between what was left of her arms and carried it into her kitchen. She made several more trips, each time carrying back one item. At least, she could still do some things in life. These, she insisted on doing herself, not allowing her handmaidens to do for her. She was now thirty-three years old, but she still had that smile that had suggested she was totally alive and happy, the kind of smile that all men found irresistible. After her husband had met with his 'accident,' Karis had allowed her black hair to grow as long as it would. Now it reached her lower back. Somehow, her hair attempted to make up for her arms.

Karis was still dressed all in black. Her handmaidens had dressed her after supper, before they left for their homes and families. Now Karis awkwardly opened the drawer that contained her black hood and retrieved it. Putting on her hood by herself was an incredibly challenging task, which occupied her a frustrating half-hour before she was satisfied with her look. Now she had only to wait.

Around midnight, the unconscious form of Drusus was carried into her secret dungeon basement. Here the thick stone muffled all sounds. Indeed, tonight, she would need these walls to contain it. Several men got the brazier going, and Karis retrieved the long poker. One end held a wooden handle, the other contained a raised letter, 'K.' Rarely did it find use, but tonight, Karis would use it once more. She placed the metal end into the roaring blaze and turned to watch the proceedings.

Drusus had his legs and torso tied securely to a bench. Next, they secured his head to the bench as well. Two side benches were placed under his arms, which were place outstretched, and the upper portions strapped to the benches. An iron bar was forced into his mouth, forcing it wide open. Karis spoke sternly, "Wake him. I will pronounce his sentence; he must know why this is being done to him."

One man splashed water on Drusus; he coughed and woke up, struggling in vain to move. He saw a number of men and women dressed in black, head to toe. He tried to scream out "Kali!" He was unable because of the iron bar.

Karis spoke, "That's right, Drusus. Kali. You have caused your own wife to lose her hands unwillingly. Your own daughters you sacrificed! Have you no shame? No, I can see that you do not. Your punishment, delivered for your wife and daughters, is to live as they must now live. So that you can never speak words that will cause another woman to undergo such torture, your tongue will be removed. So that everyone who sees you will know what you have done to your own family, your own wife and daughters, I will burn a 'K' into your forehead. Live a long life, Drusus. As your have condemned your family, so I condemn you. Execute."

The Kali were merciless. Both arms were hacked off at his elbows. He screamed and passed out from the pain. The wounds were stanched by hot irons from the brazier, then bandaged. Next, his tongue was removed and the wound there stanched. Finally satisfied with the work her associates had done, Karis awkwardly picked up the stoker by its wooden handle and carefully pushed it into the man's forehead, holding it while it burned deeply into his flesh. When she removed the poker, the letter covered his forehead between his eyes.

"It is done. Take him back to his home. Leave word with his brother that he will need attending to in the morning. Thank you." They bowed to her, and she bowed to them. She walked up the steps to her living quarters. An hour later, she managed finally to get sufficiently undressed for bed. She slept very well that night.

Six weeks had now passed and Cardinal Morpheus was ecstatic with just how well the grand plan was working out here in Patri. Fully one hundred twenty women now lay in his infirmary, recovering from the Holy Degrees, a smashing success. No resistance whatsoever, just as Pope Aison had predicted. True, Milo had been assassinated, but he cared little for the man, a nuisance. Whoever they elected as the new King would be just as useless.

"Prelate Brutus, I've just made my evening rounds in the infirmary, praying for the women. It is just magnificent how well it is all going. The first group is healing well and may be sent home in a few weeks. Soon we will have to expand our list," both men chuckled.

"Your Eminence, one small matter still bothers me. How many men have volunteered their women as you asked them too?"

"Ah, that is the best thing that has happened yet. Ten have already done so. I doubted that so many would, you know. Why?"

"What troubles me is that eight of those men have been savagely attacked by the Kali Assassins. Drusus, remember he was the first who brought in his wife and two daughters? He has had his arms cut off at the elbows, his tongue cut out, and a 'K' burned into his forehead. He still lives, though."

"Yes, these Kali are a menace to society; I'll grant you that," Morpheus said.

"Seven more of the ten men have had similar butcheries done to them, by our reckoning. I see a pattern in this."

"Yes, it is unfortunate that these men will not be able to reap their just rewards with their women we had made into Holy Degrees. Why? Does this bother you?"

"Your Eminence, this may well discourage other men from coming forth, asking you to make their women into Holy Degrees."

"Yes, now I see your point. You are wise, Prelate. Suggestions?"

"Two have not yet been butchered. I would like to put some of my men on them, watching them all day and night. I would like to see if we cannot catch these abominable Kali Assassins, perhaps putting an end to them."

"Make it so, Prelate, make it so. Very wise decision indeed."

"One other thing, Your Eminence. Have you decided what actions to take in Axos and Kefall? All our priests, Holy Paladins, and even nuns were murdered, and all churches burned down by persons unknown."

"Prelate Brutus, at this time, we do not have men to spare to rebuild. I need everyone here. We must not fail here in Patri. Later, once we have Patri completely under our control, then I will expand out from here. I want the faithful in Axos and Kefall to begin to demand that we return to their cities and rebuild their churches. I want it to appear to be a fundamental, grassroots demand that we return. We will have far more support from those cities this way."

"Ah, brilliant, excellent. I had not thought of that aspect. You are correct. I will go see to the assignment now of the two remaining men. I hope to report back to you within a week that the Kali are no more." He bowed and left.

Chapter 16 The Rooster's Tale

Back near the founding of the Church of Jehosanity, the first leader was Pope Yazi I. In those insecure and troubled times, he selected out the most highly skilled and feared assassin on Megalos, successfully converting him into the faith. He made him the first Supreme Prelate of the Mano del Dio, the Hand of God, who was in charge of church security.

Little more than skilled assassins, these men set to work, guaranteeing the safety of the priests and their facilities. The man was known in the streets of Megalos as the Rooster, because of his malformed head, shaped like that of a cock. Life had forced the Rooster to be able to carry out his missions despite any physical or emotional pain. When he formed up the Mano del Dio, he began the use of the pain-inflicting waistbands, training his men also to ignore pain. The safety of their Pope took priority over their mere bodies, no matter the pain it was under.

Over the many years that the Rooster served and idolized Pope Yazi I, he had done many missions, doling out death frequently, securing the Church on Megalos. Yes, idolized was an understatement, for the Rooster considered Yazi to be the personal representative of Lord Jehosa on Tarra. The Pope could do no wrong, ever!

The Guardians of Mont Blanc and the Santi del Dio became their archenemies. Finally, the Rooster took upon the mission of assassinating their most powerful leader, who continually interfered with overall Church plans, one Ket Bethany. In the spring of 636, the Rooster, hiding in a tree, aimed his heavy crossbow with its poisoned quarrel at Ket, and fired, hitting him in neck. The Rooster watched his most worthy opponent fall from his horse, mortally wounded.

However, what happened next had forever changed the Rooster, who believed utterly every word that his Pope Yazi I had ever said to him. Most critically was the fact that he, the Rooster, had a precious soul, unlike the lies that the Santi were spreading, that man was a soul. This Ket Bethany flew up at the Rooster, who saw the spiritual being, the soul, of Ket Bethany. Ket attacked and killed his body and yet Ket's body lay on the ground dead.

Shocked beyond all reason, the Rooster floated out of his dead body, realizing that he was not his body and that he was the spiritual being, the soul. Worse, Ket showed him that all of what the Pope, his revered Pope, had told him was an outright lie. When he realized that for a half century the man had merely used him, like a slave, doing the Pope's dirty work, the Rooster snapped at that moment. The Rooster vowed to get retribution as he floated up and away from West Reach, where his body had died assassinating Ket Bethany.

Now most spiritual beings on Tarra at this time were utterly convinced that they were a body and not an immortal spiritual being. When their bodies died, they lost everything, their identity, their body, their possessions, everything. As a result, few ever chose to remember their previous lifetime when they moved into a new baby body, starting the cycle of life over once more. It was too painful to remember all that they had lost forever. Sometimes, they had done things which are best forgotten, if you follow me.

A very few beings, such as myself, remember their previous lifetimes here on Tarra. The Rooster lay partially in between these two extremes. He knew that the Church of Jehosanity had to be destroyed utterly. He felt that in every fiber of his existence, though he often did not know precisely why.

Worse, the Rooster's next baby body, which he rushed to acquire back on Megalos, turned out to be female. After all, it is often a fifty-fifty chance with the sexes. She knew that the Church was evil and had to be destroyed. Hence, she became very vocal and outspoken against the Church. Unfortunately for her, the Church began to deal with these "recalcitrant women" on Megalos by kidnaping them, taking them into a secret underground prison, run by the Mano del Dio. There, these women had their arms encased in a metal device tightly behind their backs, making any use whatsoever of their arms nonexistent. Worse, they were forced to wear a metal headband which forced a metal ring into their mouths, so that their mouths were perpetually open. Thrown into this prison, they were left to survive like dogs. Unable to use their arms in any way, they somehow had to position their bodies on the floor and use their tongues to lap up water and the liquid paste-like food that was dumped onto the floor several times a day.

The Rooster did not survive this treatment for long. Her body became diseased and died in less than a year of imprisonment. Yes, this mistreatment only firmed the Rooster's resolve to somehow destroy this church. Unfortunately, she was so confused about things, that several years passed by before she realized that she had to go find a new mother and baby body.

Double unfortunately, she again found herself with a female body, born in 681, in Galantas, Megalos. Her mother named her Yannis, Yannis Virgos. As Yannis began growing up, her hatred of the Church of Jehosanity only rose. Soon she discovered that she could pick pockets and money pouches with great ease. Slowly, she began sliding into the dark side of Megalos society, learning all that she could. One day, she remembered the house that she had, as the Rooster, before Pope Yazi I recruited him. She walked by it and felt somehow drawn to this decrepit, rundown, abandoned home.

Yannis had entered it and found it very familiar. Soon, she was opening many of the Rooster's secret hiding places, where he had stashed his accumulated wealth and tools of his trade. These, she confiscated and adapted for her use. From this point in time onwards, she never went anywhere without many deadly devices concealed on her person, as well as various lock picks.

During her late teen years, Yannis began practicing spying and stalking various church members. She knew that she had graduated from this when she managed to follow unnoticed the Supreme Prelate of the Mano del Dio, once getting close enough to have slain him, had she so desired. Something had stayed her hands at that time, though she knew not what.

During this time, the ambassador from a new land of Demokritos came to Galantas, taking a local wife. Worse, these men from Demokritos had brought the Holy Eight Degrees of Matrimony with them. For months, she had followed Nikos Drakon and his wife, Melissa, of the Eighth Degree all over the city. Seeing the helpless Melissa, of course, brought back all of her horrid memories of being similarly utterly helpless encased in the metal devices, in which she had died in her last lifetime. Her hatred of the Church rose to new levels, though she was very wise now, and never spoke openly of her seething hatred. Her last lifetime taught her well.

A master of disguises, Yannis was drawn to be near Nikos and Melissa, often overhearing their conversations. In this way, she learned of the Church plans to begin widespread implementation of the Holy Degrees down on Demokritos. She snapped over this revelation! Somehow, someway, she had to travel to Demokritos and assassinate these men who would do such horrible crimes to helpless women!

Then luck struck. Many ships were beginning to sail to Demokritos, bearing supplies and a number of Holy Paladins. In fact, there were so many of them being scheduled for departure that she decided to use this to her advantage. At first, she thought that she might stowaway for the voyage. However, this new country was at least two months of sailing to the south, and she could never remain hidden that long. Next, Yannis considered disguising herself as a young boy and hiring on as a deck hand, jumping ship when it reached Demokritos. However, considering she would have to play this part for such a long time and in such a confined space, she would be taking too great a risk of being discovered.

Finally, she devised a better plan. Dressed for the role she wanted to play, she boarded a likely vessel she knew would be sailing for Demokritos shortly and asked to see the captain. "Sir, I would like to sign on as your washerwoman. On such long voyages, surely you could use a washerwoman. I will work for one copper a week and meager food. I am a good washerwoman." Her appearance was that of a down on her luck elderly woman, yet one who wore clean clothes, if of poor quality. She had also purposely disguised her looks so that men would not desire to flirt or worse with her. Men ignored the ugly looking women; she'd seen that many times in her wandering of the streets of Galantas.

In mid-April of 702, her ship landed at Patri. She watched the men disembark. Then came the confusion of unloading all the supplies. Men were working hard, their attention on the heavy lifts. Stealthily, she and her sack of supplies, jumped ship without being noticed at all. Quickly, she moved through the streets putting as much distance from the docks as she could. That night, in a darkened alley, she changed her clothes and appearance. She emerged from the alley a young, beautiful woman of means and checked into a nearby inn, treating herself to a fine meal, bath, and room.

The next day, she went shopping and reconnoitered the city. It was huge, unexpectedly so. Two weeks she spent walking and observing, learning the streets, shops, and customs of these people. Fortunately, they spoke the same language as she. When she needed more funds, a few money pouches were skillfully lifted.

Then, she began to hear of the abduction of the women. Her ire rose and she resolved to find out for herself the truth of the matter. Having carefully scouted the large church complex, she knew that she could not directly break into it; thousands of Holy Paladins made that highly unlikely and far too risky. She decided to try her washerwoman disguise once more.

Yannis had a good grasp of the use of a building merely by observing those who entered and who left. Carrying her basket of cleaning supplies, she approached the heavily guarded gates of the complex on a fine fall morning. As expected, the guards merely opened the gates for her, not even challenging her. She walked up to the infirmary building, where several men who looked far better dressed were standing and talking. "Excuse me, sirs. Who do I see about obtaining a washerwoman's job here? I am a good washerwoman. I clean well." She acted rather dim-witted as well.

"Ah, say that is a good idea. Our nuns are currently very overworked. They could definitely use your assistance. Come with me. Your name, miss?"

"Yannis, sir. Thank you so much. I do not ask much pay. I work very hard. You will see." Yannis poured it on heavily. The head nun was very grateful for the help of a washerwoman.

"You may call me sister Eudosia. Follow me. The pay is ten coppers a day. You have heard that we are helping so many women with their Holy Degrees that they may earn many Good Marks?"

"Oh yes, I have. Such a worthy thing to do. I must earn Good Marks. I clean very good. You see."

"Well, we have plenty for you to clean around here. Follow me." Yannis spent the afternoon scrubbing down the operating room. Dried blood covered the tables, floors, and even the walls in places. When she had finished and Eudosia had inspected her work, she handed her the ten coppers and asked, "On your way out, would you like to take a peek at all the women who are now of the Holy Degrees, who will forever more be only earning Good Marks so that their souls may go to heaven?"

"Oh yes, if this is permitted. I am only a humble washerwoman." She followed the nun down the hall to the large rooms where the women were being housed, while they healed.

"Yes, they are all recovering nicely, though do not be alarmed if some are still fighting us; the Devil within their bodies are protesting and will soon be abandoning them. Now they will be incapable of earning Bad Marks. I am so happy for them. They cannot be tempted to do bad things any longer. We, you and I, we have to be vigilant, every day. We must be alert to the worldly temptations that Lucifer casts before us. We must strive to earn those Good Marks, as you have done today by making our infirmary room so clean, Yannis."

"Here, stand in the doorway and you can see all these wonderful women, who are on their way to having their souls, their precious souls, be able to enter our savior's holy realm."

Yannis peered into the room. Beds upon beds lined both sides of the walls. Women were wailing, moaning, crying. A large percentage had both their arms bound in bandages where their hands ought to have been. A smaller percentage were bandaged at their elbows; those were of the Seventh Degree, the nun explained. Only four had no arms left at all, the Eighth Degree, she explained.

Yannis fought for self-control! Horrid memories of her death last lifetime came flooding back over her. Was this place that place? Was that place this place? Were these the women who were encased as she had been? Her mind reeling, she excused herself and left as quickly as possible, hoping not to draw undo attention to herself. Only when she was several blocks away and out of sight of the complex did she stop and vomit in an alleyway.

Yannis lost control of her mind. *I am not in time. Maybe I am in time. I am encased, I cannot move my arms. No, I still have them. Did I escape? When? No, yes. They didn't escape. They cannot escape now. I have to help them. How can I help them with my arms encased like this? No, I'm free at last. No, they are not free. Yes, they can be free. I have to help get them away from those bastard men. But I am a bastard man, I remember helping him set up this church. No, it is not a church. It's a lie factory. But I am a lie factory. I am a murderer that's why I was encased and left to die in the prison. We were all murderers there. No, we couldn't all be killers, only me. They got me. I was found out at long last. I paid for my crimes. I died there. No, I am alive here. They are still alive too. For how long? Where am I?*

She looked around, like a frightened cat, knowing danger is nearby, though it could not yet see it or the direction from which it would come. *I see assassins everywhere. They are both inside and outside. How do I know that? I am not an assassin! No, I am; no I was; yes I was; not anymore; maybe. I have to lie down, weak. Where's home? No, that's Megalos. This isn't Megalos. Where's home?* An image of her inn flashed in her mind. *Home.* Instinctively, she began walking quite fast, heading for that inn.

By the time she reached it, her mind had cleared, enough so that she realized that she needed to change her disguise before entering. Ducking into the last alley before her inn, she quickly changed her appearance, removing the handkerchief over her head, letting her black hair down. She entered the inn and went straight to her room, where she cleaned up and changed into a better dress. A half hour later with a full stomach, she sat on her bed in her room. The chaos in her mind had died down completely.

"Yannis, think, what exactly have you seen?" she said to herself to get her on the right track. She'd seen Mano del Dio men around the complex, but they were few, compared to the Holy Paladins. Yet, what else had she seen? It was something important, buried in the confusion she'd experienced when leaving. What was it? Something had really caught her attention, though she could not identify it.

She fell asleep with her clothes on. The next day, she felt a renewed vigor. *I have to go back. I have to rescue those women before they die, like I died. No, I came here to kill those priests and Mano del Dio men, who tortured and killed me. No, now I have to rescue those women first or they will die in there, just like I died. Yannis, you are definitely going to have to case this place very well today. Tonight, I'll devise a plan; yes, observe then figure out how to do it.* She went down, got her breakfast, and returned to her room. A few minutes later, she had her disguise in place once more. She ducked out of her window into the alley and headed for her cleaning woman job at the church complex.

As she approached, she noticed two unusual sets of men. Her keen eyes spied two men who were most definitely watching the entrance. No ordinary men, these had to be assassins or thieves; they were being discrete in their surveillance. That was what had caught her attention. They were being very clever about their actions. Yet, there was a second group of men, fighters perhaps, ruffians maybe; certainly they were being crude about their spying on the complex. She noticed that both groups noticed her as she walked through the gates and on up to the infirmary.

Today, six Mano del Dio men were standing around the entrance to the infirmary. She knew something was either in progress or about to happen. As Yannis went inside, one man said, "You will have a lot to clean up today." She ignored him and entered, wondering what he meant.

"Ah, good morning, Yannis. Today, we will all be earning more Good Marks. First, I need you to scrub all the floors in the recovery rooms, where the women of Holy Degrees are staying. Many have had accidents and the floors need to be cleaned. Later in the afternoon, we will need you to clean the surgery room. It will be easier this time, Yannis, the blood will not be dried. You will get a silver for your efforts today, assuming that you do as good a job today as you did before."

"Yes, ma'am, Yannis will scrub very good. Scrub now." She took her bucket filled with supplies and entered the first of the recovery rooms. Today, she knew what to expect and was not shocked by what she saw. Most of the women in this first room were recently done, in great pain, and only semi-conscious. Blocking their moans from her mind, she concentrated on cleaning the accumulated filth from the floors, mostly blood and human excrements.

Two hours later, she entered the next room. Here the women were nearly healed. As she began her cleaning, she observed many of the women. Some were barely in their teens, but none was older than perhaps their early thirties.

As she began scrubbing by one bed, the young girl lying there struck up a conversation with her. "I'm sorry that I had an accident on the floor for you to have to clean up. I'm Charessa. I'm thirteen. What's your name?"

"Yannis, Yannis the cleaning woman. Does it hurt? I mean your arms there? How awful for you?"

"It did at first, but now it's much better. I know it's just horrible. My father had this done to me and to my mother and sister. She was going to be married in two months, but now, without any arms, she won't be able to. No one will want her this way. They won't want me when I grow up either, not with only these." She raised her very short arms. "I used to scrub for mom, but now I can't do anything anymore. Neither can mom. They cut off her hands, you know."

"How awful!" Yannis tried to think of something to say to Charessa, but nothing seemed appropriate.

"I know. The worst part of is what will happen to us now? Where will we live? Who will look after us? Poor Cynthia cannot do anything now. She's next to me. See, she has no arms left at all. And there is my new friend here, see. She's Eleni Gavril. She's like me but a year older."

"Who are you talking to, Charessa," Cynthia said. She was lying down and could not either raise herself up or see Yannis, who was on her hands and knees below her sister's bed.

"I'll help you up," Charessa said. "It is hard for me, but I can manage maybe." She hopped out of bed and with great effort managed to help her sister sit up. Then, she climbed back onto her bed. "Mom's next to Cynthia, but she is sleeping. I think she is depressed about what will become of us now. She cries a lot, Yannis."

Yannis rose and her eyes met those of Cynthia. This young woman reminded Yannis of herself last lifetime, when she was encased in those metal devices, unable to use her arms in any way. Yannis felt a very deep sympathy for Cynthia. She found herself saying something that startled even herself. "Don't worry Charessa and Cynthia, I will find a way to look after you, all of you here, though I don't know how just yet. Give me some time to figure it out. I promise you I will do this."

"Please, miss, please help me too," Eleni said mournfully. She had gotten up to help Charessa get Cynthia up, but had been too slow. "We are so helpless and so desperate, please."

"Come here, Eleni," she opened her arms and gave Eleni a long hug.

"She is all alone here. Cynthia and I are her only friends. Please, Yannis, please, help us."

One arm around Charessa and one arm around Eleni, Yannis said, "I promise all of you. I will find a way to take care of you."

Just then, everyone heard loud screaming coming from the surgery room. Charessa explained, "They are at it again, cutting someone's something off. Don't worry; they will pass out, and the awful noise will stop for a while. Usually they do three each day. Then late at night, they wake up, as I did, and see what has become of them. Then, their screams are pitiful. I can barely stand to hear them. It is awful, Yannis, just awful to hear them. I don't scream any more, though Cynthia sometimes does. She has bad nightmares now. So does mom."

"I do too," Eleni added sorrowfully.

"Yannis, can I ask you something?"

"Sure, Charessa."

"What is a Good Mark? How do you earn a Good Mark? What is a Bad Mark anyway?"

Yannis noticed that nearly all of the other women in the room suddenly looked at her. More than young Charessa wanted to know the answer to these questions. She wanted to say all sorts of things, but realized that it was just too risky to say anything. "I really do not know the answers, Charessa. Maybe I can find out for you."

By the time she had finished scrubbing this room, she had made friends with well over half of the younger women in here. The head nun came in to inspect and complimented Yannis. "You have done very well, Yannis. Now we could use your services in the surgery room, this way please."

Yannis picked up her things and followed the woman in blue. As they went through the room she had just done earlier, she noticed three new women lying on what had been unoccupied beds. Two had lost their hands, while one was like Charessa, her arms ended at her elbows. All three were unconscious and Yannis was glad that she would not be here tonight when they woke up.

The surgery room was a mess. She overheard two physicians chatting. "Well that one didn't go as planned."

"Tell me about it. Damned if we didn't have to go all the way to her elbows. I hope the Cardinal will not chide us on our mistake."

"I don't expect that he will. Come on; let's get cleaned up. Leave everything for the cleaning woman there." The two left Yannis alone in the room. Quickly, she set to work. It was much easier this time, for the blood was not dried.

Sometime later, she was given her silver and asked to return in the morning. This time as Yannis headed out of the infirmary, she stopped just outside the door and looked around, pretending to stretch and get some air. The Mano del Dio men were gone as were most of the Holy Paladins. Only two men stood guard. Slowly she walked to the entrance, her eyes missed nothing. Ah, the two men pretending to be constructing a fishing net were still there, watching the complex. The other obvious men had been replaced by others equally inapt at surveillance.

She left the gates and began walking back to her inn. However, she discretely saw that the two supposed fishermen making the net chose this time to pack up. Indeed, she caught a brief glance of them behind her as she turned a corner. No doubt, they were following her. Instinctively, she knew that she had enough skill to lose them. Yet, something held her back for a time. Why were they following her? Her disguise was designed to discourage any man from desiring to even meet her. That could not be it. "What have I done?" she asked herself. She could think of nothing.

Now her curiosity rose. These men were most definitely following her from a distance. She wanted to know why. Besides, they were skilled at their craft, though perhaps not as good as she was, but certainly good enough to probably fool the Mano del Dio assassins. Yannis decided not to lose them, but getting into her inn dressed as she was would be a problem. Should she climb back in her window? No, that would only make her look very suspicious. She could not take the easy approach and change in an alleyway; they would be watching, and Yannis did not want them to see her other "look," that of a young woman of some means. Only one other avenue was left: enter at the side door of the inn and hope that no one was watching. A short while later, this is just what she did. Luck was on her side this early evening.

Once in her room, she rapidly changed her disguise. Now she looked like a fine young woman, radically different from her look upon entering. She went down into the inn and ordered a light dinner. While she was waiting, she spied the two supposed fishermen enter and take a seat. Their eyes darted from person to person and soon had examined the two dozen people in the inn. She saw the barkeeper bring them two pints, so she took her time eating her dinner of quail and yams. Yannis suspected that they were hoping to see the cleaning woman appear for diner. At last, the two men gave up their wait and left. Yannis paid her bill and quietly strolled out the main doors. She spied the two talking together, walking rapidly down the street.

Pretending to be out for an evening stroll, she followed them, keeping a block behind the two. Halfway across town and now in the wealthier section of Patri, the two men ducked down an alley behind a grand old mansion. As she approached it, she saw them ducking into what appeared to be a little used door to the mansion's basement. Now standing before it, she had a choice, go inside or return to the inn with her questions unanswered.

These men did not look like they belonged with this mansion. Perhaps they had previously cased the place and were now in the process of robbing it. That would seem to fit her observations. Now a third choice arose, she heard the hoof beats of a horse and carriage coming up to the main entrance. Interesting, the owners would be arriving, not knowing the two men were in the basement. She crept around the corner to observe. Yannis gasped when she saw a young woman being helped out of the carriage, a woman whose arms ended at her elbows!

Sympathy and worry rose within Yannis. Here was a helpless woman about to enter her home, not knowing that two seedy characters were in her basement. Yannis' sense of justice swelled within her. She had to do something. She watched the carriage pull away, heading to the carriage house some distance away, while the woman entered the house. Yannis rushed up to the door and knocked, though the door was not quite shut. This should have given her some instant concern, but her attention was on this poor, helpless woman who may well be in danger.

The woman herself opened the door with what remained of her left arm. "Yes?" she said. She saw a woman in her early thirties, with gorgeous black eyes, and straight, long black hair that reached her waist. She wore a very nice silk dress, indicating a woman of means.

"Excuse me, miss. I was walking by a minute ago when I saw two very rough looking men enter your basement door. Seedy fellows, perhaps they are here to rob you. I saw you coming home and came to warn you."

"Oh dear me," the woman said. "Please come in and keep me company, until my driver returns from the stable. I am called Karis."

"Pleased to meet you, Karis. I am Yannis. Such a magnificent dress! Expensive, I'll bet. I do love your hair." Yannis tried to be polite as she entered the room. To her surprise, Karis held out her arms for the customary shake, startling Yannis.

"Shake? They won't bite you," Karis replied, she'd often gotten the same response from others, who did not expect that she would be able to shake hands. Karis put both her arms over Yannis' offered hand and they shook. "There, see we are civilized women. Now come, let's see if these men are still in my basement, shall we? If they try anything, please run and fetch my driver."

Again, Yannis ought to have known better, what woman of the Seventh Degree, knowing that two thieves might be in her basement, would go and see all by herself? Yannis agreed and followed her, opening several doors for her along the way.

When they reached the basement steps, Karis paused and said perhaps a bit too loudly for Yannis, "I don't hear any intruders down there. Come on, let's see." Again, Yannis ought to have had her guard raised, but she felt so sorry for this poor woman, that she followed her down the steps. Yannis saw that there were a number of rooms and a long hallway. By now, the robbers could be in anyone of them. Karis walked on down the hall, giving Yannis no choice but to follow her.

Without warning, Karis said, "Take her." The two men stepped out from behind her and grabbed her arms. Karis whirled around to face Yannis. "Bring her to the interrogation room."

Startled, Yannis could not believe that she had fallen into the trap! Yet, she was more curious than worried. Mentally, she counted the concealed weapons on her person, satisfied that if she needed to dispatch these men, she could.

The men had changed clothes and now wore all black. Now that she noticed it, the silk dress of Karis was also all black. Coincidence? Meaning? Thoughts flashed in her mind. Something others had said about black. What was it?

They sat her on a chair facing another chair, in which Karis sat down, wiggling to adjust her dress, for her arms were too short to be of any use in this. Now Yannis could see the faces of the two men. They were the two fishermen she had been following! Things made even less sense to her now!

The two men stared at her. Perhaps they would not recognize her. Karis said, "Okay, out with it. What is your real name, young woman?"

"Yannis, really it is Yannis," she said.

One of the men exclaimed, "Well I'll be, damn. She is good, Karis, very, very good. I didn't recognize her."

The other said, "Hell, we sat there drinking our pints, and she was right there in front of us all the time! Clever woman."

Karis said sternly, "Why were you following my men?"

Yannis replied, "Why were your men following me?" Stalemate. Neither would budge.

Karis studied Yannis for several minutes, saying nothing. "Yannis then it will be. Your accent is strange to me, foreign. Where do you come from, Yannis?"

"Megalos." Yannis saw nothing in lying about that. Anyone could tell where she was from by her accent. Their language was the same; just the accent was different.

"Are you one of Cardinal Morpheus's associates? A Church member? You do work for him; we know that. We've watched you for days. Clever disguise, though, cleaning woman," Karis stated.

Yannis could not contain her ire; that anyone would believe that she was associated with this vile pseudo-religion was more than she could tolerate. A keen observer would catch her involuntary, but suppressed instant reaction, which Yannis strained to conceal, she said, "No to both."

Karis, however, did not miss the subtle reaction of Yannis. She thought for a moment. This woman was obviously from Megalos, yet she most definitely was not part of the church. Rather from her reaction, quite the opposite. Karis had to make a snap decision. No one could know this was the Kali headquarters and that she was their leader. Yet, this woman was a mystery and definitely despised the Church of Jehosanity. Further, she was adept at surveillance. She had eluded her own men, assassins in their own right, and followed them here to headquarters, without their knowing it. Karis decided to take a chance. If it did not work out, she would have to kill this young woman.

"Yannis, you are new to Patri, are you not?"

"Well, yes, I arrived only a few weeks ago." Karis detected no lie here.

"Have you heard of the Kali Assassins?"

Yannis suddenly had a flash of insight. Black. Now she remembered. Others had warned her about the Kali — men dressed all in black. "Yes, I was warned about the Kali. I was told that they wear only black similar to all three of you. Are you the Kali I was warned about? Why were your men casing the church complex? I've seen them there each time I entered and left." Yannis decided to be more forthright. She still had all of her weapons and the freedom of her hands. She was not tied up, as she would have done, if she were in Karis's place.

This surprised Karis somewhat, a fact not missed by Yannis. Karis said, "Yes, we are Kali. Do you know the true purpose of the Kali Assassins?"

"No. It was said that you attack, rob, and kill people; that was all."

"That is our cover, which we seldom do. Kill, yes, however, not whom you might think. Let me explain our organization a bit." She told Yannis about the Holy Eight Degrees of Matrimony and its long history. The Kali were against this mutilation of women and had been secretly watching over those women who underwent the ceremony. Karis explained, "Sometimes, the husband is unfaithful to his wife, who has given the ultimate in sacrifices to their marriage."

Yannis exclaimed, "That is horribly wrong! That man deserves to be killed! Think of how awful it is for the poor woman, who has given up her arms and become utterly helpless, utterly dependent upon her husband. That is high treason on his part. He should be killed mercilessly!" Yannis could not contain her outrage. Karis now realized what had motivated Yannis to knock on her door earlier.

"That's why you came to warn me, isn't it? You feared for my safety?"

"Yes, I ought to have seen all the signs that this was not so, but I was blinded by seeing you, so helpless," Yannis replied honestly. "I made a mistake. I seldom make mistakes."

"Yannis, the men that we kill are only those husbands who have betrayed their helpless wives. My own husband began sleeping with my handmaiden! I felt so awful, so betrayed, so completely helpless, like this," she waved what remained of her arms. The Kali assisted me and my husband met with an 'accident.'"

Karis continued her questioning, "You have been inside the church infirmary. Have you seen the women there that we know they have abducted and harmed?"

"Yes, there are hundreds of them. Most have lost both hands. Some are like you. A few have nothing left. They are in dire trouble. I've promised to help rescue them," Yannis blurted out, not intending to divulge this much information just yet.

"Yannis, we are both on the same side in this matter. We have been casing the place, looking for some way to get in there and get to the women. We want to help them too, to get them out of the clutches of the vile priests. Do you realize that some men have voluntarily ordered their wives and daughters to get mutilated against their wills?"

"Those men should be slain!" Yannis cursed.

"No, we have a better punishment for them. We have cut off their arms like mine, cut out their tongues, and I personally branded them with the letter 'K' on their foreheads. Now they get to see how it is to have to live life as we must!"

"Damn, that *is* better than killing them! Have you gotten all of them?"

"No, we still have to get to two more men who turned in their wives and daughters to be brutalized. We want to get in there and assassinate Cardinal Morpheus and the all of the Mano del Dio men."

"No, he's mine! I came here to kill Morpheus. Leave him to me. He's mine!"

Karis suspected that Yannis had had some vile previous experiences with Morpheus back on Megalos. Perhaps he had done these mutilations to her mother, her sister? She asked, "Why?"

"They killed me. They encased me in metal so my arms were behind my back. I could not use them in the slightest. An iron helmet around my head held a metal ring in my mouth, forcing it always wide open. Dozens of us were like this and left in a small prison cell together. We had to slurp up water with our tongues, like dogs, eat like dogs. It was horrible; we were more helpless than you are. I died there. I came here to get my revenge. I am going to assassinate this Morpheus myself and the accursed Mano del Dio assassins as well. He is mine!"

Karis, who had heard such stories from the Santi del Dio here in Patri, was confused. "But you are alive, you have your arms. You must have escaped."

"No, no, they killed me. That killed me. No, I am alive now. I died, yes I died, but now I am here. New body somehow. I get so confused sometimes," Yannis said, a single tear found its way down her left cheek.

Karis knew better than to press her further. "Then it is true. The Santi here have told me tales of how they rescued women that were so encased and mistreated. So many of them lost their entire arms, hundreds, I think she said. Perhaps it is just as well that your body died. It is horrible trying to live with just this much of my arms left. I cannot imagine living without even this much of them left! Now you can get revenge."

"Yes, I know how it is to live as these women are being forced to live now," Yannis replied. "I felt so sorry for you when I first saw you getting out of the carriage earlier."

"Okay, Yannis, why don't we work together? We both have the same goals in mind? Are you with us?"

"Yes, there are too many Holy Paladins in there. We need help."

"Good. Let us shake on it, Yannis. Welcome to the freedom fighters of Patri," Karis said, offering her arms once more. This time, Yannis didn't hesitate; they shook, sealing the bargain.

"Now we must get ready, Yannis. My men are bringing in some others who we saw casing the complex. We want to question them."

"Oh you must mean the ones that are fighters. I saw them there too, but they are not very good at surveillance," Yannis said.

"You saw them too? You are good, Yannis. Come on, we need to get ready. Let's get you covered in black as well. We will be wearing masks so that these cannot identify us. They have been abducted and are being brought here as we speak."

A short while later, Yannis was also dressed in black, a mask covered her face. She helped Karis don her mask. They sat in a darkened portion of one of the rooms here in her basement. Soon, the door opened and several other men in black brought in two men who had their hands tied and were blindfolded. They were seated and their blindfolds removed. Yannis noticed that Karis had wiggled her arms under her long hair, hiding the absence of her hands.

The two men looked around at their captors. One said hesitatingly, "Kali?"

Karis replied, "Yes. Why are you spying on the church complex?"

"You have heard what has happened to their churches and men in Kefall and Axos?"

"Yes, they were burned to the ground, and the priests and men slain," Karis replied. Yannis had not heard this, which was good news indeed. Others, she thought, hated this wicked church as well.

"Our doing. You have to let us go. We have to stop these men. They have been abducting and cutting up women for weeks now, and no one is doing anything to stop them, but us. You have to let us go!"

"You are not the only ones trying to stop them. What do you call your band, your group?"

The two men looked at each other, realizing that they had little choice but to answer. These were the Kali Assassins, after all. "Hektor Revenge Militia," the original man replied.

"King Hektor?"

"Aye."

"We would like to meet with Hektor. Have him come to this address at noon tomorrow for lunch. Dress nicely, if that is possible." One of the men in black stuck a piece of paper into the man's shirt pocket. "Take them back and turn them loose," Karis ordered.

After they had left, Karis asked, "Yannis, if you'll help me out of this mask, I'll make us some tea. You'll stay for tea with me?"

Yannis wondered how Karis could possibly make them tea. She helped Karis out of the mask and changed back into her own dress. Yannis joined Karis in her tearoom. Her servant girl poured their cups. "Yannis, this is my faithful servant, Katerina. Katerina, this is my new friend from Megalos, here on a visit."

Katerina was only thirteen, with a kind smile, which revealed growing gaps in her teeth. "Pleased to meet you, Yannis. I've poured your tea. Will that be all for tonight, Karis?"

"Yes, have our driver take you safely home. See you in the morning." The young girl left. "I'm helping support her family. Her mother gave up one hand when she married, but he has passed away. It is difficult for them to get by, and I am glad that I can be of help to them. Now sit and tell me all about yourself, if you want. Of course, if you would rather hear my sorry story, that's okay too. Oh, you don't have to help me with the tea. I manage well enough by myself."

Yannis knew that she couldn't really tell her much about herself. Her mind was a confusion at best — lifetimes that seemed to overlap, even though they did not. She watched how Karis managed to lift the teacup with her arms. Awkward, slow, but she did it, much to the surprise of Yannis.

"You will be here for lunch tomorrow? I want you to meet Hektor. You've heard about him, haven't you?"

"I'm supposed to work, but I suppose that I can take a lunch break. Can I sneak in here and change my disguise?"

"Certainly, I will leave that back door open. In fact, I will leave a dress there for you; consider it a little gift from me. I like giving out little presents." They chatted a while longer, and then Yannis had to leave. Karis sent two of her men to follow Yannis back to the inn, making sure she arrived there all right.

The next day, there was only a little cleaning to be done, and she easily was able to take time off for an extended lunch. The head nun explained that they were again making three more Holy Degrees and that she should come back around three to clean up the operating room. A short while later, Yannis, after making sure no one was watching, ducked into the basement door. In the first room, she found that indeed Karis had left a new dress for her. It was a black silk dress! Yannis had never worn such a fine dress before. After she changed and brushed out her hair, she slid her hands over her form; the material felt fabulous to the touch. She then headed up the steps, hoping she was not intruding or that she could find her way around the house.

She need not have worried. Katerina was waiting for her and led her into the dining room. "Well, that dress does wonders for you!" exclaimed Karis as Yannis entered. Another woman, extremely homely, sat next to Karis. "Yannis, this is my handmaiden, Kleo, she is a very close associate of mine," Karis winked at Yannis. Yannis presumed that was a reference to the Kali, and she took a seat on the other side of Karis.

"Katerina, you can go take care of your mother's lunch now. Thanks dear." Katerina left. "She does not know about the Kali," Karis explained. "Kleo is my closest associate and my hands in the Kali." From the looks the two exchanged, Yannis suspected there might be more than mere associates.

"Kleo has found the plans for the sewer system beneath the complex. I think that we have a way in there. Ah, I hear someone at the door. I'll get it," she rose and went to the door.

Yannis wondered how she could possibly open the door and longed to go watch for herself. Kleo sensed this, "She is very skilled with what is left of her arms. She can do far more than anyone believes."

"I am beginning to see that for myself. Have you been with her for long?"

"Nearly ten years, ever since her husband betrayed her. She hates men now; cannot say I blame her much. Show me an honest man and I'll lift a house. She and I get along just fine."

Karis returned with a very old looking man. His beard was unkempt, his hair barely brushed. Yet, he wore halfway decent clothes that didn't quite fit. Evidently, he'd borrowed them for this meeting.

They went into the dining room where Katerina had laid out the table. Kleo served them and sat close to Karis. "You will have to excuse us. Kleo has to feed me. While I can manage my tea, I cannot manage my fork."

"I am so terribly sorry that your husband is not here to assist you, noble Karis. I always was there for Angele, always. Such love we shared. It brought us so very close, you see, closer than I ever imagined. Now she is gone," Hektor lamented.

"My husband slept with my handmaiden, betraying me. I suspect that you have some idea how I felt when I caught them in our bed. He met with an 'accident,' shortly after that. Hektor, I've told Yannis all about what happened to you and your son. It is just despicable that Milo never did anything about it, though I believe you have already taken care of that detail."

"Yes, Milo was a pawn. We eliminated that worthless man. You know why then I am in Patri. I am carrying out my pledge to Maximus, Angele, and Lyris. I will destroy that entire church. I want Morpheus very dead before I die."

"I will see to it," Yannis declared. "He's mine!"

"Well, he's yours only if you get to him before I do," Karis teased.

"Hektor, we need to speak openly and frankly. Our goals are the same between us three. I am the leader of the Patri Kali." She allowed the magnitude of her revelation to sink home with Hektor.

"I am an assassin from Megalos, come to kill the Cardinal and all the Mano del Dio," Yannis found herself admitting openly. She added, "But I have also promised to rescue and help the women there."

"So you've heard that Morpheus is now making Sixth, Seventh, and Eighth Degree women out of abducted, unwilling women?" Hektor asked. "We've heard tales of this, but have been unable to get inside and see for ourselves. It is too heavily fortified, too many Holy Paladins."

"Yes, it is true. Yannis has been inside many times, visiting with the recovering women, and cleaning up after their bloody surgeries. It is all horribly true. We have to stop them. If we join together, maybe we can succeed," Karis suggested.

"You have my full cooperation, Karis, Yannis," Hektor said. "Yet, I know not how this may be done. That is why we have delayed so long."

"We know that they have thirty-three legions of Holy Paladins stationed there within the complex. They are housed in the three large two story barracks buildings, the ones with the little windows. There are fifty-two Mano del Dio assassins there as well. Morpheus has five priests and ten nuns to look after the poor women's needs."

"Then it is hopeless. I only have about ten legions of fighters who wish to see this blight destroyed," Hektor sadly said.

"Perhaps not by yourself, Hektor, but we are with you. We know a secret way inside their complex. What would you say if I could get your men safely inside, unseen?"

"Oh, Karis, that would indeed be a miracle! Is this possible?"

"Kleo, would you be so kind as to clear off the table and show them your map?" Kleo grinned and did so.

Kleo explained, "I stole into the city planner's office and made this copy of the sewer system around the complex. Here close to the ocean, the tunnels are large enough for a man to walk in them. Just don't go in there when it is raining. I'm teasing," she added. "See here, we can get men to these points that I've circled. The Mano del Dio and Morpheus live in the rectory building, which is this one here. All these are some distance from the infirmary. If we go under the cover of night, we ought to be able to get everyone inside without alerting any of their guards. Of course, then I don't know what we're to do, once inside, that is."

"Once we are discovered, how can we possibly defeat three times our numbers?" asked Hektor with some renewed enthusiasm.

"I've been working on that one," Karis replied. "I've taken a number of carriage rides around the area, studying it from a distance. The paladins will be mostly asleep, here and here," she pointed roughly with her right arm. "Damn, I cannot even point well. Ah well. The roofs are made of thatch. We ought to be able to set them on fire. The only ways out of these buildings are the front and back double doors. The windows are too small for a person to get through. It gives them security so that no assassin can enter that way. Yet, that may well be their undoing."

"Yes, but won't they all come rushing out the four doors?" Hektor asked.

"I've been working on that one too. What if we rolled wagons loaded with something heavy and used them to block the doors? We've spotted wagons in the stables. Once the guards are eliminated, wagons can be put into position and the fires set. Then, we go after the rectory and Morpheus. Then, we can rescue the women," Karis explained her plan.

"Yes, but how are we going to rescue the women?" Yannis asked. "They are helpless, and some will be barely done with their surgeries and in great pain. We will need wagons to carry them; there are hundreds in there. Where will we take them? I have promised Charessa that I would get her to safety somehow. Where will they be safe?"

"I've thought about that too, ever since we found out that Morpheus was doing this to women. The only possible safe place is with the Santi del Dio. They have great healers, and I have heard that they can help them learn to live better lives, though I do not know what that means."

"I do," Hektor spoke up. "I was in Velona with Angele. Karis, I swear to you that I saw this woman who is like you, of the Seventh Degree, and she was a master painter of ocean scenes, oil paintings that are so incredibly real it is as if you are there looking at them! We bought one of her paintings to adorn our halls, but now there is no one to respect it, with Angele now gone from me. We saw women of the Eighth Degree doing dances that I could not do and I have arms. It is truly amazing. Karis, you owe it to yourself to go to Velona and seek their aid. It is all free, that is what is so incredible. They have a Laird Foundation there just to help women of Degrees. You truly must go there, Karis, you must. We should see if the Santi will come to our aid and help us help these poor victims of Morpheus."

Karis was impressed. As he discussed this, the old man was so excited, so animated, that some tiny spark of hope rekindled within Karis. "Then I shall go to them this afternoon and see what can be done. The sooner we act, the fewer women will be mutilated for life. We dare not wait much longer," Karis insisted.

"Good. When shall we meet again?" asked Hektor.

"Say tomorrow evening after supper?" They all agreed and their meeting broke up.

"Come by after work and change into your new dress here. Leave it where you found it, and it will be easy for you to sneak in and change. Then, come and take dinner or tea at least with me, Yannis." She grinned and said that she would. Sometime later, the cleaning woman reentered the complex and began cleaning up the blood splattered surgery room.

Later that afternoon, the carriage carrying Karis pulled up at the gates of the Santi fortress in Patri, very close to the ocean. A small private dock was at the back of the small fortress. At the gate, her driver spoke, "Noblewoman Karis to speak with the Santi commander." They were allowed inside. Her driver opened the door for her and she carefully stepped down herself, unwilling to let them see her as helpless.

Dag came out the main door to meet her. "I do not believe that we have had the pleasure, ma'am. I am Dag Waterby, the commander." He held out his hand to shake with her, something only her dear friends would do.

A bit surprised, she held out her arms and contributed to the shake. "Karis K. Pleased to meet you at last. Is there somewhere we can talk very privately?"

"This way, Karis." He slid his arm around her waist, guiding her gently along, as they moved through the fortress and up to his meeting room. At first she resisted; she hated men. Yet, this one seemed kind and definitely in control. He seemed to sense when she would need that gentle touch for ease of balance. Karis allowed him to guide her into the room, and he knew just how to fan out her silk dress as she sat down, so that she was not sitting on it, all rumpled up.

"Would you mind if three others, my dearest friends and wife joined us? What we say will be strictly between us. Nothing said will ever leave this room, unless you so desire it."

She had wanted this to be private, but she relented. "Yes, that would be acceptable."

"Tea perhaps?" he asked.

"Of course," she replied without thinking. This man was indeed respectful of her, she decided.

Shortly, more introductions were made, accompanied by more handshakes. "This is my lovely wife of fifteen years now, Betsy, and our Healer. This is Art and Sandy Duval." After the introductions were done and everyone was seated, a servant perhaps, she was not sure, brought in a tray with tea and cups. Betsy poured out the cups, setting one before Karis.

She asked, "Can you manage or would you like me to assist you?"

Karis thought this must be a test. "No, I will manage. Thank you."

After demonstrating that she could barely manage, Dag asked, "Okay, Karis, what is so important that we must meet in private?"

Karis found it difficult to know just how to start. "How much do you know about what evil is going on within Patri, at the Church of Jehosanity complex, with Cardinal Morpheus?"

"Oh, don't get me started on that vile excuse for a human being!" Dag exclaimed.

"Dear, don't get so upset! We will find a way yet," Betsy tried to calm him down.

Dag continued, "We know that he has been abducting women, and against their will, cutting off their hands and arms! I'd like to cut off his arms! Why, he's even got normal men, well I wouldn't call them normal, family men, hell, I wouldn't call them that either! He's got them turning in their own wives and daughters to have their hands cut off! We know of one case, what was his name, Drusus, Drusus Laslos. He had them abduct not only his wife, but he had them take his two daughters! The idiot wanted Morpheus to cut off their hands so that they could get Good Marks. Ah, but somehow he got what was he deserved. I heard that his own arms were cut off as well as his tongue. What I found weird about it, they say he had a brand on his forehead that looks like the letter 'K.' So yes, we think we have some idea of what despicable, vile things are going on in that so called church complex."

"Dear, not so loud. You will frighten this poor young woman," Betsy attempted to quiet him down. This whole affair had really gotten to Dag, primarily because he was helpless to do anything about it.

"I'm sorry, Karis, if I have scared you. We Santi are so violently opposed to the mistreatment of women and I want so badly to do something, anything to help these women, but I only have barely enough fighters here to hold this fortress against these Holy Paladins, though I don't know how long three hundred of us could hold out against thirty-three legions."

"So you know how many Holy Paladins are in Patri?" she asked.

"Yes, I counted them personally when they arrived. You can see lots from our tower's roof, if you only look."

"I see." Karis decided to level with Dag. She had little choice, if she wanted their aid. She said quietly, "I branded Drusus so that everyone could see that the Kali got to him. I am sending a message that may make other idiot husbands think twice about forcing their wives and daughters to have their arms removed."

"What?" Dag nearly fell off his chair.

"Oh my," said Betsy.

"Well, I'll be a donkey's butt," exclaimed Art.

"Fascinating, she must be the local Kali leader," Sandy, their Communicator, observed. Karis liked her. She was homely, but very observant, reminding her of her dear Kleo.

"Yes, I lead the Patri Kali. I have joined forces with two others. One is an assassin from Megalos, who has come here to kill Morpheus, unless I get to him first. Then there is the old King Hektor. He's come for the same reasons, to destroy this church, after what they did to his son, his wife, and poor Lyris, who had only just become of the Eighth Degree for Maximus. He has ten legions of freedom fighters with him. The Megalos person, she has been working on the inside of the complex as a cleaning woman. She wants, as we all do, to rescue these women, get them to safety. She has given her word to some of the victims that she would do this, but we all do. I have a plan that will result, if all goes well, in their rescue. However, we have a big problem. Where can we take them? Where they can get any needed healing? Where can they go to live in safety? Hektor spoke highly of Velona as a possibility. I came to you today to beg you to assist us. If there is any way that we can get these hundreds of women safely to Velona and under the Santi care there, I am willing to pay any needed fees to have that happen."

Betsy spoke first, "See Dag, it is just like Linda said. Help will come from invisible allies. Oh, I'm sorry, Karis. Linda is the leader of the Santi del Dio, and she is of the Eighth Degree as well. Impressive woman. I do wish you could meet her. Powerful woman. Charming husband too. Sorry, I digress."

Dag replied, "Karis, you can count on the full and complete support of the Santi. No fee. We do it willingly to help these women. Do we attack tonight? I have three hundred excellent fighters, plus we four. Of course, the real problem is with the Mano del Dio. They are assassins you know."

"Yes, they are assassins, but poorly trained ones. I had a long talk with Yannis, the assassin from Megalos. Now there is a strange woman if I ever saw one. Highly competent, but well, strange. Her mind is not quite right, I think. She claims to have created their training program a century or more ago. She says that over the years, they have become mere robots, blindly following the steps she prescribed. She thinks that they will be easy to eliminate. I said she is a strange one, not quite right in the head, if you follow me, but incredibly competent. She outdid my own men and that is saying something."

She continued. "Timing is critical. We will attack at midnight. I have a way to get Hektor's men inside the complex, unseen, by using the sewer tunnels. We need to take out the guards without raising any alarms; otherwise, we are doomed to failure. Once the guards are gone, his men will move a bunch of wagons over to block the doors of the two barracks housing the paladins. We set fire to the roofs and let nature handle the thirty-three legions, while we go after the rectory and the fifty-some Mano del Dio and then Morpheus. First one to get to Morpheus gets to kill him. Then, we rescue the women, though Yannis says that we will need many wagons to carry them. She's probably right; some will just be coming out of surgery and in dire conditions. Do we then bring them here? Can you handle so many injured women?"

"Yes, Linda foresaw this coming, this mutilation of women, and sent us our Healing Caravel, fully equipped to help us. Between our own caravel and the Healing Caravel, we can take several hundred women to Velona, but will they all want to go there?" asked Dag.

"They must choose. Every day that we delay means three more women are permanently mutilated. We must act soon, but coordinating such a large action is going to take some time. Ten legions must make their way through the tunnels. Somehow, we must know when they are ready to strike. I have not yet worked how that may best be done. I will need to use all my Kali to take out the guards quietly, if we can. The number of nighttime guards exceeds the number of Kali I have, however."

"Karis, you could not have picked better allies. Sally here is a telepath. She knows Hektor well. She can be in touch with him and let the rest of us know when his men are in position. Allow me to assist you in the most critical aspect, the taking out of the guards. I have some special skills that guarantee it can be done without raising any alarms. Those two key actions are done deals. No, the incredibly dangerous part is dealing with these ruthless Mano del Dio assassins. I fear many will be harmed taking them out. They know no pain. Pain and wounds do not stop them. Plus they use poisons liberally. They are most dangerous men."

"That is almost too much to believe, but I will accept your word on this. Yes, the Mano del Dio will be the most dangerous men to handle. I am so thankful that you can help us with these poor women. I don't know what we would do without your aid. Sure is strange, our Emperor is off trying to conquer everything, including Velona, and here you are helping us out. Strange. Sometimes I think the Emperor is wrong. Ah, well. I had better get going. It will take some preparations to get all of Hektor's men in place. I'll send word to you during the day that we will act that night."

They shook hands once more and Karis left. On her ride back home, she went over their conversation in her mind, making sure that nothing was overlooked and that she had really duplicated what was said. If so, she would soon see some Santi magic, she had no other word to describe it.

Chapter 17 The Rescue

On May 10, 702, Karis decided tonight would be the night. Already nine more women had been abducted and mutilated; she could wait no longer. She had Kleo create ten detailed maps for Hektor's ten groups to follow. Each group would enter the sewers at different locations not too far from the complex, however. They would have to navigate through the filth to the correct positions, from which they would emerge inside the large complex. Just how Sally would know when they were in position, she really didn't know. What was this telepathy thing all about anyway?

That afternoon, she dismissed Katerina early. To ease her tensions, she and Kleo exchanged pleasuring. Then Kleo helped her into her black leather pants and shirt. Carefully, Kleo arranged Karis's two weapons of choice, specially made for her use. Both had cylinders of metal in which she would insert what remained of her arms. These were affixed at her sides so that she could get them on by herself with a bit of a wiggle motion. The one on her right contained a long, thin dagger blade. The one on her left had a six-inch thin stiletto, more like a nail. These were only useful for an unsuspecting strike and an upward thrust at best. She preferred to use her powerful legs, when possible.

Around eleven, all of her twenty-five associates arrived, dressed as she, entirely in black. Kleo tucked Karis's hood into her belt for her and gave her a farewell kiss. Kleo was staying behind. She was not a fighter, but rather an expert information gatherer. Karis would not risk her on this most deadly adventure. She and her group began the long walk to the agreed upon meeting location, where the Santi would join her forces. Exactly how Dag would be able to guarantee that the guards could be removed silently still eluded her. There were just too many of them.

They stopped and waited in the alleyway near the eastern edge of the complex. Not long afterwards, the Santi began arriving, in small groups, so as not to arouse suspicions. Karis noticed that most of the Santi wore chain mail, hardly appropriate for this affair where silence was golden. However, Dag, Art, and Betsy wore no armor at all. Dag whispered, "The Santi will remain here until the guards are dispatched. Sandy is up on our rooftop. If you look closely, you can barely see her from here. She will be coordinating our efforts from there." Karis did see a tiny figure in the moon light, but didn't see how anyone could do anything from such a distance.

"We should start taking out the guards when you are ready," Dag said.

"We think that there are fifty of them. It will take some time. Any idea how much longer Hektor will need to be in place," Karis asked.

"About a half hour, maybe an hour at the outside. You all stay back until the guards goes to sleep." Dag walked quietly up the street chanting softly to himself. As he passed by a guard's position, the guard yawned and dozed off. He heard the faint footsteps of Karis, Yannis, and the others moving up behind him. He continued merely walking along the street, passing by the guards, who were positioned around the perimeter. Still, to get all the way around would take some time.

A while later, Karis moved quietly up beside him and put her arm into his. She said nothing, unwilling to interrupt his chant. She was now keenly curious. These guards were magically falling asleep while on duty. Dag was merely walking on the street nearby, minding his own business. Yet, one by one, the guards continued to fall asleep as he passed by their positions. She had to see how this was possible. Although she accompanied him on the rest of the long walk, when they arrived back at the starting point, she still was no closer to understanding what he had done.

She just had to know how this was done. She whispered, "Is it possible for me to learn how to do this, to put men to sleep?"

Dag whispered back, "If you go to Velona and study with the Santi for some years, it may well be possible for you to master this Judger illusion. Ah, Sandy has just told me that Hektor's men are in place."

"How can she tell you this? She is back there. I heard nothing."

Like this, Karis. I can talk with you this way. You don't have to speak to talk back to me, just think what you want to say. Sandy sent, after Dag asked her to do so.

Karis opened her mouth is total surprise. *Oh my. This is so, so intimate! Can you hear me?*

Loud and clear. We telepaths can talk like this to anyone anywhere on Tarra. It is a rare gift that a very few of us have. You had better get going. Hektor's men do not like being in the sewers.

"Okay, show time. Station some Santi by the rectory in case some Mano del Dio men should come out. Mine will open the grates for Hektor." Both groups quietly hopped over the low fence onto the church complex. It was midnight.

Soon, the badly smelling men began climbing out of the sewers. Once oriented, the first group headed for the stables and began pulling the heavy wagons over to the barracks doors by hand. It went painfully slowly, and Karis was terribly worried that some Holy Paladin might walk out and discover them. None did, fortunately. A half hour later, all exits of the two barracks were blocked by the heavy wagons. Meanwhile, another group had dozens of torches ready, soaked in oil. Some had smaller flasks of oil. Once the wagons were in place, the men began tossing the oil flasks on to the roofs, while others lighted the many torches. Each torch was then pitched up onto one of the roofs. Within minutes, both roofs were fully ablaze. Hektor's men now rushed for the rectory, joining up with the Santi and the Kali. Now came the dangerous part; they had to take on the Mano del Dio men who

246

were inside, assassins in their own home. Cries of fire and panic began to come from the barracks, and everyone knew that shortly the Mano del Dio would be roused.

The rectory also had two floors and was a rather large building, with four different doors. No one knew the layout inside, nor who was where. The Santi entered one door, the Kali, another, while Hektor's men, led by Hektor himself, smashed in through the other two doors. One full legion stayed outside, in case others should come from the infirmary building or somehow escape the rectory.

Once inside, mass pandemonium broke out almost at once. Doors opened and these assassins leapt to their own defense. Dag allowed his armored men and women to lead, while he and Art followed from a safe distance behind them. Betsy remained outside where it was safe. The armor of the Santi served them well. Only a few blows from the Mano did any real damage. Slowly foot by foot, the Santi moved down the hallway.

Hektor's fighters fared poorly against these assassins. Many were felled, including Hektor. However, their sheer numbers forced the day, as they made progress through the long halls themselves, but at the higher cost.

The Kali members, with Karis and Yannis in the middle of the group, found themselves facing a stairs, a backstairs that led to the second floor. They heard the sounds of combat below, and began rushing up the stairs. When they opened the doors onto the second floor, they saw men rushing out, swords and daggers in their hands. Now it was assassin versus assassin; one by one, the Kali split off into single combat. There were not that many of the Kali nor were there that many Mano here. On the second floor lived those higher in the Mano del Dio organization, including Prelate Brutus, who backed up and stood beside one specific door.

Both Karis and Yannis guessed that the Cardinal was behind that door and both women inched their way towards this towering man. An assassin jumped out of a doorway at Yannis, she dodged, while recognizing the robotic motion the man had trained himself to perform. She then did the unexpected, dropping to the floor, kicking upwards with her feet into the man's groin. Howling and keeled over in pain, her dagger slit his throat.

Meantime, she spied another coming for Karis, and Yannis tried to get up to help this helpless woman. Yannis got the biggest surprise of the night. As the man came towards Karis, she raised her short arms, and the man lowered his sword slightly, looking at the stumps, realizing that she was indeed totally at his mercy. The very instant he lowered his guard and took his eyes off of her, her left leg swung up and struck him squarely on his neck. She used his neck as a fulcrum, swung her other leg up, and locked her legs behind his head. The instant she did that, her own body began to fall to the floor. Yet, she pulled downward with her lower legs, as if to use them to do a sit up to keep from falling. So sharply did she do this that the man's head flew back and his neck cracked instantly. As his lifeless body slowly fell to the floor, Karis prepared herself to hit the floor. The instant she felt the floor, she released her legs and rolled with it, out of the way of the falling man. A moment later, she hopped back onto her feet and spat on the man.

Yannis called out, "Incredible." Both women moved on towards Brutus, who prepared to take on these two women personally. The three moved slightly, each one maneuvering, looking for the hole in which to deliver a death strike. Yannis focused all her attention on Brutus, analyzing his patterns; Karis did likewise. However, Brutus was a Prelate, one of the most skilled assassins. He showed no easily used flaws. Yannis saw that he was indeed a most worthy opponent. She faked a move to see how he countered. It was as she expected. Karis did likewise. Brutus was indeed good, Karis noted, knowing that she had not the skill to take him down. She could only do so much without hands.

For several minutes, the three jockeyed for position, seeking some slight advantage. Finding none, Karis decided to trust the skill of Yannis; there was little she could do against Brutus, except one little thing, draw his attention, hoping she was not killed because of it. Without warning, she brought both feet upwards, intent on kicking him in the groin, while she herself fell helplessly to the ground before him. He saw it coming and took his eyes off Yannis for an instant to dodge the flying feet of Karis.

That instant was all that Yannis needed. The instant she saw his eyes move downward. Her left hand swung her stiletto for the kill. The long nail-like piece of steel penetrated the right ear of Brutus, lodging deep within his brain. He gave a very queer look; his motion froze. For several seconds, he just stood as still as a statue. Then his eyes closed, and his body slumped to the floor.

"Very well done, Yannis," Karis validated her companion. Yannis pulled out her stiletto and helped Karis to her feet.

"I wonder what's behind this door?" Yannis said, half in jest. She turned the knob. It was locked.

Karis said, "It has come down to you or me at last. I trusted you with my life with Brutus. I could not have taken him, not remotely. So I will give you first crack at the Cardinal. Allow me to open the door for you."

"But how?" asked Yannis. "It's bolted from the inside."

Karis moved back as far as she could and then came running at top speed toward the door. At just the right instant, she leaped upwards, both her feet hitting the door solidly. She was horizontal to the floor when she hit it. The lock and door splintered, while she hit the floor hard.

Yannis didn't wait to help Karis up. She moved through what remained of the door. Cardinal Morpheus stood there, his purple robes half on, covering his half-dressed body. He did not even have a weapon.

"I have come to kill you because you and your others have killed me and betrayed me. I have come to kill you on behalf of all the women that you have mutilated in your infirmary."

"Please, please don't kill me. I beg you. Have mercy on me. I have only been trying so hard to help these women earn Good Marks so that their precious souls may go at last to heaven. I am trying to help them. How could I have killed you?" he suddenly realized she spoke in a paradox.

Yannis looked at this pathetic excuse for a human being. Here he was facing his certain death, and he continued to spout off his good intentions, his insane intentions. "You want me, whom you and your fellow priests and Mano have shown no mercy, leaving me to die as I did; you want me to show you mercy? You, who have condemned all those women to a helpless life, show you mercy?"

She stared at him and added, "Never has the Rooster shown mercy. This night the Rooster shall show you, Cardinal Morpheus mercy, the mercy of the Rooster." He looked uncomprehending at this strange woman. However, his mind registered that name, the name of the most legendary Mano del Dio ever, the first Supreme Prelate of the Church of Jehosanity, R. Thraxton. Wham. She hit him hard in his head, knocking him out as Karis entered the room, very shaken up by her fall.

"You didn't kill him?" she asked questioningly. "Want me to do it?"

"No, he still believes that he is doing good. He begs for mercy. I shall show him the mercy of the Rooster. Karis, treat him as you did to Drusus. Exactly the same way."

A big grin formed on Karis's face; she saw instantly that what Yannis proposed was a far, far better punishment than an instant death. Give the man something to ponder for many years. The fighting on the second floor ended. Karis yelled out her orders, and her men came, carried the unconscious man down the steps, and outside the building.

While her men began their preparations, the two went to check on the other fighters. Dag and his group was just now coming out their door, helping many wounded Santi. "Is it done?" asked Dag as he saw the two women coming his way.

"We have Morpheus. Yannis has decided we show him mercy. My men will make him into another Drusus shortly. The mercy of the Rooster, she calls it, whatever that may mean. How many of your men are wounded?"

"We have ten. Betsy is starting to help them now. Art and I are also lesser healers. We need to lend her a hand. Are any of yours wounded?"

"No. We haven't checked on Hektor's men. We had better do that now. You two do what you can. We'll be back shortly," Karis ordered. She and Yannis began running for the other doors.

Wounded men were staggering out of both doors as they arrived. Many were being supported by their unwounded companions. One saw the two and said to them, "Hektor took a bad one. If you want to say any last words, you had better hurry up."

Both wove through the men coming out, calling out for directions to find Hektor. They found him slumped against the wall not too far inside. A large pool of blood covered the floor around him. He had a terrible wound to his chest, and both arms were bleeding badly. He was very weak but recognized them. He managed a whisper, "Did you get Morpheus?"

"Yes, with your help, we got him. We are going to make another Drusus out of that pathetic man. He will have the rest of his lifetime to understand fully how horrible he has made so many women's lives by living it himself. Thank you, Hektor. You have your revenge at last. We will soon be taking the women out of the infirmary and to the Santi fortress. From there, those that desire will be taken to Velona. I promise you that by tomorrow morning, this entire church complex will be nothing but ashes!" Karis declared vehemently.

"Thank you. It is done. Angele, I am coming for you, my dear. I am c . . ." Hektor passed away before the two women. Karis began crying, and Yannis put her arm around her and led her back outside.

"He was one of the very few men who really understood what it means when we give up our arms for love. He was one of the most worthy men I have ever known. He should be given a hero's burial," Karis cried.

"Boss," one of Hektor's men came up to her, not knowing exactly how to address her.

"Yes?"

"We have over a hundred wounded men. What should we do?"

"Take them over to the back side of the building where the Santi healers are now. They will attend to your men. Once you have all your wounded being handled, I need all of the wagons harnessed to carry all the women in the infirmary to the Santi tower."

"Yes, ma'am." He rushed off to carry out her request.

They heard a hideous scream. Shortly afterwards, five Kali came up to their boss. "It is done. They are bandaging now."

"Good. Come with us; we need to go into the infirmary. I do not know if we will encounter any more men or not," Karis said.

"Are we to kill these nuns?" he asked.

"I was going to kill them too, but I've changed my mind. They are to be sent to help our helpless Morpheus now. Tell them to take him to some inn and care for their precious Cardinal. Let's go."

"May I enter first? I don't want to scare the women any more than we've done already. Besides, they know me, and I have promised Charessa. I think that will help keep them calm," Yannis said.

She entered the infirmary. Standing in the surgery room, the first room, were the ten nuns. "Go outside and tend to your Cardinal. He now needs your assistance. We are sparing your lives. Go!" Yannis ordered them. Hastily, the ten left, watched by one of the Kali, who directed them to where the Cardinal was lying. They saw the burning inferno, which had held the Holy Paladins. The nuns were now in shock, but walked like zombies where they were so ordered.

Yannis went through the first recovery room filled with frightened women. She called out that it was safe and that they were being rescued. In the next room, she found the women sitting up, anxious to know what was happening. Yannis went directly to Charessa, Eleni, and Cynthia. "Hi, it's me, Yannis, your cleaning woman. I have come to tell you all that as I promised, you are being rescued. Except for the nuns who cared for you, they are all dead now. By tomorrow morning, every building in this church complex will be ashes. We are bringing up wagons to carry you all safely to the Santi fortress, where you will be checked over by their expert Healer and given sanctuary. You are now totally safe from all harm; I give you my solemn word!"

Young Charessa threw what remained of her arms around Yannis and held her as tightly as she could. Yannis did not know why, but her eyes flowed water heavily. "See, I told you, Cynthia, that Yannis would rescue us and mom! Now you and Eleni will be safe and helped. We all will be!" Her enthusiasm spread among these partially recovered women.

Just then, the three who had been operated upon this morning awakened each other with their shrieks of shock and agony. Karis was in that room when these three who had lost their limbs regained consciousness. Tears flowing from her eyes, she went to each and hugged them as best she could, saying, "It will be all right in time. I know, I'm one of you."

Yannis, with Charessa at her side, stood in the doorway to this recovery room and watched Karis. Charessa continued to hug Yannis as tightly as she could. Yannis put her arm around the young girl and held on to her as well. Soon several men came in with word that the wagons were ready for their passengers. Yannis led Charessa, Cynthia, Eleni, and their mother out first, helping them get into the wagon.

"You'll come with us, won't you," Charessa pleaded with Yannis.

"Please come. We are scared," Eleni added.

Yannis promised, "I will be along later; I have to help everyone else first. I will find you later on in the Santi fortress; I promise you." Charessa smiled and waved her arm goodbye.

An hour later, the last of the women had been loaded and that wagon headed off to the fortress. Men set fire to the infirmary and began loading all the wounded men onto the remaining wagons. Finally, five heavily packed wagons rolled off to the fortress, followed by Dag, Betsy, and Art.

Dag had asked them all to come to the fortress when they finished up here. He took the remainder of the Santi with him to help deal with this huge influx of visitors. The last building to be set ablaze was the stables. All the horses had been confiscated and removed, claimed by Hektor's men. The nuns had already left, struggling to carry the body of their Cardinal. At last, only the Kali remained, surveying the huge blazes. They noticed hundreds of onlookers were now lining the streets outside the complex. It was time they left as well. They slipped out into the streets past the gawking crowd who were talking about this massive raid by Hektor, some saying Hektor got his just revenge. His body had been buried in the courtyard, a final affront to the church, which had assassinated his only son.

Following Karis's orders, one by one, the Kali slipped silently off to their own homes. Only the two women walked on down to the Santi fortress. However, two Kali made sure they arrived safely before they silently departed.

It was four in the morning when the two at last entered the fortress. A Santi sergeant met them at the gate as they entered. "Hi, I'm Alice. Dag and the others are tending to the wounded. We have housed those who are sufficiently healed in our guest rooms. We've put at least one of our women in each room with them to assist them with basic needs. Charessa wants you to come to their room. Something about you promised her?"

A few minutes later, Yannis and Karis entered a room. Many makeshift beds allowed the room to hold a dozen women. "Over here, Yannis. We are over here. We have saved a bed for you and Karis," Charessa called out.

"Go ahead get some sleep, you two. We will come and get you if you are needed," Alice suggested.

Both women were exhausted, but carefully moved over to where the teen was lying down. Indeed, Charessa had saved a bed beside her and one beside that one. "I'm so tired I'll probably sleep all day," Karis said. Then, she realized that she was not at home. Kleo was not here to help her. Embarrassed, she asked, "Yannis, will you help me undress? I cannot do this myself."

"Sure," Yannis helped her remove the leather pants and shirt, then she removed her own outer garments, and both lay down on the beds. Charessa rolled over and put her arm onto Yannis. Instinctively, Yannis put her arm around the young teen. Karis looked at the two, rolled over, and put her short arm on Yannis as well. Soon all were sound asleep.

The only two men who survived what was thereafter called Hektor's Revenge were the two physicians, who were in a local tavern, getting quite drunk that night.

The two awoke the next morning to a bit of chaos. Karis was part of it. "Yannis, wake up. I have to go pee and I need some help with it. I can't get my nickers off by myself." Yannis woke up and hastily helped the embarrassed Karis. As the others woke, Yannis found herself going from woman to woman, helping them with this basic necessity.

"Thanks Yannis. I like you being my arms now," Charessa said as she helped the young teen. Then, she helped Eleni. However, poor Cynthia had a most awkward time dealing with this. Yannis discovered that she had a lot to learn about just how best to help those of the Eighth Degree. Once the ten were done with this, a Santi woman entered with breakfast trays. Actually, several men carried them, but out of modesty for these traumatized women, allowed only Alice to enter the room.

Yannis and the other Santi woman, who was with her, had to feed the ten. Karis, who was used to Kleo always doing this, felt even more embarrassed, but had no choice but to let Yannis feed her and help her dress. Finally, Yannis was able to eat her own breakfast.

Shortly after that, Alice re-entered. "Yannis, Karis, can you come outside with me for a short while? Many of the men are returning north and want to say farewell to you two."

They followed Alice. Outside, gathered in a large group were around eight hundred grubby looking men, who had given all to help Hektor. As soon as they saw the two women, they began yelling and cheering the two, rather embarrassing them both. One man, who had been elected to be their spokesman stepped forward and said, "Yannis, Karis, on behalf of all of us, we want to thank you for what you have helped us do. We are proud to have worked with you. Hektor has completed his mission, and so we return to our homes far from here. However, we will all carry your memories in our hearts and minds. Thank you for freeing these women and all women of Demokritos from the butchery that was this vile church." Now the group really yelled and cheered, further embarrassing both women.

The men mounted and rode out the main gates into Patri. Over one hundred of their original numbers would never return with them. Another hundred would be staying here for some time, until their wounds healed enough for them to travel home as well.

Dag came up to them as the last man left. He looked awful, covered in blood; his eyes were bloodshot. "Been up all night tending the wounded. So have we all. I'm heading to bed. Look after the women until we recover. Alice can get you anything you need. Will talk more after sleep. Sleep." While they smiled, he left, stumbling his way to his room.

"All night!" Karis exclaimed.

"Hundred wounded men to tend, that is an awful lot. We'd better get back to the women," Yannis suggested. They allowed Alice to lead them back to the right room.

When they entered, Charessa and Eleni were standing over Karis's two special weapons. "Karis, what are these strange things?" Eleni asked innocently.

"Be careful. Those are my weapons. I use them to kill bad men," Karis tried to put it in a nice way.

"But how can you kill bad men? You are like me?" she waved her short arms. "I can't do anything."

"Charessa, Eleni, we can do far more than we might believe. That's why they want you to go to Velona, to learn how to do many things that you think you can't do now," Karis replied, but began to wonder if she also ought to go to Velona. She'd seen things, magical things, things that she really wanted to be able to do.

"Will you come with me to learn too? You are like me and Eleni," Charessa begged. "I want Yannis to come with me. She promised to help me."

Karis looked into those innocent young eyes. She saw a beautiful person robbed of her life, as she was. She felt more like a mother to this child that she had just met. "Yes, yes, I do believe that I will go with you, if they will let me." If nothing else, she would look out for her and all of these others here. Karis felt it was her duty to do so.

"Great Yannis. See Karis is coming with us to Velona too," Charessa exclaimed, very happy indeed.

Poor Yannis, floods of conflicting thoughts swept through her confused mind. *I am a murderer. I've killed so many people. I am a thief. I was betrayed into killing. I have stopped Morpheus. I have rescued all these poor women. I don't dare go to Velona; they will recognize me and kill me. I must go to help Charessa, Eleni, and Cynthia. I promised them.*

The distant voice of Karis seeped into her mind. "Yannis, I need you to come with us. I need your help now with so many little things. Please come with me."

"Huh? Oh, yes, Karis. I'm sorry, I was, well confused. I will help you. It has to be so humiliating for you," Yannis said.

Karis's face had a flash of grief. *Yes, it is so humiliating, so degrading, so embarrassing, and so awful to have to ask someone to help me with so many stupidly simple things! I feel so helpless sometimes.* Yet, for these women's sake, she flashed her smile once more. She could not wallow in her own shame.

Cynthia, who had heard Yannis statement, realized suddenly the horrible truth. She would be now doomed to a lifetime of continual humiliations and embarrassments! She began crying and realized she couldn't even wipe her own eyes and bawled even harder.

Yannis went to her. Not knowing exactly what to do or say, put her arms around the young woman. Cynthia wailed, "You are right. I feel humiliated. I cannot even wipe my own eyes!" Yannis began crying along with her.

Their mother, Daphna, too, began crying. "What kind of a mother can I ever be now? I cannot even help my own daughters?" Others in the room, feeling the same way, also began crying. Soon all ten were crying away. Yannis had accidentally started a flood of tears.

Karis began crying as well. She had been valiantly suppressing her grief for years, but now surrounded by these women, it came back to the surface with a vengeance. Yannis, not having the slightest idea of what to do, just leaned over and put her other warm around Karis and pulled Cynthia and Karis close to her, allowing them to rest their heads on her shoulders.

Charessa and Daphna put theirs around the three and Eleni piled onto all of them.

Some hours later, lunch came and Alice and Yannis again fed the ten under their care. Once that was done, Karis said, "Yannis, will you come with me to my home? I need to pack some things to bring with me. On the way, we can stop and get your things."

"You are not going to leave us?" Charessa said worriedly.

"No, I promised," Yannis answered her. "We will be back in time to help you have dinner."

A while later as the two quietly walked the streets heading for the mansion of Karis, the Kali said, "I want to thank you for coming along with me, Yannis. I hate like hell to have to admit this, but I am dependent on someone to help me. I have tried to do much for myself, but I just cannot do so darn many things. That's why I have Kleo and Katerina around me. I can't take either of them with me. I guess I owe you big time now, Yannis."

"Charessa and Eleni affect me deeply somehow. They need me desperately, so do you. I just cannot turn my back on you or her or the others. No one was there to help me when they encased me, and for all that time, I was mostly like Cynthia, utterly and completely helpless. I died because there was no one for me or the others for that matter. I just have to help you all. I wonder what happened to all the others, Karis? There must have been fifty of us there, all helpless living like dogs in the one cage. Maybe they all died too. I won't let that happen to you or the others. I promise you, Karis."

Yannis quickly discovered just how much Karis needed her. The simple chore of packing her things to bring would have taken Karis days to manage by herself. Yannis allowed her to point out what she wanted and then packed it for her. Kleo was promoted to the head of the Kali, until Karis returned. However, Karis insisted that Katerina come and do house chores while she was gone so that Katerina would still have the same income.

Near suppertime, Yannis, carrying four sacks, while Karis struggled to carry one lighter one, arrived at the fortress. Charessa was extremely relieved to see the two come into their room.

After supper, Dag and the others were up and about. He had all the women who could walk come into his huge dining hall for a meeting. Six women, the most recent ones to have had surgery, were bedridden.

Betsy did the talking, however. Dag felt that seeing a man running the meeting might be too hard for these women, under the circumstances. He was right. Betsy gave them a long talk about why they should go to Velona. Not only for further healing and for the handling of their trauma, but also so that they could learn new ways to care for themselves, regain some self-respect as well. It would cost them nothing; the Laird Foundation would pay all expenses.

The complicating factor in this case was the fact that most of these women had been abducted from their homes, meaning that they had a husband or parents to consider. Hence, one family member was encouraged to accompany each woman, if they were able to get away for so long. This added another seventy sets of hands to help on the long voyage. Dag worked with the remaining seventy families, arranging for them to come and visit their loved ones later on.

The Healing Caravel was equipped to handle one hundred patients. However, there were one hundred fifty-two women going to Velona, along with seventy-one parents or relatives, including Karis and Yannis. Although none of the women had yet to have their bandages permanently removed, those who were in the best shape went on Dag's private caravel, while the remainder went on the Healing Caravel. Yannis, Karis, and the four under their direct care, who had been one of the first to be mutilated, went on the private ship.

While much could be said about their voyage of two months, I must say a few words about Yannis. She was kept continually busy helping these women and soon became quite aware of their needs. Noticing subtle clues, she was right there with what was needed. Yannis became extremely attached and devoted to Charessa, Eleni, and Cynthia. So much so, that this assassin changed her basic goals from killing others whom she thought deserved it over to helping others who really needed help. She vowed to learn all she could in Velona about healing and helping women. The two-month voyage began the fundamental change in Yannis's outlook on life.

They set sail on May 7 and arrived in Velona on July 10, 702.

Chapter 18 The Choices of Maren

All during April, Sandy had made contact with me at night, keeping me posted on what little they managed to learn. I was appalled, shocked, and disgusted at what Cardinal Morpheus was now doing in Patri. I felt helpless to do anything about it, which only added to my depression. I could not talk much with Deimos, for he was always chatting with Alexandr. Moreover, I had the reins in my teeth and couldn't talk much as we rode. During the evenings after we stopped for the night, I couldn't talk to Mia or Hans, because Eirena was always there helping us women with our necessities.

At last, I could take it no longer. Deimos and Alekos just had to know the treachery Cardinal Morpheus was doing at home. *Mia, Hans, I need the messenger illusion.* Mia nodded to me and suggested that I accompany her on a short walk around the camp.

"When do you want it and what's the message going to say?" she whispered.

"Tomorrow. When the least number of people have to be controlled by your illusion. Have the writing on the document look like Sea Prince, and I'll pretend to read it. You pretend to hold it and flip the pages. Is this possible?" I asked.

"Tough one. I think Hans and I will have to work together on this one. I will call out for you when we are doing it, have you ride back, and read it. What will we do with the dispatch when we are done reading it? Someone else might like to handle it or save it?" Mia replied.

"I don't know, pretend you are crumpling it up, put it in your pocket, and then toss it into the camp fire? I was going to say to tear it up into pieces and toss it on the ground, but then what about the pieces. I leave it up to you two."

Midmorning the next day, while they were riding along, Eirena said, "Mia, I think that there is a rider coming along side our coach. I believe it is a dispatch rider from Demokritos! Look, he is handing some towards you."

"It is a dispatch rider, Eirena!" She leaned out of the window and took the rolled package from the rider's hand. At once, the rider veered off, heading back the way he had come.

"Look, I recognize that seal! It's Santi, from fortress. Oh, I can't read it. Can you?" Eirena's face fell.

"Yes, but it's addressed to Empress Maren. Hans, see if you can get Maren back here. This is for her, and it must be very important."

"Yes, dear, right away!" He leaned way out of the coach window and yelled for me. I leaned my body, put a light pressure on my mare's neck, and we turned around and headed for the coach, not far behind us. When I drew alongside, I turned my horse around, paralleling the coach. "A dispatch rider just brought this letter. Eirena thinks it is from the Santi fortress. It is addressed to you."

I asked the driver to hold up a second. Hans helped me get down, tied my reins to the carriage, and the driver started up once more. "Mia, can you open it for me, and I'll read it aloud. I am sure glad that our teacher, Mr. Halvor, taught us to read many languages." She appeared to be opening it and then I read aloud:

Empress Maren,

I regret to inform you that the Church of Jehosanity is once more committing high treason in Demokritos. Cardinal Morpheus is having his Holy Paladins seek out young women in Patri who have spoken out against the Church. His men abduct three women each day and are cutting off either their hands, or their arms at the elbows, or taking the entirety of their arms. He claims that now they will only be able to earn Good Marks.

Already hundreds of women have been abducted and mutilated. Now he is even having husbands begging him to do this to their wives and daughters, against the women's will. King Milo is doing nothing about it. He has only about one legion while the Cardinal has thirty-three legions.

Please tell the Emperor that his cousin, Eleni Gavril, was abducted early on, and as far as we know, she has lost her arms at the elbows. She is still alive, but we do not know her condition. It seems that Cardinal Morpheus is beginning to take over control of your country.

Sincerely,
Dag Waterby

"Oh good god!" cried Eirena.

"Damn! This is very bad news," I exclaimed. "I had better go tell this to Deimos and Alekos at once! Hans, can you help me with this?" He told the driver to hold up once more. Mia made a motion that indicated she was putting the paper into Hans's pocket.

After Hans put me back on my horse, he took the reins, and we jogged up to Deimos and Alekos. Quickly, I relayed the news in detail, trying not to add anything else that I had not pretended to read. "Where is this letter?" Alekos said solemnly, he was terribly worried about the home front situation.

Hans fumbled in his pockets, "Damn, it must have fallen out when I was jogging up here, bringing the Empress."

"Never mind. Deimos, this new development is extremely serious. This Cardinal Morpheus is defying your throne!" Alekos stated in strong terms. "Your own young cousin, Eleni! How old is she?"

Deimos had a tear in his eye, but tried valiantly not to show emotion. He replied, "She's fourteen. This is an outrageous misuse of our holiest matrimonial ceremonies. This is barbarous! Alekos, this is high treason!" I hoped I was finally getting through to Deimos, that this excursion was utter folly, but my heart sank with his next sentence.

"But what am I to do about it? Here we are thousands of miles from home, two months by sea plus six more weeks overland. If I wanted to send back thirty-some legions, then that would both jeopardize our entire campaign to conquer Tarra, and they would not get there for four months. Another four hundred women would have been harmed before they could even get there. So what should I do, Alekos?"

Alekos had no answer; he just looked sadly at the ground as it moved along slowly beneath his horse's feet. I decided to ride in the carriage a while, and we two dropped back to the carriage. Once inside, I must have looked incredibly morose.

"What's the matter, Empress?" asked Eirena. "Something's wrong. I can tell."

"Deimos and Alekos — they cannot think of anything to do about it. They are going to do nothing at all right now. Maybe when we get back in a year or so. . ."

"Oh no! By then, thousands of women will be so grossly mutilated! I will speak to him myself about it tonight, though if he will not listen to you, Empress, he probably won't listen to me either," Eirena said encouragingly. I rode along until lunchtime, moping in my own depression.

Another interesting event occurred that evening when we halted for camp. The supply wagons, which were supposed to be bringing up another load of food for the army, had not come. We were getting low on food and needed the promised wagon loads that Cardinal Morpheus and his Pope had promised. Deimos ordered fifty riders to gallop back down the road to see how far behind us they were. At dark, they returned having found no trace of any such wagons.

Furious, Alexandr ordered the heliograph signalmen to send a message down to Megalos, asking just how far behind us the promised supply wagons actually were. Around ten in the morning, the heliograph man reported to Alexandr. I overheard his report. "General, your message was relayed all the way back to Sud. Not one of our heliograph outposts along the road has seen any of these wagons!"

I couldn't help but throw my opinions into the fire. "I warned you not to trust this Church of Jehosanity! Now our army will starve to death!" I was being melodramatic, I know, but then I was depressed anyway.

"If we were not so far along, I'd return and teach this Pope a lesson!"

Alexandr yelled.

"What can we do?" asked Alekos.

"Oh we won't starve. I am the General after all. I made allowances for some treachery such as this. None of you asked where our seventy-five caravels went, now did you?" he was gloating over his wise, surprise move that we knew nothing about. "Tell them Emperor."

Deimos, feeling rather pompous, said, "They are all in the Med Sea near New Barq, loaded with supplies, just in case something like this happened. As soon as we get there, we will have all we can eat again. How long will that be, General?"

"Less than two weeks, Emperor. We should begin food rationing at once. I will give orders to have all of what remains tallied and then rationed out for fourteen more days. If we run too low, I will send out hunting and foraging parties. We will not starve in this short a time, though our stomachs may be a little lean."

When the Centurions around our campsite found out about it this evening, there was some grumbling as expected. "Oh dear," was Eirena's comment.

Fourteen more dreary, depressing days passed, only now I was hungry more hours of the day, which only added to it. Mid May arrived and at last we saw the Santi tower of New Barq in the distance. Ahead of us, Deimos' mighty army stretched out in campsites for miles in the open desert around the city. Already many of the ships had docked and re-supplied their supply wagons. Ours was the last to be refilled, and all of us were quite grateful for this. Alexandr had been wiser than I gave him credit for — my stomach thanked him.

That night, I received a full accounting of the raid by Hektor, the Kali, and this new assassin, Yannis who hailed from Megalos. The details were grim and brutally savage. All those men burned alive bothered me. Yet, the tragic news of so many women brought tears to my eyes and to Mia and Hans, when I told them the news when we were alone. Mia's comment cheered me slightly, "At least they are bringing them all to Velona. Now they will have a new chance for life. Left in Demokritos, their lives would be one of utter misery." I took hope in that. Hektor had been true to his word, and I mourned his passing. Details of this I chose not to tell the others at this time.

Around the campfire, Deimos explained to me, "Maren, we will rest up here a week. The men have been marching for nearly two months now. After they rest up, we will then march on Zargarb; our glorious conquest shall begin at long last!"

"Deimos, this is wrong! The prophesy does not say you are to attack and subjugate the world. If you do this, you will be going against the prophesy."

"Maren, I have been giving this a lot of thought. I admit that I now believe that you are correct in your interpretation. Yet, here we are with our army. Alexandr is very confident that we can indeed do this. I've decided to let him try it. Maren, I don't like always having to do what someone else is telling me to do, especially when the orders come from seven hundred years ago. Yet, here we are with an opportunity that I cannot let pass. We will march on Zargarb in a week."

I sighed, "Deimos, if you get killed, then there will be no way that the prophesy can be fulfilled, not unless I marry the next Emperor who takes over after your death. If you really want to be that Emperor spoken of in the Prophesies of Demos, don't go getting killed. For god's sake, stay back here with me; don't go up front with Alexandr." I got this small concession from him, mostly because Alexandr also suggested that the Emperor should stand tall above the battlefield, directing the overall battle.

The night before the assault on Zargarb was to commence, I contacted Linda at headquarters in Velona. *Hi, it's me. I've failed; he is attacking Zargarb's lower fortress tomorrow morning.*

You have not failed yet, Maren Bethany. Zargarb has not fallen yet. I believe that you will have another opportunity to change history tomorrow afternoon. Use that one wisely.

I didn't see how I would get another chance, by then the battle would be long underway. *I need to contact the fortress Communicator or commander. I need to keep them updated. I sure am in a fine pickle here. I'm supposed to be on Deimos' side, yet I am on our side, Zargarb's side.*

No, you are on humanity's side, preventing another horrendous war, where thousands will perish, and major upheavals result. Your contact is Erika Enyo Westhall, Enyo's daughter. She married your youngest son, Adrien. She's the Zargarb Communicator and he's a Planner. They both are forty-seven, by the way. Nicolina Sue Decassas Zar is still the monarch; she's fifty-four now and married Rachelle's son, Muzzio Decassas. Your daughter, Lena and Zach are fifty-one now. All of them will be at this key fortress, excepting Nicolina Sue and Muzzio, who are staying in the city in case the fortress falls.

Damn, Linda. If it gets that serious, I guarantee you that I'll start decimating the Centurions before I let them hurt my children!

I know. I have put you into a terrible position. You have my permission to do just that, protect your children as you can. Still, I don't believe that it will come to that. Chaucer and I both feel that you will have one more chance tomorrow afternoon.

Okay, I had better contact them now. Thanks Linda.

I relaxed and reached out for Erika, who I had not seen now for over sixteen years. *Hi, Maren Bethany here.*

Bethany! How are you doing? Are you all right?

Yes, depressed because I still haven't been able to prevent this war yet. They are going to attack you in the morning.

Hang on one minute. Everyone wants to join in and chat with you. She Mind Linked in Lena, Zach, and Adrien. *Hi mom!* It was Lena. *Hi mom.* It was Adrien.

My body was crying, while I chatted with my two children from last lifetime. For an hour, we talked about everything. Dear Enyo, my brilliant, loving engineer, she too had lost her body last year at seventy. I had many grandchildren I had never met. Of course, this Maren body was not their grandmother. It would be somewhat hard on me to meet them this way.

Don't worry mom, Adrien sent. *We will be showing them a thing or two in the morning. I believe my inventions will give you that final opportunity that Linda keeps telling us will happen. I sure do hope so anyway.* Finally, I was getting sleepy — no the body was, and we broke our contact. They needed their sleep for the big day tomorrow.

After breakfast, Deimos strapped on his pieces of armor and sword. Eirena watched him and commented, "Deimos, you look like a conqueror. Good luck today." He smiled at her.

"Deimos," I said, "this is wrong, very wrong. It's not too late to change." He glared at me. I added, "Just don't go getting yourself killed!"

He left with Alexandr to inspect the troops. We climbed into the carriage, with my horse tied to its rear. We rode down into the valley. On our right was the Cedar Forest. On our left was the Med Sea. This was exactly the same place where the First Crusades had been fought! Memories of that horrible slaughter came back to me. Then, I was Ket Bethany, leading the Santi Strike Force, up from New Bark to come to the relief of the crusaders, who had been battling the Centurions from Megalos right here for a month. Some Arad fighters also swooped down and finished off the remaining Centurions and my strike force came to heal.

God, what a sight we found there. Only a very few crusaders were un-wounded. Hundreds were gravely wounded. We tended rotting wounds — men and women missing all sorts of arms and legs — their wounds grossly infected. No one was able to bury the dead, and the massive pile of thousands of rotting dead bodies littered the ground. I've never seen such horrors before. Yet, it all had happened right here where we were.

Our carriage pulled up on the last hilltop overlooking the road and narrow plains, which led up to the first of the Santi built fortresses, designed to prevent just such an attack. Here, we would have a bird's eye view of the battle as it unfolded, a view, which I desperately wanted to have avoided at all costs, yet had not. Hans helped us all to find seats, moving several boulders together so we could sit as a group. Below, we saw General Alexandr and Deimos going from legion to legion, undoubtedly encouraging them to victory, which I sensed would not happen.

"If it gets too awful, too ugly to watch, just go back inside the coach. Wars are horrible to watch, the aftermath, horrific," I said glumly.

Eirena said, "It's Alexandr. He treats Deimos like the father he never had. His real dad was a drunkard and a looser. Deimos thinks so highly of Alexandr. That's why he is going along with the general's plan, Maren. I know that he thinks you are very right about the prophesy. Maybe it will all work out fine. We have an awful lot of men down there and that is only a small fortress blocking their way." She tried to sound hopeful and was certainly sticking up for Deimos.

An hour later, Deimos rode up to our position and joined us. "Alexandr explained that he is sending in our six top legions. He says always send in first those men who are most eager and enthusiastically behind the war. They have the edge of desire on their side. Here's his plan. These six that you see moving out now are going to head straight for the fortress and engage and surround them. While they then keep them occupied, the next six legions are preparing the siege towers, and will roll them up to the walls. Once they are in position, another dozen legions will join them, and all twenty-four legions will swarm over the walls, taking the fortress. General Alexandr told me that he will have us entering the gates of the fortress by suppertime."

"Deimos, if that happens, I'll eat your shirt for my supper!" I declared morosely.

"You are just being pessimistic, Empress. You will see. Alexandr is the strongest man I know," Deimos replied.

"We shall see," was all that Alekos would say. He added a bit later, "Don't discount all the reports of their defenses that our Empress has discovered from talking with the Santi back home, Deimos."

Midmorning, the six legions in the front wave were approaching a thousand yards from the tall grey fortress walls. Boom! Boom! Boom! Boom! A thunderous noise echoed across the battlefield below us, bouncing off the hills. We saw a dozen light flashes first followed by the resounding noise. That got everyone's attention here on the hill. "Sounds like Tashien fireworks," commented Deimos. I knew better, far better.

A minute after that the fireworks exploded, not high in the sky as the magnificent aerial displays we had seen, but in a blinding ball of fire and flames just over the heads of the six legions! Ten blasts followed in quick succession. At once, another ten enormous booms broke the stillness; another volley was on its way.

On the battlefield, as the smoke cleared away in the gentle sea breeze, bodies were lying in a jumbled pattern. Over half of the six hundred men were not standing. The others stood around holding their ears in complete shock. The six legions that were behind this first assault group halted of their own accord, uncertain what to do.

Deimos screamed as loudly as he could. Mia exclaimed, "Oh my god!"

"Wow!" was the comment from Hans. The others just stared in complete disbelief.

"What is that?" asked Lyris, who found her voice at last.

"Those are the dragon cannon that the Santi back in Patri warned us about. I think their technical name is cannone assassino. More than appropriate," I replied as the next ten shells landed among the original group. The resulting explosions again were deafening. We women had no arms to cover our ears and had to endure it, while Mia and Hans covered theirs involuntarily.

I expected to hear yet another volley being fired, but an eerie silence fell, incredible silence after such a tremendous noise. My son Adrien had done his job very well. Not a man stood out of the original advancing six legions. All on the battlefield below stopped dead in their tracks. No motion of any kind could be seen.

Suddenly, Deimos realized that Alexandr was among those in this first wave. He screamed, "Alexandr! Alexandr!" He started to race to his horse to charge down there to find his general.

"Deimos, stop!" I used my commanding voice. He stopped dead in his tracks and turned to face me, his face white as a sheet. "Get a white flag, a sign of truce. Carry it high as you go down there. I am coming with you, so you are going to have to lift me onto my horse. For once, Deimos, do as I say!" He fetched our horses, while Eirena fashioned a white flag from part of her knickers and gave it to Deimos. She, too, looked awful.

Deimos struggled to get me onto my horse, never having done it before. At last, he and I slowly rode down the hill, as he held the white flag as high as he could. I had already sent word to Erika to have them hold off on more volleys. Now I knew that this was what Linda had meant. I had one last opportunity to turn this war around before it was too late and the total slaughter began.

The six forward legions, seeing Deimos and me coming down to the devastation in front of them, also hoisted several white flags and began moving slowly to help us assist the wounded men. I knew in my mind what we would find when we got there, there would be no survivors. As Deimos and I reached the back edge of what had, minutes before, been our finest legions, the carnage was clearly visible. Body parts lay scattered about; bits of iron protruded from heads, eyes, torsos, and even limbs that were still attached, as well as those that were lying about. Massive pools of blood drained into the earth or began congealing on the paved road.

Deimos began vomiting from atop his horse. I would have spared him seeing this, but I had to make the outcome of wars real to him, not the glorious images that Alexandr had been feeding him all these years. Deimos rode to where he had last seen his beloved general, who he had used as a substitute father. We found him, rather what was left of him. His head was barely recognizable, for so many iron pieces had torn away most of his face. Parts of his arms and legs were missing, and we never did locate them. Deimos began crying profusely, and I let him grieve for a short while.

Soon, however, the six legions would close the gap to us. They would be expecting orders from their Emperor now. "Deimos, your legions are coming. It is time that you grow up and start acting on your own council. You must start giving them orders. Act like an Emperor now or you will lose their respect and your throne as a result."

"But what do I order them to do?" he wailed, tears soaking his face.

"Tell them to start a burial detail and give our fallen warriors a proper burial for starters. You might also tell them the truth about all this," I said.

He wiped is face on his sleeves, just in time as the first captain arrived, leading his legion. "Captain, Alexandr's war is over. We do not attack any more. It is time that we bury our fallen comrades who died bravely here today. Please take the time to see that they are all buried properly. I will meet with all the other captains when this is done. Thank you, captain."

"Yes, Emperor Deimos!" The expression on this captain's face spoke volumes. The utter relief he expressed told Deimos that he had said the right words. I suspected that the captain had expected his Emperor to order an all-out charge in retaliation, which would mean certain death for him and his men.

"Come on; let's get back to the others, Deimos. I've dropped my reins. Will you lead my horse, please? I can talk to you as we go." He grabbed my reins and began heading back up the hill.

"Maren, what am I going to do now?" he asked.

"Be the leader that you were born to be. Act from your heart. Do what is right and just for your people and for all the peoples of Tarra. Make your own goals and follow them. Stop letting others tell you what to do."

"Do what I want to do? How strange that sounds to me just now, Maren."

"Listen to Alekos and hear his advice. Then, you decide whether you want to take it. What does your heart tell you?"

He gave a cynical laugh, "My heart? My heart tells me that I love Eirena and long to be with her. That's what it tells me. If I did that, I'd be called unfaithful to you, who are of the Eighth Degree. They'll kill me for doing that, Maren!"

"No they won't, Deimos. We were never married, remember?"

"Oh," he said, his mind racing with the significance of that. "But how can I? I mean you have been with me from the beginning. Don't I owe it to you? I mean you are dependent upon me, aren't you?"

"No, I am not dependent on you, Deimos. I live my own life. I don't need you, but I suspect that Eirena does. We should have a long talk with Alekos and Eirena immediately. We have several hours before you will have to issue orders to your army. Let us use this brief time wisely, Deimos." We pulled up before the crying companions on the hilltop.

"Is he, I mean are any . . ." Eirena couldn't say the words.

Deimos answered, "They're all dead, blown to bits. I threw up when I saw it. I won't let any of you go down there. It is beyond description. I've ordered the captains to bury our brave soldiers properly and then to have all the captains report to me here when this is done. We need to talk now." He dismounted, but forgot about me. Quietly, Hans lifted me down, a fact not missed by my friends, especially Lyris.

"I'll make us some tea, Deimos. It will help soothe your throat," Mia offered. Yes, I could use a cup myself right now.

We all sat down. Deimos looked at Alekos and then said, "Alekos, it is time that I take charge. From now on, I am going to lead, follow my own council, and follow my own heart. I must do what is right for our people. The total annihilation down there is not in anyone's best interests."

"Excellent, Emperor, I will support you all the way," Alekos said more enthusiastically than I had ever heard him sound!

"Good. Let's start with Maren here. When I went to get her, as the prophesy instructed, I was only fourteen and ignorant of many things. I thought that just going and getting her to make her mine, as one would do with a new dog. In the back of my mind, I knew this was wrong, that we should be married. I now know better, Maren; I am sorry about this whole thing."

Alekos added, "Yes, well, I must assume the responsibility for that decision, Deimos. I knew that you should actually marry her, but if you remember, I suggested that you didn't. I have never been a true believer in ancient prophesies. I was terribly worried that Maren would be a horrible liability to have around as Empress, so that is why I cleverly didn't have you two officially marry. Maren, it is all my doing. I am the one responsible for you having to have lived these years in unholy wedlock. Please forgive me. I was only doing what I thought best for Deimos here."

"You are both completely forgiven. I guessed that was the reason right away when no mention of a wedding ceremony came," I replied magnanimously.

Eirena brightened up, "But then how can Maren continue to be our Empress? I don't understand this at all."

"I have only been an Empress of 'convenience,' Eirena. I think that now is a good time for me to end this charade. Don't you all think so?"

Zenovia, Lyris, and Amara, all three gasped! This was shocking news to them. Here I was a helpless Eighth Degree woman being cast off — from the position of Empress, no less.

Alekos replied, "I agree with you, Maren. However, Deimos and I will see that you are properly handled for the rest of your life. It is the very least that we can do for you."

"Thank you. Now that being handled, Deimos, let's handle affairs of the heart first. Is there something that you wish to ask Eirena?" I winked at him.

Deimos flushed. He took a deep breath and moved over to Eirena. "Eirena, I have been in love with you for ages. Would you consent to give me your hand in marriage?"

Eirena nearly fainted. Her face showed intense joy, relief, utter shock, and surprise all at the same time. She squeaked, "Yes! Oh yes!" She added, "But I want to keep my hands, Deimos. I don't want to become a woman of Degrees. I mean no disrespect, Maren, Amara, Lyris, Zenovia, but I just cannot live like you. I am not that brave a woman."

"I promise you that I will never ever ask you to, either," Deimos replied. "Honestly, Maren, I have never gotten comfortable with you. I am just not cut out to have a woman make such a sacrifice for me. I cannot deal with it. Can you four understand me? I, too, don't mean any disrespect or to lessen what you have done."

"I understand, Deimos, truly I do now understand," Lyris answered him.

"Good for you, Deimos!" Amara added. Zenovia just smiled.

I whispered, "Deimos, you are supposed to give her a kiss about now." He needed no further encouragement.

Mia passed out the tea all around. "Now we should get down to business, Deimos. The burial detail won't take all that long," Alekos suggested.

"Maren, can I ask one more thing of you?" Deimos asked me kindly. I nodded, sipping away at my tea, content to let things roll along.

"I have been thinking about the real intent behind the prophesy and about what I see as our strengths. I know that I have snapped at you over this before, but I was listening. As I see it, right now we have many caravels, which are doing nothing. I know that the Santi in Patri have said that Velona has double that number. However, I think that our way to greatness lies in commerce. Our country is many times larger than Velona; eventually our ships could easily outnumber theirs. I think that we should open up all kinds of trading with these other lands. What do you think? Am I just dreaming or is it feasible?"

"I believe that you are precisely on target. In time, this will bring enormous prosperity to Demokritos. It is something that all people can assist in bringing into existence, something to rally all of the kingdoms. However, I would stress most strongly that you send some people to Velona to learn many of the languages others speak; otherwise, your ship crews will be facing a big barrier to communication. I say Velona, because they have traveled extensively, and many there know many languages."

Deimos broke into a huge grin; at last, he had worked a great plan out all on his own! We chatted over other details until the remaining sixty-nine captains came walking up the hill to meet with Deimos. He went from leader to leader, shaking each one's hand.

He then made his most critical speech to date. "Captains, valiant captains. The war of Alexandr's is now over. We head to New Barq, where our caravels will take us home." They broke into a round of applause, for none wanted to face another artillery barrage.

"I must apologize to you all and relay that to your men. I have been a childish fool following Alexandr's continual urging for this war of conquest. In that, I take full responsibility for what happened out there on the battlefield today. I was warned about this repeatedly by Maren Bethany and many others, but I was blinded by my misguided love for Alexandr."

"Those of you who believe in the ancient prophesy, know this, the prophesy does not say we should become a world power by conquering these lands by war. It is by establishing the largest commerce fleet on Tarra that we will take our rightful place as world leaders. When we return, I will lay out plans to double the size of our fleet, and then double that again. I will be looking for men who love the sea and wish to travel to all the lands of Tarra. We will also need some security forces to accompany them. Once we return home, I will be disbanding most of the legions. Let you and your men know that shortly all these positions will be open. I will ensure that all you men who have served me so well this trip have the first opportunities to fill these many new positions."

"Finally, a personal note. Due to an oversight, Empress Maren and I were never married." He paused to allow them to grasp the magnitude of what he just said. "That means that unless I marry her, she is actually not entitled to be our Empress. She agrees with me entirely and does not hold me to blame for this gross error. I have decided to marry for love, not for power. My maid all these years, Eirena here, has agreed to marry me and will become the true Empress of Demokritos. We will wed in New Barq, so that it is official. I ask that all you bear witness to our vows there. Please, no presents. You have already given us the best presents possible; you are still alive yourselves, and you have kept us alive as well."

"Finally, to make amends for my horrible mistreatment of Maren Bethany, a most honorable woman of the Eighth Degree, she has accepted the post of Demokritos's ambassador to Velona. Thank you. As soon as you tell your men, let's put some miles between us and this valley of death, please."

First one captain began slowly clapping. Soon, all sixty-nine were clapping loudly. Deimos had swayed them completely; their loyalty to the throne remained intact.

War was thus averted at the last minute. History calls this Alexandr's War, whether or not the man deserved full credit for it. It is also the only war in history which lasted all of two minutes — the time it took to launch two artillery barrages. It also opened far too many people's eyes to the new technology of the cannone assassino.

As we began to retrace our route back to New Barq, I chose to ride in the carriage. Not being the Empress any longer, I did not need to ride at his side. Eirena was near tears though when I climbed in and sat beside her and Mia. "Maren, I feel so awful taking the throne away from you. It's as if I am stealing it from you. You are so much wiser than I am and are of the Eighth Degree as well. It should belong to you."

"Eirena, I saw that you loved Deimos a long time ago. The throne belongs to the woman who loves Deimos and is loved by Deimos. I fit neither of those. You do. You are not stealing anything from me. I, like so many others, have been but pawns in this stupid prophesy game. My mother believed in it utterly, which is why she had my arms removed the day I was born. Deimos and his court believed that they just had to come and find me, the only Eighth Degree woman in Annelise. You see, in the end, we have all been used by this prophesy, one way or another. Had Deimos been totally ignoring the prophesy, you may well already be married to him and Empress. So you, too, have been used. Now is the time to set matters straight. Deimos and I have ended this blind-following prophesy game. We want to lead our own lives. You now have your chance to do wonderful things for your people. You will make a very fine Empress. After all, Eirena, how many Empresses have been a maid and know what real life is all about?" She smiled at that. Eirena was not of noble birth and had to work since she was a very young girl. She gave me a long hug and kissed my forehead.

That night, Erika contacted me with all the others in a Mind Link with her. *You did it! They are leaving.* She sent.

No, Adrien did it with his invention. You should have seen the results, Adrien, ghastly beyond belief. Not one survivor out of the six hundred. Arms and legs blown off, bits of metal sticking out of heads, eye sockets, chests, blood everywhere, ghastly!

I told you I would do it, mom! It worked. We had only one casualty; one man got a small burn from touching the lighted fuse. See, it stopped a war dead in its tracks, mom.

Son, the next war, the other side will also have your cannone assassino. Not even the thick walls of the fortress will provide protection. Shoot, maybe even the walls will be blown up too.

Ah, that's a long way in the future; maybe it won't happen. The main thing, mom, is this is the first time in history that Zargarb held on and wasn't conquered by the invading army. That is something to be proud of — don't you think so? I had to agree with him.

What are your plans now? asked my daughter, Lena. *Will we get to meet you?*

Not right away. We are going back to New Bark. I have Zenovia, Amara, and Lyris under my care. I've promised to get them to Velona and to the Laird Foundation. All four of us have to learn how to live better than we have been. They are still mostly helpless women, so I have to help them and myself too. I will come and visit later on, once I have them doing well.

Give my love to everyone and my thanks to saving Zargarb.

It's we who must thank you. I fully expected the other sixty-nine legions to come charging at us. Had they done that, we really didn't have enough firepower to stop that many. We would have lost the fortress, mom. We chatted some more until my body fell asleep.

Two days later, we were all back outside New Barq. Alekos found a priest of the Sun God there and brought him to our camp. Zenovia, Amara, Lyris, Mia, and I stood for the bride, while Alekos and sixty-nine captains stood for Deimos. It was a simple ceremony, but one filled with love. As they shared their first kiss as man and wife, Mia carried the simple crown that I had often worn and put in on Eirena's head. Everyone with hand clapped loudly, while the four of us stamped on the ground.

Then came the preparations for the return trip to Demokritos. We had sixty-nine legions with us, plus one legion spread out all along the north-south road to Sud. To carry us back, nearly double the number of caravels would be needed. Hence, thirty-two legions would have to walk back to Sud. Deimos asked for volunteers and found too many captains willing to make that long walk on foot. He had to choose thirty-seven legions to board the boats.

"Five months from now, these caravels will be in Sud to pick you up, if not sooner. Take your time and have fun on your way to Sud. I am sending along ample supplies to get you there and then some. When you get there, captains, I leave what you do to or with this treasonous Pope Aison up to your discretion. I will support whatever action you desire to take. As soon as these thirty-seven legions land in Patri, we will put an end to their treachery there. Good luck, men. Once again, I thank you," Deimos wrapped up his farewell speech to those walking home.

At last, we boarded the caravel, the Emperor's ship. It would take us ten or so days to get to Velona, where we six would depart. As we watched New Barq drift behind us, Deimos asked me, "Maren, are you sure that you will be all right here in Velona all by yourself? I mean you have never been there and you are, well you know what I mean. I assure you that we will send ample funds for your care, always, Maren."

"Yes, I'll be okay. I still have my handmaiden and my protector with me, and I have these three lovely women. We will go to this Laird Foundation and see what becomes of that. From all that we have heard about them, they may be able to help us learn how to live better as we are. Send all the funds to them; they will always know where we might be. I doubt that I will return to Annelise though. I have you to thank heartily for rescuing me from those stupid clothes, impossible to wear for a woman such as I am." Everyone chuckled, no more so than Mia, who had to endure them as I had, only she at least had arms.

During the days that it took to get to Velona, Mia and Hans worked with Zenovia, Amara, and Lyris to learn some basic words of the Sea Prince dialect, a crash course, so to speak. This kept their anxiety lowered; after all, they were about to enter a foreign country of which they knew nothing about and felt even more helpless than normal.

Chapter 19 Velona at Last

June 1, 702, the Royal Arc at last arrived at Velona. We were all on deck as the caravel used its spanker sail to enter this vast harbor slowly. Even Deimos was impressed with the size of the port and city. It has grown considerably since I last saw it, well more than twenty years ago, when I came for Elona Po's funeral. The docks themselves had to be at least twenty-five percent larger! A dozen ships were either loading or unloading, while two more were following us in to the docks.

I had briefed Deimos, Eirena, and Alekos on what to expect. Linda had already briefed me. She and Chaucer would be there to greet us along with Ellaina Dietz Po and her husband Felix. Ellaina was the monarch of Velona. Thankfully, Linda decided to keep the reception down to the key leaders, primarily to avoid overwhelming us. Some of Bard Tal's musicians would play a welcome fanfare.

"The sheer size is truly impressive," remarked Alekos.

"You mean it is huge," Deimos stated more plainly. Eirena just kept saying "Wow!"

I could tell that Zenovia, Amara, and Lyris were getting very nervous. There were so many people, so vast a city, all so terribly different, and they felt even more helpless than normal. I too felt nervous. Linda had been my best friend last lifetime. She and Chaucer had been spiritually freed by the Guardian of the Anuir, Jes Amir, and were so vastly more able and powerful than I was. Besides, I now had a new body. I wondered how I would fit in with everyone. I was glad that the reception would be kept small!

After the mooring lines were tied securely, the gangplank was attached. While the crew unloaded our few possessions, we six along with Deimos, Eirena, and Alekos walked down onto the timbers of the docks. Again, our forward pace was slow. Mia and I could only move so fast in our boots. Once we hit the main part of the docks, the musical fanfare began, lasting until we drew close to the four standing awaiting our arrival.

As we halted, Ellaina spoke first, surprising us by using our language, if with a decidedly Megalos accent, "Welcome to Velona. I am the monarch of our country, Ellaina Dietz Po. My husband, Felix. I don't speak your language all that well, so I hope I don't make too many mistakes." She was kindly; she had aged so since I last saw her as a young girl. She was now fifty-four, grey streaks appearing here and there in her long black hair. "May this be the official start of a long and friendly relationship between our two countries."

Eirena whispered, "She doesn't look like a queen."

"I am Emperor Deimos Gavril, my new wife, Empress Eirena. My advisor, Alekos. You speak fairly well, much better than my Sea Prince, thank you."

Linda and Chaucer stepped forward, and Deimos and Eirena were very surprised to see that she too was of the Eighth Degree. "I am Linda d'Grange, my husband, Chaucer. We are the leaders of the Santi del Dio. Very glad finally to meet the Emperor of Demokritos. We've heard a lot about you from our delegation in Patri. It is good that we meet at long last."

"Pleased to meet you both. I've heard many wonderful things about Velona," Deimos said diplomatically.

"Would you and the Empress care for a tour?" asked Ellaina.

"May we have a rain check, please? You see after this incredible mess of things that I've made, there is a crisis at home that I must attend to as soon as possible. Once I have things under control there, may we return for a lengthy visit?" Deimos asked. Gosh, I was truly surprised at how well he was handing things! He was growing up fast!

"Absolutely! Any time. I understand," Ellaina replied.

"This is to be our ambassador to Velona, Maren Elizabet Ryker, and her handmaiden Mia Kallisto Ryker, and her husband and protector of Maren, Hans. Maren has brought three of our most honored women here in hopes that they may learn to live their lives better, though I do not know how that may be possible. May I have your word that these women of the Eighth Degree will be accorded the high honor that they deserve?" Deimos was really a changed man, I thought.

"Emperor, you may count on that!" Ellaina replied most sincerely.

"Thank you. We will be sending funds for their proper care, but until such arrives, will you see to their needs? You will be repaid most fully."

"Absolutely, Emperor. They will be treated as if they were family."

"Excellent. I hate to rush off so quickly, but I have thirty plus legions of men waiting out there, and they are most anxious to return to their families. I will send a dispatch and the funds through your branch in Patri. Perhaps we will be able to come for a visit next fall; I mean spring. I get these seasons mixed up; you have summer when we have winter, so confusing."

"Yes, that is part of what makes this such an interesting world, Emperor Deimos. We look forward to your visit." With that both groups bowed and the three returned to the ship, leaving us six standing before the four.

As they left us, I had an awful feeling as if I was now leaving behind all that was familiar and known to me, stepping into the unknown, even though I knew all four from my last lifetime. I could only imagine how the other three women in my care must be feeling. Ellaina looked at us four women and said, "Before I let Linda take you off to her place, I want to let all four of you in particular know that if ever you need anything, anything at all, just send word to me. I am here to serve. Welcome to the finest country on Tarra."

She gave each of us a warm, loving hug, with an added kiss on my forehead. Then, she and Felix left us with Chaucer and Linda. Linda said, "Ladies, and gentleman, I am so very glad to see and meet all of you at long last. You are all very beautiful, well not you, Hans." That brought a chuckle to us women and I found magically my gnawing fears evaporate. I relaxed.

"I have a coach waiting for us to take us to our headquarters and the Laird Foundation. This way." We followed her while some dockhands carried our few sacks to the carriage. Hans and Chaucer helped us all inside, and soon, we were off. Linda simply allowed us all to look, keeping conversation to a minimum.

I looked at her. She ought to be at least in her late sixties, he too. Yet she didn't look a day over thirty! Her long, curly blonde hair reached her knees, and her blue eyes looked brighter than I remembered. Likewise, Chaucer looked like a dashing young man of thirty. Truly amazing how they had not aged!

As we neared our destination, Linda said, "We've made quite a few changes here over the years. With women of the Eighth Degree (she used our term for it), over these many years of helping them adjust better, we have found that if four women live in close conjunction with each other, they can help each other much more effectively. That learned, we have rebuilt all the dormitories accordingly. We have prepared a quintuple-plex for you. Five private dwellings are attached to one large common living area. Mia and Hans will have one, and each of you will have your own private space. Now please do not get concerned; on this entire estate, you will not find one door that has a doorknob on it. All doors are double hinged so that folks such as you and I can enter and leave at will by ourselves. Yet when you desire privacy, there is a sliding bar that you move with your feet so that no one can enter. Each of your private rooms is equipped with your own flushing toilet and Water Washer, one that women like us can operate ourselves. It was invented by Enyo, one of us and a brilliant engineer. You will see many of her inventions around the estate."

Chaucer added, "She forgot the most important detail that you women are going to love! Each complex has its own private bath, with hot and cold water. You can bathe to your hearts content anytime you desire. As for food, there is a small pantry there, which is shared by all, so you can have late night snacks. Around here with so many people, we have a staff of twenty cooks, and we have a giant dining hall where everyone can eat together, one giant happy family. You will find that there are enough hands around to help you dine nearly all the time. However, I suspect that as soon as you learn how, you will probably prefer to feed yourselves. I know Linda does. She hasn't let me feed her anymore in years now."

"How, how many are there around here that are like us?" asked Amara timidly.

"Ah, there are so many beautiful women here that I cannot count

274

them all!" Chaucer declared teasingly.

"Dear, that's not at all what she meant. Ignore him, Amara. She means like she and me. Honestly, Amara, I have lost count. Over the years, we have rescued so darn many women who had lost hands, arms at the elbows, and like us, that I have completely lost count. At one time, we numbered over a thousand. Now many have married. Some chose to move elsewhere with their husbands. Others have moved their husbands here. You see, the Laird Foundation pays for everything that we women need, as it will yours too. You need it, the Laird Foundation provides for it. The foundation was funded by generous people who wanted to make a difference in our lives. They certainly have done that."

"Ah, here we are. Now I know that this estate is huge and will seem overwhelming to you at first. My plans are to take you to your new home and show you around it. Then, I'll show you where you go to get your meals. Take a few days to get adjusted and then I'll give you all a grand tour, sooner if you prefer. I don't want to rush you with anything. We have all the time in the world here."

"One more thing, on Friday and Saturday nights, we have formal concerts and public dances here. They are *the* socializing events around here. Many women such as ourselves have met their husbands at these events. I will send a dressmaker around to each of you so that you too will have a fine silk dress ready for this weekend's festivities. Oh yes, Mia, Maren, your boots are all the rage around here now. All women wear them to the concerts and dances. I will make sure you three have a pair soon so you can practice walking in them. If you find them too difficult to manage so soon, you are under no obligation to wear them. If you choose to wear them, take a tip from me. It drives men nuts. I'm sure in time you will meet many new friends here. Who knows, the love bug may also bite you; it's quite common."

"Here we are. This huge three-story brownstone mansion is our main headquarters. The large building just to its left is the dining hall where you get meals. By the way, anytime you are hungry, just walk over to it. There is always a cook around to rustle up something for you, even at midnight. Now all along that wall there behind the dining hall are the newly designed living dorms. Yours is the very first one, closest to the dining hall. I wanted to make it as accessible for you as possible. Chaucer, will you assist us from the carriage?" I knew that she needed none, but was allowing him to help her out of deference to my three companions, who would need it.

"Follow me, and I'll show you around your new home. I do hope you will like it and find things around here are so to your liking." She demonstrated how to open the front door, using her foot. We four paid attention, and I noticed my three friends were most impressed. Doors would no longer be a barrier to us.

The communal room was spacious with large windows that gave a view of the inner estate area, with drapes that could be pulled easily using our feet. Couches, tables, and chairs were numerous and plush.

Each of the private quarters was identical in design. The bedroom had a large bed, small table, and chairs. Instead of drawers, shelves held clothing within easy foot reach. Each room had one beautiful oil painting. "All of these paintings were done by women artists like us, no arms. Pretty amazing, eh?" My three companions just couldn't believe it.

Off the bedroom was the toilet room. Linda demonstrated, "You see we usually wear loose fitting dresses like mine and no underwear. When we need to go to the bathroom, you catch the back of the dress on this hook on the rear and wiggle down; it pulls the dress up. It certainly is wonderful not to have to constantly ask someone for help with this."

She led us back out into the common room. "This room is your small pantry where you can keep snacks. This large one is your common bath." She showed us how to use it and proved it had hot running water, compliments of Enyo and her engineering staff.

"It's around one in the afternoon. Dinner is at five, listen for the bell ringing call to dinner; you cannot miss hearing it. It's rather loud. If you need a snack before then, wander into the dining room just there. I figure you would love to take a bath and get settled in, so I will leave you to enjoy. We can talk more later after dinner. Oh, yes, I took the liberty of have at least one dress like mine made for you four. You will find them in your bedrooms. Ah, here come your sacks from the ship now. Just tell the ladies where to place them. See you all at dinner."

"I think that Hans and I ought to take the room closest to the front door, so we can oversee things better," Mia said. You four figure out which ones you want. If you need anything, holler. We didn't and we grinned as Hans carried Mia into their room and shut the door.

Lyris teased, "I bet I know what they are going to do." We laughed. After picking rooms, I thought it was time for a bath. "Don't we need Mia to help us?" Lyris asked, as we four entered the public bath, where the huge tub sat partly below ground so we could more easily enter it.

"Hey, we got feet and teeth; let's see if we can work together to get each of us undressed somehow," I suggested. An awkward thirty minutes later, we four had done it and were relaxing in the warm waters. Six could bathe at one time.

"This is heaven! Such luxury!" Lyris exclaimed. Her sentiments we all echoed; it was wonderful.

Quite a while later, a flushed Mia joined us and helped with our hair. Then, Hans hopped in as well and lent his hands drying us off. Mia then suggested that we see if we could wiggle into the loose fitting new dresses. She watched and gave us helpful hints, but allowed us actually to do it ourselves, only aiding us by getting our long hair out of the inside of the dress after it was on. There were easy slip-on shoes for the other three. Mia and I had no choice but to slip on our heeled boots. Either that or walk around on our tiptoes all day, since our leg muscles just wouldn't let our feet go flat.

Around five, a very loud bell chimed the call for supper. We walked the short distance to the dining hall, watching hundreds of others, men, women, and children streaming out of other dorms and buildings. When we entered, rows and rows of tables filled the room. At one end, Linda and Chaucer had their table arranged so that they could look out on everyone else. Linda was there already, thankfully, and Chaucer waved for us to come to their table.

"Tonight, I want you to dine with us so I can introduce you to everyone at one time. After tonight, you can sit wherever you like. There are still several hundred of us, though you will find that they are fifty or older now. You are the youngest. In a month or so a hundred and fifty or so young women who were mutilated by the priests of Jehosanity in your country will be arriving, so you will have others your own age like yourselves. However, there are any number of other normal women your own age. I'm sure they will want to meet you and you may strike up friendships. Oh yes, these funny, tall chairs with sloping backs are for us. It makes it easier for us to feed ourselves with our feet. Watch some of the older women like us, and you will see what I mean. It takes quite a bit of learning to be able to do it, so don't worry, there are many hands to feed you as long as you need the assistance."

Soon the place was packed. Linda introduced us all to the others who gave us a round of applause. Then a number of serving women began bringing in pots of food and the dinner began. We picked what we desired from the many offerings. Linda had taken dining to a new level of sophistication, and I, for one, greatly enjoyed the ability to select out what dishes I wanted to eat.

Lyris, Amara, Zenovia, and I watched the older women eating with their feet. I noticed, and they did too, that absolutely no one paid any attention to them, as if it was perfectly normal to eat this way. It went a long way to making us feel more comfortable here, if only we could learn to do it ourselves.

After dinner, Linda walked us back to our dorm. She took each one of us into our private room for a chat. I heard the results later on from Linda. First, she visited with Zenovia, the eldest of our group. Zenovia was now twenty-six. She had black hair that fell to the small of her back. Deep black eyes shone intensely. "You want to know about me," Zenovia said to Linda.

"Perceptive of you," Linda replied.

"I have this knack of being able to know what another is thinking when I look at them. It kind of grew on me after I lost my husband and had to fend for myself like this." She shrugged her shoulders.

Linda grinned. "Looks are very deceiving, are they not?"

Zenovia grinned back, "Yes, I've killed five men myself. My legs are a lethal weapon. You are right, but they all betrayed their wives as my husband did to me. Can you imagine how I felt after I gave up my arms for him and then found him in bed with my personal maid?"

"Your world collapsed in upon you, an intolerable feeling of utter helplessness. I can understand. How would you like to greatly expand your skills in knowing what another is thinking?"

Zenovia grinned, "Is that possible? Absolutely, I would!"

"Good, I will begin your therapy sessions in the morning. How about a hug?" The two hugged in our special way.

Linda visited next with Amara, who was now twenty-two. She had shoulder length brown hair, beautiful brown eyes, and a well formed bosom to match her trim figure. Amara, like Lyris, was very pretty indeed. During their chat, Linda discovered that Amara used to love to work with flowers and floral arrangements, before she gave up her arms for her husband.

Lyris had turned twenty-one, just as pretty as Amara, with waist length dark brown hair. She was proud that her hair had never been cut, except for frazzled ends on occasion. Linda discovered that Lyris loved music, though had never learned to play any instrument. She had enjoyed our singing during the long carriage ride from Sud.

"Well, let me look at you, my dearest friend," Linda said to me when we were finally alone together. "I have so much to tell you, I don't know where to begin. Let me just look at you. I love your hair; it's turning blonde, right?" Indeed, it had been getting lighter each year and now was down to my waist, which I enjoyed. "Such pretty blue eyes too."

"Yes, but what about these knockers?" I teased. Mia's were even larger than mine were, but she had two more years of growth on me.

"You are growing melons?" Linda teased me. Mine were nearly as large as my head.

"At least they are perky and not sagging like some old maid!" I replied.

"You are sixteen now?" I nodded. "Okay, I guess the place to start is how do you want to handle things? Almost no one here knows that you were Bethany le'Goeur. They think you are from Annelise, rightly so. I love the hue of your shin, charming and pretty. Do we want to leave it that way?"

"I think that is best for now, Linda. I see so many new faces and so many I knew have died. The ones that I recognize are so old looking that if I go around saying who I used to be, too much confusion might result. How come you look thirty?"

"I am in control of the body, Chaucer too — one of the benefits of being a completely freed spiritual being. I know the last sixteen years have been very rough on you, physically and mentally."

"Yes, I have not just played for sixteen years, Linda. I just want some time to relax and enjoy life for a while, unless we have some emergency to handle."

"No emergencies, thanks to you. You can have all the time you want for yourself, Maren Bethany. I will run some therapy sessions on you as well, if you are willing. I know that you need to relearn how to care for your basic needs. You have spent sixteen years in a straitjacket, more or less. I thank you for having done that to save us all from the war." I nodded.

"There is one other thing, Maren, what about Renzo? I know that when your body passed on, you swore to him that you would look him up once you finished the assignment. Are you still desirous of honoring that promise?"

"Oh god, Linda! I would do anything to have my Renzo back with me, to feel his arms around me, to kiss me. He is the only one who ever really knew how much I love to play games. Renzo is my soul mate, so to speak. Is it possible for me to take off and go find him? I suppose that he now has a baby body and we are more or less doomed this time. Then again, maybe he doesn't want me now, not like this again. Maybe he has found someone else in these years."

Linda smiled, "Oh no he hasn't. He's madly in love with you still. He spent a number of years with the Guardian and has now become as freed as Chaucer and me. He longs to be with you once more. You remember how you acquired your Bethany Madelyn Amir body?"

Distant memories came back. "Yes, a young girl had been bitten by a viper. She decided that was the end of that body's life and she abandoned it. I took it over and helped it heal itself. Why do you ask?"

"Renzo has done a similar thing, Maren. It's taken us some time to locate a sixteen year old body that has had an accident in which the being who had that body has decided it was all over and left it. Plus, that body had to be salvageable, if you know what I mean. Anyway, he has finally pulled it off, it seems. If I am not mistaken after talking with the others you have with you, Renzo may have just pulled the coop of the century. But we will see how it works out. He will be coming to next week's concert and dance. I'm afraid you will just have to wait a bit longer for your romance," she teased. I grinned.

"In the meantime, let's get you going on re-learning how to do things, shall we?" I couldn't agree with her more. I was so tired of having my sister, Mia, look after me, so that I didn't "blow my cover." "One other thing, Maren. Your legs. Do you want me to try to do something for your legs so that you don't have to always wear these extreme heels?"

"No, don't bother. I'm so used to them now. After eleven years of constantly wearing them, I guess I rather like them now."

"Okay, if you change your mind later, Renzo probably can also help your legs recover as well as I can. Now then, I promise you that I won't talk Santi business until you tell me that you've had enough time off and are ready. All right with you?" Very much so, as far as I was concerned.

The next day, several dressmakers came to begin making our form fitting fancy dresses, which we needed by Friday. We chose our own colors for the silk dresses. I chose yellow, bright yellow, naturally, because it's cheerful. Zenovia, as I predicted, went with black. Lyris chose scarlet, while Amara went with a deep blue. Mia chose bright green.

The dressmakers for Mia and me had major problems with the fittings, our mammoth bust lines. My drastically smaller than normal waistline only added to the problems. Mia had worn her corset only a few years, and her waist was back to normal for her size. Me, I had worn it since I was five and my waist was permanently smaller than one would expect for my size. In the end, when I finally tried on my form fitting fancy yellow dress, I was shocked at my appearance in the mirror. Because of the drastic differences in sizes between my bust and waist, I looked more like a wasp than a person. Mia looked similar, primarily because she had even larger breasts than I had. I grimaced because in a few years mine would be as big as hers, compliments of our grandmother Thorsten.

The dresses were also tight down our legs, with just enough walking room for these heels. In fact, my dressmaker explained that the rage in fashion now dictated that the dress allow only for enough room for proper steps in these heels and no more. "You will see," she said, "you will look very sexy in this outfit, Maren. Trust me." I secretly hoped Renzo would like it when I saw him in ten more days!

In the mornings, Chaucer and Linda came early to give us therapy sessions. Chaucer handled Zenovia and Amara, while Linda did Lyris and me. Afternoons, several older women who were like us came and spent the afternoon helping us learn new ways of doing things. Immediately they had us all doing stretching exercises. They were not satisfied until we could touch our noses with either foot with ease while keeping our balance when they bumped our bodies with theirs. Slowly it all started to come back to me. Many things boiled down to merely a question of balance. If we had balance in some position, we could then begin to do something.

Friday afternoon was spent making last minute adjustments to our new outfits. All three decided that they would attempt to wear the fashionable high-heeled boots with their new outfits. Mia and I spent much of the afternoon helping the three learn to walk reasonably well in them. Lyris commented, "Golly, the dress is so tight that I can just barely cross my legs!"

Amara said, "I do like the style, no sleeves; it shows off our true silhouettes. Striking."

After the practice sessions, we donned our regular loose fitting dresses and headed off to dinner. I made the three wear their boots though so that they could get more experience in them before we had to walk over to the palace for the concert later this evening. After eating, we all had an hour to get ready for the formal concert. Mia and Hans assisted us because of the time factor. Looking like a million and feeling like we did, which I thought was more important, we six headed across the cobblestone paths to the twin palaces of the Laird Foundation. Mia had her arms around Lyris and me. Hans had his arms around Zenovia and Amara. The three needed their help to keep their balance well. As we walked, we saw hundreds of others heading this way. All the women wore fancy dresses and boots similar to ours.

Mia noted that some women wore corsets and poufy dresses as well, akin to those we had worn in Annelise, though not as extreme in diameter. I sincerely hoped that the Annelise style did not become the next fashion craze.

The twin palaces were as beautiful as I remembered them. One tower held the public art display on the first floor, while the concert theater was on the second floor, capable of holding a thousand people. It was always packed to capacity. An open-air bridge connected this second floor to the other tower and to a large open-air balcony used for elegant dining, weather permitting. The second tower was devoted to the many artists, providing proper facilities for them to create their art.

Linda and Chaucer caught up with us. She too was wearing a pale blue silk dress like ours and wore the same boots. Chaucer had his arm around her as well. "Tonight, you will first hear some lovely four part motets composed by the famous composer Amiria. Next on the program will be vocal and instrumental polyphonic instrumental works written by the famous composer Chara. After intermission, the one longer work by the famous composer Cymre will be played by fifty instruments. These three women all came here much like you four — I believe your words are women of the Eighth Degree. As you listen to their music, remember they created all this. Then, the showstopper group will play. It is the Expressionistic Dance group. Most of the original dancers who created and danced all these were also women of the Eighth Degree. How they could perform the moves I do not know, but I have seen them do it. Always, this group is a complete showstopper."

We entered the huge theater and Linda led us to front row seats, which she had reserved. "One of the perks for being the leader is that Chaucer and I always get front row seats." Soon every seat was filled and the show began. A man in a fancy suit stepped on stage. "Ladies, gentlemen, and children, Bard Tal's Music Group proudly presents another concert for your enjoyment. First is a collection of four vocal motets by Amiria. Those will be followed by four pieces by Chara. The last of those pieces was inspired by the bass flute playing of Bard Tal, and is dedicated to Elizabeth Ann le'Goeur; it was her favorite."

The curtains rose and we saw two women, one had no arms and was in her fifties, and two men. The four part songs were indeed angelic in nature, simple, yet I had chills running down my back, so moving and touching were their sound and words. Lyris actually cried; she'd never heard such beauty in song before.

Next, the music of Chara was livelier, and I found my foot tapping along with the rhythms. Hers were more popular in nature and brought smiles to many faces, as they recognized bits of their favorite dance tunes blended into the tapestry of sounds.

During intermission, Linda led us onto the balcony where we were served tea and various cheeses. Those with hands were kept very busy. Then, we went back inside for the second half. The curtain rose and fifty musicians were on stage. The full instrumental harmonies of Cymre's music were truly impressive, complex themes and variations galore. What a mind that woman had for invention. No wonder she was so famous.

When they were done and hastily swapped positions with another large group, the show stopping Expressionistic Dance Groups took the stage. At the back of the stage were the instruments. Linda whispered, "That's Alwanianon back there on drums; she leads them. She is of the Seventh Degree. I remembered her as a teenager; it was a shock to see her as sixty-three. My three companions stared at her. A number of vocalists then moved into position on either side of the ten musicians. One of those also was of the Eighth Degree, an older woman, a fact not missed by Lyris. At last, ten dancers took their positions on either side of the stage.

Alwanianon, drumsticks affixed to her arms, her feet at the ready looked at her group and then began thumping the bass drum with her feet, and the music and dance began. This was totally an improvisational music and dance group, though much of the dance was choreographed, especially the jumps and spins. However, I got a shock when the vocalists came in; they did not sing words, but sang sounds, making their voices into instruments. "Ah-la-le-li. Ah-ha-le-la. Ah-al-le-he. Ah-le-he-ho." I could not believe what I was hearing. I was totally moved. I found my spirits soaring to undreamed of heights only to cascade to depths of sadness, only to rise from the ashes to new heights. All the while, the dancers were telling their own story in motion. Spinning, twirling, bending, their bodies spoke unsaid words, more telling than words. They ended with the show stopping body spins that Zita had made famous and that I had once performed as well. Two women ran as fast as they could from either side of the stage and leaped high into the air. Two men caught them and translated their momentum into spinning head over heels around their outstretched arms. Ten times, they spun before their legs spread out to slow them down and touch the ground. The crowd went wild as always, and they had to repeat a portion of this display for an encore.

Lyris, Amara, and Zenovia could talk of nothing else for hours. We went back to our home and had more tea and cheese, while they continued to talk about how fabulous this had been. Lyris was completely swept off her feet by the whole evening, especially the vocals and the creative vocals of the expressionistic group. Just when they finally started to calm down a bit, Linda knocked, and Mia let her in; she'd brought Alwanianon with her.

"Oh my god! It's you!" exclaimed Lyris. "We were just talking about how incredible your group was." She was flabbergasted to be actually meeting their leader.

"Hi, Lyris is it?" Alwanianon gave her a big hug with her short arms. "Sorry I'm so late getting here. I always get mobbed by admirers after the shows. It's so good to see you with us here. Any of you interesting in singing?"

"Me!" squeaked Lyris, without hesitation. "The motets were incredible, but your songs without words — that is so unbelievable. I was crying through the whole thing! Are they really improvising as Linda says?"

"Oh yes, very much so. I am about the only one on stage that is not allowed to do much improvising. I have to keep the beat steady to give the others something solid from which to devise and create. Every performance is a little different, as they sing what they feel at the time. They are good aren't they? Besides, with just these, I am rather limited in what I can improvise. Some of the depths of sadness you heard were done for me; I lost my husband last year. They are honoring me with it too."

We chatted for a long time until at last Alwanianon had to go. "Lyris, as soon as Linda gives you the okay, come by and let's see if you can join us. I am always looking for new, youthful talent. You two are also welcome to try out if you are interested." Lyris thanked her repeatedly and gave her a solid bump hug, nearly falling over, having forgotten she was still wearing the tight dress and heeled boots.

An hour later, Mia said, "Are you four going to wear those dresses to bed or can I take them off now? I am falling asleep on my feet. Tomorrow is the big dance."

The next afternoon, several women in their twenties came by to teach we six all the latest dances. Okay, a crash course it was. However, most of the steps were actually very simple, and we all caught on quickly.

After supper many carriages lined up to take us the short mile to the huge dance hall, where the old Santi estate had been many years ago. Several thousand younger people jammed the dance floor, and a live band played all the popular dance tunes. Linda explained to us beforehand that young men and women came to these dances to meet and make new friends, often leading ultimately to marriage. It was the socializing activity of Velona and that they should expect to meet many young men tonight.

That was an understatement. While we saw a large number of married couples, the vast majority were singles, like us. I had twenty different men asking for a dance, while my three companions had just as many. We thoroughly enjoyed ourselves; however, I longed for Renzo even more after the dance!

Back at our estate, Amara commented, "My dance partners — they just could not keep from sliding their arms up and down my back side!" She giggled, "I liked it. It felt really good."

"We don't have anything like this in Demokritos," Lyris added. "This is just fabulous, though I really wasn't attracted to any of the men who danced with me."

"Me either," echoed Zenovia and Amara.

"That's the whole point. You get to meet tons of new people. Eventually, you may find just the right one for you. At least that's what Linda says," I added.

The therapy sessions were rolling along. Mine were done fairly soon. Linda helped me wipe out all my discomforts, upsets, and especially the depression I had felt for the last sixteen years. I felt like a new woman, rejuvenated at least.

Chaucer had made remarkable progress with Zenovia. She came out of the last session laughing her head off. "I can read other's minds and thoughts at will without even trying. He calls it telepathy. Now I have to learn more about how to do it. He says I'm a natural born Communicator. I feel so incredibly alive, Maren! I've never felt this way before!" I also noticed she was out of her head now at all times. Chaucer had done a super job.

"Yes, I know that Chaucer has done a super job, Maren." She laughed and laughed. "I hated all men, but not anymore. There are good men around; you just have to find them. I'll tell you a little secret, Maren. I knew before I married him that he would be unfaithful to me, but I went ahead with it and did the Holy Degree Ceremony anyway, when I knew I should darn well not do it. I did this to myself." She roared with laughter once more.

Some days later, Amara came out radiant! "I feel like a flower about to blossom. I am so alive! Maren, I can actually feel and sense the aliveness of others and even the flowers. I can tell what they need. You, for example, are hungry and longing for some guy named Renzo. This is utterly incredible!"

Not long after that Lyris came out of her session, serene and tranquil. She looked at me and said, "I am." I knew what she meant. She was sitting outside of her body now. Lyris was now in control of her body and her life.

On Friday afternoon, Linda came to visit with us four. She had us sit in the common room where we could talk. "As you all are now well aware of your own spiritual natures, and have seen some of the lifetimes that you have led, I can explain more easily about Maren. Last lifetime she and a fellow named Renzo were madly in love with each other. This lifetime both have expressed a sincere desire to continue where they left off when their bodies passed away. I have located Renzo, who is now known as Marcel. Tonight, they will meet each other for the first time since they were separated be the death of their bodies. Does this make sense to you?"

"So you and Renzo were married and now you both want to marry again?" Lyris asked.

"You bet, if he likes me. Maybe he won't be attracted to me in this body, but I want to try," I replied. The three accepted this explanation, but Linda was not finished.

"I seldom try to play match maker. Who can predict affairs of the heart? Certainly not me. However, this is a most peculiar set of circumstances with this Marcel Perrin. He has three older brothers. It seems that his parents died in a boating accident when he was five years old. His older brother, Emery, looked after the boys, while they grew up, kind of like a substitute father. None of the four is married, though not for lack of trying, as I understand it. I guess you could call them picky men. More than likely, they were too busy trying to stay alive. The older brother, Emery, was sixteen when he suddenly had to support his three younger brothers, so I suspect they didn't have a lot of time to meet and date women. Until recently, they didn't have a lot of money either, and that may have been a factor."

"They live in north Velona, about five miles from here. There, Emery is mayor of North Gate, the newest section of Velona, built as an extension beyond the old northern gates to the city. He is twenty-six. Jasmin Perrin is a florist and has his own gardens now. He's twenty-two. Alain Perrin is a vocalist in the Bard Tal Music Group. He sings tenor; I've heard him and he's quite good. Alain is twenty-one. Marcel is only sixteen, perfect for Maren."

"When I met all four, it struck me that you three might possibly be just the women that these men might like from the viewpoint that you have much in common with them. Of course, you may think that they are pigs, or vice versa. However, I have taken the liberty of setting you four up with a date with them tonight to go to the concert. If you don't hit it off with them or you don't like them, it's just for the few hours of the concert. If you do find them at least worthy of a second date, there is always the dance tomorrow night. By no means are any of you under any obligations to these men. I just thought that mutual interests might make for a more enjoyable evening for you three."

"However, if you don't want to do this, let me know. I will not be offended if you refuse. As I said, when I met them, they seemed like good men and had interests similar to yours. What say you?"

"Well, it's only for a concert," Zenovia said. "We ought to meet new people, lots of them. Perhaps one day we will meet someone special again, though I personally have already resigned myself to becoming an old maid. After all, who's going to want half of a woman, when they could just as easily have a whole one?"

"It's the being that matters, Zenovia, not their current body," Linda replied.

"That's true, I was just being pessimistic again," she admitted.

"One other thing, apparently, Marcel was bitten by a viper when the four of them went on a fishing trip three weeks ago. For a time they thought that Marcel had actually died. Yet, he recovered, but his brothers claim that his mental state is confusing. He doesn't remember much of what happened to him and them before the snakebite. It's as if he's forgotten sixteen years of his life. They are most concerned for him. I promised them that I would run some therapy on him."

"I suppose that we should start getting ready sooner. I ought to take a bath at least," Lyris suggested. "I should look as good as I can, you know, present the best appearance and then hope for the best." We all agreed with her. Give it a chance.

We four took a bath and slowly began to get ready. Amara said, "Well, honestly this won't be much like a date, we will just be watching the concert together, that's about all." Still, we wanted to put our best foot out there. I began to get more and more nervous about finally meeting Renzo. What if he really didn't want to put up with me like this a second lifetime in a row? What if he didn't like the way I looked?

Finally dressed after dinner, my hair brushed the way I liked it, flowing down over my shoulders, hiding my lost arms, my nervousness peaked as Linda knocked on our door, but I knew she had them with her. Mia opened the door and brought them in for introductions. We four stood in our common room, nervously waiting.

Renzo! I couldn't help myself. Although he had a teenager's body I had never seen, I knew my Renzo's presence.

Bethany! At last, we can be together again! I've waited and waited! Oh, we'd better act cool.

Linda did the introductions. "Maren Bethany Ryker, this is Marcel Perrin. Marcel, Maren Bethany. He's still got a bit of a limp from the snake bite infection."

"You are so beautiful, Maren. I brought you a rose, but it wilts compared to you," he presented me with a rose and carefully put it into my hair. I leaned forward for a hug, not much else I could do. He remembered the tiny hint and gave me a good hug, whispering in my ear softly so the others couldn't hear, "I love you already!"

"Zenovia Philon, this is his older brother, Emery Perrin, Mayor of North Gate. Emery, this is Zenovia, she is from Kefall, Demokritos," Linda continued.

"Very pleased to meet such a beautiful woman. Linda said that you were an elegant woman, but she has a way with understatement, you know. Allow me," he presented her with a red rose as well, following Marcel's lead, putting it in her hair the same way. Zenovia leaned forward and he at once accepted the offer and gave her a hugging welcome.

"Amara Gavril, this is Jasmin Perrin, the florist. Jasmin, this is Amara, from Axos, Demokritos."

"Wow. Linda said you were very pretty, but you are so much more than that! She said that you were interested in flowers, so I brought one of my own creations, a hybrid rose, white to bring out the best in you." He put it into her hair as his brothers had done. She leaned forward and he gave her a welcoming hug as well. She was about to comment on the rose, but Linda continued.

"Lyris Georgios, this is Alain Perrin, the musician, who you have yet to hear, though I know you will get that chance next week. He's scheduled to sing at that concert. Alain, this is Lyris of Theolopolis, Demokritos."

"Welcome to our Velona, fair Lyris. Your face is like that of an angel. Linda lied when she said that you were merely very pretty! Allow me," he also put a red rose in her hair, and hugged her. "Please allow me to escort you to the concert. We have had many women such as yourself in the large music group. Some of our most famous composers have been what was your term, oh yes, of the Eighth Degree." Like a pro, he slid his arm under her hair and around her waist, gently guiding her to the door.

The others followed suit. Zenovia was quite surprised when Emery deftly slid his arm around her waist under her hair. "You've done this before, dated a woman such as I?" she asked.

"Oh there have been many fine women here at the Laird Foundation over the years such as you four. I made it my responsibility to know how best to assist such women. After all, I am the mayor, and I must set a fine example for my people," Emery replied.

Jasmin mimicked his older brother and slid his arm around Amara's waist. She said, "Thanks, I am new to these boots and am still a little uncertain on my feet. Say, did you really grow this white rose yourself?"

"Oh yes, it took a lot of trial and error, but now I have a small pair of white rose bushes. No other in Velona can boast of having white roses."

Marcel, Renzo, side his arm around my waist as he used to do thousands of times before. *God, how I have missed you all these years, Renzo! Rub your hand — yes, like that.* He had picked up my intention and was now sliding his hand up and down my back. Oh did that ever feel fabulous!

I looked after our kids as I promised you that I would, but every day that I would look at them, I saw only you and missed you. The only thing that allowed me to keep my sanity and not rush down there to Annelise was going to the Red Desert. I'll tell you about that later. Right now, I just want to be with you and hold you!

Wait a second. I forgot to maintain my telepathic link to you. You just — you're a Communicator now? I sent, startled by his ability to connect with me.

I can do many things now that I had forgotten how to do, my love. I am more worthy of you now than I ever was. You will find it much harder to beat me when we play our games once more.

God Renzo! Do you realize that I have had to go sixteen years without being able to just relax and play a simple game? I am going to play you out!

I don't think so, my love, not this time, he teased and squeezed my butt gently. I swayed my butt into his side and smiled.

Say, what are we going to do about these new names? I am afraid I have confused my brothers by insisting that I am called Renzo now.

I'm really Maren Elizabet, so Maren Bethany is okay for me. How about doing the same, Marcel Renzo? Will they buy that alteration?

Let's hope so. The concert is about to start. Are we going to listen or we can continue to chat like this?

Oh, the music is fabulous, Marcel Renzo. I haven't heard anything this good in so long. Let's listen. We can talk afterwards. God, I am so glad you still want me, because I want you so badly I could scream! He squeezed my side slightly, and I rested my head on his shoulders, as I loved to do all last lifetime.

After the incredible concert, we all went into the dining hall, where a cook made us a pot of tea. I ordered the tea, not caring whether the others wanted tea or not. I certainly did. We sat across the table from each other, gazing at our new bodies, making small talk, while we chatted away telepathically.

I was afraid you might not want to have me like this, armless, again.

I want you no matter what!

I hope you like big breasts, because these are still growing. Mia and I are growing melons! Comes from our grandmother Thorsten, we were told. Might get as big as my head; god I hope they don't droop and sag like an old woman.

More of you to love, my dear. If they do, I will adjust them for you. I can do that to bodies now, you know, adjust them. I can do many neat things that I had long, long forgotten. My fondest wish is that one day you will be able to go to Jes and become as free and able as I am now. I will work hard for that day, my love.

Nearby, Lyris and Alain were chatting about music. Both were impressed with how the voice could be used as an instrument. Alain explained how when he performs, he becomes one with the feelings of the music and then adds his own refection of that back into the music. I got lost on their subtleties of nuance.

Amara asked Jasmin about his florist shop. "I love to grow my own flowers. Yes, there are many flower stands all throughout the city. I differ because I grow my own flowers from seed. I try to make arrangements that speak to the recipient or to convey an emotion. I only wish that I could tell what my plants really need," he said.

"Oh, you mean why they might be getting a fungus or wilt? Do they need more water or less sun?" she asked.

"Yes, I want them to be very healthy. Sometimes I just know something is wrong with one of my plants, but I don't know what. I just experiment until I get it right or I lose the plant. Now another problem I have is getting the floral arrangements just right. I am never quite sure I have it right, you know, when you have this feeling it could be better, only you don't know just what to change?"

"Oh yes, I certainly do. I have always had a love of plants, you see. I talk with them and they tell me what they need. If you like, I can come by your garden and see what I might find out for you. It is an easy thing for me to do, kind of like empathy for plants. Now my mother always said that I had an eye for floral arrangements. While other children were playing dolls, I was making the flower arrangements at our house. I have a real talent for that too. The next time that you feel something is not quite right, let me know and I will be glad to have a look," Amara replied.

"That's incredible! You can just talk to plants and know what it troubling them?"

"Sure, I thought everyone could do this when I was growing up," Amara confessed.

He retrieved the white rose he had given her earlier from her hair. "Can you tell anything just from the rose itself and the few leaves on it? This is my pride and joy plant, but I swear that it needs something."

"I usually talk to the living plant, but let's have a close look at its leaves and stem." Sometime later, she suggested that perhaps the plant needed some more minerals and suggested some to try. "I really should see the plant to make sure you know." The two of them chatted on about plants.

Emery and Zenovia's conversation was somewhat more interesting in a number of ways. Like the rest of us, they were facing each other across the table. Periodically, the guys would hold our teacup so we could take another sip. Emery said, "I've always wanted to be in politics. . ."

Zenovia added, "Since you were a little boy."

"Yes, precisely. I got this golden opportunity to become mayor of North Gate. . ."

"When they built the subdivision beyond the gates. Makes perfect sense."

"Right. I've been a good mayor now for five years."

"You were the youngest mayor in Velona?" she asked.

"Yes, I was. Of course, my biggest problem is being able to just know. . ."

"When they are telling you the whole truth and not altering the fact to fit their needs," she said.

"Exactly so. Why I just had the devil of a time recently. A man claimed that our council should pay for the repaving of the street in front of his business because all the wagon traffic had made deep ruts in the road. .

."

"Ah but you suspected he was not telling quite the truth, so you sent someone to investigate?"

"Exactly so. Well, the road was definitely damaged there in front of his store."

"But you suspected it wasn't made by wagons?"

"Yes, indeed. I hired a Santi Planner to check on things."

"And he found out from the neighbors?"

"That he had been out there with a pickaxe late at night causing the damage so that we. . ."

"Would pay for a new road, making his business look finer. Clever attempt. I am glad that you saw through it," she complimented him.

"Yes, this sort of thing does happen. Had I not. . ."

"Been so vigilant. . ." she added.

"He would have gotten away with it costing our suburb money." He paused and helped her take a sip.

"Thanks. I really wanted it just then," she smiled at him.

"I know. Now where were we?" He paused and exclaimed, "You, you have been, well you knew just what I was about to say and said it before I said it! Zenovia, this is so incredible. I've never met anyone like you. Do you do this with others?"

"Know what they are going to say?" she asked.

"Yes, I can see that you do. Incredible. Impressive. This is just too amazing. I have never, ever been so. . ."

"Impressed by a woman?"

"Precisely so. I've met any number of women, especially here at the Laird Foundation and the dances, but none. . ."

"Really interested you. Pretty face, no mind. Or worse, no mind, not much to look at either. . ." she added.

"Nor could I respect. I've always told my brothers, you must respect a women and admire her, before you ever. . ."

"Try to get into her bed. . ."

He flushed, "Er, well yes, I was thinking that. More on the lines of considering serious dating."

"That is a very astute observation on your part, Emery. Linda and I have been discussing this at some length. Love is a combination of admiration. . .

"And respect," he finished her sentence. Without asking, he helped her take another sip, knowing now was just the right time.

She smiled at him. He said quizzically, "Doesn't everyone just know when you need something? It's plainly obvious to me. . ."

"When I need something? No, I usually am forced to ask. I've had so many others that just. . ."

"Offer you something when you really don't want it or need it just then. That has got to be very annoying, I'd find that quite. . ." he said.

"Obnoxious, and it shows me that the other person cannot. . ." she explained.

"Even observe you or really look at you. Incredible!" he added.

"Ah, but you have another concern about me, don't you. Ah, I see, yes it is about my lack of arms isn't it?" she said. He flushed.

"Well, as a matter of fact, yes, yes I do. You know that there are always, well, hooligans and . . ." he began.

"Riffraff and thieves out there in the streets," she continued for him.

"Yes, I am being polite about them. I would be so utterly worried about you, if you. . ."

"Were out there walking the streets by yourself. You think that I am so helpless this way?" she asked.

Again, he flushed. "Yes, I didn't want to embarrass you or make less of you, but I would worry constantly that something. . ." he confessed.

"Bad would happen to me," she finished and looked him squarely in his eyes. After a moment, she added, "Yes, genuine concern I sense. Emery, I'll share something with you. You need not worry about me, on the streets I am able to take care of myself if someone attempts to rob me or harm me. I used to be the head of the Kali Assassins in Kefall. I've killed men." He gasped.

"No, it's not the way you think. Let me explain." She told about the Holy Eight Degree ceremony and what it meant for a couple to partake of that ceremony. She also described what it was like when a husband became unfaithful to the woman who had sacrificed all for him. Those were the men she had assassinated.

Emery looked into her eyes and said, "I am so terribly sorry for you, Zenovia. I see that this has indeed happened to you. I can see it in your eyes. God, how awful you must have felt when you saw him with her." He leaned over and put his hands on her sides. "I'm so glad that he got what he deserved. That is high treason in my book!"

"But you want to know how I can kill. I can see that percolating in your mind." He grinned and nodded, holding up her teacup for her to take a sip before replying, just as she desired.

"My legs are lethal weapons. I start a circle kick with one leg, hooking it around the victim's neck. Using that as a fulcrum, I pivot the other leg up and lock the two together. Of course, my body begins to fall over backwards, but I then use his neck as a lever's base, attempting to do a sit up, snapping his neck. I hit, release, and roll out of the way of his falling dead body."

"Absolutely incredible, Zenovia! I am more impress with you than I have been with any other woman ever!"

"And you still wonder how I am in bed?" she added. He blushed.

"And you wonder how I will be in bed?" he countered and she flushed, that was what she was thinking at that moment.

I stared into Marcel Renzo's eyes, and he, mine. We longed to be together all the time, but we had both decided for the sake of everyone else, we should pretend to date some and not marry instantly, because that others could not have so easily. In his brother's eyes, we had just met.

Just then, Mia entered, heels clicking on the stone floor, catching our attention. "Hi all. Say, do you realize that it is now midnight? You've been sitting here talking for nearly three hours. I am getting tired, so if you want to continue, you will have to find a way to undress yourselves."

"Okay, okay, Mia, I can take a hint. Ladies, we had better get some sleep. The dance is tonight right after supper. You are taking me, Marcel?"

"I will be here with bells on, dearest Maren!" he replied.

The other brothers said that would most certainly take their partners to the dance as well. Emery said that they would bring their coach for us. While they wanted to see us safely back to our dorm, Mia reminded them that it was only a hundred feet away and she would do it. Renzo gave me a farewell hug and kissed my forehead. His brothers, seeing his move, duplicated it much to the desires of my three friends. We watched them leave and followed Mia to our dorm common room. All four of us felt like we could float there on a cloud.

Of course, all we did the next day was talk about the four brothers. Amara, Lyris, and especially Zenovia, claimed that they never had such an engaging, heartfelt, relaxed talk with a man before. "Are all men here in Velona like these brothers?" Zenovia asked. "If so, they put Demokritos men to utter shame!"

"No, I think by some incredible luck, we came across the right four," I suggested.

"Each one is so different from the other," Amara declared. "I like the other three, but Jasmin is so incredible. You know, he is interested in me and what I sense with plants. He's asked me to come and check out his gardens. Do you suppose that is allowed here?"

"Sure, go ahead and have a look at his many plants, Amara," I suggested. We chatted way the morning and early afternoon. Then we spent the later afternoon getting ready for the big dance. As you can probably guess, we had a fantastic time. When the last, lights dimmed, romantic slow dance of the night, we four were also passionately kissing our knights charming.

Chapter 20 Therapies

July 10, 702, the Healing caravel and the Demokritos Fortress caravel docked in Velona, bringing one hundred fifty-two women from Demokritos, who were in dire need of our therapy and assistance. Linda thought that it would be wise for the four of us to be there to meet them, since we were their countrywomen. Marcel Renzo came with me, as well as Mia and Hans. A slew of carriages parked along the northern edge of the docks, ready to carry the women and their relatives to the estate. Because of the intense stress that these women were under, Linda kept the reception small. Linda had it timed perfectly. Ellaina Po, Linda, Chaucer, and our group gathered together in our welcoming line just as the two caravels slowly inched to their mooring locations.

We saw most were on deck watching the spectacle, gaping at the immense size of this port city, many times larger than Patri. In fact, Velona dwarfed Patri. Slowly, the women were assisted on to the docks, and the shipboard Santi formed them into a group before us.

"Welcome to Velona, I am the monarch of Velona, Ellaina Po. I wanted to welcome you personally to our city and country. If there is every anything that you need, please send word to me. I am here to make your stay in Velona a most pleasurable one."

"I am Linda d'Grange, my husband Chaucer. We are the leaders of the Santi del Dio. You will be staying at our estate, which houses the Laird Foundation. We will do everything we can to help you over this horrible trauma and to learn new ways to life. Obviously, I have had to do this myself. I believe some of you may know your fellow countrywomen. Maren Bethany is now your ambassador to Velona. This is Zenovia, Amara, and Lyris. I have coaches waiting to take us the short distance to our estate."

By design, Zenovia, Mia, and I assisted the key group into our carriage. Eleni Gavril, Charessa, Cynthia, Daphna, Karis, and Yannis climbed in with us three. Karis explained to Yannis, "Zenovia is my counterpart in Kefall." Yannis knew what she meant, that Zenovia led the Kali Assassin there, and she could not help stare in awe at Zenovia, discretely of course.

"Velona is so big!" exclaimed Charessa. Eleni agreed enthusiastically with her.

Lyris, overjoyed to find someone closer to her own age, chatted away with these two and Cynthia. "Yes, I am still getting used to just how large this city actually is! You would not believe the shops! I must take you all shopping, later, after you are settled in; it's so amazing what you can find. Only last week, I found this shop which sells paca clothing, the softest dresses imaginable."

"You, you go shopping like, well, like we are?" Cynthia asked. "How can you manage?"

"Oh, you will soon see, Cynthia. We are all learning new ways to do things, even Maren is learning with us. You are only about a month behind us, so you'll catch on quickly, I'm sure. I even am able to feed myself, well mostly," Lyris explained.

Daphna asked me, "Empress, I'm sorry, I keep forgetting, Ambassador Maren, I feel so helpless now you know. I can do nothing for my two daughters anymore. I don't know what we would have done if it were not for all the help that we are getting from the Santi. Are we really going to be able to live like this? Am I ever going to be able to help my lovely daughters with, well you know, the necessities of living? I feel so bad for them; now they are never going to be able to find husbands of their own. Cynthia was engaged before this happened, but he broke it off once he found out."

Before I could answer her, Amara spoke up, "Oh, I'm sure they will. Can you believe that already we four are dating some of the most wonderful men I have ever met? There are many fine men here in Velona. Well, there are some not so nice ones too, met a few at the dances."

"You, you have a boyfriend, Amara? He isn't turned off by, well, the way we are, so completely helpless?" Cynthia asked in disbelief.

"Not at all, we have so much in common; he's a florist, growing his own plants. I am helping him once a week now, when I can get away from all the training we are getting. I'm sure that you will find a handsome, great man here who will love you very much. I'm sure of it, Cynthia." We chatted away and got to the estate in almost no time.

By Linda's design, Eleni, Charessa, Cynthia, and Daphne were housed in the next dorm down from ours, and Karis and Yannis were in the one next to theirs. She wanted us all close together, though why she singled out these six from the many others, I didn't yet know.

As had been done with us, the new arrivals were taken to the dorms, shown how things worked, assigned a Santi family who lived in the fifth room and who would assist them. The next day, the therapy sessions began in earnest, after each was checked over by Linda herself to make sure the wounds had fully healed. I discovered quickly that those who could deliver Jenna's therapy sessions were now far too few; many had died. Essentially, the deliverers were Linda, Chaucer, Mia, Hans, three other women, and me. Linda asked us to handle three patients each day.

I was asked to handle those next door first, and Daphna pleaded with me to do her last. However, I had the others listening in as I ran the session on one of them. While it tended to bring their own horrors to mind, they could see what was expected of them and what may lie underneath this one occurrence, namely traumatic incidents that happened much earlier and in other lifetimes. We spent the rest of the summer working with these many women, undoing the terrible trauma they had endured, all to excellent results.

Once a woman was finished with her therapy, her life and vitality returned, she was then sent to the Laird Foundation for "education and training" in how to do life things for herself, in so far as such was possible. A side effect of this large number of therapy sessions was that Lyris, Amara, and Zenovia all volunteered to learn how to deliver sessions and were soon in the thick of things with the rest of us. I will spare you the details of all this, however.

Yet, I must explain what happened with Yannis. Chaucer was assigned to handle her as his first patient. Soon, I discovered why that was. Both Linda and he knew that she had been the infamous Rooster, the first Supreme Prelate of the Mano del Dio, and responsible for many assassinations, including my own as Ket Bethany, to say nothing of the mutilation of women in the Sea Princes.

Yannis was psychotic. There is no kinder way of putting the state of her mind. Chaucer began by asking, "Do you believe that the truth, no matter how awful it may be, will ultimately set you free?"

"Yes, I have come to see this may be so," she replied hesitatingly.

"Good. Are you willing to tell me about whatever we discover in your past, no matter what guilt you might feel about having done it?"

"Yes, I deserve whatever punishment I get," she sighed.

"I'm sorry; we don't deal in punishment here. I am not here to make you wrong for what you might have done or should have done. I'm here to help you get better, to be free of the past, as far as that may be possible. Shall we begin?" Chaucer explained.

Yannis still had her attention stuck on all the women she was helping. Chaucer began treating what she had recently seen, the horrors there in Patri, as a traumatic incident, even though she herself was not harmed in any way. Quickly, he asked for an earlier trauma that was somehow similar in nature. Bang, he ran headlong into her previous lifetime, where she had been too vocally against the Church of Jehosanity, had been abducted, and her arms encased in those nasty metal enclosures.

This one took a good deal of time to handle, since she was encased and left to fend in the most miserable, inhumane conditions imaginable for nearly a year, before her body sickened and died. After days of working this long incident, getting all the gruesome details re-experienced, he found that Yannis experienced some relief, but it was not fully going away. He then asked her if there was still something else that was earlier in time and similar. Of course, he ran into the seeds of the Sea Prince mutilations, which began late in the Rooster's lifetime. This still refused to erase and blow off of Yannis. Again, he had her look earlier for something similar.

Sure enough, Yannis had run into the mantis creatures! A mantis creature had removed and eaten her arms. The whole mess blew completely when Yannis realized that the priests who were supervising the removal of her arms by the mantis commented while she was unconscious and recovering for the hideous ordeal, "Well, she is just another worthless woman now." Yannis took that to heart and believed that she was worthless as a person.

That decision, heavily embedded in pain, unconsciousness, and the mantis saliva drug, had underlay her next lifetime as the Rooster. Compounding the problem was the fact that the Rooster's head was malformed, and he was teased and beaten relentlessly as a boy. The combined result had been a complete and total loss of the last vestiges of his own self-respect. Since he was a worthless person, it did not matter in the slightest what he did, and the Rooster's lifetime of criminal behavior began.

Chaucer spent a week going over the many harmful actions that the Rooster had committed, more than half had been as the enforcing arm of the Church, culminating with his assassination of the Santi leader, Ket Bethany, me, in other words. Back then when I, as a spiritual being only, my body lying on the ground assassinated, blasted into the Rooster and killed his body and then showing him the errors of his beliefs, little did I know that I had totally altered this basic decision, which was controlling his life. I am glad that Chaucer was doing the therapy sessions on Yannis, because I don't know that I could have sat there listening to crime after crime, assassination after killing.

After two grueling weeks, Chaucer finally achieved the result that he was after with this patient. She began laughing wildly, all yawns had ceased a little before her laughter. "I see it so clearly now. Yazi spoke just the right words that convinced me that I wasn't worthless! That's why I was so fanatically supportive of this vile church and their screwed up beliefs! He was nothing more than a super con man and not a priest at all! He conned everyone on Megalos!"

From this point on, Yannis was always seen around this group of one hundred plus women, helping them in every way possible. She adopted a new purpose for her life, the helping of others who were in need. Chaucer had actually salvaged one spiritual being who had been one of our worst enemies during her lifetime as the Rooster, an incredible feat indeed.

The therapy sessions continued until mid-September before we had handled all of these women fully. During that time, all were undergoing daily re-learning experiences, run by the Laird Foundation women. By this time, all were able to fend pretty much for themselves at the dinner table, as long as their plates were filled for them and things cut into bite-sized pieces. With the help of the loose fitting dresses and Enyo's inventions, all were able to handle their own hygiene issues, mostly.

Not until December did Linda feel confident in their skills to allow them to return to Demokritos. However, a few remained behind for further Santi and Guardian training. Among these were Zenovia, Amara, Lyris,

Eleni, Charessa, Cynthia, and Karis. Some twenty women were now stable outside their heads, prime Guardian material. Yannis was not, but was very content to help these twenty with their needs.

In late August, Marcel Renzo proposed to me, and his brothers, concerned about the suddenness of it, threw conservatism to the wind and proposed to Zenovia, Amara, and Lyris. In September, after the last of the therapy sessions was finished, we four couples got married in a mutual ceremony. The men moved into our dorm with us. We were not yet fully re-educated on how to fend for ourselves and the brothers did not want us to leave until we were completely ready. Besides, we all knew that Linda's order that four of us rooming together was the ideal scene so that we could help each other with our daily needs. If we had gone our separate ways at this time, each would likely have needed a live-in personal assistant to get by.

In December 702, we received a dispatch from Annelise, sent to us via the Emperor of Demokritos, Deimos. It seems that our parents had just passed away, and now there was a major problem of who would be their next king and queen. The letter explained that our older brother Erik had died some years back of food poisoning. A year ago, Poul, my cousin and the older brother of Hans, had died in a shipwreck during a surprise storm. By Annelise rules of succession, the throne belonged to Hans now, with Mia becoming their queen.

"If I refuse the throne, what happens next?" Hans asked after we all read the dispatch.

"I think that they must find some other family to replace the Rykers," Mia said. "It doesn't go to us women, only to the males, unfortunately. I suspect that we could have Deimos make a request that Maren and Marcel have the throne, since she was the Empress of Annelise."

"Thanks, but no thanks!" I declared. "I've had all their fashion I care too. If I still had my arms, it might be manageable, but not like this; it was pure torture for me, those fourteen years there. No thanks."

"But I've promised to look after you, Maren! I cannot go," Mia argued.

"Hey, you have done a most incredible job of that, sis, thank you, thank you! Now that I have Marcel Renzo back, I release you from that obligation, Mia. If you want to go with Hans, I think that is terrific. Maybe you can get them to wear more sensible clothes."

Linda and Chaucer were present with us. She said, "Mia, Hans, you have done an exemplary job of looking after Maren Bethany. I salute both of you, except I've a slight problem with that. Chaucer, you salute them for me." He did and we all laughed.

"Seriously, Hans, Mia, I think that this would be an ideal thing to do. I'll send along a Communicator and Healer to join you, if you decide to take the throne of Annelise." After some discussion, the two decided to do it. We had a tearful farewell on December 21 when they set sail for Annelise. I knew that the two Judgers would make a fine king and queen. Finally, they were free of having to look after my needs and could make their own way with their own goals.

After Mia left, I had a long talk with Linda. I was pregnant with our first child, but I was also very frustrated. "Linda, I really don't want to have to live another fifty more years like this. Renzo and I are so frustrated. I just cannot play games with this body. You know how much I love to play, and I feel so constrained in this body. I don't know how you have managed it for so long, Linda. I feel trapped by my own body."

We talked at length. "It is your body, after all. It is yours to do with as you desire," Linda quietly pointed out. That was true. However, after all the trouble that Renzo had gone just to be with me again, I felt miserable about making him once again have to give up his loving spirit of play that we used to share, that was the strongest bond between us. Complicating matters, so many others looked up to me as their example, as well as Linda, of course.

In June 703, the festering problem was finally resolved. I gave birth to a boy, who we called Raphael Perrin. However, my body had a severe problem, stemming from growing up from the age of five wearing that restrictive corset. My organs had been shifted around, and the birth ruptured my spleen. I knew something might be wrong because I felt so weak after the birth. I fell asleep that night, and the body never woke up.

Renzo, Linda, and I had a long talk, via Mind Link the next morning. He promised that he would raise our son, and I told him that it was fine with me for him to find a new wife and mother for Raphael, if he desired. We both agreed to see if we could get together in the future. Me, I just felt relief. I was free of that debilitating body at last and did not have to face another fifty years dealing with it. Surprisingly, none of us felt any huge grief over my body's premature death.

Linda said that things would be calm and quiet now for many years, which had been my biggest concern — that something else major would soon appear to threaten the peace and quiet of the world, only that I would not be there to help in calming it. Linda promised she would contact me periodically with updates and lend me any assistance I might need in the future. Renzo also promised me the same thing. It was very reassuring indeed.

Linda sent, *Maren, you haven't yet asked about how the Santi del Dio are doing, nor about what Hektor has left for you in my care. I should tell you now at least. He sent along two hundred thousand gold coins worth of gems. Also, Demokritos has been sending you funds as well. I took the liberty of combining them. You have at your disposal close to three hundred thousand worth.* I was flabbergasted at the sum!

The Santi, as a group, are quickly becoming obsolete. Already all the Sea Princes and the two Greenway kingdoms have created their own security forces or armies. Velona's armed forces greatly exceeds our entire combined strength. We've accomplished our original mission, that of guaranteeing their security while they developed into prospering countries capable of handling their own affairs. Worse, the number of actual Guardians is now down to an all-time low, barely a hundred still are active, though we still train new recruits.

Tarra is entering a new era of extensive trading between far-flung countries. What is needed is some way to handle payments or transfers of large sums of money from one distant location to another. As you can imagine, this is a major problem and concern. One theft could result in humongous losses for the sender. Hence, our organization is moving into a universal banking system called the World Bank.

We have established branch offices in every major city on Tarra, and we are now working on those of lesser size. Instead of people having to find some secret place to keep their money, they can bring it to our bank and open up a secure account. We store their money with an iron clad guarantee that when they desire their funds, we will provide them anywhere in the world.

For example, a merchant in Patri wants to buy a load of silk from Velona. They deposit their funds to pay for it there in our bank in Patri, and we see that the trader in Velona has the funds transferred into his account. Now neither buyer nor seller must worry about the physical transfer of money, which has always been fraught with difficulties, robbers being the largest.

We keep the real money safe in a secret location known only to a few and it is heavily guarded as well. It is working very well; far less real movement of gold is needed. You see, we are rapidly getting to the point where all we need to do is adjust the balance figures on the buyer and sellers accounts. I think it is a slick operation. No one will dare interfere with us, because we control so much money worldwide.

More to the point, Maren Bethany, I have opened an account under the name of Elizabeth Stanton. You can go to any World Bank in the world and ask to withdraw funds from your account. They will ask for your secret password. I chose Linda Chaucer for you. For example, in say sixteen years you want say a thousand for traveling expenses. You go to one of our banks and give them the name of the account, Elizabeth Stanton. They will ask you for your secret password, you say Linda Chaucer. They will then give you the thousand.

But how do we make any money? How do our banks pay our workers?

Ah, we charge a tenth of a percent on the total amount of the transaction. On your withdrawal of one thousand, you would get back nine hundred and ninety nine gold pieces and the bank gets to keep one gold coin. It gets better, Maren. Since we have your funds, we will pay you *for allowing us to hang on to your money. Each month that the three hundred thousand gold coins are in our bank, we pay you a tenth of a percent interest on it, adding another three hundred gold to your account. We are basing each month's interest on the original amount, so the next month, only another three hundred is added. Maren, if you do not touch your funds, in sixteen years, we will have added about sixty thousand gold to your total amount!*

Wow! That is a clever scheme indeed.

Thanks, Chaucer and I thought it up. Now that it is established worldwide, soon no one will ever dare touch us. We have slowly been transferring key Santi people over into the new organization, World Bank. We guess that in another twenty or thirty years of peaceful commerce, the Santi will be no more, and we will all be part of the World Bank. I promise I will keep you posted and up to date on things.

This is sheer genius, Linda! Control the money and you have incredible influence in stabilizing the entire world!

Yes, plus we insulate ourselves from direct attacks. The Church of Jehosanity has always been after us Santi. Now we will become essentially free from their influence. If they try to go back to mutilating women again, we merely increase the fees charged for each of their transactions, making it terribly expensive to continue that path. Just don't forget your account name and your secret password. Only three of us, besides you, know it: myself, of course, Chaucer, and Renzo. I promised.

After we broke the Mind Link, I was free for a time now of my heavy responsibilities, at least until my new body would grow up. I took off floating over the Sea Princes and the Appian Way looking at all the changes that had occurred since I had last seen these lands. For once, I was not in a hurry to pick up a new baby body and I didn't even have a location or mother all picked out. Yes, it felt good just to observe a peaceful, prospering Tarra for a time, knowing that I had a figurative hand in this tranquility.

The End.

Other Books by Vic Broquard

Without Warning (fantasy)

The Trident Series: (fantasy)
 Volume 1 The Trident and the Book
 Volume 2 The Trident and the Scepter
 Volume 3 The Trident and the Resurrection

The Adventures of Elizabeth Stanton Series: (science fiction)
 Volume 1 The Evolution of the Path
 Volume 2 The Great Messiah
 Volume 3 Of Kings and Queens and Troubadours
 Volume 4 Chaos in the Aftermath
 Volume 5 Power Plays
 Volume 6 Age of Exploration
 Volume 7 Abducted
 Volume 8 The Emperor and Empress
 Volume 9 A Job Worth Doing
 Volume 10 Degradation
 Volume 11 The Second Crusade
 Volume 12 When Worlds Collide
 Volume 13 Dark Ages

The Lindsey Barron Series: (fantasy)
 Volume 1 The Rod of the Apocalypse
 Volume 2 The Board of Governors
 Volume 3 The Crown of Moses
 Volume 4 Dominus for President
 Volume 5 The National Health Care Program
 Volume 6 States Justice
 Volume 7 Cross and Double-cross

Zoran Chronicles Series: (fantasy)
 Volume 1 A Dragon in Our Town
 Volume 2 Dragons, Power, Courts, and War

Planet of the Orange-red Sun Series: (science fiction)
 Volume 1 When Kingdoms Fall
 Volume 2 Dark Ages
 Volume 3 Age of the Towers
 Volume 4 Difficillis Exitus
 Volume 5 Age of the Lords
 Volume 6 The Renegade Tower

Vic Broquard

Volume 7 Rebellions
Volume 8 The Aliens Return
Volume 9 Power Struggles
Volume 10 Guilds, Genetics, and Gods
Volume 11 Magi, Witches, Swords, and Superstitions
Volume 12 The Voyage of the Eagle's Seed
Volume 13 Eagle's Seed and Origins
Volume 14 Justifications
Volume 15 Responsibilities

The Return of the Wizards: Twelve Companions – The Making of Wizards
(fantasy)